THE FRUMKISS FAMILY BUSINESS

The
FRUMKISS FAMILY

BUSINESS

A Megilla* in 14 Chapters

MICHAEL WEX

 *Alfred A. Knopf Canada*

*Megilla: 1) a scroll, as in *The Megilla of Esther*; 2) a drawn-out, complicated matter.

PUBLISHED BY ALFRED A. KNOPF CANADA

Copyright © 2010 Michael Wex

All rights reserved under International and Pan-American
Copyright Conventions. No part of this book may be reproduced
in any form or by any electronic or mechanical means, including
information storage and retrieval systems, without permission in
writing from the publisher, except by a reviewer, who may quote
brief passages in a review. Published in 2010 by Alfred A. Knopf
Canada, a division of Random House of Canada Limited.
Distributed by Random House of Canada Limited, Toronto.

Knopf Canada and colophon are registered trademarks.

www.randomhouse.ca

Library and Archives Canada Cataloguing in Publication

Wex, Michael, 1954–
The Frumkiss family business / Michael Wex.
Also available in electronic format.

ISBN 978-0-307-39776-8 (bound)

I. Title.

PS8595.E93F78 2010   C813'.54   C2010-901422-7

Text design: Jennifer Lum

First Edition

Printed and bound in the United States of America

2 4 6 8 9 7 5 3 1

For Bonnie,
who gives ear to a kvetch

One never knows, do one?
—*Thomas "Fats" Waller*

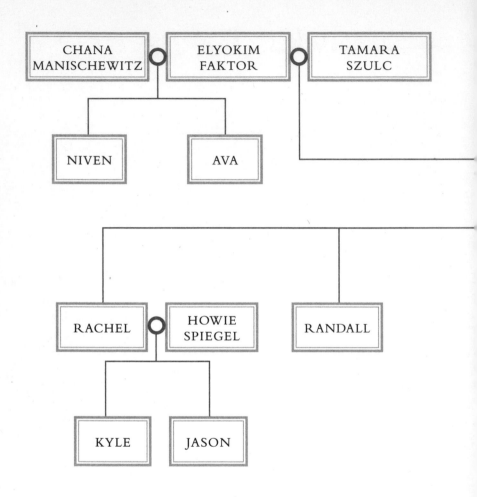

Frumkiss Family Tree

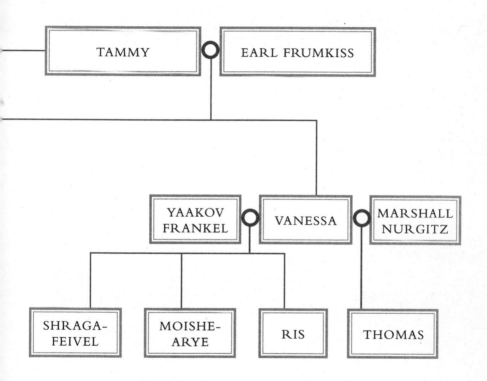

PROLOGUE
Toronto, 1955

I N THE EARLY DAYS OF TELEVISION, when the CBC had dominion from coast to coast and not even those fortunate few with access to American networks ever dreamt of missing *Cross Canada Hit Parade*; in the days before *Juliette* or *The Friendly Giant*, days when the Canadian version of *Howdy Doody* was still new, there sat a boy, a very strange, enchanted boy, who didn't care if he ruined his eyes watching TV. He wasn't sure what "ruin your eyes" was supposed to mean. The last thing he ruined was a teddy bear that he doused in 3-IN-ONE oil so that it would slide better when he raced it across the rug against his plastic Uncle Remus saucer, and he couldn't imagine his mother holding his eyes under a faucet and then throwing them into the garbage like she did with the bear: his eyes were too far inside his head to come out.

He didn't understand what ruining his eyes had to do with sitting too near to the TV. "We got a nice big one," his mother used to yell, "so you could sit on a chair and watch like a human being." But when he sat in the chair, he was too far away; when he sat in the chair, his mother winced for the chair. She kept coming in from the kitchen and making him put his feet down—"You can't sit like a person?"—until she finally told him he should sit on the floor right in front of the chair, because if he sat too close and they had to get him glasses, don't ask her how they'd pay for the things—did *he* have a job? And as soon as she went back to the kitchen, Allan would start inching up to the set, sliding his bum across the rug on the floor where his bear hadn't liked to slide at all until he was less than a foot away from the twenty-four-inch Admiral that they won in the Lodzer Society raffle celebrating ten years of a Hitler-free world.

Allan wasn't old enough to tell time yet, but he knew that after Popeye finished on Channel 4, the only kids' programs were on CBC. He passed most of his mornings with Maggie Muggins, Uncle Chichimus, and his favourite of all, *The New Curiosity Shop*, starring Omar Pieman. Omar, the portly, fez-topped proprietor of a ramshackle secondhand store, was a soothing fusion of Major Hoople from *Our Boarding House* and Sydney Greenstreet in *Casablanca*. He spoke in a slow, deep baritone, enunciating every word very, very clearly. Each episode began with Omar looking up, slightly startled, from the new acquisition that he was studying—a sandglass or crystal ball, a repeating rifle, toy fire engine, knight's helmet or fox-fur stole with the head and paws attached—then telling a story or singing a song about it with his two hand-puppet side-kicks, Pip the Porpoise, who used to poke his head up from the soft-drink cooler that Omar used in place of a counter, and Stanley the Squirrel, who lived in an oak but entered the store through a seemingly glassless back window.

Native-born grown-ups, proper Canadian mothers and fathers who were out of work or down with the flu, recognized the cast right away. Omar and the puppets were played by the popular radio comedy team, Willan and Healey. Omar was Willan, Healey did both the puppets, using the voices of characters from their old radio show, and much of the dialogue was improvised. They'd been working together since vaudeville and were milking their resuscitated fame for all it was worth. Not that Allan cared about any of that, or that his parents, for whom Poland had never been home but was still their native land, had ever heard of Willan or Healey or gave a damn what they were up to now.

Allan had always liked the show—there probably wasn't a kid in Canada with a TV who didn't watch it—but like had blossomed into love a short time before, a love that had nothing to do with Omar or Stanley or Pip. Allan fell for a new character, a puppet that had made its debut about two weeks earlier, just long enough for Allan to have trouble remembering what the show was like without it. It was a bird, a dodo, though you would never have known if the bird hadn't told you: the waves of aggressively curly white hair—half Liberace, half Gorgeous George—and the thick horn-rimmed glasses pasted behind its beak to the side of its head worked against any sense of authenticity, as did the fact that the dodo could talk. The other animal puppets talked, too, but they talked with the kinds of voices that puppets always had; they sounded like puppets, not people, even though they never seemed to think of themselves as anything but human. But the dodo, the dodo sounded like Allan's mother and father and some of the other mothers and fathers on his street and like all of the *bubbes* and *zeydes* who came to visit the kids whose parents didn't sound like Allan's, and he talked a lot about being a dodo.

"Mama, he's on!" Allan was all excited. "Come in already. I want you to see him." He had been telling his parents about the dodo all week, and he squirmed through the weekend, waiting for Monday morning, waiting for right now, when *The New Curiosity Shop* was on. Allan didn't want to miss anything, but he started to back away from the set as soon as the dodo appeared. He called again, this time in Yiddish. "*Tateh, mameh*, run fast, you can see him now."

It was one of the intermediate days of Passover and Allan's father wasn't going to work. He was a cutter. The owner of the factory where he worked was very religious and paid his Jewish employees, who were all his employees, not to work on Jewish holidays, even though most of them, like Allan's father, never entered a synagogue if it wasn't Rosh Hashana, Yom Kippur or a day when memorial prayers were recited. "*Nu*, come fast. He's on. You have to hear. He talks like us." Nobody on television, not even Molly Goldberg, whom his parents never watched and Allan had never seen, sounded anything like anyone whom Allan had ever heard.

His parents came into the living room and saw the dodo. He had a pronounced accent and spoke only in rhyming couplets. There was almost nothing that he liked. Whenever any of the other characters came out with a sunny observation or shared a piece of good news, the dodo would throw his head forward so that the bottom of his beak rested on the lid of the soft drink cooler. He'd open his mouth, with only the top half of the beak in motion, and ask in a way that moved hundreds of thousands, maybe millions, of children from coast to coast to scream along with him through their laughter; that crazy dodo would look at Omar or Stanley, or more often at Pip the Penguin, and ask, "So it's good for the birds?" Then he'd get really upset and start muttering and sputtering, although the vitriol that he seemed to be spewing was nothing but schoolyard tongue-twisters in Yiddish. "*Trugt a fiks a biks in pisk*," he'd spit, like it was something too dirty to be allowed in English. It means "A fox is carrying a gun in its mouth."

"You see?" Allan asked. "Just like you!" He turned to his father with an air of seriousness. "But without the bad words when he's mad, *tateh*."

His parents both laughed. They didn't have much, but they had a bright kid. "Listen to his Yiddish," said Allan's mother. She was talking about the dodo. "He sounds like a Lodzer."

"What else?" asked the dad. "He sounds like he knows what he's doing, too. With English like that, he must have been some kind of actor in the old country. He doesn't make any mistakes."

They waited until the end of the show, eager to check the credits and see who played the bird. "You see?" Both of them were yelling and pointing to the screen. "E. Yakima Faktor? You see? It's gotta be him. E. Yakima. Get it? Elyokim, Elyokim Faktor. The *Mazik*"—the little devil—"it's got to be him."

"Could be. I never saw him perform in English, though."

Allan's mother explained it to him. "We think that the man who makes the puppet for the bird was famous before the War in newspapers and the theatres in Poland. He was very funny and all his stuff was in Jewish. We think it's him that's the voice of—what's the name of the bird again?"

"Yankee," Allan said. "Yankee Gallstone."

PART 1

The Death of the Last Famous Yiddish Poet Still Young Enough to Know Who He Was

Toronto, 2008

1

THE FINAL DAY

I T WAS PROBABLY THE ALL-KUGEL DIET that killed him.
Probably. It's hard to be sure with a man of 103: he
could trip down the stairs, get hit by a car, succumb
to the kind of illness that young people don't get any
more—phthisis, diphtheria, the neurosyph—but Faktor was
never accident-prone, and not even his bitterest enemies—
a good three or four of whom lived long enough to see him
die—could recall him ever having so much as a toothache
or runny nose. A touch of scurvy during the War, when it
was almost compulsory—unless he induced it to keep out
of the army—but Faktor? Sick?

When the Yiddish paper of record called for details of
his death, his wife repeated the question as if she didn't
quite understand. "Sick? I don't know about sick." It was
like they'd asked if he had two foreskins. "Faktor was never
sick." Mrs. Aubrey, the professional name she insisted the
paper use, had been in Toronto since 1927, but she never
entertained any idea of calling her husband by his given
name, not even when they were alone. He was Faktor

when they met and Faktor is who he stayed. It was a sign of affection and respect, and was what everyone else called him, too. "He was too busy getting under people's skin to spend time getting sick. We were married for sixty years, I know what I'm saying."

She didn't know the half of it. Faktor's whole life was about getting under skins, driving others up a wall. "I want to be a *yatesh*," he wrote, the gnat that burrowed into Titus's head to punish him for his mockery of God. It banged against his brain and didn't give him a moment's peace: its claws were made of iron, its beak of brass. "That's me all over," he said. "A *yatesh*, but without the God. Every time a Jew is born, the rest of the world gets a headache. Most of us do it inadvertently; the difference between me and the rest of the Jews is that I want to cause headaches on purpose. We have to work on the world like the *yatesh* worked on Titus after he burned down the Temple and ruined our lives. Heinrich Heine had the same idea. And now—there's me."

He started in 1926, when he was living in Paris and frequenting brothels that specialized in religious themes. He was young, naive enough to fall in love with a whore who appeared everywhere, in private and in public, in the brothel or in church, in full Carmelite habit. She told Faktor that she was in the middle of her temporary vows when she lost her vocation, as well as her faith. She didn't say why, and he wasn't naive enough to ask how or why she became a whore. He just knew that he felt a real bond with her. "We had a great deal in common, having both been religious once." When Faktor realized that it was strictly business on her end, he published a book of French sonnets called *Ma Soeur, Ma Fiancée: Chants d'amour pour une Religieuse*. He used the pseudonym André Zhid.

Mrs. Aubrey, his second and most long-lasting wife, knew nothing about this. She didn't know that back in Poland two years later, he published his first novel, anonymously and at his own expense. A contemporary critic described *Memoirs of Jesus' Moyel*, the man who circumcised Christ, as "the first plea for a pogrom ever to have been issued in Yiddish." It was condemned by the government, forget about the Church, and not a single copy is known to have survived. Those who saw it—and there were plenty—said that it was a virtual encyclopedia of foreskin jokes and anti-Christian slurs, including a number invented by Faktor himself, all of it presented as the after-dinner speeches from the banquet portion of Jesus' circumcision. The Nazarene's foreskin was described as broad, leathery and marked with the sign of the cross; no matter how often the narrator sliced it off, it grew back again in a very few minutes, which is why he was able to make so many speeches.

Faktor had the book printed by *ostjüdische* anarchists living in Berlin. They had it smuggled into Poland, where copies were handed out on street corners, in front of popular theatres and restaurants, and beside newspaper kiosks all over Jewish Warsaw by boys yelling, "Extra! Extra! The truth about Yoyzl's *bris!*" It was distributed for free, and they gave away five thousand copies in a single day. Faktor also sent one to every bishop in the country. Insiders, including Yiddish-speakers in the pay of the police, were pretty sure that they recognized the anonymous author's style. Faktor was a well-known journalist by then, and his weekly columns in the Warsaw *Haynt* were stuffed with slightly milder near-blasphemies. Faktor threw his hands into the air and denied everything. There was nothing to connect him to this regrettable perturbation: at the Tachkemoni seminary where he had studied, Jesus, with a foreskin or without, had no place in the curriculum.

He never admitted responsibility for the *Memoirs*. Neither of his wives knew anything about it, and the secret of its authorship would have died with Faktor, had he not explained the whole affair to his biographer only a few weeks before he died. Loud as Faktor could sometimes be, self-restraint for the sake of a punch line or prank was one of the guiding principles of his life, perhaps the only guiding principle of his life. He was a *tzaddik* of *shtik*, a saint of shenanigans. He had a talent for strategic self-effacement and was willing to sacrifice anything, possibly even his life, to safeguard the purity of his japes. In the real world, Faktor craved all the attention he could get; when it came to hoaxes and provocations, though, he could conceal his name and forgo any credit, while patting himself on the back for his near superhuman self-abnegation: he craved efficacy, not renown—he got enough of that in literature and the theatre. He didn't want a vulgar craving for reputation to come between the work and its victims: "Crazy ol' Faktor, up to his crazy ol' tricks again," could dampen the most incendiary prank.

And Faktor could afford to play pranks. His father was one of the wealthiest textile manufacturers in Lodz, and Faktor grew up in the very bosom of early-twentieth-century Polish-Jewish luxury, all velvets and tutors, music lessons and Hebrew grammar. His father saw him as heir to an empire, a new, better educated sort of businessman who was just a bit of a rabbi on the side. Along with the usual religious education, Faktor received extensive instruction in French, German, Russian and English—the language of any country where he might have to do business with people who didn't know Yiddish or Hebrew. His father was an old-fashioned Orthodox intellectual who believed in the kind of education that he himself could never have obtained. In 1923 he sent Faktor abroad to learn the international end of the business. Though the boy was only eighteen, he was bright and eager and, as even his father realized, temperamentally unsuited to the rabbinate. He had finished at the top of his class at the recently established Tachkemoni school in Warsaw, but showed no evidence of any feelings of piety. He was as ambivalent about God as he was about work: he knew that they existed, but could see no reason to bother with either.

He lived in Manchester for a year, a stay that marked his English forever after, giving it more in common with *Coronation Street* than with Isaac Bashevis Singer, his classmate at the Tachkemoni. He spent another year boarding with his father's French agent, a religious Jew from Poland who kept a kosher home, but finally got up the nerve to take digs on the Left Bank and throw himself wholeheartedly into student life and *la vie parisienne*. He was beholden to no one, not even his father; his maternal grandfather, who had taken his father into the business, passed away not long before Faktor went to Paris and left him a monthly stipend: Faktor was an Old-World trust fund child who could do whatever he wanted and buy his way out of any trouble that he'd either caused or gotten into. He quit the job at his father's firm and spent the next two years writing poetry and mailing the results to French, Polish and Yiddish journals, where he started to gain a reputation as a talented youngster who didn't take himself or anything else too seriously.

He chased girls but didn't get very far. Faktor was heavy and pale, with a spare tire that seemed to sag from his navel to his knees and that no amount of vigorous walking ever changed. Floppy, with folds of hidden skin almost everywhere, he had the curly red hair and pasty, freckle-splotched skin of a Japanese demon. He was known variously as di *miyeskayt*—the ugliness—*le rideau à chair* and *le cochon cacher*. His granddaughter Rachel described a photo of Faktor taken around that time as, "Bozo goes Poland.

With schmaltz on every side." For all his wealth and all his wit, Faktor spent three or four years in Hemingway's Paris and never had sex with anyone but prostitutes; some of his cheaper conquests actually winced on going off with him, but Faktor pretended not to see.

He went back to Poland for his mother's funeral and found himself with enough of a reputation to be invited by one of the editors of *Haynt*, the Warsaw-based Yiddish daily, to contribute a weekly column of humorous verse on issues of the day. He called it *Der Mazik*— the li'l devil, the trouble-maker, Lucifer Junior or Satan in shorts—and the name soon stuck to him: in Yiddish circles he was known as *Der Mazik* for the rest of his life. The column ran until September 1939, and was picked up after the War by a succession of failing Yiddish papers in the States, finally ending up in the *Forward* once there was nowhere else for it to go. Faktor faxed the last one to New York on his final Monday; it came out the day that he died.

His mother died of a heart attack at the age of forty-one, and all of her doctors said that it was because of her weight. She was five feet tall and weighed 255 pounds. Her death affected Faktor in ways that a whore's sneer could never have done; as soon as he established himself in Warsaw after his mother's *shloyshim*, the thirty days after her death, he joined one of the Jewish gymnastic associations and began to swim—once he'd been taught how—and work out with bowling pins and medicine balls, kettle bells and pommel horses for an hour every day. He went on a strict vegetarian diet, eating meat only once a week, for a full twelve months, until he looked like Douglas Fairbanks from his neck to his knees. He kept exercising until he was close to ninety, doing push-ups, sit-ups and other exercises that needed no equipment even while fleeing the Nazis and starving in Soviet Asia.

Faktor had an iron will and a rare sense of discipline; he could go days without sleep in order to meet a deadline or follow an unusually hot inspiration. Whatever he wanted to do, he did; and for reasons that not even he could explain, Faktor wanted to piss people off. The older he got, the more adept he became. Eight years after the Jesus memoir, he published an art book, a collection of nude photos of a model who looked so much like Magda Goebbels that he had no trouble calling the book *Die erblühende Magda*, "Magda in Bloom," or describing the pictures as "figure studies" of "a now famous lady" made just before her first marriage in 1920. The girl was a domestic who'd once worked for Faktor's parents in Lodz, but the pictures were taken in Warsaw. The book was printed in Buenos Aires at a press owned by former members of Zvi Migdal, the Jewish pimps' association, and was bound by a left-leaning *volksdeutsch* pornographer in Teplitz, who smuggled all 250 copies into the Reich. Faktor himself took over from there, driving all over Germany in a Hispano-Suiza and mailing the books from eighty-odd post offices, whence they were delivered to prominent journalists, political figures, foreign diplomats and government officials, including Himmler, Goering and the *Führer* himself. He sent two to Dr. Goebbels.

No one knows how many arrests were made or the number of executions that might have followed. Word of the book leaked out through discreet reports in *Le Monde*, the *London Times*, the *Neue Freie Presse*, and the *Neue Zürcher Zeitung* concerning the mysterious appearance of a volume of highly artistic photos of a certain matron, "now well placed in the New Germany," in her somewhat more free-spirited youth. All four papers found the pictures "excellent propaganda, as it were, for the German mastery of streamlined form."

The book quickly acquired legendary status among the Nazi-obsessed, probably because so few of them ever saw it; a copy from Berchtesgaden with Hitler's personal bookplate sold for $100,000. There were abundant theories as to its origin—including one that held the photos to be authentic and attributed their publication to the family of Gustav Ritter von Kahr, the Bavarian *Staatskommissar* who helped quash the Beer Hall Putsch and was murdered during the Night of the Long Knives—but its true origin remained unknown until Faktor, once again, spilled the beans to his biographer.

Faktor, of course, earned nothing from such a book, just as he never asked to be paid for his column after the War. Between what he had from his family and what he earned from Yiddish plays and performances—even then, poetry didn't make anyone a living—money was the one thing that he didn't have to think about. In 1935, a year before the beginning of the economic boycott of the Jews in Poland, he and his father, with whom he remained very close, despite his defection from the *shmatte* trade, began to shift most of their own money, as well as anything that the business didn't immediately need, to Switzerland. They took good care to convert it all to sterling before socking it away. Faktor's father was run over and killed by a delivery truck owned by a prominent Endek, a member of the fascist National Democrats, in 1938, after which Faktor sold the business for a fraction of its real value, went to Switzerland and consolidated all the accounts into one vast holding of his own.

So why didn't he get out of Europe? He didn't have a clue, except that he was a celebrity in Poland and nothing but a foreigner in America. A year or so after his return from France, Faktor had been approached by Zaynvl Nurgitz, a writer of popular dramatic shlock who made the leap to impresario and become the manager of a number of popular Yiddish theatre stars, including Shula Kutscher.

A good ten years older than Faktor and with a century's more knowledge of the world, Shula Kutscher, "the Hebrew Duse," was also the Lillie Langtry of Yiddish theatre. Mistress to the wealthy and powerful, tall and majestic looking, with bright red hair, a gentile nose and a bosom that made grown men long for infancy, she was remarkably reticent about her origins and early life. "I was born," she used to declare, rolling her shoulders back and lifting her nose into the air, "the day I stepped onto a stage." No one knew her real name or where she was from; her off-stage Yiddish came straight from the Warsaw fish market, and her inability to suppress that accent in anything but Yiddish kept her from performing in any other language. She was incomprehensible in German, and her Polish, though fluent, sounded like something that a Hebe comic might use in a not-so-subtly anti-Semitic cabaret sketch, a fact that the reviews of her performance in Nurgitz's Polish-language production of *Camille* hadn't been slow to point out.

Madame Kutscher was stuck with Yiddish, but there had never been a better time to be stuck. Yiddish culture between the two world wars extended all over the Western world and was able to keep its stars in Hollywood style. Sholem Asch had a villa outside of Nice, where he hobnobbed with the likes of Stefan Zweig and Gerhardt Hauptmann. Anna Held crossed out of Yiddish and became one of Ziegfeld's biggest stars, while actors like Boris Thomashefsky and Jacob Adler were stars and Ziegfelds, actors and producers, all at once. Yossele Rosenblatt, the megastar cantor, turned down an offer to appear in *The Jazz Singer.* Though Madame Kutscher's wealth had more to do with gifts from well-heeled admirers, especially the two plutocrats whom she allowed to keep her at once—she owned two apartment blocks in upper-class, goyishe Warsaw—the theatre was what really mattered to her. She still had her looks, was only a couple of years past thirty, and had a face that adorned cigarette and candy packages, coasters and postcards and magazine covers all over Yiddish-speaking Europe.

After the *Camille* debacle, she decided to forgo her tragedienne's dignity. It would be too easy for them—critics, audiences, Jews and Poles—to see any serious performance in the light of *Camille* and begin to pick holes in her style and interpretation. "I have to do something new," she told Nurgitz. "Give them what they don't expect from me. Comedy, satire. The real thing. Sharp and mean."

"Since when," he asked, "were you so worried about changing society?"

"Since I realized that I can't throw that son-of-a-bitch critic for the *Kurier* out of his apartment just because he wrote that all that separates me from the real Camille is illness and inspiration. I don't think that asshole knows that I'm his landlord."

"So, nu," Nurgitz was rubbing his pince-nez against the summit of the mountain formed by his vest and paunch. "What are you going to do? Move to Russia?" He started to laugh. "Play Hedda Gabler, the frustrated housewife? With *your* reputation?"

"Was she funny, Hedda Gabler? I want to do satire. Funny stuff that makes fun of the way things are."

"So what have you got in mind?" Nurgitz asked. "What repertoire, I mean."

"*My* repertoire," she said. "Find me someone to write it."

Nurgitz had been with her long enough to know that "someone," rather than a name, meant someone she'd never either worked with or slept with. This let out most of the better young writers, and the ones she didn't know tended not to be funny. He went through his files, asked his friends, went for long walks on which he deliberately thought about other matters, but still couldn't come up with a name. La Kutscher had to do something quickly to make up for her Polish flop, but Nurgitz couldn't come up with anyone who could give her what to do. Hungry and desperate after walking half the length of Warsaw one rainy morning, he decided to have lunch in the Literary Union restaurant on Tlomackie Street. He found Faktor before he'd even found a seat. Faktor's physical fitness program was still too new to be showing, and he was far too ugly for someone like Madame Kutscher to consider even in a moment of weakness. He wrote that funny column in *Haynt*—which meant that his name could help sell a show—and he seemed to love making fun of everything.

"Excuse me, *Pan Mazik*." Nurgitz used the Polish for Mr. as a sign that there was business afoot. He called Faktor by his pseudonym to give him some idea of the nature of that business. "I am Zaynvl Nurgitz." He reached into his vest pocket and found a card. "The impresario." He handed it to Faktor.

"Yes, I recognized you. A pleasure to make your acquaintance, *Pan* Nurgitz." They shook. Faktor gestured for Nurgitz to sit down. "What can I do for you?"

Nurgitz decided to get straight to the point. "Do you think you could write me a play?" Nurgitz lit a cigar while Faktor picked at a doleful bowl of kasha and cabbage. The impresario explained what he needed for Madame Kutscher, why he needed it, and how soon he'd have to have it.

"I've never written any plays, but why not?" said Faktor. "A month is plenty of time." Faktor told him how much he wanted for the script itself and how much for each performance.

"But what if it's no good?" Nurgitz was relieved to get back to real business. "It's not like you have any track record in this area."

"You don't have to pay me unless you accept it." Nurgitz was so taken aback that he forgot to keep haggling about the price. They shook hands once more. By the time they met the next morning, Faktor had roughed out the first act and already completed two scenes.

Madame La Malkeh, "Madame Queen," was about someone just like Madame Kutscher who attains international stardom but is treated like an idiot by everyone around her. One of Madame Kutscher's lovers, the financier who had given her the larger of her apartment buildings, had once said that "She's between her legs what I am between my ears," and her off-stage accent and diction kept her from living down this reputation for stupidity. In the play, she outsmarts both her lover—the German-Jewish head of a fictitious Zionist organization—and the British government, winning independence for a Jewish Palestine and installing herself, as her character described it, as "queen for life."

The show was Madame Kutscher's greatest hit; in its nearly four hours, it managed to make fun of Jews, Poles, Arabs and Englishmen, along with Zionism, orthodoxy and assimilationism. Faktor even wrote a scene in Polish in which Madame Kutscher's character is supposed to be pretending to be a simple girl straight from the shtetl who is forced to speak Polish in order to get something or other out of a horny Polish deputy during a performance of *Traviata*. Everybody got the joke, and laughed so hard that Madame Kutscher wound up recording a couple of comedy 78s in Polish.

With the shame of *Camille* finally out of her system, she and Faktor became a team. All of Jewish Poland assumed that they were also a couple, but she never gave Faktor a tumble, not even out of pity or for the sake of form, not even after Faktor lost all that weight and started to perform in their shows himself, delivering comic monologues and patter songs. And Faktor, to be quite honest, had never even tried to give her a shot. Hot as he admitted Madame Kutscher to be, she wasn't his type. Too large, too pale; he didn't like the freckles that started on her shoulders and trailed all the way onto the tops of her chests. "Too much like what I've got already," he said. He wanted someone who looked the way he felt, and he didn't get serious with anybody until years later, when Madame Kutscher hired Tamara Szulc as her wardrobe girl. Tamara—Temme or Temke, in Yiddish— soon moved up to playing maids, monosyllabic younger sisters, and yea-saying friends of the female lead. She had the legs for the maid's little dresses, anyone could see that, but Faktor liked her slight, somewhat pensive overbite and lightly slanted black eyes, not to mention the bust that others might have thought too big for her hundred-pound frame. Madame Kutscher once described her as looking like "coco-nuts on a fishing rod," and *ventke*, "the fishing rod," became the second part of her name.

Temme Ventke, Tammy the Fishing Rod, was dark, with mahogany-hued skin and an encyclopedic knowledge of day-to-day religious practice. Her private life was austere: no men, no women, no pictures in her trunk. The company assumed that she must have been carrying a torch for some-one who had seduced and abandoned her. When she wasn't with Madame Kutscher, to whom she was clearly devoted, she was by herself.

Faktor was drawn to her loneliness. Relentlessly social himself, she stirred feelings of *Weltschmerz* in him, feelings that seemed to deepen his poetry—the stuff that *wasn't* written for the newspaper. He always said that if it weren't for her, he would never have written his first and greatest hit, "Dem Pogromtshiks Viglid," The Pogromist's Lullaby, which was set to music by his friend Chaim Lehmann and took on the status of beloved folk song within weeks of its publication. No matter what the show, Faktor would have to take a curtain call at the end just to sing it; it received more and more encores as the War drew closer. The audience joined in at its close:

Almekhtiker got hot indz kristn	Almighty God made us Christians
Bashafn tsi hershn di velt	To rule his world, yes, indeed
In yidn bashtimt indz far kistn	And gave us Jews as storage bins
Fin alts voos di shparberlekh felt.	For anything vultures might need.

Faktor didn't approach Temke immediately, and when he finally did, the courtship lasted only a couple of hours. They celebrated their wedding with the members of the theatre. Temke was astounded to discover how much money Faktor had; he asked her never to breathe a word of his fortune to anyone, not even Madame Kutscher.

Mrs. Aubrey, the second Mrs. Faktor, knew only slightly more about Faktor's first marriage than she did about his anonymous European publications, but that still doesn't mean that she knew nothing about him. After sixty years of marriage, she knew plenty.

She knew, for instance, that Faktor was a hero to

millions of Canadians born from the forties to the seventies, and she knew that there was no truth to the one rumour that had dogged Faktor for decades: Isaac Bashevis Singer did *not* call him "the Soupy Sales of Yiddish literature." It wasn't Singer at all; it was Yankef Glatshteyn—Jacob in English—the Yiddish poet, critic, novelist, and longtime Singer antagonist, and he wasn't really talking about literature. Mrs. Aubrey knew all about it, because Mrs. Aubrey helped to bring it about, six years after their marriage.

Between the Swiss bank account that Faktor could get to again after the War and what his wife, whose real name was Chana, brought in as Mrs. Aubrey, they were well enough fixed not to have to worry about money. But Faktor was bored. He was publishing nothing but the *Mazik* column. He was writing real stuff, too—poetry *and* prose, everything except plays—but with diminishing enthusiasm. "Why bother?" he used to ask. "Thirty years from now, Yiddish will be nothing but hieroglyphics."

He was so frustrated that he started to work on a book in English, a memoir of life in Soviet Asia during World War II, a book that he never finished. Mrs. Aubrey read the first fifty pages one day when Faktor was out, mostly to see if he confessed to any affairs. Most of it was about his love for the first Mrs. Faktor, which didn't really thrill Mrs. Aubrey, but she could see that his English was now good enough for him to write in. She had a cousin who was a producer at the CBC; she phoned him up and called in a couple of favours. "Believe me, Morty, he doesn't write with an accent. He sounds like he comes from England. I want you to look at what he's written. . . . Experience? Please, Morty, you're twenty-six years old, don't start with the experience. Faktor's plays were being produced all over Europe when you were still in diapers and I can tell you that every one of them made money. He could always write, and now he's writing in English. Tell your bosses over there the kind of bargain they're getting—it isn't as if he doesn't have a worldwide reputation."

She took a drag from her cigarette, looked at the lipstick on the cork tip and silently counted two beats. "And Morty, don't forget. You were no quiz kid; the scholarships all passed you by. You would never have gone to university if it wasn't for the money that I gave your mother." The last thing Morty needed three days before his scheduled elopement with a French-Canadian continuity shiksa was an angry phone call from his mother. He told Chana that he'd do what he could, but she shouldn't forget that he worked in the children's department.

"If he has to write for children, he'll write for children. Don't you worry about Faktor."

There was at least a bridge game's worth of CBC board members or their wives among the clientele of Chana's china store, and Mrs. Aubrey didn't hesitate to contact them all, apologizing for her temerity but asking for their intercession on behalf of a *fascinating* man whom she'd recently met, a writer who had been famous in Europe before the War but was having trouble establishing himself over here. "Apparently, he used to write in Yiddish. 'Can one write in Yiddish?' I asked him. 'I thought it was only a spoken language, a sort of bastard German.' At any rate, he mentioned that he had an interview coming up with Children's Programming and was hoping that he'd be given a chance to write scripts or teleplays or whatever they're called—I swear, his English is more up-to-date than mine"—and, due to his current involvement with one of Mrs. Aubrey's oldest and dearest friends, she'd take it as a great personal favour if he could be given a chance. "I'm not saying you have to keep him, darling. If he's no good, chuck him out. But give him a chance to prove himself."

After a quick apprenticeship on the Canadian version of *Howdy Doody*, where he became friendly with James Doohan, who played the Canadian counterpart of Buffalo Bob, Faktor was assigned to a new fifteen-minute, five-day-a-week series that was about to go into production, *The New Curiosity Shop*. It ran for the next twenty-five years. Faktor became a member of the cast when it expanded from fifteen to thirty minutes, and by the end of the third season he had joined Willan and Healey as an executive producer. By the mid-sixties they were turning out kids' shows that sold all over the world.

His television job was driving his friends in the Yiddish literary world out of their minds. They didn't mind him working; some of the greatest Yiddish poets of the twentieth century had been housepainters, shoemakers, paperhangers.

None of them had had Swiss bank accounts, but if Faktor *wanted* to work, so what? No one had anything against honest labour, and if Faktor had stuck to writing scripts, no one would have held it against him. It was what he did on the show, in front of gentile eyes *a mari usque ad mare*, that caused veins to throb so threateningly in so many literary Yiddish foreheads. It was undignified, it debased an entire culture. Faktor talked like a Limey in real life; his shitty English wasn't even real. It eventually got Glatshteyn mad enough to compare Faktor with Soupy Sales. Faktor pretended not to understand, just as he had pretended not to know who wrote the memoirs of Jesus' *moyel*. Only this time, no one believed him. The character that Faktor played on *The New Curiosity Shop*, an ill-tempered, verse-spouting puppet called Yankee Gallstone, was a dodo bird whose white hair and horn-rimmed glasses had both been modelled on Glatshteyn's.

Glatshteyn hadn't done anything to upset Faktor; acerbic as he could be, he always spoke highly of Faktor and reviewed his work positively and perceptively. Faktor picked on Glatsheyn only because the idea that there was a puppet based on him on Canadian television—which no one in New York City was able to see—would be sure to drive someone as high-strung as Glatshteyn straight up the wall. There was no malice; it was a question of opportunity. Faktor voiced the bird, and so many Canadian children learned to dismiss so much of life with Gallstone's ironic, Yiddish-accented catchphrase, "So it's good for the birds?" that a countrywide chain of chicken restaurants hired Faktor to repeat it on their TV commercials.

Faktor's wife knew that he was perfectly capable of enraging a friend and ally solely for the sake of seeing him get mad, but even she had to wonder if the stunt he pulled at his hundredth-birthday party was anything more than one last, desperate attempt to piss *anybody* off. Faktor's keynote speech was supposed to have something to do with his life and career: anecdotes about the famous people he had known, his experiences in the Yiddish theatre, or in the Soviet Union during the War. Instead, he strode to the lectern, lit one of the unfiltered cigarettes that he'd been smoking for more than eighty years—"No plant is going to do to me what even Hitler couldn't"—and exhaled like a man who's just heard that his son was caught cheating on an exam. "Friends," he said, "I want to thank you all for joining me to welcome the dawn of a new era in my life. I don't know about any of you, but I've been noticing an increase in anti-Semitic sentiment that's starting to remind me of Poland when I was young. In order to take a stand against it, I pledge here, with all of you as my witnesses, that from today forward, June 7, 2005, I will eat nothing but kugel, the most Jewish of all the world's foods, for all the years that I have left, except on Friday nights and Yom Kippur, when I will continue to have my supper delivered by Sea-Hi Famous Chinese Food on Bathurst Street. I also promise to drink a glass of orange juice every morning to forestall any recurrence of scurvy." He spat three times after mentioning the disease. "I'll be chronicling the effects on my mind and body on my new website, www.noodlepudding.ca. And remember, please, if *I* can eat kugel, the anti-Semites can eat cake."

It was not the speech that anyone expected. As Mrs. Aubrey told the Yiddish paper, "I had a freezer full of meat at the time."

Faktor wasn't kidding about the website. The video clips in which he describes his bowel movements appeared in YouTube's Featured Videos window more than once and were pulling hits in the Elvis or Michael Jackson range. "Check it out," viewers messaged one another. "It's Yankee Gallstone from *The New Curiosity Shop* and he's really an old Jew." Faktor's adventures in indigestion sent thousands of young people and older non-Canadians, people who had never seen or heard of Yankee Gallstone before, to the *Curiosity Shop* clips that were available on line; from there they went back to Faktor's website for gastrointestinal status updates.

Willan and Healey had both died around 1980, but Faktor was being invited to fan-meets and nerdfests where people dressed as characters from old TV shows had a chance to meet the people who played those characters, many of whom showed up in character: kind of like Larry Parks as Larry Parks meeting Larry Parks as Al Jolson in *Jolson Sings*

Again, which starred Larry Parks as Jolson, except that Parks and Jolson are both supposed to be real. The number of Gallstones at such events was growing all the time. Someone came out with a book of Gallstonisms, effectively if somewhat predictably titled, *So It's Good for the Birds.* Faktor received a respectable licensing fee and royalty, as well as an author's discount so that he could buy copies to flog at the fan conventions.

Whatever was left of the Yiddish literary world from which he'd come now hated him almost as much as they hated his old classmate, I.B. Singer; *he* had got too much attention, too, and they still hated him for it. It didn't matter, not to Faktor, not to his Yiddishist foes and certainly not to the legions of salvia-smoking latter-day hasidim of Yankee Gallstone, that Singer had been dead since 1991. What mattered was that he got too much attention and how much they hated him for it.

The delegation that flew in for Faktor's funeral was more interested in proof that Faktor was dead. As far as they were concerned, he had been a nudnik for a lot longer than he'd been a provocateur, and this so-called death might be just another trick to get people to look in his direction. Faktor was like a tree standing by the water or ten last pounds of diet-proof fat on the cusp of swimsuit season: they really believed that he'd always be here. All they could do now was complain that there was no one left for them to hate.

His end came at 11:30 on a Friday morning, while he was eating lunch—a noodle kugel with cheese, two shots of Crown Royal (one neat, the second with soda) and a glass of tea—and trying not to choke over his self-appointed biographer's asshole questions.

"*Zug mir*, tell me, Getsl." *Getsl*, yet—the Yiddish version of Elyokim that Faktor never used and no one ever called him. Mrs. Aubrey would have liked to give the shmuck a Getsl, but Faktor was determined to get a biography out of him. "How good could it possibly be," she once asked, "given that he's such a shmuck?"

"Good enough," Faktor told her, "to make somebody better want to do a decent one."

So he put up with Milner's *narishkayt*, his foolishness, leaving Chana no choice but to go along. "Tell me, Getsl, did you, uh, did you have many . . . love affairs when you were living in Paris?" As if it were his business. And as if he needed to ask in front of his victim's wife. But Chana knew that Milner didn't like her any more than she liked him.

Faktor was about to launch a flotilla of prurient whoppers when he grabbed his chest and stared hard into a void that no one else could see. "Faktor, are you all right?" Chana asked.

"All right?" he gasped, before falling face first into his kugel. "Of course I'm all right. I'm a blogosphere celebrity."

And then he was dead.

"Faktor!" Chana tried to shake him. "Faktor. *Oy vey.*"

"Move." Milner barked an order and pushed her out of the way. Luz, their housekeeper, was out doing the grocery shopping and someone had to take charge. "Call 911." He lifted Faktor's head from the kugel and tilted it back, ignoring the noodles and cheese plastered across his nose and dangling off his cheekbones. He opened Faktor's mouth and tried to perform CPR. Milner had been watching hospital shows since *Medic* debuted in 1954, the same year as Yankee Gallstone, and he knew that he knew what it looked like. Chana was on the phone shouting out her address, while Milner wiped away some noodles and decided to try the artificial respiration that he learned in a pre-teen swimming class.

"Idiot, hit him in the chest!" Chana urged him on in Yiddish. "Don't you ever watch TV? You need to hit him in the chest."

Little as she knew about CPR, she knew all about Milner and was pretty sure that he didn't know what he was doing. Milner, for his part, was just as sure that Faktor was way past help already.

They were both right. Nothing short of the general resurrection could have done Faktor any good. Chana, in a Dior suit, got the paramedics to lift her into the back of the ambulance. "I'm ninety-five years old, I can wear what I want. If you're lucky, I won't need a ride back home." She watched plenty of television herself and kept repeating "Flatlined" all the way to the emergency room, as if she were calling on the god that she worshipped.

2

CHANA

THEY'D BEEN MARRIED SINCE 1948, though neither of their kids did more than send a card for their diamond anniversary a few weeks before Faktor died. Her friends had warned her about marrying him; they all thought that she could have done better. She *had* done better the first time around, but that was never going to come back. Still, she was no DP like Faktor. As far as she was concerned, the old country was England, where she went when she was five and a half years old, just after World War I. She was born in Stashov, in Poland; she lived there for a little while, but didn't have more than half a dozen memories of the place, most of which revolved around mud or her mother.

Her father was shot by Cossacks on Yom Kippur when she was eighteen months old—not that she could remember it—and as soon as the War was over her mother's brother in England brought them both to London. They stayed there until 1927, when her mother's second husband decided to take the family to Toronto, for reasons that he never explained. He walked into the house one night with three ship's tickets and told them to get packing, they were leaving in two weeks. When her mother asked why, he told her to shut up before she got hit. No one ever found out where the tickets had come from; if her stepfather had been earning that kind of money at his crockery cart in Petticoat Lane, the three of them wouldn't have had to live in one room.

Chana, or Anna as she became in public after she started school in England, was a bright, bookish kid with a passionate interest in the movies. Theatre was okay, but it was relatively expensive and, since her parents bought the tickets, was always, but always, in Yiddish. Her mother and stepfather both burned with a love for the language that was unusual even then, when Yiddishism was in flower and the cultivation of Yiddish became a virtual religion for thousands and thousands of its speakers. There was no other language in their house. Her parents read novels and poetry, attended readings and lectures and plays *because* they were in Yiddish: if they chanced to go to a concert or museum that had program notes or descriptive plaques in English, her stepfather would read the text himself, then translate it orally into Yiddish for their benefit; neither Chana nor her mother was allowed to look.

There wasn't much in Yiddish to appeal to a girl Chana's age who couldn't remember Eastern Europe, and the little that did—most of it by Sholem Aleichem—she'd already read more than once. The plays were even worse, with the cast bursting into song every five minutes for no apparent reason, no matter how dire or serious the situation was supposed to be. Give her the movies every time: Valentino, Douglas Fairbanks, the Gish sisters, Clara Bow, and Jetta Goudal, who was even rumoured to be Jewish. There were no Yiddish plays like that, nowhere where Chana could see anybody on a stage who was half as funny as Chaplin or Harold Lloyd.

The biggest disagreement that her parents ever had— or the biggest one that Chana ever heard—was over her mother's insistence that Chana stay in school even after they came to Canada. Her stepfather wanted her to work in his china shop.

Chana went to high school and graduated in 1930 with 98.7 per cent, the highest average in the province. She went to Yiddish school on Tuesday and Thursday afternoons and Sunday mornings, and tried to get to the movies at least twice a week. The Yiddish school kept her off any athletic teams, but she was captain of the debating society, and never lost her English accent; the prejudices of the Ontario school system even helped refine it so that she didn't sound quite so East End any more. No one who heard her would ever have guessed that she'd spent her whole life in areas that any outsider would have characterized as ghettoes.

The University of Toronto offered her a full scholarship; so did McGill and a few other out-of-town schools, but her parents made it clear that she wasn't moving anywhere without them, and they weren't moving anywhere. Chana majored in English at the U of T, took a minor in French, graduated with a ton of awards and was voted valedictorian. Her stepfather had no desire to hear her make a speech in English and refused to come to the convocation.

It was 1934, the depression was at its worst. Chana was teaching at the Yiddish afternoon school, but the wages weren't enough to get by on. Her parents' store was barely limping along, and her stepfather decided to retire. He made an official announcement: "Starting today, *I'll* be the parasite for a change."

Chana had always been a good girl, and had put up with plenty of crap from her stepfather over the years. Her mother's marriage had been a terrible mistake, but there was no way he'd give her a *get*, a Jewish divorce. They knew because he'd said so. There was nothing to be done.

Chana was in the store at nine o'clock the next morning, alone. She checked the books and bank statements and found that everything was in her mother's name. At eleven, she started phoning movie theatres that sponsored dish give-aways and arranged meetings with the managers for later in the week. She had never used her accent for business purposes before and she surprised herself at how fluently she was able to lie. The fibs seemed to come out on their own, without any conscious thought or effort from her. She gave her name as Arabella Aubrey and told them that she was calling on behalf of Montagu Aubrey China, which had finally opened a long-awaited Canadian branch here in Toronto. Forget about "Chana," which only other Jews could pronounce, she knew that most of the managers would never think of meeting with *Anna* Manischewitz, and the one or two who might—there were a couple of *yidn* in the bunch—wouldn't have paid any attention to the deal that she wanted to make. She took the name of the firm from the movies, half Montagu Love, half C. Aubrey Smith. The Arabella was her own idea; it was supposed to convince the suckers of her impeccable Limeyosity.

After making the appointments, she got hold of her best friend, Stella—née Sheyndl—Balaban, at the law firm where she worked as a secretary. Stella's father was a printer who had even fewer customers than Chana's stepfather. "Do me a favour, Stella? I need you to ask your father to print me up, oh, maybe a hundred and fifty, two hundred business cards and let me have them on account for a little while."

"What's the rush?"

"I'll tell you when I see you. It's kind of complicated, but it's strictly business. That damned Herschel is forcing me to run his stupid store, so I've decided to take over for real. Here's what I need the cards to say," and she gave Stella the details.

"What is this, anyway? Who in the name of God is Mrs. Arabella Aubrey and what the hell is this Montagu Aubrey store doing at your address?"

"Just sprucing the place up a bit. I'll tell you the whole story when I see you."

"But how am I going to explain to my father that the cards are for you? He'll do them for free if he knows they're for you, but now, I don't know, Annie."

"Just tell him that *ikh miz farblendn di oygn bay a pur titz areylim*. He'll understand."

She was out to pull the wool over the eyes of a couple of dozen gentiles and remake the business in someone else's image. Her stepfather simply sat in the store, waiting for customers and arguing out loud with the editorials in the Yiddish papers. Herschel refused to read novels and poetry in a place devoted to commerce; he kept such pleasures for home or the library of the Friends of Yiddish Culture, which he would never have left had it not closed at nine o'clock. He let Chana's mother deal with salesmen and wholesalers; he gave expression to his artistic nature by arranging displays in the store and its front window that might well have brought in some trade had the passersby been more refined and had a little more money to spare.

It was a miracle that they lived as well as they did, and they owed the miracle mostly to Mrs. Manischewitz's ceaseless wheedling. She was in and out of the kitchens of every synagogue and benevolent society and wedding hall, trying to convince them of the advantages of buying from her rather than directly from manufacturers or restaurant supply houses. The basic message was: it won't cost you any

more to put food into Jewish mouths, and once you're putting it into Jewish mouths, you might as well put it into the
ones that speak Jewish. She relied on speed more than logic.
Her sales patter, full of widows and orphans and those who
martyred themselves every day for the love of a Jewish
word, worked remarkably well. Years later Chana said, "If
my mother had been twenty years younger, she would have
been the greatest fundraiser who ever *shnorred* a nickel."

Chana had a better idea, though. Rather than beg from
the Jews, she decided to fuck them. She would never have
put it that way, but that's what she was out to do. It worked
so well for everyone else, she was sure it would work for her.
At eleven-thirty, she called Khazkel "Chuckles" Fastow,
whom she'd known since she came to Canada; they were
members of the same Yiddish book circle. Chuckles was
short, bespectacled, and nearly bald at the age of twenty-two.
He wrote vast amounts of metrically regular love poems,
most of them dedicated quite openly to Chana or Anna,
depending on whether they were in Yiddish or English. She
had refused more invitations from him than she had received
from all the other boys she knew.

"Khazkel," she said into the phone, "It's Anna
Manischewitz. How'd you like to take me to the movies
tonight? *It Happened One Night* is on downtown."

"Anna." Chuckles felt a peculiar mixture of awe,
terror and resentment. "Why *dafke* now, Chana? What is
it you want?"

"I need a sign." Chuckles worked in his father's sign business.

"And you have no money." She could see him through the telephone wires, shaking his head. "I thought you were better than this."

"Then don't take me. It's a bit of an emergency, but if you don't want to help, I certainly can't make you." She paused, sighed. "I can hold my own hand in the movies just as easily."

She bit her lip that night and let him touch her bra. By the end of the week, the sign reading "Z.H. Manischewitz and Sons" that overlooked their awning on College Street— the sons were part of a dream that never came true—had been replaced with an understated white-on-black shield so distinguished-looking that it could pass muster in the heart of downtown:

MONTAGU AUBREY

FINE CHINA

DINNERWARE TEA-SETS GIFTS

LONDON TORONTO

Beneath the cities was a coat of arms that Chuckles had copied from the colophon of a book by a long-defunct publisher that Chana had given him. It had some lions and things that looked like bowling pins and a panel of stripes, and directly under it, in much smaller print, the words "By appointment to HRBM Anna I." The HRBM, she said, stood for Her Royal Bushwa Majesty.

The business cards that came a day or two later read the same, but added the store's address and phone number. The coat of arms was lacking—probably a good thing—but the words by themselves were enough to make the rather threadbare store in the middle of a completely Jewish neighbourhood sound like a highly exclusive showroom.

Armed with the cards and her pseudonym, her English accent and a noticeable resemblance to Merle Oberon, Anna dressed in a tight skirt and blouse—a "come hither" body with a "back off" voice—and met with the theatre managers, a good dozen of whom she managed to persuade to use dishes and cutlery from her shop as prizes in their weekly give-aways. She met with school friends who worked in hotels and at the provincial legislature; nearly twenty years before the first Tupperware party, she got other friends, wealthy ones whom she had met in various clubs at the university, some of them not even gentile, to arrange parties for which Chana supplied all the dishes. Rather than be so crass as to try to sell anything at the parties themselves, Anna—who was in mufti as a guest—had the hostess mention, offhandedly and for a five per cent commission, that these were just a few of the masterworks that Mrs. Aubrey and her husband had devoted themselves to making available at last in Canada.

Two years of ass-kissing, lying and scheming turned a poky alcove on the verge of failure into a retail powerhouse in the heart of the fanciest shopping district in the city. Aside from her party-giving friends, no one ever knew that Mrs. Aubrey was really Miss Montajew. Mr. Aubrey entered a state of official non-existence after the shop window was framed in black crepe while the store stayed closed for two weeks: Mr. Aubrey, *Colonel* Aubrey to be strictly accurate, had been killed in the *Hindenburg* disaster and was now interred in his native soil. Chana spent the two weeks vacationing in New York, where she saw at least one double feature a day.

The widow never stepped out of character at work, and people who knew her from the Yiddish reading groups that she still attended began to remark that Chana looked like a different person if she happened to come straight from the store. Because she was in trade, she didn't mix socially with her customers and never gave much thought to the possibility of being found out. Once the store had moved downtown, she was no longer worried about her Jewish acquaintances seeing her inside. She told them that she'd been hired as a salesgirl under the name Anna Mannix. She continued to go to the movies at least two or three times a week.

In 1938 she married Milton Cooper, the six-foot owner of a proudly non-sectarian surname. He was a year or two older than Anna and was considered one of the most promising younger Jewish lawyers in Toronto. They met a year or so before their wedding at a showing of *Nothing Sacred* with Carole Lombard and Frederic March. Each recalled having seen the other more than once at earlier showings of the same picture, and each finally admitted to having sat through it and its accompanying second feature at least twice on every occasion.

Fate brought them together in the popcorn line. Milton found himself right behind Anna. He ignored the tingle in his stomach and tapped her on the shoulder. "Excuse me, miss, but I couldn't help noticing—well, I couldn't help noticing that I've noticed you at a number of showings of this movie and I was wondering . . ."

"Yes?" said Anna, who almost *plotzed* with delight when she turned around and saw that she'd been tapped by the guy she'd noticed in the lobby two or three times already. A couple of days before, when she was there on a blind date, she found herself wondering why *he* couldn't have come to her door instead of the *zhlob* who was waiting for her in the loge while she pretended to powder her nose. "You were wondering . . . if I might be having difficulty following the plot, and if I were, you'd be glad to take me somewhere where you could explain the whole thing to me?"

Milton was getting happier all the time. "Almost. I was wondering if you'll go out with me and let me, uh, since we both seem to be so devoted to this picture, whether you might care," Milton was thinking as fast as he ever had in a courtroom, "to meet me for a cup of coffee at the Childs just down the street where we can discuss it after it's over. It's public and well-lit there—it's Childs, for God's sake, how sinister can it be?"

Anna laughed, ditched her date by claiming a headache—he went into Childs himself after the movie and never spoke to her again—and found Milton in the restaurant. "You're a lawyer and Childs is the best you can do?"

"Would you have met me for a drink in a bar?"

She chuckled. They talked about movies for a while. He gave her his card. She said that she worked in the china shop. As soon as she mentioned the name, Milton said, "I think I'd better tell you then that I'm Jewish."

Anna had never been so relieved. She pressed an index finger to the centre of her lips. "So am I," she whispered in Yiddish, "may Mrs. Aubrey never find out."

She didn't tell him the truth until their fourth date, right after she'd accepted his proposal. "That's a relief," he said. He was wearing a white dinner jacket and the hotel band was playing Jerome Kern. "I didn't like the idea of you working for *antisemitn*, and I've been trying to figure out why you liked *Nothing Sacred*"—about a girl who pretends to be dying of radiation poisoning so that she can get out of Vermont and be a celebrity in New York—"so much."

"But at the beginning, Carole Lombard really thought she was going to die. I came into this dishonest."

"That must be what attracted me."

"And what about you, Dr. Jekyll? What made *you* see it seven times?"

"Carole Lombard. I'll see anything she's in seven times."

"Shiksa *krikher*! Carole Lombard? I don't look anything like Carole Lombard."

"You don't sound anything like her either. I saw *My Man Godfrey* ten times."

"So who *do* I look like, Mr. Wisenheimer?" She was expecting the usual answer.

"Uh . . . Eddie Cantor? Edna Mae Oliver?"

"I could pour this wine over your head, you know."

"You look, you look most like, you know as well as I do—Merle Oberon, of course."

"Not in *Henry the Eighth*, I hope," where Oberon played Anne Boleyn. "I'd like to keep my head."

"No, more like *The Scarlet Pimpernel*, though I have to say that your accent reminds me of Boris Karloff."

"You sure know how to make a girl feel good. Would you think me unladylike if I told you to bugger off?"

"Just don't let anyone call me Mr. Aubrey."

Milton joined the RCAF not long after the War broke out and was killed over Dieppe in August, 1942. Anna was convinced that his death was a punishment, a sort of payback for the lies she told about the death of Montagu Aubrey. She never really got over Milton, perhaps because they'd had everything but children. For almost five years after his death, she did everything alone. She was spending less and less time on Yiddish literature—in the middle of World War II, it was the last thing to help take your mind off your troubles—and more and more time in the movies, going as often as seven nights a week when the loneliness got especially bad.

Despite her mother's pleas, she didn't move back to their house on Shaw Street. Milton had inherited his parents' home on ultra-fancy Palmerston Boulevard, and it, like everything else he left behind, was now Anna's. Between the money coming in from Montagu Aubrey and the money left by Milton, Anna, the girl who had been forced to go to work in her stepfather's failing business eight years earlier, had quietly—very, very quietly—become one of the wealthiest Jewish women in Toronto. She didn't stop working, though. The endless days of the early years were now as remote as the years themselves, but Anna was still in character as Mrs. Aubrey for at least eight of every twenty-four hours. Once the Blitz had got underway, while Milton was probably still in training, Anna—Mrs. Aubrey, really—had sponsored a two-night Dresden China Blitz near Grenadier Pond in High Park. Torontonians of all ages and backgrounds, especially those with loved ones in the service, were invited to come out and smash their Dresden plates and figurines, and have the shards refashioned, free of charge, into tiny ornamental toilets with Hitler's face at the bottom of the bowl.

This stunt turned Montagu into the Patriotic China Shop, the shop that was On Our Side; almost any girl marrying a serviceman or someone who was going to be a serviceman wanted to get her china from Montagu Aubrey. Chana had no trouble keeping busy, but the nights were long and lonely, and when there was finally nothing playing that she hadn't already seen, she'd go to the odd Yiddish social or literary evening. Toronto was like Stashov on Lake Ontario; a large part of Chana's hometown ended up there before the War, and a disproportionate amount of literary time was devoted to the son of a Stashover mother who was one of the most popular Yiddish writers in Poland in the decade before the War: "*Der Mazik*," Elyokim Faktor, whose mother's youngest sister was living in Toronto. Faktor's mother had been dead for nearly twenty years, and her sister assumed that the rest of the family, like most of the rest of Stashov, had probably been murdered already.

Faktor's satirical verse, his stories and plays, and, of course, "The Pogromist's Lullaby," became their elegies. Where traditional Jews read the Book of Lamentations every year on the anniversary of the destruction of the Temple, Toronto's Stashover Literary Heritage Society recited one or another of Faktor's works every week, weeping in anguish at the same time as they laughed at his jokes and wordplay. His pieces *were* the culture that they were mourning; their little shtetl, which Faktor had probably visited two or three times as a child and never seen again, had made the whole Jewish world smile.

And now, in January 1947, his aunt had found him on a Red Cross list and was sponsoring him and his daughter, about whom she knew absolutely nothing, as immigrants to Canada. She'd tried to send Faktor some money for a ticket, but he wrote back and told her that he didn't need it. All he wanted was enough to get to Zurich. From there, he said, he and his daughter could make their own way to Canada.

The members of the Stashov reception committee were used to meeting shabby, furtive-looking DPs in clothes that the Sally Ann would have turned down. Faktor emerged from a first-class compartment in an unfashionable but unquestionably new morning coat and top hat, with a monocle in his left eye and a walking stick in his right hand. "Give a look," he said in his George Formby accent, "it's me, Charlie McCarthy." His three-and-a-half-year-old daughter was dressed like a little princess.

Years of exercise, illness and privation had prevented any resurgence of his weight problem. His custom-made pants had a thirty-inch waist, and as fat as he ever got in Canada was to wear a thirty-two from 1970 to '85. His complexion had cleared up, his skin was no longer mottled, and he hadn't lost any hair. Overdressed as he was, with a cigar in his hand and his big fleshy lips sticking out of his face like fungi on the side of a tree, he looked to Chana and everyone else there, especially his aunt Gitl, like a clueless gangster on his yearly trip to the synagogue. Whatever happened to him during the War had also left him with a hunted, slightly crafty look that he didn't lose for a number of years. It was partly in his eyes—so light blue that his irises almost disappeared in the sun—partly in the set of his mouth, its thick lips always nervously pressed together as if he were planning an escape from a difficult position.

Chana felt that he'd let her down. She'd never seen a photo of Faktor, and couldn't reconcile the humorous, even corrosive, yet strangely tender writing with his vulgar features and tasteless self-presentation. She told herself that any further relations with him would be strictly on the printed page. Looking at him made her uneasy. She shook his hand rather gingerly when they were introduced and pretended not to notice how his eyes ran up and down her body as he bowed to kiss her hand. He said something in what she recognized as Polish but couldn't understand. "You understood?" he asked in English. She shook her head, no. "I said, my daughter asks if perhaps you have a child." He switched into Yiddish. "She said the other women all look like bubbes."

This was the clumsiest pickup line that Chana had come across in quite a while, and the only one she'd ever heard from a refugee dressed up like a ventriloquist's dummy. A lady is always a lady, though. "No." She wasn't going to screw around; she answered in Yiddish. "I'm a widow and I have no children."

Faktor nodded rather solemnly and turned away from her without a word. He knelt to the little girl and stroked her hair—so black and straight that it could have been Chinese—and said, "I'm sorry, Temkele. The lady doesn't have any children. But don't worry, we'll find you someone to play with soon." He went back to Chana. "We were three days on the train—no children at all. On the boat"—he covered his mouth with his hands and puffed out his cheeks. "No matter where we go," he was speaking Yiddish again, "we can't find any Jewish three-year-olds." Chana looked at Faktor and saw no more sleaziness around the eyes and mouth. "She's never played with anybody but me for more than a few minutes."

Chana's opinion was starting to change.

3

EARL

"Ninety-five years old and I'm still doing everything." Arranging the funeral and getting the
house ready for the shiva hadn't given Chana
much time for grief. "If I don't get help soon, it's going
to be too late." She'd been speaking English to herself
ever since she wasn't supposed to as a kid. "Kids—you
break your back all your life and you're lucky if they can
be bothered to kick you in the ass. Can't even get off their
own to help put their father away with a little bit of dignity. Faktor was right." She thought about her children
and was finally starting to cry. She pulled the folded
Kleenex out from under her watchstrap and held it up to
blow her nose. "Tammy, *ala ha-shulem*, was the only one
worth a damn," and Tammy wasn't even hers. She landed
in Canada with Faktor, a little girl whose mother had
died in childbirth and whom Chana adopted when she
married her father.

About all you could say for the two kids that they had
together was that other people had much worse. Don't

misunderstand: Chana was full of maternal feeling, but these were not the children she would have chosen.

Neither Ava nor Niven could be bothered to live in Toronto—which is mostly what Chana had against them. Ava, the elder, lived with her wife in the Queen Charlotte Islands, but wouldn't allow her parents to tell anyone. As far as Mrs. Aubrey was concerned, if Ava's wife had to keep her lesbianism such a deep, dark secret, she didn't deserve to sleep with her Ava. She and Faktor had never met this girlfriend, and Suzy, whose last name they didn't even know, had no contact with the family. "Maybe," Faktor had said, "she doesn't know that Ava's Jewish."

Her brother, Niven, five years younger, had been teaching Old English and Old Norse at the tiny but prestigious College of St. David in Weston-super-Mare for the last thirty years. He wore plaid flannel sports jackets and had been rumoured by his fellow grad students at Leeds University to cultivate his dandruff on purpose. He'd never married, but talked to his parents on the phone every Sunday.

Both children had their mother's dark hair and their father's natural girth. For most of Niven's years in school— from the Sholem Asch Hebrew Day School, which taught more Yiddish than Hebrew, through William Lyon MacKenzie Collegiate Institute and on to the University of Toronto, stuffed as it was with alumni of the earlier institutions—Niven was known as Herbie, after the obese, lollipop-sucking Herbie Popnecker, hero of the eponymous comic book. Niven's round horn-rimmed glasses and half-Beatle, half-bowl haircut were exact matches for Herbie's. He heard "I'll bop you with this here lollipop," Herbie's catchphrase, so many thousands of times in school corridors, from moving cars while he walked on Wilmington or Sheppard Avenue and even Bathurst Street, the Broadway of Jewish Canada; he heard it in stores and on buses; he heard it so much that he already knew where he was likely to hear it and he therefore avoided any elevator with male passengers under the age of twenty and developed a lifelong aversion to suckers of every flavour. As soon as he was able, he moved to England, where he still received invitations from high school and university reunion committees addressed to Herbert Faktor.

Chana, at ninety-five, still took care with her wardrobe and had her hair done every week. Her kids both looked like they'd been raised in Dogpatch. For all she saw them, they might as well have lived there. Tammy is the person she would have gone to at a time like this, beautiful, sweet, devoted Tammy, who lived fifteen minutes away. But because Tammy wasn't here any more, Chana—to these people she was always Chana; Mrs. Aubrey rarely came home—Chana had to fall back on Tammy's husband, Earl.

Tammy had been dead since 1990, but everyone, including Earl, went on thinking of him as part of the family. He offered to contact the funeral home while Chana signed and collected the papers they were going to need. "Earl," she added through her sobs, "One other thing, if you don't mind."

"Whatever you want, Chana."

"Hold on a second." She found the tiny leather-bound phone directory in her purse and flipped the E–F tab open. "Could you let Ava and Niven know? I don't have enough change to call from a pay phone." Earl rolled his eyes. "I'll give you their numbers."

"That's all right, Chana. I've got them here." Earl was telling the truth. "I'll call them as soon as we're off the phone."

In spite of his beautiful house, well-stocked bank account, enviable professional reputation, and a retirement in which he could do almost anything he wanted, Earl Frumkiss was just about the unluckiest guy that Earl Frumkiss had ever met. His kids hated him. Hated him? Not really. It was worse. They were ashamed of him. He could tell. They thought he was was an embarrassment, a national disgrace. And why? Because he tried to do his best. He could have been like them and done nothing. He could have lived off his in-laws' money, but Earl was determined to make his own way, look after his family on his own, become the biggest man in his field in the whole country. And you don't turn an office above an Italian bakery into a nationwide chain of clinics without making a few commercials. "Hi, I'm Dr. Earl Frumkiss." He first said it during commercial breaks in the late show, back when there was still a late show. He said it and said it, in better and better time slots on stations with higher and higher ratings until "Hi, I'm Dr. Earl Frumkiss" became a kind of password to national identity. People turning up in the wrong place at the wrong time would blush and introduce themselves as Dr. Earl Frumkiss; police reports noted that muggers and home invaders had been using it for years, much to the chagrin of both Frumkiss and their victims.

"I'm Dr. Earl Frumkiss" introduced every commercial for every Frumkiss Family Foot Care Clinic ever made. Earl's favourite featured a disgraced Olympic sprinter sighing, "Oh, my aching feet," but the most popular, the one that transformed his children's schooldays from loci of workaday teasing into an uninterrupted campaign to drive them mad, was the one that introduced the Frumkiss Family Foot Care jingle:

> When my feet are feeling beat,
> I don't waste time on gimmicks.
> I bring 'em in, with spouse and kin,
> To Frumkiss Family Clinics.

Earl was rather proud of having written it himself. The first time Faktor heard it—it aired after the station break between *Kraft Music Hall* with Perry Como and *Hodgkins!*, a short-lived CBC drama about an incorruptible restaurant health inspector—he phoned Tammy and advised her to file for divorce. "The old man"—*old man* was just one of his pet names for Earl—"is bringing you a shame that you'll never live down." Faktor, as usual, was right. Within hours—minutes—the jingle had been revised by kids from coast to coast:

> Trick or treat,
> Smell my feet,
> The Frumkiss family
> Beats its meat.

All three of Earl's kids blamed him and his commercials for every untoward event that ever befell them, every personal or social failure all the way into high school, and Earl could never forget it. As far as he was concerned, they might as well have blamed him for giving them the wherewithal to go on failing right into their forties. Three nothings he had, and only one with a real excuse. And the excuse was one of his other kids. That took care of the girls. His son was harmless enough, he'd never done anything but kill Earl's dreams. Some reward for having worked his way up from nothing and nowhere, all on his own: he had his pride, Earl, and after Faktor called him "Mr. Dynamite" for the first time, he vowed never to accept any help from him. Ever. It was rough those first few years, establishing himself and his practice while Tammy worked for

Burroughs Adding Machines and gave music lessons on the side, but Earl almost succeeded. He was the kind of guy who couldn't walk by a brick wall without banging his head against it, and he knocked an awful lot of them down.

His life had always been hard—that's the way he liked it. But it had turned burdensome and stale since his wife, the best thing that ever happened to him, died suddenly and pointlessly while she was still in her forties. Earl had been on cruise control ever since. Tammy was the only woman he'd ever loved, the only woman he'd ever been with, the only person—man or woman—who ever paid enough attention to Earl to find out who he really was.

He never understood why. Even Earl knew that he wasn't up to much on the outside. He was a grain of human sand, enough like all the other grains that no one ever thought of looking for the difference. His height was average, his weight was average, his hair, when he had it, was sandy. It was hard for him to start a conversation; he had trouble making friends. If he'd disappeared when he was in high school and the cops had questioned his classmates about him, they'd have found no more than half a dozen who had ever said a word to him. And they would have described him as a fussy, over-particular kind of guy who was never quite satisfied. Abundance was just another headache. A kid could have got the best pair of skates that money could buy or got hold of a Jaguar to drive to school, and all young Earl would have thought—and thinking was about

all he could do, in view of how few people he spoke to—
was, "Aaah, who needs it?"

He was a born old man. He came into the world a couple
of years before the War. His parents had come from Lithuania
just before the Depression and figured that their childbearing
days were long past. Earl's youngest sister was twelve years
older; he hardly ever heard English until he started school.
His eldest sister, who was already married when his parents
decided to leave, stayed in Kaunas with her husband and baby.
Earl never met her. His youngest sister was dead now, too,
while the middle one, Feyge-Brayndl was in a home for
seniors with Alzheimer's four or five blocks from the Frumkiss
family home in Bathurst Manor, where Earl still lived.

He grew up in the old Jewish neighbourhood, not far
from where Chana started out. His family was plain, not too
anything—not too religious, not too smart, not too rich, not
too poor. They kept kosher and observed the Sabbath as a
matter of course; Earl's father was convinced that daily
synagogue attendance was the fount of all self-discipline.
"I don't go because of God," he used to say. "I could stay
home and pray. I go because it's a very good habit." Earl
went with him every day until he moved to Cleveland to
attend the Ohio College of Podiatric Medicine. He once
tried to stop going when he was about twenty-one.

"What? You don't believe in God any more?" his
father asked.

"No. Yes. I don't know. I guess so.

"So why don't you wanna go then? Do you eat pork, God forbid?"

"No," Earl lied. He did it mostly in the cafeterias at the university where he wasn't likely to run into his parents or any of their friends.

"Do you smoke on shabbes?"

"No." This time he was telling the truth. Earl couldn't get away from his family long enough to sneak a smoke and have time for the smell to wear off.

"So you must believe that God gave the Torah to Moses on Mount Sinai or you wouldn't be doing any of this."

"No." Earl wasn't sure if he was lying or not. "I don't believe it. I only keep shabbes and eat kosher because you won't let me have any choice. But don't think that means I believe it."

Earl's father was about five foot one and couldn't have weighed much more than a hundred pounds. Earl gave him a look of defiance and braced his knees against the storm he was sure was coming. He wasn't quite sure what form it would take, but he knew it was going to be rough.

Instead of saying anything, though, his father turned his back to him and walked over to the bookcase. "I admire honesty." He turned around as if he'd been surprised by a visitor while searching for one of his rarer volumes. "I respect a man who isn't afraid to give an honest opinion. You don't believe? You don't believe. Your uncle, my brother Meyshe—you never met him—he didn't believe, too. A socialist, that Meyshe? He would have eaten lobster sandwiches on Passover, if they'd had lobsters in the Soviet Union. Or Passover. Or bread. I didn't agree with him, but I respected him. Some of his fellow non-believers shot him in Moscow in the Lubyanka. You don't wanna believe, trust me, you don't have to believe. And if you really don't believe, it's stupid to make you go to *shul*. Just do me one favour." The old man turned back to the bookcase and pulled a book off one of the shelves. Earl could see that it was a *khumesh*, the first five books of the Bible, Genesis to Deuteronomy. His father held it out to him. "Take it. I want you should do me just two little things and then I'll never bother you about going to shul again." Earl stood there looking stupid; a complete lack of chin fooled many people into thinking that he was dumb. "Take the book like I told you." He took it. "Now open it up. Anywhere. Just open it." Earl opened it; he landed on a passage in Leviticus about abominations. "It's open? Good. Now spit. Go ahead, give a *shpay*. You don't believe, then you don't believe. It's okay. You can spit. No? You won't do it? If I ask you nice will you tear out a couple of pages? Just rip them out and take them into the bathroom with you and use them to wipe your ass. Nu? Get in there . . . You're not going? To tell you the truth, I'm relieved." He smiled, but not at Earl. "You're not an atheist. You're not an unbeliever. We both deserve a mazl tov. Now pick up your tefillin and haul yourself to shul with me now. We're going to be late."

There was a theory among those who thought about Earl at all that he chose podiatry because there were no schools for it anywhere in Canada and he had no relatives in Cleveland. He stopped going to shul every day and began to eat treyf openly as soon as he commenced serious study of the human foot. He graduated summa cum laude in 1963 and decided to reward himself with a vacation before starting his residency in the fall. Since neither Earl nor his family had any money, he went to Israel, where he could work on a kibbutz without having to worry about paying for meals or accommodation. "But you'll be working, won't you?" asked Tim Norval, his best friend at podiatric college.

"And what would I do with myself all day if I wasn't?" Earl answered.

He ended up on one of the loser kibbutzim where most of the other volunteers were church-goers from Canada or the States, sorrowful Germans, or Australians looking to party. Tammy was there because the loser friend with whom she went to Israel wanted to be on the same kibbutz as her Australian cousin and Tammy was too nice to put her foot down and fight for something better or dump the loser altogether and make the trip with someone else. Tons of her friends were going that summer, and Tammy was one of the most popular girls in her circle. She was concerned, though, that if she didn't go with Bryna, the loser, Bryna would end up alone. That's the kind of person Tammy was. "I would have ditched that Bryna in a second," Earl had lost track of the number of times he'd said it or even just thought it, "but that's why I'm not as good a person. Tammy never thought about herself."

Earl was struck by Tammy's voice before he'd ever seen her. She had the kind of Joan Baez soprano that was popular at the time and which Earl always found particularly attractive. The volunteers used to sit around in big circles and sing after they'd finished working for the day. Unless they had a bonfire, the nights all smelled of lilac and the manure they used in the fields. Someone would bring out a guitar and they'd all start singing: "Tom Dooley," "Blowin' in the Wind," "Michael Row the Boat Ashore," that sort of thing. Tammy was singing Israeli songs that she'd learned from records by Theodore Bikel and Hillel and Aviva, as well as some Yiddish stuff that was also in Bikel's repertoire and had become severely unfashionable, especially in Israel. From the way she was singing, Earl could tell that she knew what she was saying. Although he had scarcely spoken to a female since he'd landed in Israel— he hadn't spoken to very many males, either—he pushed past the smooching couples on the periphery of the circle to get a good look at the singer and maybe try to say something to her if she looked like she might be friendly.

She was small and so dark that she could have been anything—Indian, Italian, Arab, some sort of weird tribal Jew from Libya or Samarkand. Earl couldn't have known that Tammy looked just like her mother, or that she'd been born in Alma Ata. He didn't know anything about talking to girls. He skipped his high school prom because none of the six girls he asked said yes. He'd been on a few blind dates without ever being accepted for a follow-up. The more nervous he got, the fussier he became. He knew it was happening, but he didn't have the strength to stop it. The thought of silence was enough to make him panic, and he could go on at length about everything that was wrong: "He won't do this, he don't like that. Something else is a waste of time and what the hell does he need it for—if I wanted to date my zeyde, I'd buy a shovel and dig him up." Earl had never got to first base; he was twenty-six years old and had never been kissed.

He didn't know that Tammy was from Toronto or even that they'd lived in the same neighbourhood up until four years ago, when he left for Ohio, anyway. There probably wasn't a boy on earth who didn't find Tammy cute, but Earl thought she was the most beautiful thing he'd ever seen; she was like the pictures of Pier Angeli and Natalie Wood that he used to tape to the walls of his room. He had to be sure to say just the right thing. No dismissive hand gestures. No kvetching. No pointing out how pointless it was to have a fire when there were no marshmallows anywhere in the country and the nighttime temperature never went below twenty degrees Celsius. He had to say something friendly, something smart. It had to be memorable, had to make an impression that would leave her asking for more of him. "Hi" wouldn't do it. "Where you from" was so overworked that even Earl wouldn't consider it. He looked towards the ground, thinking, looking at the criss-crossed Band-Aids sticking out between the straps of his sandals; he'd bought them on his last trip to town and they were shredding his feet into sauerkraut, but he didn't want to be the only guy at the bonfire in work boots.

None of the pick-up lines that he knew was going to work any better here than anywhere else. Poetry? Too silly, and he also didn't know any. "You sing beautifully" or "Where'd you learn to play the guitar?" Strictly feh.

She was looking at him now. He knew that she could tell that he'd come all that way to talk to her, but she wasn't making it any easier for him. She stood there, every last bit of her, and looked. She wasn't smiling, but she looked approachable. If only she'd speak, make that all-important first move that would give Earl's self-confidence a bit of a boost. She waited a minute or two. Earl felt himself blushing; he was sweating so heavily that he felt like he'd wet his pants. Tammy turned ninety degrees, bent over and opened her guitar case. Oh shit, she was going to go. It was now or never.

Earl moved a step or two closer. He coughed and cleared his throat. Tammy looked back up at him. "Um, excuse me," he said, kicking himself inwardly for the delay, "*Tsi reyt ir yidish?* Do you speak Yiddish?"

"Some question," she answered in Yiddish. "*Un ir*, and you've been over here so long that you can't remember any English?"

"I remember, I remember. *Ober ikh vil aykh nisht klingen azoy vi yeyder khayim-yankl vos vil zikh bakenen mit aykh*, I just don't want to sound like every Tom, Dick and Harry who wants to get to know you."

He never really understood what she saw in him and, in all the years they spent together, it was the only thing she would never tell him. Whenever he asked, she'd give him a kiss and say, "What does it matter? I love you because you're you; what I see in you is that you aren't somebody else."

"Who else?" He'd press her occasionally.

"No one else." She'd give him another kiss.

She was afraid to tell him the truth, in case she hurt his feelings and he developed a complex. Aside from the fact that in Yiddish Earl was actually funny—they didn't speak it enough that it made much difference—she liked what everybody else hated about him: his dogged stodginess and love of routine, the fear of disorder that led him to wake up sometimes in the middle of the night, worried that a pair of his argyle socks might have got into the drawer with the solids. After a lifetime with a professional madcap for a father and a stepmother who spent much of her time pretending to be an English widow who didn't exist, predictable and slightly dull was just what she was looking for.

Fussy as Earl could be, he was totally compliant when

it came to Tammy, and Tammy could hardly be called demanding. After living with two eccentric adults and having to look after her spoiled and weird, really weird half-brother and -sister, Tammy's biggest ambition was to run her day-to-day life. To pick the china patterns, decide on the furniture, determine a menu for the week. Earl was as close to Ward Cleaver or Jim Anderson from *Father Knows Best* as she was going to get, but instead of having to manipulate him, all she had to do was ask. They got engaged on the kibbutz. Her friend Bryna never spoke to her again.

The only real problem was Tammy's father. "*Oy, gevalt,*" he yelled in Yiddish, "*a square, a square fin Delaware,*" and if there was one thing that Faktor couldn't stand, it was squares. "He's what? Twenty-six, twenty-seven? So how come he's older than I am? You marry him, Temke, and you'll be dead from boredom before you're thirty."

Chana agreed that he was a little bit dull, but she admired his drive. "He's pretty smart and he works like a dog. And he follows Temke around like a dog, too. Faktor, she's no dope. She knows what she wants. And if this is it, *gezinterhayt,* let her enjoy it. You don't have to live with him."

"No, but I have to make small talk."

"He could be a lot more interesting and still not get a word in."

They were married two years later, after Tammy finished her bachelor's degree in music. The wedding was in June;

they honeymooned in Israel, even revisiting the kibbutz where they'd met, then went back to Ohio so Earl could finish his residency. Tammy taught Yiddish at one of the Jewish day schools in Cleveland and started performing in local coffee houses, relinquishing a budding showbiz career when she was into the sixth month of her pregnancy and couldn't reach the guitar for her midriff. Their daughter Vanessa was born at the tail end of 1966; when Earl's residency finished in the spring, they moved back to Toronto, where he set up a practice.

Faktor and Chana bought them a custom-built house in the fanciest part of the nearly all-Jewish enclave known as Bathurst Manor: the far east end of Blue Forest Drive right next to the entrance to the day camp in the valley. The valley is really a ravine, but ravine must have sounded too Jewish. With their indoor and outdoor pools and a billiard room, with pool table, cues and pool-room lighting on the lower level, the Frumkisses didn't need any stinking day camp.

Earl would have turned the house down if his in-laws had offered it, but Tammy convinced him not to look a fait accompli in the mouth. He opened an office on the Italian part of Dufferin Street, figuring that all those construction workers and bricklayers and labourers were going to have plenty of foot trouble, and was pleasantly surprised to discover a virtual epidemic of bunions and hammertoes among old ladies dressed in black. He worked hard and he prospered; he and Tammy had sex and they had twins. If Earl's pleasant surprise took place on Dufferin, Tammy's had come earlier, on their honeymoon. Earl had been so shy during their make-out sessions that she'd been fretful about the man-and-wife part of their approaching marriage, but Earl told her not to worry. He was a little old-fashioned, as if she hadn't already noticed, but as soon as everything was official, no power on earth was going to hold him back. She saw what he meant on the night of their wedding: if cocks needed bras, he would have worn a double D. *Now* she understood why he refused to be seen in a bathing suit. Remarkably for a male virgin, he had no trouble controlling himself after their first time—he told her that he'd been practising "techniques" that he'd read about in various manuals since he was a teenager—and Tammy had very few sleepless nights after she and Earl were married.

He went on working and saving. Without rent or a mortgage to worry about, he put aside enough to open a second office inside of a year, and it wasn't long after that that he began to hire chiropodists and other podiatrists to work under his supervision. The chiropodists split their fees with him, the podiatrists paid for office space, administrative personnel and supplies. He started advertising as soon as he opened the second office, but before he did that he gave Tammy the gift that he'd *wanted* to give her at their wedding but hadn't been able to afford. He booked studio time for her and her guitar, hired a prominent folk music producer and waited a couple of days for them to come up with a dozen finished songs. He took the acetates to a mid-level ethnic label in the States and, unbeknown to Tammy, subsidized an album for them to release.

By the time it was ready, Tammy had three children and was starting to wonder if she'd put a gun to the head of her youth when she married and pulled the trigger when she started having kids. She wasn't even thirty, but felt that she'd missed her whole young adulthood. Although it wasn't exactly a complete surprise, Tammy was thrilled with the record, even more by the idea that it had come out on a real label and that people could go into stores and buy it. *Introducing Tamara* used one of Tammy's publicity photos from Cleveland on its cover. It showed Tammy with a beehive hair-do in the middle of a field of clover. She was wearing a white blouse under a dirndl and was apparently playing a guitar.

The record received decent reviews and sold steadily, albeit in relatively modest numbers, for decades. *Woofer Report* called it "an accomplished reading of some overly familiar material. Tamara's voice is the highlight here. Let's hope her next outing is a little more adventurous." Thirty years later, after Tammy was already dead, *Introducing Tamara* was reissued on CD for the sake of the cover, which had popped up in a few anthologies of campy-looking old LPs. Copies of the original were going for up to twenty-five dollars on eBay.

By the time Tammy died in 1990, Earl had been national for close to fifteen years and had four clinics in

Toronto alone. Any Canadian who had ever turned on a television knew who he was, and he used to get stopped on the street like a real celebrity, much to the mortification of his children and the delight of his wife, who was surprised and delighted by how far out of his shell he'd come in the time that she'd known him.

They went on screwing four times a week except when Earl was out of town. On top of everything else, he had the best sex life he'd ever heard of, even if it had all been with the same person. Fussy as he was, Earl knew what he liked—and he liked Tammy more all the time.

And then she had to go and die. On a Sunday morning when he was in Victoria getting ready for the grand opening of the city's first Frumkiss Family Foot Care Clinic. It was Frumkiss: Family Foot Care, not Frumkiss Family: Foot Care, or at least not yet. Earl's son, Randall, was in his last year at York University in Toronto and had just submitted his application to Dad's alma mater in Cleveland. With any luck, the signs outside every location would soon read: Frumkiss Family Family Foot Care Clinic. Earl was lying in bed half awake at six o'clock in the morning, able to see the signs in his mind and absently stroking his boner, when the phone rang. It was Rachel, the smartest of his kids and probably the sanest, in spite of her nervous breakdown. She was the only one who seemed to understand that those commercials were the reason that all three kids had had their own cars since they learned how to drive.

"Dad?" Rachel was also the only one of the kids still living at home. "Dad?" Earl was swimming towards consciousness. Rachel didn't sound right. "You need to come home right now. Mom just died."

Earl woke right up. "What?"

"Mom just died." He could hear her struggling to keep her voice level.

"How? What happened?"

"I don't know. Just come home now."

Earl checked out of his hotel, got into a cab, went straight to the airport, booked a seat on the next flight from Vancouver to Toronto and got onto the next flight to the mainland. He could remember thinking how lucky he was to be rich, because these last-second flights were costing him thousands. He called his assistant at home and had her cancel everything for the next little while. He dialled Faktor's number and hung up as soon as he heard the wailing on the other end.

Everything had stunk ever since. It started at the funeral, where he tried to hold hands with all the kids as they walked into the chapel, then got mad because he had three kids but only two hands. By the end of the shiva, Earl was an old man again. Not just an old man, but an old bachelor, someone who had never bothered to adapt himself to other people. The kids noticed right away. "This is what he would have been if he'd never met Mom." No one believed them at first, but six months later, when Earl was still telling

everybody to fuck off and leave him alone, they knew that
the kids were right.

"The weirdest was when he ran away." Rachel managed to stick it out at home for the first six months, and then
some. "I was only twenty-two and Mom and I had been
pretty close, so you can imagine how messed over I was.
I was still in school; I'd moved home because I was drinking
too much and trying to be popular. I wanted to stop party-
ing, when wham! In the middle of my self-administered
rehab, my mother dies and my father starts to go nuts. I was
cured in a second. Our cleaning lady didn't do meals, so
he hired a cook to come in and make us supper every day.
One day we're sitting there, having supper together, and he
says something about how pretty soon I'll probably be moving
out again and he wonders if it makes sense for one person
to live in such a big house all alone. And I said, yeah, but
the house was paid for and Mom had loved it so much, even
if it was a little bit old, but then again, so was he, ha ha ha,
and he just went nuts. Completely ballistic. Jumped up and
started screaming that we were all just waiting for him to
drop dead, too, so we could take absolutely everything.
'That's how you want it?' He started to really scream.
'That's how you want it? Well, fine by me. I'll pack a bag
and go.' And he ran upstairs, cursing all the way, saying
'fuck' and everything—things I'd never heard him say
before—then comes stomping back down with a plastic bag
from the liquor store, where I guess he's got a couple of

shirts and a toothbrush, and goes straight to the door and yells back at me, 'Don't worry about me. Don't you worry about me. I'll get a place. I'll be fine.'

"I called Ran right away, but we couldn't stop laughing. I was still on the phone with him when Dad came home, looking a little embarrassed and pretending that nothing had happened. He just said hi and went straight to his room. He used to play that record that Mom made over and over, I think so I wouldn't hear him crying."

Earl finally got tired of listening to Tamara's record, but nothing else changed much. He never stopped grieving. He screamed "Drop dead" at someone who came up to him on the street one day and said "You're Dr. Earl Frumkiss" just the way Earl did on the commercials. After he read his victim's letter to the editor in the next day's paper, Earl stopped taking his grief out on others. He went so far as to cultivate a look of haggard saintliness, an aura of compassion born of suffering. One of the last commercials that he did before selling the business and retiring on his millions had him come out and say, "I'm Dr. Earl Frumkiss, and I know what it's like when the pain won't stop."

He grew closer to his in-laws, insisted on turning up at their house every Friday night and paying for the dinners that they ordered from Faktor's favourite Chinese restaurant. He delivered homilies on the importance of family and togetherness over foil casseroles of sweet and sour chicken balls, as if Faktor and Chana could never understand what he was going through. Faktor, who had lost a wife when Earl was still a little boy, would wait for him to leave and then tell Chana, "I'm Elyokim Faktor, and I know what it's like when a shmuck won't stop."

Chana thought he was being unfair. "Enough, Faktor. Can't you see he's suffering?"

"And I'm not? You can turn your hearing aid off, I've got to listen to him prattle on like he's the only one who lost something. I've been telling you since Temke first brought him home, he isn't a person, he's a whine, a ravening kvetch that swallows everything it sees."

Faktor might have been unfair, but that didn't make Earl any the less sorry for himself. When Chana called with the news of Faktor's death, he was ready for anything but his own children. Dealing with the funeral home was easy. Calling Ava was easy and calling Niven was even easier; he wasn't home, so Earl just had to leave a message. He told both of them to get to Toronto by Sunday and that the funeral would probably be on Monday morning.

Then it was time for the kids. This wasn't like calling Faktor's children; these were his, and Earl couldn't just dial a number and leave a message: he had to tell them why and how and how important it was that they get here post haste and not mess around, and there simply wasn't time for all of that right now. Calling Vanessa was out of the question, anyway. It was Friday here and it was already shabbes in

Israel; she wouldn't pick up a phone until roughly this time tomorrow. Besides, Earl was in no mood for her hostile religious shtik, her refusal to speak anything but Yiddish. She sure didn't want to speak it when he was sending her to the Sholem Asch school. Back then, she spoke it badly and with a horrible, he hated to say it, gentile accent. She was trying to prove something—she usually was—and at this particular moment, Earl didn't give a damn what it was.

No point in calling Randall, either. Earl had come close to sitting shiva for him once already, and he was pretty sure that Randall would deny or screw up any request just because it was Earl who asked. On the other hand, Randall had been closer to the old man than the other two, and with only twenty minutes left before his appointment at the funeral home, Earl was too busy to sit through anyone's extravagant grief. According to Rachel, Randall was depressed these days. Probably served him right, whatever the reason, and Earl already knew that he'd probably take whatever was bothering him—lack of girlfriend, lack of job, lack of money or hope or future or brains—and recast it as grief over Faktor, so that the dead zeyde, to whom Randall will suddenly have been bound like Jacob to Benjamin, David to Jonathan, or Peter to Gordon, could provide him with at least twelve months of a concrete reason, a plausible excuse, for his droopy letdown of a life.

So it was Rachel. It had to be Rachel. He'd known it all along, but wanted to kid himself into thinking that he had the kind of family where there was some kind of choice when something needed to be done. She was the only one of the kids on Earl's speed-dial, and she was on it twice: once for home and once for her cell.

She was in the middle of her daily divorce when the phone rang, standing under the shower while muttering her real feelings about her husband in a voice that rose sporadically to a desperate, almost demented scream, the kind of thing you used to hear when the drunken couple next door would get into another one of their fights back in the old neighbourhood that you're still telling your kids how lucky they are never to have had to live in. Two, maybe three octaves below her normal tone, she'd growl out some crowning, marriage-ending insult, put both hands on her hips and stare down to the floor of the shower and the bright red nails on her size four feet.

Rachel lived in the Jewish part of Thornhill, a suburb of Toronto that was like a Photoshopped update of the Bathurst Manor she'd grown up in. Atkinson Avenue, only two blocks from her house, is crowned by a hat trick of Hebrew schools—Orthodox and Reform bang bang right together, so kids on either side can see each other every day and know who not to play with, and a "Mainstream" day school on the next block, as if to say, "We have no part in your petty squabbles"—while drivers trying to park at the Promenade shopping mall, two blocks west on Bathurst Street, have to stick-handle their cars around men in prayer shawls cutting through the parking lot on their way to and from any number of local synagogues on Saturdays. While remnants of the town's white working-class past can still be found in its older sections, neither Rachel nor anybody that she knew ever ventured into them; not much of her Thornhill was more than twenty years old. The street where she lived was created in 2001, her house finished two years later. Before that, she and her family lived in a smaller house that dated back to the late eighties, half a mile away.

Despite the house in the suburbs, the mini-van parked outside, the kids' endless roster of hockey practices and the chartered-accountant husband with an MBA, Rachel was probably the strangest of Earl's kids. She was the most normal, and certainly the hardest to understand. She should have been at Caltech or MIT, or working with E.O. Wilson at Harvard, instead of driving her kids to hockey practice twelve months a year. She had a Ph.D. in invertebrate paleontology—prehistoric ants were her thing—and absolutely nobody could figure out why she turned down a postdoctoral fellowship in order to marry a guy who was studying to become a trustee in bankruptcy and didn't want his wife to work. He couldn't understand why an heir to the Frumkiss Foot Care fortune would *want* to work, especially not when it meant futzing around with a lot of dead bugs and comparing them to even more disgusting live ones. The first time he came to pick her up, he saw the aquarium full of marine woodlice that she'd moved into the living room after her mother died, and under-stood why a little hottie like her would even consider going out with him.

They met at a Jewish Graduate Student Union Anti-Valentine's Dance. Howie, her husband-to-be, had been pushed into going by some of his friends, who made up the remaining two-thirds of the crowd. They were worried about Howie, genuinely concerned that his total absorption in sports—all sports, any sport, though hockey was his favourite—might have something to do with his apparent lack of interest in women.

"You don't think he's trying to hide something, do you?" one of them asked when the topic came up in Howie's absence.

"Hard to say for sure. I mean, he never tried to 'mo me or anything, and I never caught him staring in the locker room, but there's something weird there."

"I think it's just that he's really shy. He hardly even talks to *us*, just smiles and laughs at jokes and nods a lot." Either way, they were afraid that Howie would never get laid and that he'd spend the rest of his life alone. They could tell that he thought a lot, and when he did say some-thing, it always made sense and was often even pretty smart. His marks in school were really good; the only trouble he had was that nobody could hear his oral presentations.

"Don't you like girls, Howie?"

"Sure, I do."

"Well, wouldn't you like to, you know, fuck one sometime? Do you ever think about it?"

"Yeah, all the time."

"Yeah, but have you ever fucked one? Really stuck it in and fucked?"

"Fuck off, eh? I never knew any girls who'd screw me."

"Look around, Howie. This is a big university. It's as close to a cunt farm as you're ever gonna get." Howie shrugged. "And you never went out in high school, either."

"I didn't know any girls then, either."

He really didn't. He rarely spoke to anybody who didn't play hockey with him; there were people who'd been in his class all the way through high school to whom he'd never said a word. His parents didn't talk much, either. If silence had any moral value, Howie would have been a saint. He became an accountant instead. Growing up as a top floor tenant in the ghetto of triplex apartments on Pannahill Road, near the western edge of Bathurst Manor—the landlord lived on the second floor and the landlord's mother had the basement; in buildings where neither the landlord nor his wife had any parents, they would rent the basements to goyim—Howie became very interested in money. Just because he didn't talk, didn't mean that he didn't think. He was no genius, that's for sure, but he was smart enough to know it, smart enough to know that the best way for him to get to money was to get into a profession that wasn't about anything else. He was determined to be a millionaire—that's how old-fashioned he was—by the time he was thirty. He worked like a dog in school, graduated third in his class in business school, and was well on the road to becoming a trustee in bankruptcy when he met Rachel.

She was more than cute, she was really quite beautiful if you could ignore the bright red Princess Leia cinnamon buns over either ear, the calf-length gingham dress from a vintage clothing shop, the Dr. Martens boots, and her thick-rimmed black plastic glasses. She was bursting with money; she was weird enough that almost nobody wanted to go out with her twice—she not only kept marine woodlice, she talked about them, too. And about giant hissing cockroaches and the ancient ants she'd studied for her Ph.D. She was dying to show him a tape of her favourite movie, *The Hellstrom Chronicle*. "The science is shit," she said, "but it's got the best bug footage you're ever going to see. And Dr. Canfield from Doogie Howser." She was so weird—unlike him, she showed up at that JGSU dance voluntarily, the only person in the entire university who hadn't helped organize or staff it to do so—so—Howie wasn't sure how to think this delicately, so it just came out as: so beneath him socially that even though she'd be like a goddess or something if she didn't make herself look so weird, the second she opened her mouth she reminded him of a super-intelligent version of the hillbilly couple on *The Simpsons*. So socially clueless that Howie didn't feel scared or nervous or anything; he could talk to her like he'd talk to a guy and that's exactly what he did, with maybe a little less detail when the subject was sports.

At the beginning, it looked like they were made for each other, two opposites attracting, each supplying what the other one lacked. She was a Doogie Howser type herself, a female version of the kind of young scientist, often a mathematician or physicist, who spends his free time watching pro wrestling and the Three Stooges, with maybe a little *Monty Python* tossed in for variety. A highly developed intellect with a pubescent sense of aesthetics. The main difference between Rachel and the boy scientists who made up most of her social circle—had she only known that there wasn't one who didn't dream of marrying her and living in a castle where he could drop his adult dental retainer into a goblet of gold before Frenching her until the sun came up—the main difference is that Rachel was never tongue-tied, not even among strangers or when she was scared. She never stammered, had never gone mute. She talked all the time, even when there was no one else around—that's how she worked out her ideas—and her mouth could turn from tool to weapon at the merest whiff of any threat. It came naturally; without a tongue like the angel of death, she wouldn't have made it through junior high.

Rachel had managed to sidestep most of the problems that smart kids are supposed to have in school. She was a bit of a tomboy, but didn't put on airs; she made damned sure that everybody knew that Yankee Gallstone was her grandfather and that she could go to the set of *The New Curiosity Shop* whenever she felt like it, but unlike Vanessa or Randall, she let them know that she was allowed to bring friends. She watched the same TV shows as everybody else, knew the pop songs that kids her age would know, and knew enough not to use words like "ganglion" or "obtuse" anywhere within earshot of her classmates. Lots of boys had crushes on her, she had crushes on some of the boys; she read comics and the usual kids' books, thought Judy Blume was the bendin' end and found the Narnia series unreadable. Aside from the powers of mind hidden everywhere but on her report cards and test papers, Rachel fit right in with other kids her age who lived in Bathurst Manor in the seventies.

Her giant brain finally seemed to screw it all up, though her sister Vanessa's tiny one was really the culprit. Vanessa, born while her parents were still living in Cleveland, was two years older than Randall and Rachel, who came along in 1968, a good half hour apart, and as far as Earl was concerned (and probably Tammy, too, though she'd never have broadcast it the way Earl did), God or nature or whatever was in charge of such things had certainly saved the best for last: the later they were born, the smarter they were; the newer they were, the nicer. Character and ability seemed to improve, "without prejudice, Dad," as Rachel herself once put it, "in inverse proportion to birth order"; physical distinction seemed to fade in and out, like AM radio stations on the highway.

Vanessa was the beauty, Rachel the brain, and poor Randall was the comic relief. There was a system, a balance—beauty, funny, brainy—that worked fine for everybody until the dividing lines got blurred.

The Sholem Asch Hebrew Day School, named for the Yiddish novelist who wrote three books about Jesus, was largely supported by Elyokim and Mrs. Faktor. It wasn't one of the bigger Hebrew schools in Toronto: four grade one classes became two classes per grade from grades two to six, and then one each for grades seven through nine, which was as far as the school went. Its mandate was to teach Yiddish and Hebrew simultaneously by reviving the old-fashioned technique of teaching all Hebrew subjects pertaining directly to religion in Yiddish, reserving modern spoken Hebrew for the more secular classes. Most first-grade students had no knowledge of either language. Like the dissident Hebrew school teachers who first approached him for a donation, Faktor was a firm believer in the sink-or-swim method of pedagogy. "It doesn't work for everybody," he admitted, "but when it works, there's nothing like it."

It didn't work for Vanessa, who had no interest in school at all. She didn't pay attention or do her homework. Her Yiddish was embarrassingly limited for a student in a school where its use was compulsory for half of every day, including lunch and recess. Vanessa didn't care until she realized that

Rachel and Randall were using Yiddish to talk about her behind her back. *That's* what led her to pay attention to the language, but it did nothing to increase her interest in the material being taught in it. The Torah and its dopey commentaries left her utterly unmoved—if God wanted you to know that "black" here really means "white," why didn't He just say so?—and she looked at any difficulties in the Hebrew texts they were studying as deliberate assaults on her personal dignity. She felt the same way about math. If Farmer Brown were herding 463 steers through a gate at the rate of thirteen steers every eighteen seconds, how long would it take before he butted heads with a local sheepman? Vanessa would crinkle up her beautiful face and begin to sob with the quiet intensity of a woman whose pain would never end, as if she were watching a train carrying all her family to her wedding plummet over a five-hundred-foot cliff.

Earl and Tammy got her tutors; they threatened her with punishments; took her to psychologists. She was sullen in school, rather than ill-behaved, and there was no question of her being disruptive; she wasn't interested enough. She didn't have the brains to get by without any effort, but she had enough willpower to resist any inducements to exertion: "I won't do it. You can't make me try." Trying per se wasn't a problem. Vanessa practically ran to her ballet classes and Tammy had to keep such a close eye on her to make sure that she wasn't disobeying her teacher and practising at home that she finally gave up, installed mirrors and a barre in the basement and hired a private teacher to come give Vanessa individual lessons, over and above the group classes that she did at the studio.

Her problems in school grew worse from year to year. She scored slightly above average on the intelligence tests that they gave her, but came in well below the norm on personality tests designed to measure responsibility and motivation. She barely scored at all on responsibility, a result finally confirmed when the school, wary of offending the man who had paid for its building but feeling a responsibility of its own to the other students and to the rules prescribed by the Ministry of Education, had no choice but to flunk her and make her repeat grade six. This put Randall and Rachel one year behind her instead of two. Rachel, meanwhile, seemed to have swallowed the whole curriculum in a single gulp. By the end of September of her sixth-grade year, she'd been through all of her textbooks from start to finish and had started to show off in a way that was disrupting the class.

The principal knew that he couldn't win. Keeping Rachel in the sixth grade finally struck him as worse for everybody—Rachel, her teachers, the kids in her class— than kicking her up to the seventh, a move that he had already considered before Rachel even started grade six, but hadn't wanted to go through with because of his reservations about putting her into the same class as her duller but prettier sister. It took a summer for the principal to convince himself that Rachel's presence would stimulate Vanessa to put some effort into her schoolwork, but he didn't really persuade anyone else. And nobody talked to Vanessa. Tammy wanted to send Rachel somewhere else, maybe even some place for gifted children, but Faktor intervened with one of his rare tantrums, screaming about all the money he'd spent to make sure that his grandchildren would get the kind of education that would enable them to read his work, and said that he'd disinherit Tammy if Rachel didn't graduate from Sholem Asch.

"Screw him," said Earl. The idea of Faktor telling him what to do was enough to make him take Tammy's side. "We don't need his money. I've made plenty."

"But he did pay for this house back when you didn't have any money at all."

"And I said to you then that I didn't think we should take it. But you started to cry and go on about he's your father, he wants to help, he feels bad that you never knew your real mother. But didn't I tell you that we'd end up paying for it?"

They were careful to let the kids know nothing about the plan until they came to a decision.

"It isn't the money, Earl. Or the inheritance. I've never seen him so, what's the word, so adamant about anything. Soon as we mentioned taking Rachel out, he just went nuts."

"But what about the kids? I really don't think it's a good idea." Neither did anybody else, but Faktor screamed long enough about how pulling Rachel out would nullify everything he'd ever worked for. "You want I should live in vain? Is that what you want? Well, I can tell you, I won't be living very long. Break my heart—I'm seventy-five years old, I should be easy to kill."

Earl was appointed to talk to Rachel, Tammy dealt with Vanessa. Rachel was excited at the idea that she was going to skip a grade and didn't think much about being in the same class as Vanessa—"We get along all right at home"—but Vanessa took it as an insult, a humiliation. She said nothing to her mother. Later that night, she came into Rachel's room. "Hey," said Rachel.

Vanessa punched her in the stomach. "I'm going to make you wish that you'd never been born." She turned around, walked out and slammed the door behind her.

"Jesus," Rachel thought. "I'm living in an after-school special."

If she had been, it would probably have been called *The Getting of Rachel*, because nothing less was going to satisfy Vanessa. She, Vanessa, was well aware of her status as coolest girl in school; where Rachel was considered pretty, Vanessa was in another class entirely. She had the sort of looks that made everyone who saw her feel blessed to have looked. She was small and dark like her mother, olive-skinned, with a heart-shaped face, huge black eyes, a slender nose and lips like invitations to a kiss. By the time she made it to the seventh grade, she also had the beginnings of a set of knockers that could only have come from her grandmother. Boys went on calling her Frumtits well past the end of high school.

She dressed well, too, better than any other girl at school, and had managed to attract a sizable group of co-educational sycophants. Who cared if she was good in school or not? Vanessa was a star, and they all knew it. Anyone who doubted that she could have done just fine in school if she'd wanted to had only to look at the campaign that she mounted against Rachel: Vanessa had a powerful sense of logic and a deep understanding of human nature. "They're all afraid I won't like them," she told Fred, her favourite stuffed animal. "But I'm gonna let them think that I'll like them if they hate Rach. And that I'll like them even more if they let her know." She rubbed Fred against her cheek. He was a donkey who wore a straw hat made of felt with holes cut into the brim for his ears.

She started out with tricks, the kind anyone might play on their baby sister, tripping Rachel as she walked up the aisle, flinging a bag of dog shit into her locker just as it closed so that it would sit and fester all day—the kind of pranks that make for memories. But these only paved the way for the real campaign. "Look at how ugly my sister is, eh? I know she tries to make the most of what she's got, but what can you do when you start out with *that*? We like to stand in our front window, you know, bare naked. I go out and the cars all stop; when the traffic jam gets too long,

Rachel comes in and they peel away. Don't they, Rachnik? Don't they, Rachnik? Don't they, Rachnik?"

Rachel's first period came in the middle of a school day and Vanessa made sure that the whole class found out. "She wasn't even wearing a Kotex. She's spreading her cooties all over the building." Cooties, the Rachnik's cooties, became a big thing in that tiny junior high. Kids wouldn't sit at a desk or a bench that she'd just got up from; they developed elaborate purification rituals centred around punches and pinches to cleanse themselves of any inadvertent physical contact with her. Vanessa got six of her biggest fans to sing a song she wrote to the tune of "I Will Survive," "Rach makes me retch."

It didn't take long. On the first day of Chanukah, Rachel stopped talking altogether. Tammy found her in the morning, trembling under her covers, pulling handfuls of hair from her head. Nobody knew what was wrong, and Vanessa looked as puzzled as everybody else. Randall had some idea of what had been going on, but the elementary grades ate lunch earlier than the junior high kids, so he hadn't seen very much for himself. Vanessa had also warned him that if he said anything, he'd be next. The sight of a nearly catatonic Rachel shook him enough to open his mouth, but a glance from Vanessa shut it right back up again.

Tammy and Earl sent the two kids out of the room. Rachel's head was in Tammy's lap now, she was sobbing and moaning and still not talking. Tammy was stroking her forehead and shushing her while Earl walked back and forth across the room as if someone were about to give birth, talking to himself. "It couldn't be a dream. Nobody gets that way from one bad dream."

"Rachel, darling, what's the matter? Who did this to you?" Visions of rape were curdling Tammy's brain. "Did somebody hurt you?" Rachel just shook her head and trembled. "Can you speak?" Rachel nodded. "Why don't you?" She shook her head and trembled some more. Tammy stroked her forehead again, then bent over and kissed it. "Okay, okay. Everything's going to be okay. I'm going to call Daddy. Okay?" Rachel trembled. "Earl. Earl. *Gey, kling oon tsim dokter,* call for a doctor," as if Rachel wouldn't understand her Yiddish.

"Who? Which one?" He was speaking Yiddish, too. "We don't know what's wrong. I'll call an ambulance. And then I'll call Dr. Schpaitner and let him know what's happened."

They both sat with Rachel until the ambulance arrived. Tammy went with her, while Earl stayed home to talk to the kids. Vanessa had already left for school; the note on the kitchen table said that she was sorry but she had a test first period that she simply couldn't afford to miss. Randall was still wandering about, as upset at his complicity as he was at Rachel's condition. Vanessa had warned him again before she left the house. "Open your mouth,

Bozo, and life as you know it will come to an end. They'll be taking you out of here just like they're taking her."

The "Bozo" did it for him; if life as he knew it was going to be nothing more than being thankful for *only* being called Bozo, he had nothing to lose by talking.

So he talked. Told his father everything he knew; told him how Shoshanna Stone and Tiffany Shadlyn, Vanessa's best friends—Randall called them her henchgirls—led most of the public confrontations in order to keep suspicion away from Vanessa, who issued her orders in the background. Vanessa had been careful to make sure that no teacher ever twigged to the anti-Rachel campaign; it was all conducted in signs and whispers. A word had only to be said aloud once or twice, after which it could be mouthed just as effectively. And, of course, there was no respite at home. Later on, when Rachel was able to talk again, she said that the worst part of the whole ordeal was when Vanessa used to drop into her room and say, "See you in the morning" every night and "Can't wait to get to school today" in the mornings.

"And you just stood there and watched?" Tammy asked. "Or did you join in, too?"

"I didn't do nothin'." Looking back years later, Randall always saw himself in a pair of Tom Sawyer overalls. "And you guys, you don't know how scary Vanessa can be. You only see what she wants you to."

"So how come none of the teachers has noticed?"

Randall shrugged.

"Has she done this kind of thing to anybody else?"

Randall shrugged again. "Not that I ever heard about, but the whole school's afraid of getting her mad at them."

"The whole school?"

"Maybe not the real little kids, but the grade fives and sixes, and the whole junior high."

"And you?"

"I already told you."

"And did she ever do anything else?"

"No."

"That's it." Earl was out of his seat and grabbing for his car keys. He'd already called the clinic and had them cancel all his morning appointments—thank God he wasn't out of town. "This is all your old man's fault," he said to Tammy. "Insisting on that cockamamie goddamned Yiddish school just to stroke his own fuc-*farkuckter* ego." He didn't want to swear in front of Randall. "I'm going there right now and put an end to this. If you haven't called dear old Dad by the time I'm finished, I'll go over myself and let him know what a big favour he did us by threatening to cut you out of his will. And then I'll tell him what he can do with his beautiful bloody school. You," he was talking to Randall now, "get in the car. You've missed half the morning already."

The school secretary had already picked up the phone to dial the police when Earl turned back from the door to the principal's office and slammed his fist onto her desk so hard that he later realized that he'd broken his baby finger. "Bitch, you touch that phone," he said in Yiddish, "and my father-in-law will be in here firing you before your afternoon coffee break." Earl didn't say anything when he came into the office, just reached over the counter, popped the lock on the little door with the knob at about waist height, and stepped on through. Now he turned back and walked to the door to the principal's private office. He opened it without knocking, took the phone from the principal's shocked hand, and told the Ministry of Education official on the other end that Mr. Rubinstein would have to call him back. "We've got an emergency here."

Rubinstein was a minor poet, very active in local Yiddish circles, who had been teaching Hebrew and Yiddish for decades and who generations of students were absolutely certain was the real-life model for Elmer Fudd. He owed his position to the fact that he'd once written a review in which he called Faktor "a dangerous hooligan, a blight to whom our youth—the tender shoots of a cultural crop still many a season from harvest—should never be exposed." Faktor couldn't think of any better way to punish him. "An emergency?" he chuckled at Earl. "This is a Jewish school, Dr. Frumkiss. The only emergency, if the building's not on fire, is going to come with guns and bombs."

"Shmuck! My daughter Rachel is in the hospital, thanks to you and your brilliant ideas," and Earl explained everything that had happened so far.

Mr. Rubinstein reached for his heart pills and ran for the toilet in one swift motion. He came back looking ten years older and Dr. Frumkiss explained that he was taking both the girls out of school, as of now.

The principal's investigation revealed that Vanessa and her friends had been running an extortion racket, too: kids in their class would pay Vanessa—a dollar, two dollars, five dollars—to keep her off them, "Unless you want Shoshanna and Tiffany to say something about *you*." Similar threats had also been used to ensure participation in anti-Rachel activities. Once word got back to the parents, Mr. Rubinstein was unemployed; registration for the next year was so low that the school was forced to close.

Rachel was hospitalized for a couple of weeks of observation and therapy. Her parents had anticipated the recommendation that she be kept away from Vanessa for as long as her wounds took to heal by sending Vanessa to a boarding school for the blind: though the doctors who examined Vanessa made a big deal about her cold-bloodedness and lack of any sense of remorse, they also said that there wasn't a great deal that they or anybody else could do about it. As long as we lived in a society in which beauty was a form of power, Vanessa would always have followers, sycophants, someone to do whatever she wanted just for the reward of being near her.

"Nu," said Faktor, "send her to a school for the blind."

"Easy for you to say. Just one little thing: she isn't blind."

"And there's no schools for the blind that wouldn't mind a little bit of money? Make a donation, and get the kid a shrink."

It cost Earl a new gym—building, equipment, and all—to get her admitted, but Faktor stepped up and covered the costs. Rachel was moved to Associated Hebrew Schools, the largest of the mainstream Hebrew day schools. She didn't like it; socially, it wasn't much different from Sholem Asch, and by January she was at Hollyhock, a private school for gifted children. Randall ended up at Associated, too, and became the only one of the kids to graduate from a Jewish school.

Vanessa spent two years at the Milton Academy for the Blind in Colorado. The psychiatrist whom she saw once a week determined that, while Vanessa was neither warm nor selfless and probably never would be, the situation at Sholem Asch had been the result of extreme feelings of inadequacy and sibling rivalry on her part. Likewise, her terrorizing the other students had had more to do with Vanessa's sudden discovery that she could get away with it than with any truly criminal or psychopathic tendencies. The girls at the Milton Academy never really stopped hazing the sightie, whose sullenness and initial lack of academic prowess didn't make up for the sudden invisibility of her face and figure. Vanessa not only found out what it was like to be on the wrong end of the pecking order, she also realized that the minute the lights went out or the eyelids came down, she had nothing to offer and no power at all. It didn't make her humble, but she learned to be a lot more careful and realized that there had never been any need to worry about Rachel. As long as people could see, there was no competition: she and Rachel were playing completely different games. Vanessa came back to Toronto and graduated from William Lyon MacKenzie Collegiate Institute, Bathurst Manor's public high school; it closed on all important Jewish holidays. She and Rachel didn't hang out together.

Rachel's recovery wasn't as quick, as thorough, or as instructive as Vanessa's. Her experience in the seventh grade seemed to seal her into a nerdiness from which she never tried to escape. She never really regained her self-esteem. Even if nothing had happened between her and Vanessa, no one could say for sure that she might not have turned awkward or developed a fondness for dressing in rainbow suspenders and boldly striped tops like Robin Williams in *Mork and Mindy*, but her transformation into the kind of person who kept her marine woodlice front, centre and out in public—her metamorphosis from very smart, pretty girl to very smart, pretty girl who led the life of one of the least popular boys—was traced back to Vanessa by the rest of the family, and then forward to her husband Howie. His friends should have realized that his lack of interest in girls wasn't feigned and had nothing to do with fear of rejection. It was all in his body, or what wasn't in his body; he didn't have much of a sex drive, and didn't understand people who did.

Rachel, on the other hand, thought about sex as often and as intensely as any other post-adolescent who wasn't having enough of it. She was shy, she was scared, but she wasn't hung up in any unusual manner; the guys she knew were too wimpy to make the first move and too scared to accept any advances from her. The couple of times she'd tried a "Let's fuck" strategy with the kind of guys with whom she usually hung out, the guys were so rattled that they couldn't perform.

She wasn't terribly experienced. She'd slept with a couple of guys she'd met at parties, and hadn't wanted to see either of them again when she woke up the next morning. For a while, she convinced herself that she might be gay, even though she'd never felt any physical tug in the direction of other women. She made out with two or three, was surprised to find how much she liked it, but couldn't tell how much of her excitement was based on gender and how much on simply smooching with people who knew how to do it. She let them play with her breasts and suck them, straddle her leg and rub themselves against it, even put fingers and tongues inside her. She enjoyed it, but she couldn't do it back. Other women didn't really attract her in that way; something about putting her mouth where they'd put theirs struck her as icky, so she resigned herself to waiting for a better class of men. She had two or three vibrators and used one of them nearly every day. She thought she might enjoy being on top.

She and Howie met at the right time. They liked each other briefly, Rachel was horny as hell and Howie felt that he had something to prove, to his friends and to his girl-friend. Although he didn't think of sex with Rachel as the gateway to the Frumkiss fortune, nothing can alter the fact that it was. His resolve wore out almost as quickly as his endurance. Their average encounter didn't last more than a couple of minutes, and most of the time he was just as happy to skip it. She was back to using a vibrator, only now she kept it hidden.

Trying to talk to Howie about his problem turned him hostile, and the hostility never really went away. Why she couldn't be happy with the occasional tumble was beyond him. It isn't like he ever claimed to be some kind of ladies' man or something; sex just wasn't that big a thing to him, and once he and Rachel started sleeping together, he found out that he really didn't like the way women smelled when they went into heat.

He'd had the same bunch of friends since he was in junior high. They played hockey and went to the movies together, and still played cards roughly twice a week. The game had started at lunchtime in high school—he was a couple of years ahead of Vanessa at MacKenzie—and had continued in one of the cafeterias at York University, to which they carpooled every day. It was easy, since they were all in most of the same classes. The first house that he and Rachel had in Thornhill was close to all his old friends; the newer one marked the fulfillment of the gang's biggest dream: they bought a crescent, and all eight of them built their houses on that one little street. "This is so great," he said to Rachel the day they moved in. "We'll be with the guys all the time now." Rachel was the only wife who didn't come along to the card games.

She got along with the other wives, though, a couple of whom she knew from Bathurst Manor. They thought she was a little weird, reading all the time and not even fiction, but heavy stuff about bugs and evolution, but they liked her and accepted her and, most importantly, considered her one of them and felt sorry for her. Her bedtime problems with Howie had long since been eclipsed by his moodiness. Things started to go bad as soon as his dream came true and he not only became a partner at J.L. Shawfett, where he'd been working, but was appointed vice-president in charge of corporate restructuring. When it came to bankruptcy, all of a sudden he was the Man. The paper side of it was nothing; it was the people who scared Howie. He'd never been much for leadership or team-building; his notions of managing people were summed up in the sign that he hung over his desk the day he started at Shawfett and that had gone with him from cubicle to office to better office as he worked his way up in the firm: "You just keep doing what you're doing until you do it right. You've got five minutes." It was

easy enough for him to assign tasks and delegate assign-
ments; keeping everybody productive and happy didn't
come easily, though—he was doing it, but it was hard—and
the people aspect of the job was starting to wear on him.
He was becoming snappish, short-tempered, turning up at
work with an air of belligerent hostility that he forgot to
leave at home. He never quite said or did anything that
anybody could put their finger on—there was a lot of talk
about tone of voice—but he was making everyone uncomfortable. And he knew it.

The rest of the guys on the crescent noticed it, too.
Mid-life crisis? He got what he wanted and found out that
it wasn't what he wanted? So what? Wasn't that the story
of everybody's life, or just the lucky ones'? They all knew
that they'd never be Bill Gates or Bruce Springsteen and
that they probably wouldn't like it if they were; they were
as happy as any regular person was likely to get, and any
one of them would have told you that he'd attained a nice
balance between work and family, pleasure and duty, inner
and outer. Every one of them was living better than his
parents had, and they were exactly the kind of guys who
would never forget it.

So what was with Howie, then? They really didn't
know. They asked him and he said that everything was
fine; Rachel hadn't told anybody that he'd started waking
up with panic attacks in the middle of the night, but they
all saw how nasty he was getting on the rink, how little he

was playing for fun and how much he was playing to win. They asked their wives, who said that everything was fine; Rachel would have done the same for them.

Things just got worse and worse. Rachel and Howie hadn't really gotten along for years, and hadn't had sex at all since before Jason, their younger son, was born in 2001. But now, instead of pretending that there was nothing wrong and that this was the way things were supposed to be, he was trying to make out that it was all her fault: she was too chirpy, too bird-like with her pointy nose and pointy little breasts: "You look like a fuckin' chicken."

The other wives on the street knew about the sex stuff; Rachel was so inexperienced that she wasn't sure if this was standard, if most marriages didn't wind up this way sooner or later. Whatever problems the women on her street might have had, there was nobody who had gone without it as long as Rachel.

"The vibrator's great if I'm feeling tense, but I thought the whole point was some kind of human contact." All of them but one had at least one vibrator; most of the husbands knew, but none knew how often they really used them. One of her neighbours, Cindi Pomerantz, had had a couple of casual affairs; Paula Adelstein and Rhonda Kravitz occasionally paid some guy who claimed to be a boxer; he was about thirty, a bit rough, but hard and muscly and basically an outcall gigolo. He'd come over in the afternoon or meet them at a hotel and fuck them.

It cost, sure, but it was worth it. "We can put you in touch, or you can come with us. We only do it three or four times a year, usually during the playoffs. Sometimes he does us one right after the other." These women knew everything about each other; anyone who talked out of turn would soon find herself in just as much trouble.

Rachel knew she could always get laid if she wanted to, but she didn't have it in her to cheat and didn't think it would help much if she did. "Really, at this point, I'm more lonely than horny."

Plenty of the hockey dads had come on to her, but she had one of those already. "Just what I need, another Jewish sports fan. I don't want anything to do with any man who's watched a hockey game since 1972."

"You're living in the wrong country," said Rhonda. They were drinking wine together one afternoon. "If that's what you're looking for, you'd better learn to love your hand, 'cause I don't think you're gonna find many men like that around here."

Rachel's marriage wasn't much more than a matter of convenience, and it was Rachel who was the convenience. She drove her kids to the Associated every morning, picked them again in the afternoon, took them to hockey practice three times a week. The kids weren't much comfort; their attitude towards her wasn't much different from their father's. She cooked and cleaned and drove them around and bought them stuff, but Howie had instilled his love of sport into them so deeply that they had no use—almost literally no use—for anyone who didn't play hockey. They played with and against other kids for most of the year, and spent much of the rest of their time playing with their dad, who was still waking up at three or four in the morning to go play hockey with grown-ups when ice-time was cheap.

Rachel had started to drink in the daytime, but the school was only a couple of blocks from home, about the same distance as the hockey arena on Clark Avenue. There was nowhere else where she needed to drive and the trips were so short that nothing could really go wrong as long as she was careful. Her purse was filled with chewing gum, breath strips and pocket-sized mouthwash shpritzers. None of the girls knew about her drinking; she kept her vodka with the cleaning supplies where neither Howie nor the kids would ever look. She took nips at intervals, or poured a shot glass into a litre bottle of pop. She didn't want to get drunk; she just didn't want to be so sad. She was looking for the energy to sit and read a book, the strength and courage to drag herself through another pointless day.

She was getting angrier and more frustrated all the time. Through Facebook, she'd got back in touch with friends from graduate school, all of whom were teaching and doing research. They complained a lot about academic life, but they had actual lives to bitch about. She was doing what Howie had told her. She'd accepted it for the same reason that she'd gone to the stupid desperation dance where she met him in the first place: fear of ending up alone. There hadn't been any other serious takers. She'd tried talking to Earl about it—should she marry him or not? Who else was there for her to ask?

Earl liked him at first. Howie was a business type; unlike his own son, he had drive and ambition. Howie had goals. "He's a decent guy," he told Rachel. "Got his head screwed on right. Not like those insect assholes. You're not getting very far with them, are you? You asked me what to do and here's my advice: grab him. Grab him now while you've still got a chance. You gonna stay home the rest of your life like some kind of spinster who spends her life looking after her aged father? That kind of care, I can pay for. You don't know how it tears me apart to come home and see you wasting your time with ant farms, for Chrissake, or those sea monsters you keep in the living room. You're a good-looking girl, a smart girl. Why do you wanna turn yourself into a freak? I blame myself. You know why. It's my fault, but for the past fifteen years you've had freakish interests, freakish friends. And your mother, *ala-ha-sholem*, noticed it, too. Like I said, I don't think you're to blame, but this Howie, he's the first normal thing you've ever almost done. So do it and don't be a weirdo all your life. If he isn't quite the man of your dreams, I got news for you, you probably aren't the woman of his."

She blamed Earl, too. She'd felt that she owed him something for having had a breakdown, as if she'd failed him by not being able to cope with Vanessa and her friends in the seventh grade. She thought that if she tried to soothe her father, who'd been crazy and inconsolable since the death of her mother, maybe God would see that she was trying to do a good deed, that she was getting married for good, unselfish reasons, and would let her be happy. She even lied to her therapist—she didn't want her to know that she still worried about God sometimes—and had been kicking herself ever since. When she finally confessed that she didn't think that she really loved Howie any more, and probably never really loved him to begin with, the therapist said, "I was wondering when you were going to admit it."

Lately, she admitted it every day. She was so angry all the time—she'd take the kids to school, come home, have a drink and jump into the shower. That was the usual setting for her divorce ritual, a ten- or fifteen-minute daily screed in which Rachel let loose with what she really thought— about Howie and their marriage, their way of life, the stupid crescent and Howie's reluctance to leave Thornhill and go into the city to do something, to go anyplace that wasn't an ice rink or part of a plaza. Everything she was going to say to Howie if she ever got the guts to leave him.

It came out every day in the shower. She was just hissing out, "Slack-dicked selfish prick, it's not even like you're a nice guy otherwise. You're gonna die one day, Howie, and your goddamned 1967 Stanley Cup Champion Toronto Maple Leafs aren't going to give a shit and neither am I.

I hope our kids turn out to be gay, I hope they hate hockey; and if they like hockey, I hope they hate the fucking Leafs and have boyfriends on the Habs."

She was just in the middle, hadn't even got to "I hope you end up with a life just like mine," which was usually the beginning of the good part, when she heard her father's ringtone. Unhappy as Rachel was, she was always in reach of her cell phone, just in case anything were God forbid to go wrong with her boys, and even though she could tell from the ring that the call had nothing to do with the boys or their school, she had problems, big problems, ignoring a ringing telephone.

"Everything okay, Dad? Lemme call you back." She hadn't bothered with a towel and was dripping onto the mat while the water kept falling in the empty shower stall.

"Don't hang up, Rachel. This is important." Earl paused to make sure that Rachel had obeyed. "Your zeyde passed away this morning."

"Oy." Her throat was closing up and she felt the first stirrings of tears. "Hold on a second. I was in the shower. Lemme get a towel." She put the phone on the counter by the sink just long enough to get herself wrapped up. "Okay, Dad. I'm back."

"I've got to go to the funeral home with Bubbie now, so I need you to call Randall and Vanessa and let them know. Tell them the funeral will be on Monday, so they'll both have time to get here. Do you know where Randall is right now?" She didn't. "But you have his cell number, right? I think you should wait until shabbes is finished in Israel and then call Vanessa. Who knows if she checks her messages? Tell her that there'll be a ticket waiting for her at Ben Gurion for the Sunday ten-to-one-in-the-morning flight to Toronto on El Al. And if she starts any crap about Zionist airplanes, tell her that the only other choice is Lufthansa."

"But what happened to Zeyde? How did he die?"

"He was a hundred and three, he didn't *need* a reason. I'll call you once I'm back. Wait, you gonna be home this afternoon?"

"Except to get the boys and take them to hockey."

"So I'll come over—oh, wait, I'm gonna have to take the bubbe home. I'll call you when I'm done."

4

RANDALL

FAKTOR DIED A FEW DAYS AFTER Randall killed his first man and started smoking again. It was the end—he *hoped* it was the end—of five or six pretty awful weeks. The shit started with his girlfriend, Shelley. They'd been together for two and a half years. Randall knew that she was difficult a lot of the time, and it was certainly no secret that no one in his family liked her. Rachel, with whom he was closest and got on the best, hated Shelley, and would go blocks, she'd go miles, out of her way to avoid her; she was convinced that Randall could do a lot better, and neither she nor anyone else could understand what he saw in her. For all his flaws, Randall was a bright guy who could be a lot of fun to be around when he wasn't depressed; even at his worst, he was a nice person who meant no harm to others. Shelley—as he was finally forced to agree—was a cow, pure and simple, bitter as poison, always ready with a bad word for anybody and a sneer for everything. Rachel was hardly alone in disliking her. Earl had actually begged Randall to dump her—"She's wrecking what little life you've got"—and Faktor and Chana threw her out of their house five minutes into her very first visit, after she berated Faktor for not warning innocent visitors that he and Chana and who knows who else had been smoking in the house for so long that just walking in and taking a deep breath would probably put her into a lung ward somewhere—and don't think she'd be slow to sue—and then announcing, unbidden, that she wasn't familiar with any of Faktor's work because she didn't know Yiddish and never watched *The New Curiosity Shop* as a kid because, "I didn't have time to waste on being a moron."

"And I don't have food to waste on bitches," Faktor said, lighting a Pall Mall and blowing the smoke in her face.

Shelley's behaviour, or Faktor's response to it, caused a bit of a rift between him and Randall. Randall had no choice. Shelley insisted that he not have any contact with a man who called her a bitch, and Randall wasn't the kind of guy to put up much of a fight. He was even less the sort who'd smile and nod and then wait until she wasn't looking to call from his cell or a pay phone. Randall was away a good deal of the time, he could have called Faktor whenever he felt like it, but Randall was honest: if he said he wasn't going to do something, he wasn't going to do it.

Like when he quit smoking, probably the only good thing he got out of his relationship with Shelley. She didn't like cigarettes; they made her dizzy and sick, and she told him when they first met that she wouldn't have anything to do with a man who smoked. Randall, who weighed 280 pounds and had started smoking when he was fifteen, was no paragon of willpower, but he wanted Shelley badly enough that he managed to stop, cold and on the spot. He flipped away the butt he'd been smoking, took Shelley by the hand and led her over to the garbage can. He reached into his jacket pocket, removed a nearly full pack of Du Mauriers, tossed them into the garbage and said, "I'd rather have you than a smoke." Shelley leaned in to him and said, "Go gargle with some mouthwash so I can give you a kiss."

That's the kind of guy Randall was. When he got home that night, after a few more kisses and a promise to meet that evening, he threw out whatever was left of the carton of cigarettes he'd just bought. He submerged each pack in a sink full of water, then bundled them all up in a plastic shopping bag, walked out to the nearest sidewalk trash bin, one of those that you can't reach into, and shoved them into the garbage. He still wanted to smoke, but he wanted to keep his promise even more.

There was no more promise, though. No more Shelley, no more need to hold back, not when he needed some kind of help. He was lighting one right after the other, giving the car's lighter a good workout as he headed for Syracuse. Every smoke was another nail in the coffin of his life with Shelley; he'd picked up a carton at the duty-free when he crossed the border and hadn't spent a single minute since without a lit cigarette in his hand. He'd really forgotten how much he enjoyed smoking, how much he'd missed cigarettes. He didn't try to pretend that they were healthy, but that didn't mean that they weren't good for him. He was able to focus again. He was thinking faster and better than he had for two and a half years; he was back to being himself. He realized that he'd let that bitch take over his life. "Unbelievable," he said to himself, shaking his head and sliding another Frank Zappa CD into the player, "how stupid I got from being lonely." "White Port Lemon Juice" was coming through the speakers, Randall was letting the butt dangle from his lips. With no more cell phone, he could sit in the car and listen and relax and not have to deal with anything that he didn't feel like dealing with. He knew that the pain would be coming back, which is why he was so determined to enjoy himself while it was still away. He also knew that he was going to have to drive like hell to get to his gig on time.

He had overslept after having one shot of whisky too many at the stag he'd done the night before, and by the time he got to Syracuse after sitting in Friday afternoon traffic at the border for nearly three hours, he was going to have to head straight for the campus without even stopping to check into his hotel. The stag at the Jewish Home for the Aged had gone well; a man of eighty-seven was marrying his seniors' residence sweetheart on Sunday, but now that the days were getting long they didn't know if they'd be able to stay awake long enough after the end of the Sabbath to have it on Saturday night. There were no strippers, no movies; plenty of kosher delicatessen for those who were allowed to eat it, and a litre and a half of Crown Royal. The guests who were able to drink at all were each allowed a single shot. Most of them developed debilitating heartburn before their ration was halfway down, and there was plenty left in the bottle for Randall to put to use.

He emceed the evening, introducing those friends of the groom who wanted to make speeches, chanting words of mock-wisdom for the groom himself, as though he were instructing a seventeen-year-old in the old country on what to do on his nuptial night. The rest was dick jokes in Yiddish, most of which Randall had learned from Faktor, who'd never forgotten any of the material that went into his book about Jesus' circumciser, and toasts to the groom made by guests on whose behalf Randall was to do the drinking. The evening was starting to remind him of the scene in *The Big Sleep* when General Sternwood talks to Philip Marlowe about having to indulge his vices by proxy. These old men were transferring their liquor into Randall the way some of them once exported their sins into chickens on the eve of Yom Kippur. Randall was their substitute, their stand-in; he embodied their regret for all the fun they could no longer have. After each old man made a toast, Randall was supposed to swallow a shot: he knew he'd been sent home in a taxi, though he couldn't remember the ride. He had to take a bus the next morning to pick up his car.

Geriatric stags were Randall's most lucrative sideline. As the only working comic in Toronto who could still perform in Yiddish, he had a lock on all the Jewish ones. Sure, there were hazards involved with crowds that were generally incontinent; Randall had one gig cancelled in the middle when the groom, who had been laughing too hard, suffered a heart attack. The groom recovered, but the engagement didn't and Randall was still trying to get his money. The stags were probably the only places in the world where Randall could be introduced as "A talented young man, and he should be. He's the grandson of our beloved *Mazik*, and he's doing everything he can to keep real Jewish humour alive. Imagine, in this day and age, a youngster who can still perform in our dear, dear *mame-loshn*, the tongue of all of our forebears." By this point, the audience would be crying, but out of admiration for Randall. So what that he weighed 280 pounds? He was fighting for a cause, *their* cause, and they knew that he had been schooled by the best.

They were right, too. Randall had idolized Faktor since he was a little boy and spent as much time with him as he could. He was over there so much, talking to Faktor and Chana, that he could speak Yiddish like he'd just got here from the old country, even though he hadn't studied it in school since he left Sholem Asch. Still, as the only Frumkiss kid to go all the way through the Jewish day-school system, Randall had the background to understand

Faktor's literary work, and Faktor was everything that Randall had always wanted to be: smart, funny, popular despite being ugly. He was famous—twice over, if you counted children's television, as if Jean-Paul Sartre had also been the voice of Pepé Le Pew.

Faktor looked at Randall and saw himself as a very young man, but tainted, slowed down by the Frumkiss genes that his daughter had insisted on introducing to their bloodline. "The boy has a great deal of potential," he told Chana, "but he needs to be de-Earled." Faktor tried, but it wasn't possible. Part of Randall remained irredeemably Earlish—square and slightly plodding—no matter what Faktor did to try to free the youngster up. Helpful as Randall's nerdiness was in keeping Faktor on top of new cultural developments and technological innovations, Faktor would happily have relinquished all his anachronistic expertise if it would have helped his grandson get laid.

Randall wasn't quite a virgin when Shelley came along, but he hadn't had a girlfriend in more than ten years or gone on a date in maybe seven—"His father all over again," observed Faktor. "Like two drops of water"—so when he met Shelley at a party at C-FAT, the Canadian Filmmakers' Alliance, Toronto, and she gave him a hand job in the bathroom after he'd run out to a drugstore and gargled with some mouthwash, he was willing to overlook a lot of her faults. They'd both had screenplays read aloud there as part of C-FAT's weekly screenplay-reading competitions, and had many of the same complaints about the actors and judges who had kept them both from winning. Shelley wrote product monographs for a pharmaceutical company and did a bit of journalism on the side, but she really wanted to break into television and film.

Randall was a fairly literate stand-up who had had no need to resort to a day job in a very long time. Artie Goodtimes, the comedy club impresario, had been Randall's best friend since grade nine, when Artie was still called Arthur Gutzeit. They bonded over a Residents album and started their showbiz careers as the founding and sole members of Ocean of Foreskins, the Hammond-organ-and-drums punk band that they put together a year or so later. Randall played the organ, and all their gigs but two took place in Randall's basement: a Sunday afternoon at the YMHA on Bathurst Street and a dance at the B'nai Brith house on Hove Street, where their refusal to play anything that the kids knew got them kicked off the stage in favour of a mix tape featuring Rick Astley, Barry White and ABBA. Randall still dreamed of recording the one really good song that he wrote for the band, "Stoned Shmuel Picnic," but until he got himself together and it became a hit, he never had to worry about earning a living; Artie was always sending him somewhere.

When he met Shelley, Randall was either a headliner or a middle, depending on the size of the town or his previous reception at the club where he'd been booked. He wasn't famous; he wasn't great, not quite, but he was good and he knew what he was doing: making over a hundred thousand dollars a year. While the rest of the comics were chasing pussy or snorting coke, Randall was working on more sophisticated material, stuff that he could sell as theatre or performance pieces and that Artie could book into theatres and colleges instead of his clubs, which all smelled like beer-soaked men's underwear.

Shelley would never have admitted it, but she was attracted by Randall's relationship with Artie. She could also see that he was interested in her, and no matter how dumb a bitch she might have been when it came to most things, she had enough animal cunning to know that a balding guy with frizzy red clown hair who must have weighed around 275 pounds was begging to be stepped on once he volunteered to flirt with a trim and reasonably attractive woman who had brought her neti pot to the party in case something there triggered one of her allergies. She advertised her hate-crime of a disposition in the expression that never left her face and kept most people who had any choice from ever saying a word to her. When Shelley was having an orgasm, she looked as if someone had just smeared her lips with dog shit; the rest of the time, she looked that way because she was angry.

She'd been born like that. But just because she was pissed off, it didn't mean that she didn't have feelings. She deserved better than her crappy freelance life, fawning over talentless assholes who'd been lucky enough, for the most part, to be born with a different bodytype from hers: to keep herself at 120 pounds, Shelley, who entered adulthood at 180, ran for at least an hour a day and ate a subsistence diet of her own devising, heavy on root vegetables, from which she deviated only when someone else was paying. She deserved better than a lifetime of loneliness and poverty. And she knew damned well that she deserved to be loved—even if her parents and sisters had long since given up on her.

She was the sort of person who cares "in their way," and she made it clear that she really did care for Randall. She wasn't very nice to him because she wasn't very nice; if she could have been, she would have saved it all up for Randall. Randall understood; frustrating as life with Shelley could get, he knew that their relationship was hardly one-sided. Which is why he went into such shock when they finally went phffft.

Shelley had come up with an idea for a TV series, "Celebrity Science," which would use an *Entertainment Tonight* format to teach kids about great scientific innovators and their ideas. She wasn't much of a writer, though; even she could see that her proposal never came to life, never displayed any of the humour or irreverence or innovative educational methodology that it described in such detail from a distance. "I might as well fucking kill myself," she said.

About a minute and half later, Randall asked, "Did you say something, dear?"

"Yes, I did say something, you big-eared buffoon. I said that I was going to kill myself. Glad to see that it won't get in the way of your reading."

They had a version of this conversation at least once a week. "Why this time? What is it now?"

"This damned proposal." She'd filled Randall in on all the details as she went along. The original idea had been his. "It just lies there like a dead fish. And I'm having trouble coming up with a sample segment."

"Lemme see." Randall got up and went over to Shelley's computer. He read through the whole proposal, then started fixing, deleting, polishing.

"What the hell do you think you're doing to my stuff?"

"Fixing it so that someone might read it and not throw up. Why don't you go out for a bit? I get nervous when you stand over my shoulder like that." He didn't reach his hand back or give her a playful slap; he really wanted to be left alone.

Shelley wandered over to a movie while Randall got to work on the segment. "Einstein's Sweater Speaks," he wrote, then had the sweater do a voice-over in which it described the man, his work, his B.O. and body hair in a Yiddish accent: "I din't mit Elbert until he came t'Amerikeh an' found me in epes a men's store in Princeton." Shelley nearly smiled after she got back from *Rashomon* and read what Randall had written. "This is great. Really. I think you should come in on it. We'll be like a company: you do the writing, I'll handle the science and research and the business stuff."

Randall had nothing to lose. Although he had been making a living from stand-up comedy for the past few years, he was smart enough to realize that he'd gone about as far as he was going to get with it. That's why he'd started thinking in terms of theatre and why he'd started writing stuff that could be performed by somebody else, preferably by lots of somebody elses in lots of different places, all at the same time. Randall didn't think of himself as an actor; he wanted somebody to see what he was doing and go, "Hey, this would be great if you could get a decent actor to do it." Shelley's idea was just another step in the right direction, and if it went anywhere, he might even be able to get a co-producer credit out of it.

After Shelley's fight with Faktor, they couldn't even ask him if he still had any contacts in the industry, but that was all right: Shelley knew somebody at TVOntario who knew the guy who was in charge of something or other and was willing to pass the proposal along. The guy to whom the first guy gave it, whose name Randall never did find out, called about three weeks later and asked Shelley to come in and have a talk. "He didn't really like the idea," she told Randall afterwards. "He said it was too sophisticated for kids and not scientific enough for grown-ups. But he loved the sweater! He said it was the best-written proposal he'd ever seen and that the segment was a brilliant piece of screenwriting. He didn't call about the show, he called about the writing." Randall was starting to feel pretty good. "He said that there were a couple of shows looking for people—he said that they were always short of good writers—and, because there were both of our names on the proposal, he wanted to know if I was responsible for writing it. This isn't the kind of chance you can afford to pass up. Face it, Ran; it couldn't have been an accident that he called me instead of you. So I told him yeah, I did the writing." Shelley smiled for the first time since Randall had known her, really smiled, with her teeth and cheeks and eyes. "I start a writing job on a kids' show next Monday! The one with the talking Canada goose!"

Randall's first thought that didn't involve murder concerned a lit cigarette. "I thought I was the writer here and you looked after the business." There were tears in his eyes and a hollow feeling in the middle of his chest, in the part that felt hot when he ate spicy food. "Why did you lie to him?"

The hardness was back on Shelley's face. "I thought it was the best thing to do, for both of us. I mean, really, it *was* my idea."

Randall wasn't sure if she went on talking or not. He stood up. "I'm going to the store. Pack your shit and get out. If you're not gone by the time I'm back, I'm gonna throw you and all your ideas right out the fucking window. I treat you well and take you into my life—I'm not stupid, Shelley, it didn't take me too long to figure out why you don't have any friends. But I thought that with me you were different. That's what I told everybody, anyway. 'Oh, I know she looks like a miserable cunt who's never satisfied with anything and likes to make everybody around her feel like shit all the time just so she can feel good, but *really* she's really very sensitive and nice.' Shit! You just stole my life from me. I loved you and helped you and stuck up for you, and this is what you give me back? I hate you, you bitch. I wish you were dead."

He went downstairs, walked to the corner, bought a pack of smokes and came back home. Shelley was still there. Randall, who was at least twice her size, grabbed her by the ears and blew smoke into her face until she threw up. He cleaned the mess up with some of her clothes, threw them into a suitcase and told her that he'd have the rest of her shit shipped—he even giggled here—to her parents. Then he picked up her neti pot and smashed it on the floor. He shoved her outside and put the chain up. Then he called a locksmith.

As far as he knew, Shelley was still working at TVO; it was just over a month since she'd sold him out. Randall made good on his promise about her stuff—Shelley had as little to do with her parents as possible—and had started looking for a new, memory-free place to live. If things had gone better with Shelley, he might not have killed a man a few days after she betrayed him.

He had been looking for apartments, leaving messages

with people who'd placed ads in the paper and making appointments with the ones who called him back. Normally, Randall didn't get too many calls from people he didn't already know. Most of his work came through Artie and the agency, and if he hadn't been apartment hunting, he'd have let the call from Wintringham, T. that came up on his cell phone around six o'clock go straight to voicemail.

"Hello?" he asked, in his stage voice.

"This is your neighbour," said Wintringham, T.

Randall didn't know all his neighbours. He rented a flat in a house on a street full of houses that had been divided up into flats; people came and went all the time, and there was no reason that Wintringham, T. couldn't have been one of them. Randall dropped the more formal tone and lapsed into his normal voice. "Oh, which one?"

"You know which one."

This wasn't quite the answer that Randall had been expecting. "I'm sorry but I don't."

"Oh yes, you do, asshole. The one whose paper you've been stealing every morning."

"Sorry, but you've got the wrong neighbour and the wrong number. I get my own paper delivered every day."

"Yeah, sure you do, asshole, straight from my doorstep. Well, I'm here to tell you that I'm coming over there right now and teach you a lesson."

"Look, I'm really sorry about your paper, but you've got the wrong number."

"Like fuck I do."

"For God's sake, I don't know who you are, but I'm telling you that I never took your damned paper. I get my own, get it?"

"I can see you right now through your window, you little shit. I'm comin' over right now and I'm gonna kick your ass. You hear me, shit-for-brains?"

What the hell? Randall figured. The guy's clearly out of his mind, might as well have a little fun with him to make up for all the stupid insults. It might even help cheer him up a bit, keep him from thinking about what Shelley'd just done to his life.

"Kick my ass?" Randall erupted into a stage laugh. "Kick my ass? You and how many of your friends, you dipshit son of a douchebag? You couldn't kick your mother's ass if she was down on her knees in front of you sucking your flaccid little faggot dick."

"What?" Wintringham was starting to choke.

"You're too busy *taking* it up the ass to kick any, you she-male fuckin' dickwad. So why don't you stop making empty threats and go back to jerking off?"

Randall pushed the button with the little red telephone on it and rang off. For the first time in months, he felt a glow of real satisfaction. He returned immediately to his brooding and beer.

When he turned on the television the next morning to check the weather, one of the anchors on the all-news station that ran weather pictures in the upper right-hand corner of the screen was saying, ". . . wife and teenage daughter are in serious but stable condition. Terence Wintringham, forty-seven, has been charged with one count of murder and two of attempted murder." Randall checked his cell phone's log of recent calls. There it was: Wintringham, T. He jotted the number down, lit a cigarette, found the phone book in the cupboard under the kitchen sink, looked up Wintringham, found the number and jotted down the address. He poured a shot just in case and sat down, waiting for the news stories to go full circle. He chain-smoked his way through weather and sports, then craned forward as the fanfare to the local news began to play. "A west end man," blah blah blah. Terence Wintringham of the same address that Randall had written down burst into the home of Sergio di Paolo shortly after six p.m., shooting di Paolo fatally and critically wounding his wife and daughter. Di Paolo's son, Tyler, sixteen, who managed to flee through the back door and call 911 on his cell phone, said that Wintringham, who lived three doors away, was hollering, "We'll see who's a faggot, you thief!"

Randall drank his shot and then had another. He couldn't tell if it was shock, alcohol, or his incessant, circular path around the apartment that was making him dizzy, but he managed to make it to the bathroom in time to throw up into the toilet. "Jesus Christ! Jesus fucking Christ!" was all that came out of his mouth besides vomit, while "What did I do?" was all he could think. He didn't know who to call, couldn't decide if it was safe for anybody to know. He took another drink and sat down at the kitchen table with his head in his hands. His brain was cloudy; another drink would make him throw up again. He wanted to smoke a joint, but he had no dope. It didn't really matter; he was drifting in and out of alertness, watching the bad movie that started as soon as he closed his eyes. Wintringham was moving through the di Paolo house, screaming and threatening to shoot. Randall couldn't see the gun, thought it might have been in a holster under Wintringham's armpit or blocked from view by his massive, protruding chest. When Wintringham reached inside his jacket, Randall didn't see a Glock or a Colt or anything else they ever mentioned in the movies; he saw himself, fresh from the holster, stretching out to his full length and moving in for the kill. "Jesus shit-ass nothing, I'm not the killer, I'm the weapon."

He ran out to the corner and bought a paper with better murder coverage than the *Globe*, then came home and collapsed onto the couch before he read it. He woke up four hours later, with a headache and a weird, numb feeling all over his body, as if something unpleasant was about to happen in the next few seconds. The taste of vomit in his mouth was even stronger now; he lit a cigarette to help take it away. "I could go to the cops," he thought, but what good would it do? They knew who did it; they knew why; and they knew the guy was nuts. Letting anybody know about the phone call would just cause the dead guy's family need-less suffering and make them turn their grief or hatred or whatever they felt towards Wintringham onto Randall. No, better to keep quiet and try not to think of it. Randall checked his book. He had a 9:30 gig in Fort Erie and it was already four o'clock; there was no time to go messing with police.

Wintringham's phone call came on Monday and Randall realized what he'd done on Tuesday. He thought about going to di Paolo's funeral, but couldn't figure out how he'd explain himself if anybody asked what he was doing there. He said nothing to anybody, not even Artie, just tried to go on as if nothing had happened. Shelley's leaving had been a piece of good luck; Randall wouldn't have been able to keep something like this from her, and she would have freaked right out, at the top of her lungs, until one or the other of them went to the police. Of course, he probably wouldn't have answered the phone if they hadn't split up, so maybe it wasn't so lucky after all.

One thing was for sure, though: Randall was finished with cell phones. If Wintringham had contacted him by semaphore, he'd have been done with flags. He didn't want anything more to do with the phone, didn't want the phone anywhere around, just in case the police decided to check the killer's phone records for some reason or other. He'd been on with the guy for close to five minutes, so there was no way he'd ever be able to deny having spoken to him if he was still in possession of the phone. He picked up the land line and called the cell phone people, asking what to do about a cell phone that had been lost or stolen sometime yesterday, he guessed, since he hadn't left the house since one or two in the afternoon. Randall felt so clever saying this that he wondered if he was starting to blush. They asked him if he'd looked for it in the house, if he'd tried calling it, if he'd called wherever he'd been when he had it last. He said yes. Then they told him that since he was on a month-to-month plan (because he'd forgotten to renew his fixed contract) he could either purchase a new phone for $250 or sign on for a three-year term and get a free phone. He said no thanks and rang off. He got a hammer out of one of the drawers and pretended that his cell phone was Shelley. Then he took the carcass, got into his car, crossed the border and went to the Anchor Bar, the birth-place of Buffalo chicken wings. He ordered thirty wings, ate them along with two pints of Genessee Cream Ale, dropped the carcass of the phone into the garbage can in the parking lot, filled up on cheap American gas, swallowed a package of Sen Sen that he'd bought in a candy store that focused on nostalgic brands and crossed the border back to Fort Erie. If he'd wanted any of this to happen, it would have been the perfect crime.

And now he had two nights in Syracuse. If Rachel had known anything about the last few weeks, she'd have flipped a wink of thanksgiving to heaven when she had to leave a message. She didn't get feelings about Randall; never knew if he was happy or sad, healthy or ill, in danger or in love, unless she spoke to him or he sent some kind of message— and Randall had told her the same thing about herself. They had no mystical twin thing at all. Close as they were, especially when it came to making common cause against Vanessa, they were more like identical cousins than people who had once shared a womb, except that they looked nothing alike. Randall was big and heavy; he favoured black T-shirts, knee-length black shorts, black socks and Dr. Martens boots. People who didn't know him assumed that he had something to do with either computers or film. He was smart, not as smart as Rachel, but with more traditional artistic and literary interests and just about none in science or technology. They were twins in name only.

Rachel tried his cell phone six, eight, ten times, and received a "customer unavailable" message. She texted him: She even sent an e-mail. Reluctantly, she called his house, and pressed "one" to leave a message for Randall, who still hadn't got around to recording a new greeting. "Hi. It's Frumkiss. I'm away for the weekend, but Shelley's here, so don't think you can steal my newspaper. If you'd like to get me directly, please call my cell at" the number she'd been trying all afternoon.

She hadn't heard from Ran in a couple of weeks, which usually meant that he was out of town, working, so she gave Artie a call to find out where he was. Artie had had a huge crush on Rachel when they were kids and she knew how much he hated Shelley. Rachel called him on his private line. "Artie?"

He recognized her voice immediately and she told him what had happened. "I don't understand why I can't get hold of Ran."

"He's got two nights in Syracuse, tonight and tomorrow. I don't know if he's there yet, but I can tell you where he's staying and you can leave a message if he isn't already there. You heard about him and Shelley, eh?"

"No, what?" Rachel was almost trembling. "They didn't get married, did they?"

"God forbid. They broke up. And Ran dumped *her*."

"Well, at least there's some good news today. What happened?"

"You better let him tell you. I don't know how much is for public consumption."

"What's public? I'm his sister."

"I'll tell you what, just because I like you. I guess I can tell you that he smashed her neti pot."

Rachel started to laugh. "Really? Did she start to melt?"

"If you want to call me back and tell me what Ran tells you, I promise to fill in any blanks."

"Sounds good, Artie. Thanks."

"And Rach?"

"Yeah?"

"If you ever decide to do anything about Howie, well, I'd still like to be your boyfriend."

"Artie, my grandfather just died."

"This isn't the first time I've offered," he said.

"I'll talk to you later, Artie."

"I'll be at the funeral. Your zeyde was a hoot, and I loved Yankee Gallstone."

Rachel left a message with the desk clerk at Randall's hotel. They didn't know what room he was going to be in, so she couldn't leave a voice message. "Call me. It's urgent. Rach."

Randall called her at about midnight, cheerier than he'd been since splitting up with Shelley. The stuff he did at the college went over even better than he'd hoped; it looked as if he was really on to something. It was sort of a character piece. He had himself rolled out on a wooden platform with wheels on the bottom, the kind that pencil-sellers and harmonica players used to have, except that it was four feet high. It was slanted and slatted so that Randall looked like he had no legs. He was wearing a tailcoat. His hair was frizzed out and he'd coated his face with kabuki-style make-up to bring out his unstintingly lugubrious stage face. The character was called the Toyless Boy, and Randall's opening line was: "I'm what happens when Gallagher meets Carrot Top," and went on to let everybody know that "my legs were my only toys." He mused about the possibility of converting to Christianity and transforming himself from the Toyless Boy to the Oyless Goy, and even improvised a good five minutes, giving them an eighty- instead of seventy-five-minute show.

He got a standing ovation and eight curtain calls; the whistling and clapping went on for ten full minutes. Not bad for the first real performance of the whole thing to an audience of strangers. And, miracle of miracles, a woman, a good-looking woman hung around while he got his legs out of the platform and waited for them to wake back up so that he could stand and asked him if he wanted to maybe go for a drink or something. She even waited while he got his props stowed away in the back of his van.

By the time they got to his hotel, Randall had forgotten that Shelley was alive and di Paolo wasn't. He had his arm around Alexa's waist; she taught in the English department and had written her dissertation on the novels of John Cowper Powys. Randall had to ask who that was, but she didn't hold it against him. He told her about his grandfather, the famous Yiddish poet and Canadian TV star; she moved onto his knee while he recited "The Pogromist's Lullaby." Randall couldn't help but think how proud Faktor would be of him right now. When he got Rachel's message from the desk clerk, Alexa lent him her cell so he could call her and Randall was feeling so revitalized that he didn't think twice about taking it and walked across the lobby.

The first hint that real life was on its way back came when Howie answered the phone. "What kind of asshole phones anybody at midnight?"

"Howie, it's Randall. Sorry to call you so late, but I got a message from Rach that said urgent."

"Oh, that. Just a minute. Rachel," Howie shouted her name as if he'd just slammed the car door on his thumb and was calling Jesus Christ, "it's your brother. Who else would call in the middle of the night?"

"Shit, Rach." Randall was hoping that Howie was listening in. "I guess this means that you weren't phoning to confess to murdering Howie."

Rachel rather wished that she was. "No, Ran. Zeyde died this morning." She spoke slowly, to make sure that Randall, who sounded drunk, could follow everything she told him. "The funeral's probably on Monday. Artie said you're only in Syracuse until Sunday morning, so it shouldn't be a problem."

Randall felt like he was about to go into anaphylactic shock. The phone was shaking so hard in his hand that he could hardly talk into it. "But how? How could it happen? And when I'm away, yet. I never had a chance to say good-bye or tell him I loved him. I hadn't even spoken to him for two years, thanks to fucking Shelley. I guess Artie told you that she and I split up."

"Yeah, but we can talk about that later. You don't need to cancel your gig, but you do need to come home on Sunday."

Randall's tears had started to flow. "Didja talk to Vanessa yet?"

"It's shabbes, remember. Dad already bought her plane ticket, so I guess she'll probably turn up. She might be able to shnor something for Le Clown," Rachel meant Vanessa's husband. "I think things are pretty grim for them moneywise since he decided to stop pimping her out on the lecture circuit."

"Maybe he decided that a woman talking is just a woman singing without any music, and it's a sin to listen."

"Yeah, maybe. Anyway, be here, okay?"

"Okay."

Alexa could see that he was crying as he came back through the automatic door that led outside. "Randall, are you okay?"

"My grandfather, the one I was telling you about? I just found out that he died."

"I'm so sorry. Really." She took his hand, the one without the phone in it, in both of hers. "Do you want me to go? Would you like to be alone?"

"I'd like a cigarette." Randall sat down abruptly in one of the 1960s Scandinavian modern chairs in the lobby and held his head between his hands. *Vus volt der zeyde getin*, he asked himself, "What would Faktor have done?" And the answer came as clear as if the heavens had opened to show him the way. "He woulda done it with gusto and he woulda told me to do it the same way—as a memorial, if nothing else. And besides, I really like her."

She went up to Randall's room with him—fooling around in hotels always made her hornier—and they went at each other all night, falling asleep about five in the morning, then starting all over at one the next afternoon. Randall was doing his usual stand-up routine that night at the comedy club in the same hotel; they stayed in bed until eight that evening, messing around and eating room service. Randall wept over the time he didn't spend with Faktor because of Shelley. Alexa tried to bring his two hemispheres of hair together on the top of his head and recited passages of Flann O'Brien that she'd memorized. While they were eating barbecue after that night's show, Alexa agreed to call her department chair sometime on Monday and tell him that there'd been a death in the family and she needed the rest of the week off. She'd join Randall in Toronto right after the funeral.

5

MILNER

IF YOU ASKED CHANA, she'd tell you that this whole *meshigas* with the memoirs and biography and the rest of the foolishness started the day that Randall turned up with that bitch girlfriend of his and vanished from their lives as if he'd never been. Not a phone call, not an e-mail, not even a message on Faktor's Facebook page, forget about a visit or an "accidental" encounter somewhere or other. And Faktor was either too proud or, to hear him tell it, too subtle a student of human nature to do anything about it by making the first move.

"Nu, Faktor, *you* could send *him* an e-mail or write on his Facebook thing. If you can't bring the mountain to Mohammed. . ."

"Please, Chana, leave the Arabs out of it. I've seen this sort of thing before. A man falls for a *klafte*"—the Yiddish for bitch is closer to "vile cunt" in English—"and turns into a ventriloquist's dummy. Women like that think in speeches, the cry of the aggrieved, and they're always aggrieved. She's been dying to deliver one ever since we threw her out, and Randall's sat through it so many times that he thinks he made it up himself. The minute he sees anything from me, he'll sit down and type the thing out as if it just occurred to him. And he'll really believe that he's speaking his own mind."

"So he's gone? We've lost him?"

"For the moment. I'm sure he'll be back. God, I hope he comes back." Faktor sniffed and wiped a tear from his eye. "I love him like a son, even if he is a bit of a nebbish."

He was certainly directionless. He'd fallen into comedy as a stop-gap, partly by accident, partly out of desperation, after years of aimless occupational drifting. He broke his father's heart after graduating from the Ohio College of Podiatric Medicine, Earl's alma mater, by announcing that his three years of residency had taught him one thing: he hated being a podiatrist, he sometimes thought that he hated feet. The idea of spending the rest of his life looking after them filled him with horror. He'd already seen how his mother died without having a chance to pursue her dreams—they all assumed he was talking about her folk singing—and he didn't want her to have given them up in vain. He was planning to take a couple of years of arts courses and then go to graduate school, where he could devote himself to the things that were really important to him. Eventually he decided on media studies and completed a master's degree. His thesis, "Too Fat to Thrive," examined the careers of Laird Cregar, William

Conrad and Orson Welles as symptomatic of certain aporia of male body-image in modern Western culture.

Aside from Tammy's death, Randall's refusal to go into podiatry was the worst thing that ever happened to Earl, who still felt wounded by the decision, and who didn't speak to Randall for two full years after he made the announcement. There wasn't much that Earl could do but sulk; Randall paid for his humanities education him-self, with the money he got from Tammy's will and insur-ance. But after four years, all he was was thirty-two years old and unemployable.

Faktor was solidly behind all these decisions and even offered financial help. Randall wanted to do it on his own, though. He took nothing from Faktor but a free suite, with private entrance, yet, in Faktor and Chana's Forest Hill mansion: they saw even more of each other now that Randall was a grown man than they had when he was a kid. He became Faktor's fan and disciple, heard all his stories. When he couldn't find work after graduating, it was Faktor who told him that Artie's offer to start him out on amateur nights until he got enough material for a full set was worth accept-ing. In the interim, Artie put him in charge of one of his local clubs, figuring that if worst came to worst and it turned out that he couldn't perform, Ran could at least learn the bar business well enough to keep from starving.

Randall stayed with Chana and Faktor for two more years. Faktor went over all his material, tightening it, showing Randall how to milk a set-up and get the most out of a punch line, and unintentionally teaching him large numbers of now lost Yiddish showbiz terms for joke delivery and audience reaction. There might not have been any such thing as stand-up in pre-War Europe, but Faktor had tummeled in some of the greatest houses on the continent and knew what he was talking about. He and Chana were sad to see Randall go once he started to earn enough money to live decently on his own, but they were happy to see him doing well at last. He'd taught Faktor all about e-mail and social networking and they kept in constant touch even when he was out on tour. When he was home, he talked to Faktor every day and came over at least once a week; after the hundredth-birthday party he even published a piece in *Maclean's* about Yiddish culture in Canada, stressing the fact that two of the three important Yiddish writers still working were in Canada: Faktor in Toronto and the novelist Chava Rosenfarb, formerly of Montreal, in Lethbridge, that city and mother in Israel.

It's no wonder, then, that Chana compared losing Randall to losing a limb; it was like he'd been amputated from their lives, and Faktor, at least, didn't want to waste any time in getting a prosthesis. "I'm not doing it for myself. At my age, I need a catheter more than a fan club. But I've got things to say, not because of who I am but because I'm just about the last person left who knows some of this stuff, who experienced some of the things that millions of people used to do every day but that nobody's done in years now, in decades. If I don't tell someone, it'll die when I do. I was giving it to Randall—I was trying to teach him a forgotten language. I don't know if he knew it or not, but those stories weren't really about me, they were about a civilization that's soon going to be as remote as the Etruscans'. I don't know what I'm going to do without him. I'm a hundred and one; it's too late to start over with anybody else. If there's no one else to speak that language, to live it, then I'll have to get someone to take down a description. If I can't leave behind a vernacular, I'll have to be satisfied with leaving a grammar."

Allan Milner was supposed to be that grammarian. To tell the truth, Faktor liked him only slightly more than Chana did, but no one else seemed to be interested in what Faktor had to say. Lucky for him, Milner was a Canadian and a long-time Yankee Gallstone fan.

A law school graduate whose website described him in his own prose as "the premier contemporary link to the glories of the East European Jewish folk tradition," Milner practised law for a month or so sometime in the seventies before fleeing into graduate work in ethnomusicology and writing a thesis on ethnic recordings in 1920s America, with special emphasis on Yiddish 78s. He'd grown up in Toronto with parents who were liberated from the Lodz ghetto by the Russians and he spoke Yiddish well. He learned Russian and Polish in grad school—Milner might not have had much style, but his ear was one of the best around and he was willing to do plenty of homework. Long before he'd ever been near Poland or Russia, he could speak to Russians or Poles for up to ten minutes before they realized that he wasn't one of them and had learned the language over here. He could go another ten minutes before it would occur to them that he might have learned the language from a book, and not at home.

What he was going to do with those languages was something else. The boom in ethnic consciousness sparked by the success of *Roots* on TV sent thousands upon thousands of young people on a quest for the kind of culture that their parents and grandparents had done their best to forget and even suppress. The first stirrings of the revival of the klezmer music that occupied so large a part of his thesis gave Milner an idea. He moved to New York, got himself a "job"—he used quotation marks for it, too, because "I had to put on a tunic and play the balalaika in a Cossack-themed restaurant five nights a week to cover the rest of my rent." He was working at PAYCOS, the Presidium of American Yiddish Cultural Organizations and Societies, which ran a clubhouse disguised as a bookstore in two rooms of a fourth-floor walk-up in the East Twenties in Manhattan. Customers had to buzz on the street to be admitted, and a large part of Milner's job consisted of making sure they were kosher; the Trotskyists, anarchists and DeLeonites who formed the core of PAYCOS' administration had an absolute ban on Stalinists, who kept trying to worm their way inside by disguising their voices and using fake names. Milner was given a list of questions designed to root out any supplicants still loyal to Moscow, starting with "What about Kronstadt?" and extending to "Describe to me in your own words the kind of shmuck who could have supported the NEP."

The store didn't sell many books, but it was always full of people arguing about literature and politics and reminiscing about the days when they could pee at will. A year or two shy of thirty, Milner was the youngest by over forty years. The old men liked him; since none of their relatives wanted to listen to their stories or hear about their quarrels, he was popular for the first time in his life. He started to tape their memories, especially any songs they might remember, any local customs or peculiarities of the sort not likely to be described in standard histories. He listened to the tapes over and over the way he'd listened to 45s in junior high school, until he absorbed not only the words but the spaces between them, the tone, the delivery, the accents of the people on them. He became a one-man tribute band for pre-1925, maybe even pre-1915, Yiddish popular culture.

Jewish kids all over the continent were putting on fedoras and trying to play the music to which they imagined their grandparents and great-grandparents used to make out, and there was Milner, dressed like a pushcart peddler in a photo from 1892, dishing out a way of being

Jewish so authentically rooted in the lives of real Jews that some of it hadn't been written down or recorded until he came along. If there was a Yiddish culture festival any-where on earth, Milner turned up on staff. If he hadn't been hired, he showed up anyway, and got his fans to raise such a stink over this insult to one of the true pioneers in the field, a man who was both the first of the Mohicans *and* the last, that he'd finally be given a classroom and a spot on the staff concert just to shut them up, even if he didn't get paid.

Milner's career was a cavalcade of the unknown and the forgotten, and as the years went by and he learned more and more, he found less and less of either. Time was killing his career: he was running out of old guys. He had to find new lodes to mine, fresh sources to replace the ones that had died or dried up on him. He sifted through senior citizens' homes, took trips from Toronto to obscure Brooklyn bars that featured old-fashioned music from Europe and were full of post-Soviet pensioners who still played it and liked it. Milner liked to say that the collapse of the Warsaw Pact was just about the best thing that had ever happened to him.

Friends and acquaintances, awed by the apparent transmigration of his soul from a world that is no more into a body always trying to get laid, would parade their grandparents before him as exhibits, or audition worm-eaten cousins, twice or thrice removed, who'd never quite cottoned to North America but might still be good for something. They were mostly a waste of time, but when Milner came up with a good one, he didn't let go. He let them know that what they had was unique—if it hadn't been so to start with, it had become so with time—and they were lucky that he was the one who'd found out. There were all kinds of *mamzers* out there looking for opportunities to take advantage of their bad English and lack of money by cheating them out of copyrights, royalties, recognition and everything else that was rightfully theirs, while promising them the blue-plate special direct from the Lord's open kitchen of luck. Milner was their friend, though, probably the only one. He'd sought them out, hadn't he? Their children or cousins had come to him because they knew already that Milner was a mentsh: all he cared about was what was good for them and good for the Jews. *For them*—as people with material and emotional needs. *For the Jewish people*—whom they'd be paying back for having made them so unique.

He promised to produce CDs so that their songs and stories would live forever, and in their very own voices, but there was rarely enough money to buy the kind of studio time that Milner said he needed, and even when there was the album never seemed to get mixed. Milner could do anything but finish. The labels to whom he sold the projects wanted their advances back; since Milner's discoveries never received any part of these advances or even knew of their existence, a fight would always follow, with Milner yelling about his fees as producer, payment for the sidemen, miscellaneous expenses and the moral debt they owed him. Until he came along they were nothing but a bunch of retired custodians and mechanics. "And," the old guys all had the same response, "being retired means that I converted to Christianity? My name's on the cover; the stuff on the record, it all comes from me—you could have handed me a little something when you were paying everyone else."

Milner became a serial collector of old guys, flitting from one to the next as disillusion set in, and turning anthropology into a kinship ritual in which a freelance, floating son adopted any number of successive, but sometimes competing fathers.

There was more to him than Yiddish, though; he hadn't gone into popular culture for nothing. Indeed, it was TV that first let him know that Yiddish had *stuff* in it, that it was more than a strange way that his parents and their friends had of communicating among themselves. The idea of Yiddish culture—not that he would have known the word—first reached him as a five-year-old, when he called his parents into the living room to show them his hero, Yankee Gallstone, and they told him that the man playing Yankee had been a big Yiddish star back in Poland. Milner remained a big *New Curiosity Shop* fan, and he was naturally well aware of Faktor's published work. What he hadn't realized until Randall's article appeared was that Faktor was still alive and living in Toronto; it was such an obvious thing that he'd never thought to look. He also discovered that the vicious pre-War folk ballad, "Pogromtshiks Viglid," was not a real folksong at all, but had been written by Faktor. Milner had collected versions of the song from a couple of dozen different informants and was about to record it himself for the very first time for his forthcoming self-released CD, "Songs in a Milner Key." He'd had so little reason to suspect that the song was anything other than genuine folklore that he hadn't tried to track down any rightsholders.

Milner googled Faktor and found the kugel website. He sent Faktor an e-mail, in Yiddish, congratulating him on his birthday and thanking him for all the pleasure his work had given him over his lifetime. Milner was sure that he was one of a very few fans who was equally conversant with Faktor's achievements in both English and Yiddish. He quoted a couple of lines from one of Faktor's poems, went on to lament Faktor's neglect at the hands of serious Yiddish critics—punishment, it seemed to Milner, for having been born with a sense of humour and having had the chutzpah to support his art by stooping to vulgar entertainment in English.

The hunch paid off. Faktor answered him within a day or so and Milner began to cultivate the old man the way you'd cultivate a field in order to plant and harvest a crop. He tilled, he sowed, watered and waited. They'd been corresponding for about a year, an e-mail every week or so, when Milner, picking up on some references that Faktor had made to his work in the theatre, asked Faktor where he might be able to find copies of his plays.

He asked only a few weeks after Randall had stomped out of the house with Shelley, and Faktor saw an opportunity of his own. He replied that none of the plays had been published in book form, but because he acted in all of them and had a memory that was nothing short of miraculous, if he said so himself, he could still recite all ten of them from start to finish, with nary a variant to indicate the seventy years that had passed since the last production.

Milner had done his homework. He knew that the plays had never been published and he wondered if Faktor talked about his sex life the way he boasted about his memory; his bragging was important because it gave Milner the opening he had been hoping for. He wrote back and asked if he might be so bold as to suggest a project to Mr. Faktor, a collaboration between artist and scholar. He, Milner, would transcribe the plays from Faktor's dictation, and then, once Faktor had vetted the transcriptions and corrected any errors, Milner would translate them into English and try to sell the bilingual volume to a publisher, a university press, most likely.

"And what," Faktor asked, "if they only want one? If it's too expensive to publish both languages and you're forced to make a choice?"

Milner was pretty sure that he had Faktor sized up by then. "Then we go with the English, the one that's likely to sell and be read and—God willing—performed."

Faktor told him to come over to the house. If they could get along well enough to work together, they would make it official.

Milner hadn't been so happy since he shook hands with Leonard Nimoy. No matter what happened after Faktor signed a contract, Milner had to win. If Faktor didn't live long enough to finish dictating even a single play, Milner would be able to play the disciple and make all the hay he could out of whatever they'd done together. And if Faktor didn't die for a while? Milner becomes editor, translator, authorized authority, keeper of the flame and the I-got-it-straight-from-the-man-himself irrefutable expert, the last living link to the last living link.

They drew up a contract after a week's worth of meetings, and had it witnessed by Mrs. Aubrey and Luz, their housekeeper. The first twenty-five thousand dollars in advances, royalties and the like were to go to Milner in payment for his duties as amanuensis and translator, after which he and Faktor or Mrs. Faktor would divide any proceeds fifty-fifty. They agreed to record a new play on the first of every month.

Milner never lived with Faktor the way that Randall did, but he was over there four or five times a week, for anywhere between four and eight hours a day. Faktor rarely slept for more than three or four hours at a time any more, and Milner was perfectly willing to work from three to seven in the morning, say, or even four to noon. It was a small price to pay for exclusive access.

Going over the plays and their casts, their reception, the venues in which they were performed, virtually forced Faktor, who didn't need any prompting, to describe the people and places he'd just mentioned, tell stories about them, answer Milner's questions, explain topical allusions and fill in the social and political background of many of the plots and jokes. It was a social history—a social encyclopedia—of Yiddish literature and theatre in Poland in the '20s and '30s, and it led Milner to broach a more ambitious idea: a biography of Faktor, an authorized, with-the-co-operation-of-the-subject sort of thing, starting with his childhood and tracing all the vicissitudes that led to Faktor's career in Canadian television.

They drew up more contracts, releases, notarized documents—Milner used his legal training to do everything according to the laws of Moses and Ontario.

Milner transcribed the tapes of Faktor's reminiscences. They were in Yiddish when he was talking about Europe and his first years in Canada, in English once he started working for the CBC. He and Faktor went over the transcriptions together, and once any necessary changes had been made, Milner notarized a document in which Faktor vouchsafed that the transcription of such-and-such an interview, done on such-and-such a date was a true and accurate record of what he, Elyokim Faktor, had said.

In less than a year, Milner had transcribed over four hundred pages of autobiography and recorded complete texts of all of Faktor's plays. He was behind in his play transcriptions, figuring that Faktor's memoirs were going to be a lot more marketable than a bunch of plays that, much as he hated to admit it, could only be described as stale-dated. They might have been great in interwar Poland, where an audience would have recognized the names, understood the references to current events, and been able to follow the multilingual wordplay, but today they were fodder for footnotes, ephemera of no real interest to anyone who wasn't a professor. He couldn't imagine even an academic press having any interest in these things; they were strictly the stuff of theses.

Milner was beginning to understand why Faktor never really distinguished between his theatre work in Poland and his years in Canadian television. "They warmed me up for the real thing, kept the easy stuff out of the books. I'm not one of those guys who can just stay home and write. I'm restless, I like to go out. I knew that the plays and the *Mazik* columns couldn't survive for more than a few minutes, but that's what they were there for: to make those few minutes more pleasant. Theatre was my fun, and so were the columns. For me, they were what a bottle is to a drinker; I couldn't relax without them. But once I was relaxed, I could do my real work."

Milner tried to talk to him about "the real work," but Faktor wasn't biting. He'd talk about his life and the plays, but he had nothing to say about his poetry. Faktor wanted to be remembered as more than Yankee Gallstone, but he didn't think that discussing his own themes and imagery was the best way to do so. The memoirs were the key. He'd grown so enthusiastic about the recordings that he started to talk directly into his computer when Milner wasn't there, then transfer the files to CDs without waiting for Milner to show up and ask questions, "in case my hundred-and-twentieth birthday should come sooner than I was expecting." If nothing else, it let him see less of Milner.

Where Faktor preferred to avoid Milner, Mrs. Aubrey actively hated the little asshole, whom she thought of as a particularly snot-nosed kid, even though he was almost sixty. Calling Faktor Getsl was the least of his sins in her eyes. Like Faktor, she knew that he wasn't there out of love for Faktor's work, but for the greater glory of Milner and his flagging career. He'd never married—a huge red flag in Chana's books, partly because of her own kids—and the girlfriend they'd met when he first started coming round, a plain-faced drudge in her twenties who affected billowy long skirts, generally of six or eight colours, goats'-wool socks and clunky pumps with buckles, had finally dumped him for a cimbalom player who wanted to start a family, and now he had nothing but Faktor. Chana went out of her way to make him uncomfortable; she didn't need that greasy little *yutz* in the house. Why did he have to come at three or four in the morning, when Chana was asleep, if all Faktor needed was a typist? You could find a typist anywhere. Was there no limit to Faktor's need for attention?

If there was, he hadn't reached it by the time he died. Faktor recorded so many CDs on his own that Milner would need months just to do the transcriptions. He finally levelled with Chana after she'd been complaining about Milner one night. "I'm afraid, Chana. There's no way around it; how much longer can I live? And I'm afraid it's all amounted to not very much. I made a lot of people mad and had some laughs, but look: none of my poetry is translated, our kids didn't turn out the way we wanted, and Tammy doesn't exist at all. And all of it—everything I wrote after she was born, everything I did, it was only for her. You understand?"

Chana nodded. Faktor had been a good husband and a good father to their children. He never slighted them for Tammy, but everybody knew that there was something different between Tammy and him, something stronger: probably those years of being alone together, and Tammy's having had no mother at all, not even a substitute, until Faktor married Chana.

"You know better than anybody that when she died, so did most of me. But I owe her the truth, even if both of us are dead. Just so the world won't think that her father was nothing but a braggart and a clown. The stuff I've recorded is the truth, but I don't want it released until after I'm dead."

"And me, Faktor?" Chana asked him. "Do you talk about me?"

He beckoned her over and took her hand. Together, they were 198 years old, and it was like laying parchment on top of rice paper. "We've been married sixty years." Chana stifled a sob. "I talk mostly about you."

He died three days later, after recording what he said was the hardest part of his life. Chana guessed that he was talking about losing Tammy.

6

THE FUNERAL

FAKTOR KNEW WHAT HE WAS SAYING when he called himself a blogosphere celebrity. His YouTube posts about his stomach and its kugels, along with the Yankee Gallstone clips posted by fans, had expanded his reputation farther and wider than either he or his family suspected. Not even Randall knew about the Faktor and Gallstone fan sites, the unauthorized translations of Faktor's poetry, including some of the *Mazik* pieces, by fans who claimed to be studying Yiddish, most of whom were really Milner in disguise. It was Milner who got hold of the wire services with news of Faktor's death. The Gallstone angle got the obit into every daily in Canada, the Yiddish big-shot bit into the *New York Times* and thence the hundreds of papers that subscribe to its service. The headline, "Soupy Sales of Yiddish Is Dead," probably attracted a few more readers than "Elyokim Faktor, Yiddish Writer," would have. There were video clips on the TV news, soundbites on the radio. Yankee was suddenly back and bigger than ever, and no one, not even Milner, expected the hundreds, maybe it was thousands, of fans who laid siege to the funeral home on Monday morning, calling "Yankee, come back," the way Omar used to whenever Yankee tried to stomp out of the shop. There were teenage internet addicts and baby-boomers well into their sixties; entire families—parents, children, grandchildren—in Yankee Gallstone wigs and glasses, some of which had been Halloween costumes in 1957 or '58, and carrying signs and placards reading "So long, Yankee," "Yankee, we'll miss you," "Yankee, come back," and "Death is not good for the birds." They filled the chapel, the hallway, the foyer and most of the parking lot. Neighbours and members of the Stashover Young Men's Fraternal Society, the Yiddish culture activists who had flown in from out of town to honour one of their own, and everybody else who actually knew Faktor had to try and fight their way in with the help of funeral home employees and policemen, who were more likely to trust the little old Jews who said they were friends than the decidedly hippyish types who were saying things like, "Yankee was my life-coach. I've gotta get in to say goodbye."

The whole mob followed the cortege to the cemetery, only four or five blocks away, some in cars, most of them on foot, on bicycles, on skateboards, piped along by twenty fans in kilts playing "Yes, We Have No Bananas," the *New Curiosity Shop* theme song. Nearly all had brought offerings of kugel.

The funeral had been arranged through the Conservative synagogue that Earl belonged to, and the rabbi, a weedy, thick-spectacled kid in a bow tie who looked like he enjoyed wearing galoshes in May, had heard of Faktor like he'd heard of fun—some kind of distant rumour. Milner stood waiting in the empty "Reserved for Clergy" parking space, so that the rabbi wouldn't be able to avoid him, and started to pump the rabbi's hand before he finished getting out of his car. "Rabbi Zimmerman, glad to meet you. We should only meet in future on pleasant occasions."

"That's Zuckerman."

"I'm Arye-Leib Milner, I was—"

"My name is Zuckerman, not Zimmerman."

"I'm glad. I'm Mr. Faktor's authorized biographer. I was also a close friend. He asked that I deliver the *hesped*"—the eulogy—"at the graveside."

"When did he ask?" The rabbi knew all about bullshit at funerals. "And *when* did he ask it? This is the sort of thing that the family usually mentions to me."

"He mentioned it at one of our sessions. 'Arye-Leib,' he told me—do you speak Yiddish, Rabbi?"

The rabbi was looking at his watch. "No. And I'm in a hurry."

"It was his—"

"Strangely prescient request from a man who I'm told dropped dead in the middle of a meal." Milner shoved himself between the rabbi and the door to the chapel. "The family is waiting, Mr. . . . ."

"Milner, as I said." Rabbi Zuckerman put a hand on Allan's shoulder. He was a good half-foot taller and had no trouble getting Milner out of his way. He had no idea why the guy behind the Yankee Gallstone puppet that he still sort-of remembered from his childhood should need or deserve an authorized biography, but he'd been a rabbi long enough to know the real meaning of urgent importunities outside of a funeral parlour's family room. "Shall I ask Mr. Faktor's family about your proposal?" he inquired, but Milner was already heading in the opposite direction.

Rabbi Zuckerman knew that he'd done the right thing when he noticed, to his great satisfaction, that the twerp hadn't bothered to come inside for the service. A *nudnik*, that's all. Some kind of troublemaker. The world was full of them and too many of them seemed to be Jewish. Fifteen minutes after the service had ended, when the parking lot was almost empty—the rabbi was always careful not to get to the cemetery before the rest of the crowd, in order to avoid trouble from the kind of idiots who would decide that he'd started without them and then ruin the graveside service with their kvetching—Rabbi Zuckerman was more than a little dismayed to see that he had four flat tires. They appeared to have been punctured. He already knew who did it, already knew why, but there was little he could do and nothing he could prove. "Moishe," he headed straight for the owner's office, "can you run me over to Rock of Israel and get someone to call a tow truck or something. Some S.O.B. punched holes in all my tires."

Milner, meanwhile, wasn't missing a beat. "I don't know what could be keeping the rabbi"—he had elbowed his way to the graveside and started to address the crowd as if they were expecting him— "but until he gets here, I'd like to say a few words about the man whose memory we're here to honour, Elyokim Faktor."

There was time for plenty of words about Elyokim Faktor. The road inside the cemetery was clogged with Yankee Gallstone fans who weren't about to move for any *vehicle*, and the rabbi's ride was having trouble getting him through, while the family stood at the edge of the grave, twitching and scratching themselves in embarrassment while someone who wasn't one of them was howling and gesticulating as if the destruction of the Temple had somehow popped up on his TiVo instead of the celebrity cooking show that he thought he'd saved. No single-language sentence escaped his mouth. He was gliding inexplicably from English to Yiddish to Polish and Russian to German and a strangely error-ridden Hebrew.

With every word of Milner's, Mrs. Aubrey screamed and cried; she raised her clenched fists to her shoulders and pummelled the air while the cemetery employees, who thought that Milner must be some new rabbi whom they hadn't yet seen, made sure that she couldn't get anywhere near him. He went on for at least half an hour.

"The old boy must have been slipping him money," Earl thought. No one seemed as crushed by Faktor's death as this stranger whom he'd never seen before.

"Avekgerisn undzer mazik!" Milner was screaming. "Our little devil has been torn from us, our beloved little devil. We've sinned against our culture and he has borne our punishment. Who will make our folk mischief now?"

Even the people who knew what he was saying had no idea what he was talking about. Milner had thrown his jacket to the ground, good side out, the way James Brown used to do with his cape. He was kneeling on it, pounding the earth and screaming, "My heart is in the coffin here with Faktor." The few who understood had no idea why he was quoting Shakespeare in Russian.

"Who is this asshole?" Randall whispered to Rachel, who was standing beside him near the gravesite.

"A linguist without borders? A broken-hearted polyglot? I don't know." She shrugged. "Maybe he learned English from watching Yankee Gallstone. Who else would wear a polka-dot shirt to hijack a funeral?"

"Voos reyt er nokh?" Chana was stamping her feet and screaming away in Yiddish as if she could no longer understand anything that was happening around her. "Why is he still talking? Why is he even here? I wanna speak to the rabbi. Where's the rabbi?"

Milner was going on as if Chana was talking about someone else, but his attempt to switch into Hebrew was only partly successful. "I first entered the man . . ." He wanted to say that he'd first got to know him.

"Thank you, Mr. Milner, for this glimpse of your feelings and memories." Rabbi Zuckerman was moving through the crowd, less like Moses than a roller-derby jammer, shoving Yankee fans and Yiddishists out of his way with the same skilled elbows that made him the terror of many a rabbinical school scrimmage in spite of his scrawny physique. Immediately behind him, washing up in his wake before the crowd could come back together, trudged a strikingly beautiful woman, well past the first or even second blush of youth, but no less striking for her age. In spite of her long sleeves, ankle-length skirt, and the kerchief pulled tightly across her head, the crowd fell silent when it caught sight of her. They'd all turned to look at the rabbi and they all lost sight of him as soon as she came into view.

Vanessa's airplane sat on the tarmac in Tel Aviv for three hours without moving, and by the time she'd gone through customs and picked up her luggage in Toronto, it was already eleven o'clock. If not for the Yankee Gallstone fans slowing everything down by blocking the road and Milner slashing the rabbi's tires to give himself a chance to speak, Vanessa would have missed the funeral completely. As it was, she had to get the cab driver to call the funeral home on his cell to find out which cemetery to go to. The driver knew the area and parked, illegally, in the tiny plaza next to the cemetery gates; he tagged along as his fare went looking for her father. She had nothing but Israeli shekels in her purse and was hoping that Earl had enough in his wallet to cover the fifty-odd dollar fare. The crowd watched Earl follow her out of the cemetery with the cabbie in tow. Earl and Vanessa came back by themselves a couple of minutes later, each of them dragging Vanessa's suitcase for a few feet then turning it over to the other, until they were able to load it into the funeral home limo that would be taking the family to the shiva.

By this time, no more than five minutes, really, the rabbi had managed to shut Milner up, calm Faktor's widow, invite the huge crowd to move in a little closer and—at a high sign that he got from Rachel the second that Earl returned—to begin the graveside service. He said a few words of consolation, intoned a brief prayer for the soul of the deceased, and summoned the widow and children forward to say the first Kaddish for Faktor. He invited all those present to throw a shovelful of dirt into the grave, and nearly an hour later, for God's sake, announced the address of the shiva once more. The bagpipes started up again as people were beginning to leave, playing "Yes, We Have No Bananas" as a minor key dirge; the rabbi and Chana and the Yiddishists winced. Most of the fans shuffled out. No one did the Freddie.

7

VANESSA

LUCKILY FOR EVERYONE, especially Chana, none of
the Yankee Gallstone fans paid enough attention to
the rabbi to be able to find the shiva. This was the
first time in years that the whole family had been together,
the first time since Tammy's funeral: Vanessa had declined
her invitation to Faktor's hundredth-birthday party. She
sent an e-mail that read "Mazl tov. May you live to 120,"
and signed it "Feygl," the name she had reclaimed from her
Sholem Asch days after getting involved with her husband,
Yankel; he was born a Jacques. His name didn't appear
beside Feygl's in the e-mail, nor did those of their children.
Feygl, however, took care to explain that she was sure everyone understood that she was unable to attend for reasons
of propriety. Holding the event at Swineberg's Original
Smokehouse—"We're Kosher on Yom Kippur 'Cause It's
the Only Day We're Closed"—made it virtually impossible
for her to walk through the door; doing so could harm her
children's marriage prospects. And even if she went in
through the back or they changed the venue, there were

other moral considerations militating against her presence. Chief among them, mixed seating: a woman of her stature, the wife of a rabbi, could not put herself into a position in which there might be even the shadow of an appearance of impropriety. In light of her grandfather's past and, she regretted to say, present activities, she had every reason to suppose that the content of the evening—whatever speeches or entertainment there might be—would be highly offensive to her as a religious woman, as well as to general community standards of modesty and decorum. She was sorry, but she just couldn't come.

"Remind me," Faktor told Chana, "if she *does* show up, I'm gonna take off my pants."

Vanessa—or Van Feygl, as Rachel and Randall had dubbed her, short for Klafte van Feygl, *klafte* being the bad thing that Faktor called Randall's ex-girlfriend—rarely wavered in her dedication to making those who were stuck with her as uncomfortable as possible. She'd rejected a sweet-sixteen party, claiming that she didn't know enough people who deserved the pleasure of spending an evening with her, and settled for a celebratory meal at the steakhouse where Richard Burton proposed to Elizabeth Taylor. Just before dessert, she turned to her mother and asked, in a voice that carried from one end of the restaurant to the other, "You honestly don't think I'm a virgin now, do you?"

Admitted to York University's dance program, Vanessa turned out to be nothing special. She did an MFA in modern dance and it got her *bupkes*. She auditioned and auditioned for a whole year, and heard the same thing everywhere. One particularly acerbic artistic director told her to go back to the suburb that she came from, find an empty storefront in a plaza and open a school. "With your looks, all you have to do is put your picture in the window and they'll be lining up around the block with their little girls, hoping that some of you will rub off on them."

She moved to New York and started introducing herself as a performance artist. She met a guy at a party, a bit of a downtown power, who said that he could get Vanessa a show of her own at Findlay Stove, the now legendary performance space that had opened only a few weeks earlier. She showed him some videos of herself in dance class, as well as a tape that she made in Toronto after giving up on dance for good: Vanessa, in a 1950s housedress and high heels, in front of an open refrigerator from which she pulls Jewish ritual items—prayer shawls, mezuzas, yarmulkes—while wondering how a tradition "that's been boiled down to nothing but eating" is supposed to sate her spiritual hunger.

The downtown big shot, an alternative film critic named Marshall Nurgitz who was on the editorial board of both *Lucubratio: The Journal of Luca Brasi Studies?* and *Paradigm Morgue*, was also a frequent contributor to other, similarly ironic postmodern journals. He was an adjunct professor of film form and practice at the New School and made short experimental films of his own. A great-great nephew of the Nurgitz who brought her grandfather together with Madame Kutscher almost seventy years before, Marshall would probably have laid himself vertically under a moving subway if he thought it would get him any closer to Vanessa. The thought of dirtying himself between the tracks while commenting ironically on the problem of romance in times like ours gave him a real *frisson*.

The night he met her, he went home and told his longtime girlfriend that they were through: he didn't want Vanessa to have any excuse to reject him. He didn't want to cause Laetitia, his ex, any undue pain, either, and he arranged for her to move into another apartment in the building they were in. Marshall's father, a big *makher* in the State Department and former ambassador to a number of strategically important countries in Southeast Asia, owned the building—he had been born in it—and, diplomat though he was, was also happy to do anything to help Marshall escape from that whining shiksa and her goddamned vegan diet. Everybody was quite surprised when she threw herself off the roof a few weeks later, after taking a magnet to the hard drive of her computer and shredding all the printouts of her just-completed book on the poetics of clowning. Laetitia didn't die, but she sustained enough brain damage to spend the rest of her life in a wheelchair, wondering where she was. Marshall simply thought she'd moved out.

He was in that little-boy state of mind in which anything to do with Vanessa was the best of its kind. After looking at her stuff, Marshall used discussion of it to initiate a process, with Vanessa speaking her ideas, Marshall reacting, offering suggestions, lobbing revisions to Vanessa, until the back-and-forth finally blossomed into a script. Close as they were getting, their relations remained platonic, but Marshall had pledged himself to Vanessa and nobody else. Vanessa had guessed as much, just watching him try to walk or sit down. While she could never have liked Marshall, or anyone else, as much as he liked her, she felt a definite personal interest. She needed to be sure, though, that he was as taken with her art as he was with the rest of her.

Once they'd finished the script, for which Marshall refused any credit, he took it to the artistic director of the Stove, along with a very carefully edited reel of Vanessa in performance and a lengthy *bubbe mayse* about how she had renounced her prominent position in the Canadian dance world in order to engage more directly with politics, life and the nature of sexuality. The director shrugged: this girl's face could get the Stove a lot of notice. He'd been looking for something that would bring them to the attention of people who could afford to buy tickets and maybe even become donors. Vanessa made up in patron-appeal what she lacked in talent.

The artistic director talked to the rest of the collective sometime in the middle of January and they decided to take a chance. It wasn't any crappier than some of the stuff they'd already done, and this crap, at least, might do them some good. They gave her two solid weeks in May, and Marshall promised to write a major piece that would do duty as both interpretive essay and public relations brochure.

Much to the surprise of everybody but Vanessa and the now utterly enslaved Nurgitz, *Yiddisha Mama Goes to Horseradish Hell* received glowing, in some cases ecstatic, reviews and had its run extended three times. The Anti-Defamation League tried to have it labelled hate speech; B'nai Brith thought it deplorable; Republicans in Congress didn't say anything, because no federal or state money was involved. The most controversial scene had Vanessa speaking about the custom of dipping an apple into honey on Rosh Hashana as a talisman for a sweet year. After she'd taken an apple and a jar of honey out of the fridge, she pulled her dress up over her hips and appeared to slide apple slices into her honey-pot (Marshall, who had read *Candy*, thought that it fit better than the "snatch" in Vanessa's original), which she then offered for audience members to eat. There were never any leftovers. She cheated a bit and rubbed them against her clitoris when she was having her period.

Once the show was up and running, she could go back to thinking about other things. She was so overcome with gratitude on opening night that she gave in to Marshall's supplications, and once the show was over, they were married in City Hall. Both sets of parents were there for the wedding and neither set was happy: they would have preferred a synagogue and a rabbi. None of them guessed that Vanessa was pregnant.

Tammy died six months later and they named the child Thomas in her memory. Marshall got a tenure-track position as professor of performance studies at Ingarfield College, a progressive liberal arts school in Adams County, Ohio, about three-quarters of an hour from Cincinnati and a whole lot closer to Kentucky. It's the last dry county in the state. "You're joking, right? You're not really talking about leaving New York and going to Buttfuck Deliverance Porkland are you? What's the county seat there, Foreskin?"

Marshall was serious, though. He loved academic life and Ingarfield was an up-and-coming school with a reputation for hard-core avant-gardisme, the kind of place where he would have a chance to put some of his bigger ideas into practice. The success of *Yiddisha Mama* virtually guaranteed that he could get Vanessa on as an adjunct, at the very least; she was certainly well positioned to get some major grants for her next project, too. "There's plenty of time off," he told her. "We can travel, get out of there. But once we're out there, there's nothing for us to do but work. It's going to be fantastic."

"Do they have daycare?" Vanessa wasn't convinced. She liked Marshall, but she liked him a whole lot more in New York. He was right, though; she needed to come up with a new project and submit the grant applications while she was still hot, and there was no way she'd be able to do it without him. Marshall had a native fluency in the language of applications, as if he'd done peer reviews in nursery school and sat on kindergarten juries, and he knew exactly what they wanted to hear. Six months later, after they'd been in Ohio for three months, Vanessa got a fair whack of money to write and produce *Borscht Matrix*, an exploration of female flux as the root of all rhythm.

She wasn't getting much done, though. Thomas needed constant attention, Marshall was busy teaching, writing, reviewing articles for the magazines, helping his students with their films and performances and working on his own. Much to Vanessa's dismay, he'd started to hint that it might be nice if supper were waiting for him when he got home, and that both he and Thomas would appreciate some clean clothes once in a while. "You're home all day. All you have to do is put the stuff into the washer, take it out twenty minutes later, and then put it in the dryer and press a button. That's all."

"If that's all, then why's it such a big deal for you to do it yourself?"

A year ago, she would have bet money that she could have smeared her face with pigshit and Marshall would have licked it off. "Because," Marshall's fists were clenched even tighter than his teeth, "I work all day and most of the night. I know that Thomas takes time and that you need to work on the new piece"—his tone was more pre-emptive than conciliatory, but he was still trying—"but Jesus,

Vanessa, you don't even wash out your coffee cups. I come home and have to do all the housework? What kind of bullshit is that?" He looked down towards his shoes. "Have you ever washed a floor in your life?"

Marshall must have said the wrong thing. Vanessa's eyes narrowed. She spun around and threw a cup full of coffee right at him. Marshall jumped back, got splashed a little bit—thank God, Thomas was already in bed—but wasn't quick enough to be able to save the laptop on the table in front of him. It belonged to Vanessa.

"Did you expect me to be your housewife? Is that what you dragged me out here for, to turn me into your fucking mother? Shit on you, then! And shit on this place and your teaching and all the rest of your bullshit. I only got together with you so you could get me into the Stove. The real question is why I ever bothered to stay with such a second-rate talent." She stopped, lit a cigarette and looked over to her laptop. "Well, so much for anything I've done on that fucking *Matrix*." Naturally. It was his fault that she'd backed nothing up. "Thanks for all your support, Mush-hell. Can't even fuck properly. You're no goddamn use to anybody. Why don't you just kill yourself now and get it over with?"

Marshall thought she might be trying to goad him into hitting her so that she could walk out and get custody of Thomas. He stayed where he was, clenching and unclenching his fists; he hadn't been in a fight since he was twelve.

He won, but he'd never done it again and he wasn't about to start now. Especially not with Thomas up and screaming; thank God he couldn't climb out of his crib yet. Marshall took a deep breath.

"Thanks for making that clear. I was under the mistaken impression that you loved me."

Vanessa smothered a chuckle. "For about two minutes, right after the premiere of *Yiddisha Mama*, when I let you convince me that you had something to do with it."

Marshall wouldn't let himself be drawn in. Vanessa had been impossible since they got to Ingarfield and he'd been expecting some sort of confrontation for months now. Nothing this final, though; he was wondering if she'd been drinking or snorting coke. He didn't say anything, just turned around and started back for campus and the editing suite.

Vanessa was like a beast of prey that had just got a taste of blood; she was angrier with Marshall for leaving before she finished yelling than for anything he might have said or done. If he could walk away, even if only for a few minutes, he could imagine himself without her. "Shit." She'd overplayed it again. "When will I learn to leave well enough alone?"

She and Thomas were gone when Marshall came home the next morning, grateful, for once, to be unable to get a drink. She'd taken the car, too, driven to Louisville, where he was less likely to look for them than Cincinnati, parked in the long-term lot at the airport and bought a ticket on the next flight to New York, which would get her and Thomas to JFK with just enough time to get onto a direct flight to Paris. She booked that in Louisville, too. Vanessa was lucky that she kept her passport in her purse and that she'd had Thomas's name added almost immediately after he was born in 1990. The grant money, which she kept in her own account, was more than enough for travel expenses and a good few months in Paris; she had inherited enough from Tammy to do whatever she wanted when the grant came to an end.

Marshall called their friends. No one had seen her. He called acquaintances and the highway patrol. He figured she'd driven off in a fit of pique and would be back fairly soon; if he couldn't find out where she was—she could just be driving, who knew?—he wanted at least to be sure that she and the baby hadn't met with any kind of accident, God forbid. Two sleepless days later, an unshaven Marshall took his balls in his hands and called Earl in Toronto.

"They're gone, both of them." He never knew what to call Earl. "No note, nothing. I thought maybe she'd come to you."

"Me?" Earl was incredulous. "Are you sure that you're really married to her? I'm just about the last person in the world she'd come to, unless she was out of money. Have you talked to Randall or Rachel?" Marshall had never even met Randall or Rachel.

"What about her friends from down there?" Vanessa hadn't made any friends; the faculty was tiny, she was stand-offish and smarmy with the other wives and every husband there had already tried to fuck her. No one had succeeded, including Marshall for the last five months, but that didn't make her any more beloved among the rest of the wives. "Then I don't know what to tell you, I'm sorry. I'll let you know as soon as I hear anything, and please do the same on your end."

Marshall was about to call his own father when he got a call from his department at the college. There was a fax for him, from Vanessa. Great, thought Marshall, now the whole fucking world will know what's going on. The people in the office were very discreet, but it wasn't possible that at least one of them hadn't seen the fax. It was sent from Paris and said: "Sorry for any inconvenience. It's over. V."

"Fucking bitch." Marshall called his father then. "I don't give a shit about her any more—"

"Please watch your language, son. We can solve this without turning ourselves into savages." No one would have guessed that Marshall's father, Ralston Nurgitz, was born as Rachmiel and attended Yeshivas Tiferes Yerusholayim high school on East Broadway in New York. "You want Thomas back, correct?" Ralston was as well-connected as they come. "And her?"

"I never want to see her again."

"Of course not. I didn't mean to ask if you wanted her back. What would you like to happen to her?"

"Dad, I don't care about her. But if you could help me get Thomas back, I'd . . ."

"Don't worry. Are you still in Kentucky?"

"Ohio."

"Of course. Get yourself out of there and onto the next flight to Paris. Let me know the details. There'll be someone in Paris to meet you." Ralston got on to the American embassy in Paris a few seconds later and his friends there got hold of Interpol. Vanessa and Thomas were in a cell inside of three hours. Marshall arrived the next day and took Thomas home. He never saw Vanessa again, nor did she ever see Thomas. Vanessa never sent him a birthday present or a postcard. Earl stayed in touch, as did Faktor and Mrs. Aubrey, and both Marshall and Thomas used to come to Toronto at least once a year, almost always with Marshall's second wife. Vanessa had never even mentioned Faktor to Marshall, and though Marshall spoke no Yiddish, he was amazed to meet someone who had known people like Isaac Bashevis Singer and his great-great-uncle and had also worked in live television. Earl even called Marshall with the news of Faktor's death. "I'm sure he'd understand why I can't be there," Marshall told him. "And I can't imagine the trauma for Thomas if he should meet his mother."

Thomas was going into his junior year at MIT and was spending the summer as a research assistant to one of his professors. He knew the whole story of what had happened with his parents and had no desire to meet anyone who could forget about him so easily. He knew about Vanessa's remarriage and new kids and he wanted nothing to do with her. At this point, he didn't think that she'd even acknowledge him, and that suited him just fine.

After Vanessa was released from prison—as soon as Thomas and Marshall were on their way back to the States—she decided to stay in Paris for a while. There was nothing waiting for her in Canada or the US, she still had the grant money for *Borscht Matrix*, and she'd never been to France before. She rented an apartment in the Marais, the old Jewish neighbourhood, and didn't even think about looking for a job. She had no idea why she'd felt compelled to run away, no idea why she'd come to Paris, no idea why she did almost anything. Following her impulses didn't seem to explain it. By the time she realized that she'd had an impulse, she'd already finished doing the thing that the impulse had pushed her to do. She didn't really remember packing a bag or getting Thomas ready to go. She must have had food for him, and diapers; must have had to change him sometime between Ingarfield and Paris, but she couldn't remember doing any of it. There was no picture in her mind, just a feeling behind her eyes. She had an image of Marshall, when they were fighting; she could see a wholly imaginary mid-shot of him and her in the house, and could even see herself throw the coffee. She saw Marshall leave. And could see nothing at all after that.

She had no idea why she'd done it. She was bored, frustrated—and what was she now? She'd hooked herself to Marshall and Marshall no longer had time to make her look like she had talent. She stank, and she knew that she stank. She never really loved Marshall, but she never loved any other man, either. He was a perfectly nice guy, though, and she knew he'd been crazy for her. All she loved right now was Thomas, and he wasn't just gone, she threw him away. He's her kid. She threw him away and she's never going to get him back.

Losing him got her thinking for the first time in her life: she could write off the last twenty-six years. She wanted things to be different. She wanted to always know what she was doing. "It's got to be in front of my eyes from now on, not behind." She decided to swear off men for a while, until she figured out what she wanted to do with her life. She knew that romantic entanglements would take her back to the past. It wasn't a huge sacrifice. Hot as she looked, Vanessa wasn't especially sexual. She liked it, but didn't *need* it; she never felt that she might go nuts from frustration or deprivation.

She started to read, for almost the first time in her life, and went to lots of movies. She'd always liked the movies; she probably got it from sitting with her bubbie when she was little, watching any old movie that happened to come on while Chana named all the actors and then grilled her during the commercials. "And who played George Kerby?"

"Cary Grant."

"He's dead. And Topper is . . .?"

"Roland Young." Chana would give Vanessa's cheek a pinch and let her know that Roland Young was also dead.

Vanessa cut off all her hair and started to wear a kerchief over her head whenever she went out, along with shapeless, oversized trousers, badly cut and loose in the seat, that would help keep her from being bothered by men. She bought the ugliest pair of glasses she could find and had window glass put into the frames: no Frumkiss had ever been bespectacled. She read Camus and Beauvoir, the stuff you're supposed to read in Paris, and a lot of English-language stuff about philosophy and spirituality. She read Buber's *I and Thou*, then wrote a long letter to Rachel, apologizing for everything that she'd done to her as a kid. She wrote Marshall, explaining, as best she could, that it was her fault, not his; he was a nice guy and had been a great husband and companion. She knew she'd treated him badly and hoped that one day he could forgive her. Rachel answered, Marshall didn't. She tried to write to Thomas, but couldn't bring herself to do it. "Marshall would have to read it to him. How tacky can you get?"

She read more Buber and thought she might try going to shul. Sitting behind a wooden grate in the women's section on a Saturday morning didn't make her feel closer to anything but the scattering of friendly old ladies who were keeping her company. She probably should have gone to the big shul on the rue Pavée, but this one was almost next door to where she was living. It was more Orthodox than she'd expected: the men had beards and many were dressed like hasidim. All of them seemed to be in their sixties and spoke Yiddish with the same accent as her mother and grandfather. Vanessa had at least had the brains to put on a long skirt, and with the kerchief on her head, she looked completely at home.

As the service was ending, one of the few old ladies who hadn't already spoken to her came over. She wasn't really that old, about fifty, Vanessa would have guessed, the same age as her mother would have been. She was wearing an expensive blonde wig and a dark brown, "modest" suit—by Chanel. She asked Vanessa in French if she had been invited anywhere to eat. When Vanessa said no, she said, "You'll come to my place for lunch, then."

Her place turned out to be a kosher hotel on the next block. The lunch was catered and it was good. Soon as they sat down, the woman started in with the usual questions.

"Are you married?"

"Divorced."

"Jewish?"

"Why else would I go to shul?"

"No, the divorce. Did you get a Jewish divorce, a *get*, from three rabbis?"

Vanessa had to confess that she hadn't.

"Were you married Orthodox?"

"Hardly," said Vanessa.

"Then it isn't a problem."

A problem? What was this, Chanel goes *shadkhn*? An *haute couture* marriage bureau? "*Je m'appelle Vanessa*," she said, to change the subject. Thank God, they'd forgotten to introduce themselves. "Feygl in Yiddish."

"Feygl. A beautiful name. In Hebrew it's the same as Moses' wife, Tzipporah. A little bird. I am Ruth Frankel, Rebbetzin"—Mrs. Rabbi—"Ruth Frankel. Do you speak Yiddish?"

"Some," she answered. "Not as much as I should, I'm afraid. You see, my grandfather is Elyokim Faktor." Nothing. Just the Rebbetzin's blank blue eyes. "*Der Mazik?*" Still nothing.

"You don't go to shul often, do you?" asked the Rebbetzin. Vanessa confessed that she didn't. "And all of a sudden? Something must have happened to you. Nu?"

"I'd rather not talk about it. At least not yet."

"No, of course not. We barely know each other. So here, let me tell you about myself instead. I wasn't always Rebbetzin Frankel, you know."

She wasn't always a Jew either. Ruth was once Ghislaine, Ghislaine Leclerc. She was born during the War and grew up in the Communist Youth Movement, grew disillusioned and left it behind. Went to drama school, acted in theatre and did bit parts in films. "Got married, had a baby, Jacques. How old are you, Feygl?"

"Twenty-six."

"Jacques, too!" Not long after Jacques was born, she came across a copy of Martin Buber's *Je et Tu*. Vanessa, who'd been getting twitchy and bored and had even had a sudden uncharacteristic urge to go into the toilet and get herself off, suddenly perked up. Ghislaine read the book six times in as many days, in between feedings and diaper changes, then began to run all over Paris, pushing Jacques in a stroller in front of her, scouring the bookstores and public libraries for anything by Buber that she could find. His books on hasidism led her to others, which led her back to books on Judaism in general. She signed up for a Hebrew class and consulted a rabbi about converting to Judaism.

"But I don't want to be a Jew," her husband protested.

"You don't have to be. But you can't stay with Jacques and me and remain a goy." She and Jacques were in Israel within a week, then God intervened directly. A week and a half after Ghislaine had landed in Tel Aviv, Yves, possibly drunk, stepped out into the street in front of a taxi and died while he was still in the ambulance. She found out three weeks later, after she'd finally written to her parents and they had written her back. A rabbi told her that there was no need to observe any rituals of mourning for the deceased; she laughed and said that she didn't need a Code of Jewish Law to tell her *that*.

Ghislaine took her new name at her conversion; Jacques was circumcised a week later and became Yaakov, Yankel in Yiddish. It didn't take her long to find her new commitment to Judaism wanting. She needed more—more learning, more observance, more things to reject. The need to stand out for her Jewishness led her farther and farther from the modern Orthodoxy into which she had converted—a world of observant people who were also doctors, lawyers, scientists—into the more insular, less acculturated world of hasidism. She enrolled Yankel in the most extreme kindergarten that would accept the converted son of a husbandless convert; at least he'd be learning Yiddish, a task to which she also set herself. It was the sole language of the community to which she wanted to belong.

The triumphal feeling engendered by the 1967 war had yet to evaporate; for the first time ever—or perhaps only since the days of the Bible—there were people living in physical fear of Jews. These strutting, overly confident boys and girls were the antithesis of everything that appealed to Ghislaine about Buber and Judaism. They relied on themselves; she wanted to rely on God. The Zionism that had once drawn her so powerfully was starting to look like another branch of the egotistical pride that seemed to keep any Israeli from waiting his or her turn in line; she embarrassedly found herself reverting more and more to a Latin saying that she remembered from school: *radix omnium malorum superbia est*, pride is the root of all evil. And if belief in a Jewish state is pride, then Zionism must perforce . . .

She wasn't what you'd call a subtle thinker. Nor was she married, which was beginning to be a bit of a problem. The only men willing to have her were the widowed or divorced screw-ups: idiots, adulterers, wife-beaters, mama's boys, and all kinds of other refuse that Ghislaine, who was blonde, busty and fairly bright, didn't need to have changed her life to end up with.

God helped her again. The wife of Rabbi Shraga-Feivel Frankel had passed away and the rabbi was looking for a replacement. Frankel was the founder and leader of Moginey Erets, "Shields of the Land," a group of fanatically anti-Zionist hasidim, mostly of Hungarian origin, who rejected all co-operation with the state of Israel or any of its institutions.

Rabbi Frankel had a bit of a problem, though. During a 1967 protest against the reunification of Jerusalem, an off-duty fireman whose son had been killed in battle kicked him in the nuts over and over again, probably a good half-dozen times, until the police finally sauntered over to stop him.

Frankel claimed to have sustained permanent damage, a tragic fate for any man, even one who already had seven daughters and a son. His real problems began when his wife died: a Jew with crushed testicles or a damaged penis is allowed to marry only a convert or a freed slave, and strong as Rabbi Frankel's faith in the Almighty may have been, he had begun to despair of ever finding either in the circles in which he moved.

He didn't look at women, but he couldn't have helped hearing about the zealous and attractive convert who had become so active a part of the community of the faithful in Jerusalem. He sent his aides to check her out; aside from her origins, she seemed completely kosher. Her son, who was about seven years old, was registered at a school run by Frankel's allies and was distinguished from the other children only because he could remember being circumcised.

The age difference—Rabbi Frankel was seventy—seemed about right to him, and he decided it would work. He sent emissaries to the Frenchwoman; she was so moved by the request, so incredulous that such a thing could be happening to her, that she fainted dead away. When they revived her, she said yes. Three days later, she was taken to meet the groom and sign an engagement contract. They were married within the month.

Rabbi Frankel's kids refused to attend the wedding; Rabbi Frankel promptly disinherited them all on the grounds of disobedience. His new will left all his money and property to his wife; if she predeceased him, it would go to his adopted son. Leadership of Moginey Erets was also to pass to the boy.

Vanessa was captivated, especially by the idea that Ruth had given up a stage career for the Torah. They arranged to see each other again, and yet again, and were soon doing so almost daily. Vanessa's story came out pretty quickly, everything from her childhood and the school for the blind to the death of her mother and the whole mess with Marshall and Thomas. Ruth took Vanessa's hand. "Him again." She gestured upwards with her eyes.

"I don't know, though, if we're sisters or mother and daughter." Vanessa felt just the same way.

Ruth was in France to tie up some family business arising from the death of her father. Probate in France goes on forever, though; Rebbetzin Frankel was back and forth to Jerusalem a few times, but was never away from France for more than three or four days, and over the next few months Vanessa began to study Torah and Jewish texts with Ruth. She stopped eating treyf, began to pray every day and observe the Sabbath. She was wearing nothing but long skirts now and seemed to feel, well, calmer, if not actually happy. She had hardly been to the movies at all. Martin Buber was starting to look primitive now; Camus and Beauvoir were completely forgotten.

Ruth told Vanessa that she and her son wanted to do something for other people like what Vanessa had just done on her own: help them come back to Torah. Ruth was about to get the money from her parents' estate, and she and her son were going to start a program. He was coming to France next Sunday. Ruth had told him all about Vanessa and he was eager to make her acquaintance. "A man like my Yaakov, a hasid—a rebbe—doesn't usually have much to do with women." Especially after his tragically awful marriage to the spoiled and probably psychopathic daughter of another rebbe. She—Ruth could trust Feygl, couldn't she? Yes, of course—she refused him for months, then finally kicked him in the same place as his adoptive father had been kicked when he approached with a request for his conjugal rights.

Ruth wasn't lying about any of this. She referred to her son either as Jacques—a mother's prerogative—or Yaakov, only because she didn't want to hear any giggling once Feygl realized that she was going to be marrying a man named Yankel Frankel. Ruth had been talking Feygl up to Yankel in their daily phone calls and on every one of her visits home. "She's perfect. She's lived through everything we'll be trying to sell. She's from Canada and speaks English. Can talk to these people in a way they'll understand. She's made a mess of her life and she'll consider it a mitzvah"—a good deed—"an honour, even, to help out. And she'll really believe she's unworthy."

"Yes," said Yankel. "And . . ."

"And what does she look like?"

"Azoy. Is she pretty?"

"Pretty? Lots of women are pretty." Yankel was starting to get scared.

"She isn't pretty." Just what he was afraid of. "She's— she's just as beautiful as you are."

Theirs was a world in which all marriages are arranged marriages. They agreed that Yankel would come to Paris

for two days, just to be sure. Since Ruth had been mould-
ing and vetting Vanessa, all they had to do after that was
leave her to Ruth till the end of the week. She'd deliver the
proposal on Saturday night, a couple of hours after the close
of the Sabbath.

Feygl almost fainted when she walked into Ruth's
hotel suite and laid eyes on Yankel for the first time. Ruth
had deliberately not shown her any pictures of him,
saying—not entirely truthfully—that they only got their
pictures taken when it couldn't be avoided, for passports
and other such necessary documents. Ruth was lying for
the sake of a worthy cause; she thought it better for Feygl
not to know what to expect.

Feygl couldn't believe what she saw. Take away the
payes, the tightly rolled, shoulder-length sidelocks that
looked like a pair of sausages dangling from either temple;
take away the payes and Yankel was a dead ringer, an
exact double, for Jeffrey Hunter, the most beautiful Jesus
of all, in *King of Kings*. Forget about Jesus, Vanessa had
never seen anybody this beautiful. She was getting squidgy
just looking.

Yankel didn't know from movie stars, but he knew
that he'd never seen anybody half as beautiful as this Feygl.
Ruth could see both their faces on posters and in advertise-
ments: if people who looked like this couldn't attract hordes
of sex-obsessed, lust-drenched North American Jews, then
nothing could bring such people to the Torah.

The three of them spoke together for a while, then Ruth started to putter about at the far end of the room to give the two youngsters a chance to get acquainted. Feygl went home and had the dirtiest, most erotic dream of her life.

Ruth popped the question on Yankel's behalf on Saturday night. They fixed a date for the ceremony after Feygl's next period.

The wedding took place in a good and auspicious hour. Faktor refused to come—"A rebbe, yet? She couldn't get herself a caveman?"—but the immediate family all turned up and managed to hold their tongues, which wasn't so hard when no one but Feygl and Ruth would talk to them. None of them had ever been near a hasid before, let alone surrounded by hundreds. They didn't enjoy it. Earl's Lithuanian parents were very religious, but they disliked hasidim only slightly less than they hated Christians. Earl and Randall could at least talk to each other. Poor Rachel, stuck alone on the women's side of every room or hall in which they found themselves, had no one to whom she could even express her dismay. "What a farce," she was muttering to herself. "My brother-in-law won't speak to anything without a penis. His mother is Prince Metternich wrapped up in a Torah and their followers make a sixth-grade graduate"—she pronounced it, *gradgee-et*—"like Jethro Bodine look like the Golden Age of Athens. Shit." She took a Hebrew copy of *The Origin of Species* from her purse and pretended to read it. There was ten feet of breathing space on every side of her.

Once her family went home, Vanessa was Feygl forever. A week after the wedding, she and Ruth sat down and began to map out a strategy for what was essentially a revival crusade. They worked together on speeches—they decided that they needed five different topics, enough for a multi-day booking—and then began to try them out, to edit and refine them. They offered free lectures to every religious English-language program and institution in Jerusalem, including plenty of places in which Ruth would never have normally set foot, so Feygl could gain experience and Ruth could watch and take notes. She didn't speak much English, but she could read a room like the pro she had been once. In about four months, Feygl had perfected her material and presentation; she sometimes gave two or even three lectures a day. Then they started to book modest halls and hotel rooms, and to take ads in local papers in the U.S.

Feygl would be speaking to coed crowds in English. Ruth and Yankel decided that there was no real problem with having men and women in the same venue at the same time, and even okayed their sitting together: these were people who sat together, anyway. Feygl was supposed to wean them into wanting to sit apart.

Her picture in any Jewish paper was sure to bring in a crowd. Feygl thought it was kind of ironic that she and Rachel both had the same haircut now, and that it looked just like Jean Seberg's in *Breathless* or *Saint Joan*, but the frumpy hasidic clothing and the kerchief drawn tight across her head so that not a millimetre of hair would ever peep out did for her what a nun's habit and wimple did for Ingrid Bergman and Audrey Hepburn: made her all the hotter.

The Frankel Outreach Program, whose English initials nobody ever bothered to check, provided Moginey Erets with a steady stream of donations and made Feygl very happy. She got to stand centre stage and be the centre of attention just as she was, with no need for any more talent or brains than she already had. She was a bit of a star in a very small world, and it gratified her, it really did, whenever a young woman would come up to her after one of her talks and say, "I want to learn to be like you." Feygl would smile and look down shyly, then say, "No. I'm the way God wants me. You need to be the way God wants you."

It worked well for years, even after the children were born. They branched out into inspirational DVDs and an interactive website; Feygl was one of the few women in her new world to have unrestricted internet access with the approval of her husband. Hundreds of thousands of religious women were copying her clothes and make-up; Feygl Frankel became the standard of Orthodox femininity even for women who had been keeping the Sabbath since they were born. If nothing else, she was a living illustration of the difference between modesty and dowdiness.

She was lonely on the road, but saw just enough of Yankel to forget that they didn't do much together but screw. They both liked it, and they did it as often as the law allowed: neither of them had ever seen anyone else who couldn't fail to arouse them just looking. She and Yankel didn't have a lot to talk about, but couples in that world tend not to do a lot of talking. Yankel still looked like a movie star and when Feygl was home, she could look at him for as long as she liked, and even do something about it. She had Ruth there when she needed to talk. She'd sometimes unburden herself and harp on her guilt about her past, and Ruth was there to show her how it was part of God's plan.

It worked well for ten years or so, right up until Ruth died. God's plan for her was breast cancer, and there was nothing that either prayer or medicine could do. With Ruth gone, Feygl and Yankel not only had to think for themselves—something that Yankel had never done before—but they had to deal with each other. To Feygl, Yankel was a beautiful package for Ruth's thoughts and ideas; once he got over the shock of losing his mother, he tried to get ambitious. Along with the heads of a few other minor, Jerusalem-based hasidic groups, he declared war on the Israeli Conversion Authority. Standards, in their view, had fallen so low that Israel was now full of goyim masquerading as Jews. They were marrying real Jews and unleashing a flood of bastardy that was threatening to wash away an entire people. Because of his own background as a convert of unquestioned kosherness and unimpeachable legitimacy, Yankel was chosen to head the League for the Purity of the Jewish People.

Feygl thought he was being used. "What do you need with this stuff? With these people? They've got no money, they've got no power, and they've got no followers. We've got all three. How are you going to go up against them? Mother chose this path to keep us safe and make us prosper. She was a *tsadeykess*, a saint. You and I both know that we're just regular people beside her. We don't have her drive or her brains. When she was stubborn, there was a reason for it. She didn't want her own way just because it was hers; she wanted what was right and what was best. Yankel, I'm begging you, don't change to another path."

Yankel stood up and put on his *shtrayml*, the round fur hat that was also the sign of his office, as if he were at a public gathering. "You're very beautiful, Feygl. You always have been. You've been a good wife and a good mother. My mother couldn't have picked any better. But a wife is one thing. A rebbe is something else. You be the wife; I'll be the rebbe."

Four years later, with Feygl staying home and Yankel so utterly out of his depth in the byzantine turf wars and alliances that define the hasidic politics that his mother had been careful to keep him out of, Feygl was growing dissatisfied. She and Yankel weren't getting along any

more. Their sex life had turned into the grudging fulfillment of a halachic duty, no different from having to eat
when you aren't at all hungry. Ruth had been gone for
four years when Faktor died, and Feygl was beginning to
find both hasidic life and life with Yankel about as stimu-
lating, as satisfying, as a dip into a lukewarm mikve; if she
didn't close her eyes, she was afraid that she'd see little
hairs from a previous bather on the surface of the murky
goop. Without Ruth to lean on, her whole way of life was
starting to remind her of a sweater that used to fit but was
now so tight that she had trouble breathing in it. With her
mother-in-law gone, she realized that she'd been married
to Ruth and only sleeping with Yankel.

They had to get more money coming in, and even
Yankel was talking rather cautiously about trying to resus-
citate the outreach tours. Donations had just about dried
up, but Yankel had to admit that the DVDs of Feygl's
lectures in America, the ones with her photo on the cover,
were all that was selling. When Feygl picked up her voicemail and found out that Faktor had died, Yankel took it
as another sign from God. He told Feygl to stay in Canada
and the States for a few weeks and give some lectures to
raise a little money. She tried to explain ideas of lead-
time, hall rental, accommodation and travel, but Yankel
simply waved his hand and told her to do it.

8

THE SHIVA

THE SHIVA MIGHT HAVE BEEN the first time the family had been together in years, but Vanessa—who would never be Feygl to anybody there—was a little upset about having to be in a room with men to whom she wasn't related. Chana told her that she couldn't be much of a rebbetzin if she didn't know that grandchildren have no obligation to sit shiva for a grandparent; they're there out of respect for the dead, as a comfort to the bereaved parent, and as gofers for the shiva-sitters, who aren't supposed to leave the house. "You don't want to be in a room with men? Go into a different room. But before you do, go down to the corner and get me a carton of Du Mauriers. If there's a man behind the counter, don't wink."

Chana herself didn't know how she'd suddenly got so calm. They'd practically had to keep her from throwing herself into the grave at the cemetery, but her anger with Milner and what he'd done to the service, her desire to put her ninety-five-year-old hands around his balls and twist till they dropped like crabapples in September, must have brought her—back to earth, she knew, was the wrong metaphor—must have helped her to overcome her emotions and act with a calmness that she wasn't really feeling at all. Having all of Faktor's survivors in the house where some of them had lived and all of them used to come for birthdays and Jewish holidays and any other special occasions; where Randall had sought refuge when his father kicked him out; and where her own children had grown up and somehow learned—Chana had no idea where, because they sure didn't pick it up at home—that satisfaction was more important than duty, because satisfaction belongs to you, while duty could benefit someone else—having everybody together again had Chana in tears: the next time they'd all be here would be to sit shiva for her. And then her children and grandchildren would start to fight over the house, which they'd finally have to sell to pay the lawyers before it was torn down or gutted by arrivistes who'd fill it up with their own lives, as if she and Faktor had never been there to begin with; as if the Faktors, including Ava and Niven, Earl and all the grandchildren, were a rough draft, a page full of strike-outs and blotches that could be tossed away without any loss.

Chana, Ava and Niven were the only ones sitting shiva. The grandchildren and their father all knew that they were there to fill in for Tamara. She would have been sitting shiva if she had managed to outlive her father, and they all felt a need to be there on her behalf. They weren't pretending to sit shiva themselves; they kept their shoes on and sat on regular couches and chairs, unlike Chana and the rest, who were going around in their socks and sitting in little baby lawn chairs supplied by the funeral home. Earl offered to say Kaddish for the traditional eleven months; if Niven was as weird about religion as he was about everything else, Earl wasn't sure that he could be counted on to turn up in shul. He was sitting there on a mourners' stool in a pea-green tweed Norfolk jacket and argyle socks like something out of P.G. Wodehouse, describing this year's annual meeting of the Viking Society for his mother and sister in Yiddish, while spitting tobacco juice into a paper cup that he carried for just that purpose. According to Niven, chewing tobacco enjoyed something of a vogue among British specialists in Old Icelandic and he'd picked up the habit not long after he arrived in England. "I guess I wanted to fit in," he said, "and I've never been able to break it. I sometimes wonder if it kept me from getting married, or at least from going out on many dates."

"Nice coat, that," said Earl, pretending to change the subject. He told Niven how much he—Earl, that is—had always loved Faktor and that he—Earl again—was willing to get up and go to shul every morning and run his evening schedule around the afternoon and evening prayers, which are usually said together at sundown.

Niven stood up and put his hands on Earl's shoulders, even though Earl was about four inches taller. "Would you?"

he asked. "Would you really? I've been wondering what I'm going to do. There's a couple of shuls in Bristol—I go Rosh Hashana and Yom Kippur—but it's about a twenty-mile drive from Weston, and to get there for 7 a.m. and be back in time for my classes, I don't think I'd be able to manage. And forget about *minkhe-mayriv*," the afternoon and evening services, "altogether." He wiped a tear of gratitude from his eye, then said in English, "I'd be ever so grateful, Earl."

There was a lot of sudden communication; people wandered in and out over the course of the week: celebrity co-workers from the CBC and private television, famous fans and regular neighbours, Chana's relatives and a few of Faktor's, through the aunt who brought him to Toronto in the first place. There were Yiddishists big and little from Toronto and New York, including those who came up for the funeral, some of whom had written disparagingly about Faktor at one time or another but who recognized that with Yiddish in the state that it is, he was the last of a particular line. They didn't have to have liked him to admit his importance. They could disapprove of him and everything he stood for or did; what really mattered was that he was still doing it when history and logic, literary theory and common sense all decreed that he shouldn't have been. As long as he was living, they could say that their work dealt with more than the past; they weren't fusty antiquarians, they were fussy critics. Now that he was gone, they remembered how close they were to being next.

They'd been anticipating this moment for years now, some of them still angry that it hadn't come earlier, but Faktor, as usual, had been way ahead of them. "In 1939," he said at his hundredth-birthday party, "I walked into a Jewish bakery in Lvov and asked the owner what he had on special that day. Ten years later, archaeologists were asking me to describe what I saw in that store and tell them the names of all the breads and cakes." He pointed towards the window of the restaurant. "There's more of Pompeii left out there than of the world I was living in when *The Wizard of Oz* came out."

Ava and Niven spent a long time talking with the Yiddishists. They'd both been away from Toronto for so long that neither of them really knew very many of the people who were coming to visit. They hadn't kept up with their school or university friends or seen anything of their relatives or former neighbours in roughly thirty years, and they were surprised at the number who did turn up, all these years later, to offer their sympathy. They'd all seen the obituary in the paper and, of course, remembered Yankee Gallstone coming to their schools when he wouldn't visit any others, because there weren't any others with his kids in them. And, aside from the initial shock of realizing that Yankee wasn't really Yankee and that the guy who played him wasn't like that all the time, what most impressed them at the Sholem Asch school was that Yankee Gallstone came and spoke to them in Yiddish. If someone like Yankee spoke it, it might not be a complete waste of time, after all. These kids all knew that they were learning Yiddish to make their parents happy; they had no use for it in their day-to-day lives—what other kids were they supposed to speak it with?—and there was nowhere that they'd be able to speak it when they grew up. Shlep out a few phrases for the family, have a brief conversation with the grandparents and get a quarter for your trouble—that's about all it seemed good for. But when they heard Yankee speak it for real, when he told them stuff in Yiddish that he didn't tell the kids who could only see him on TV—they all said that that was when they realized it was something special.

There were people who'd been in high school with them, too. A couple of guys who'd been on dates with Ava, a couple of Niven's old friends from his days as a teenage Albert Ayler fan, back when Albert was still alive. They'd dropped by on the off-chance that Ava or Niven would be there and they'd get a chance to catch up; if not, they figured that they could at least satisfy their curiosity from a distance while paying their respects, in the case of the high school friends, to a mother who was sure to remember them.

Milner turned up, too. Didn't pay a visit so much as mount an assault aimed at changing the focus of the shiva from Faktor and his family to himself. No one noticed him come in; without the polka-dot shirt, it's unlikely that any-body but Chana would have recognized him, but there he was, suddenly, braying away to the Yiddishists about all the hours and days he spent with "Getsl," working on "Getsl's" official biography, of which he, Milner, was the officially designated and "Getsl"-approved writer. "Perhaps you'd like to share some of your memories of Getsl with me?" he asked each of them in turn, in a voice that could be heard across the room.

"Oy vey," moaned Chana. "How did he get in here? Didn't I tell him to keep away?" She stood up and left the room to go take a nap.

"Getsl?" Ava and Niven looked at each other, bewildered. "Who the fuck is Getsl? Is he supposed to be talking about Daddy?" she asked.

"I honestly don't think he knows what he's talking about," said Niven. "Isn't he the asshole from the funeral?"

"You're right." Ava answered. "There's something familiar about him, but I can't put my finger on it. You don't run into a putz like that every day."

Suddenly, though, the putz was in front of her. "Ava?" it asked in English.

"Yeah?"

"I guess you don't remember me." It switched to Yiddish.

"I guess not," she said in English.

He took the hint. "We went to high school together. Allan Milner. Your dad and I were very close his last few years. I'm working on his biography and was here almost every day, working with him. A wonderful man, a *tayerer yid.*" He put a comforting hand on her mortified shoulder. "Do you remember me yet?"

Ava shook her head and thanked him for coming, anyway. Milner took the hint and turned away, briefly muttering "*af simkhes,* let's meet only on happy occasions," in her general direction. He swivelled, like a tank turret in search of its target, surveying the room for fresh meat. There had to be plenty of contacts here, plenty of—*holy fucking Jesus, will you look at that*! His brain lit up as his eyes landed on what might really have been the best-looking woman he'd ever seen. She was standing in the doorway of the den directly across the hall from the living room where the mourners were sitting shiva. A hippie of some sort, early forties, maybe, like some kind of Mother-of-Jesus Madonna in a floor-length skirt and a pair of Mary Janes, with a kerchief over her head that emphasized the screaming, regal perfection of her face. Milner's cock went rigid and his feet went forward. He held out his hand as he approached.

"Are you a member of the family? I'm Allan Milner, Mr. Faktor's biographer."

Vanessa stepped back from his hand like it was a poisonous snake; Jewish law forbids mixed touching. She looked modestly down to the floor. She recognized Milner from the funeral and noticed that he'd been so carried away with himself that he had no memory of having seen her there. "*Ikh reyd nisht kayn* English, I don't speak English," she muttered in Yiddish.

"No problem." Milner carried on in Yiddish, after hastily sticking in his hand into his jacket pocket. "I'll bet you're Vanessa, Feygl, I mean. Your grandfather, may he intercede for us in heaven, told me so much about you." Now that he'd placed her, he knew better than to say anything fatuous about how good she looked. "I hope that this is the last sorrow you'll ever know."

"Amen." There was no harm in being polite. He spoke Yiddish very well, a lot better than she did. He looked to be around the same age as her aunt and uncle, and had the kind of faded, slightly intellectual air that had appealed to her in Marshall. "A talented, brilliant man. Too bad he wasted it all on foolishness."

"Do you really think it was foolishness? An oeuvre of *that* quality, of *that* range, how can you dismiss it as foolishness?" Milner was starting to smile inside. If there was one thing he liked, it was girls. He tended to prefer them under thirty, but this wasn't just any girl; the way she looked, she could have been sixty, and neither he nor anyone else would have cared. But any idiot could see how gorgeous she was; what Milner had was an eye for vulnerability, or vulnerability to his own peculiar charms, at least—which helped explain the fairly undistinguished looks of so many of the women he'd had to do with. And there were hundreds of them, literally. He preferred them either married or virtually so; it cut down on trouble when he decided to move on, and he had to admit that he enjoyed the thrill of putting something over on someone, especially if the husband or boyfriend was someone he knew and who thought of him as a friend or colleague. Fucking wives or girlfriends wasn't much different from getting an old song from some immigrant, recording it himself and copyrighting the so-called arrangement so that nobody could ever use it again without Milner getting a cut. They were both ways of marking his territory and expanding his sphere of influence. Where most people dream of being stars, Milner always yearned to be the éminence grise who knew all the secrets and made the real decisions: influencing a marriage turned him on just as much as influencing a generation of neo-Yiddish folksingers or the woman he was trying to bed. He got the same hard-on from all of them. He could sense the likely prospects, practically smell insecurity and unhappiness in a woman's face or carriage; in a room full of women, he could almost always zero in on the one who was going to respond to him. He was drawn to Vanessa by her looks; but her willingness to argue—about culture and religion; with a stranger; in the midst of mourning rites for a member of her family; and to do so against all the rules of her hasidic way of life—told him that she was worth pursuing. There were chinks in that pious armour. And for the first time in years, Milner thought that this was someone with whom he might want to spend a good long time.

"Whatever isn't Torah is foolishness. My grandfather is ample proof of that. A grown man hopping around pretending to be a bird in front of millions of people."

"Hey." Milner put his hand on the door jamb, directly over the shoulder where he wanted to rest it. "Not a word against Yankee Gallstone. I can remember the first time I saw him. I was so excited. You're a lot younger than I am, you can't imagine what it was like for a kid like me, five years old, from a DP family, with parents with terrible accents, and I turn on the TV and hear somebody, *somebody on television*, who sounds exactly like them. And as if that's not enough, to find out that he wasn't doing imitations. He sounded like them because he was them, a Jew from Hitlerland—but he was on the fuckin'—*oy vey iz mir*, excuse me," Feygl had to giggle here; she'd scarcely heard anybody speak so freely in the last fifteen years. "He was on the television."

Feygl could feel herself getting warm and sweaty; she was sure that she was starting to blush. Even though they were speaking Yiddish, they were talking—no, she was hardly talking at all; this Milner guy was talking in a way that came naturally to her, too, the way she used to talk all the time. She was starting to feel like Vanessa instead of Feygl; aside from her immediate family, he was the first person of either sex to talk to her like she was a woman, an actual person, instead of the spokes-rebbetzin for her husband's never-ending campaign to get people to send him money.

"Okay. He was on television." She laughed. "I haven't looked at a television in more than fifteen years now, so I don't know if that's such a big *mayle*," a great good quality.

"Fifteen years? Really?" If Milner had been holding a martini, the moment would have been perfect. "You have no idea what you're missing."

"And I'd like to go on having no idea."

"I don't believe you." Milner was scolding her facetiously. In the old days, this would have been the time to offer her a cigarette, but this wasn't the old days. "I think you're trying to convince yourself that you can do without something that, really, you miss a lot. Culture isn't like cigarettes. You stop smoking—did you ever smoke?"

"I was a dancer, what do you think?"

"So you know what I'm saying. When you first stop smoking, it's hard. You want a cigarette all the time. You eat a meal, have a drink, do something else that you associate with smoking and there's something missing. But only at the beginning. Pretty soon you stop missing it and a little while after that you even forget that you've forgotten to miss it because it just doesn't enter your consciousness any more. Right? It's like why you never missed smoking when you were taking a shower—who the hell would ever think of doing it?"

"Yeah, so? I don't understand. Why can't you give up TV the same way you can give up smoking?"

"Because television and movies and the music you used to listen to and the books you used to read and all the dance you did taught you how to think a certain way, to approach the world from a certain angle and you can never get rid of it, no matter how hard you try, because it's hard for you to imagine any other way of looking at things. You have more in common with a Catholic priest who grew up in Toronto than you would with the Baal Shem Tov or the Gaon of Vilna. You might admire those other guys, but you'd *understand* the priest—and the priest would be able to understand you."

This was the most complicated bit of thinking Vanessa had run across since she ran away from Marshall, and she blamed herself for its not making sense. "I'm starting to get a bit of a headache." She was feeling confused.

"It's stuffy in here. All these people. You're not in any kind of technical mourning—why don't we go into the yard? I know there's some furniture out there." Vanessa looked hesitant. "There's nothing but a chain link fence"— he had to stoop to English for "chain link"—"so people will be able to see us. And we can leave the door to the house open."

"How do you know so much about the place?" She was walking down the hall behind him.

"I told you. I was here just about every day with your grandfather, *alav-ha-sholem*. I've been everywhere except where people sleep."

"My mother grew up here, you know."

"Yes. Getsl mentioned it many times."

"Getsl? Who's Getsl?"

"Faktor, your grandfather. Getsl is short for Elyokim."

"I never heard anybody call him that before." Milner opened the door to the backyard and bowed with mock courtliness while extending his right arm outside in a gesture of welcome. Vanessa stepped through and Milner closed the door. Randall and Rachel were sitting on thickly padded patio chairs by a white metal table with an umbrella in the middle. Randall was smoking. Rachel was holding a hip flask.

"Look," said Rachel. "It's God's gift to mikves."

"With her friend, the guerrilla eulogist." Randall leaned back and blew a smoke ring. "Why am I not surprised?"

"Ignore them," Vanessa said in English.

"We'd leave," said Rachel, "but you're a religious woman, and married. I guess we'll have to chaperone them, eh, Ran?"

Milner didn't like this, but he didn't want to mix in. Rachel took a pull from the flask and offered it to Randall. He ignored it and stood up. "I'm Randall Frumkiss, Vanessa's brother, and this is our sister Rachel." He stuck out his hand.

Milner shook. "Allan Milner. I'm sorry about your grandfather. I'm working on his biography."

"My sister's married to a great hasidic leader, did she tell you? Yankel Frankel, can you believe it? That's his name. Of course, his followers call him the Shnorrer Rebbe. I'll let you in on a little secret, though: it's Vanessa who does the shnorring."

"Come, Mr. Milner. Let's go back in. Something

smells out here." Milner had a horrible feeling that all his plans were about to go up in smoke.

"I'm finished my cigarette." Randall stubbed his butt into a plastic ashtray. "Let's go back in, Rach." Rachel followed like a kid on her way to the dentist. "What are you starting up for?" he asked once the door was safely closed. "I wanted to get away from that asshole as quickly as we could, not engage him in dialogue about the tragic family background of Faktor's final days."

"You wouldn't be saying that if you weren't the one who killed him."

"Who, me?"

"Yes, you." Rachel nodded sternly.

Randall shook his head. "Couldn't be."

"*Fungu.* You broke his heart and he died in the flower of his youth." Rachel sang the words out rhythmically, like she was picking teammates in a kid's game.

"Barely into his second century. You might be right."

"Once he found out that you weren't inviting him to any of the stags you've been doing—he couldn't face the rejection."

"Didn't have time for the pain." Randall shook his head. "He wanted to watch the dirty movies."

By this time, they'd walked right through the house and were about to head for the sidewalk outside so Randall could light another smoke. "Hey, you guys!" Ava was waving at them. "Come over here a minute." They didn't have to.

Ava had been halfway out of her stool when she called them and had caught up with them before they could go anywhere. "Come here." They went into the kitchen.

"Yes, auntie?" asked Rachel. "Is there something we can do?"

"Don't call me auntie. But, yeah. Did I see that shmuck Milner heading outside with whatever Vanessa's name is now?"

"Yeah," from Randall. "We went out there for me to have a smoke and they came out a little bit later. We left right away."

"Shit." Ava bit her lip.

"Why, what's the matter?'

"Didn't you hear? Maybe you were already outside. I went to high school with him."

"And?" Rachel took over the questions.

"He's the biggest worm I ever met in my life. And I didn't even know him that well, but after more than forty years, he still stands out. We can't let him anywhere near—" Ava was waiting for Vanessa's Jewish name.

"Van Klafte," Randall said in a James Bond voice, "Feygl van Klafte."

"Not funny, Ran. I'm really serious. This guy is bad news."

The twins were waiting for more information. Ava sighed and opened a bottle of pomegranate juice that she'd spied on the counter. "He was a weasel, a total creepy weasel. Always sucking up to the teachers, but obviously not sincere about it. You guys ever see *Leave It to Beaver*? Yeah? So, Milner was kind of like Eddie Haskell talking to parents: 'Good afternoon, Mrs. Cleaver. My, but you're looking radiant this afternoon.' You see what I mean? So sucky that nobody, or almost nobody could buy it—unless they were a teacher. Every kid in school knew what a scumbag he was, but some of the teachers thought that the sun shone out of his ass. He had good marks, too, and seemed like such a nice, polite interested young man. Very socially aware. Civil rights committees to send money to the NAACP, early anti-Vietnam stuff. Talked about moving to a kibbutz after he graduated. Nothing but bullshit, and even the teachers figured it out eventually.

"He was kicked out. Expelled, which meant he couldn't go to any school in Ontario. His parents had to go to court and file an appeal to get him back in after a year had passed. Before that, everybody thought that he was having an affair with our physics teacher. Her name was Miss Legge, I still remember her. We called her Miss Leggy—what else, eh?— because she was about six-foot-two. She wasn't very pretty and she had a beehive hairdo that made her even taller. In heels and the beehive, she was really six-six, six-seven. The big joke was that she should have been the basketball coach, but the real joke, if that's what you want to call it, is that she was a bit of a beatnik. She taught physics and something else, biology I think, and she was gangly and awkward, but

Miss Legge was a total hipster." Ava lowered her voice to a whisper. "She had a black boyfriend. They were still called Negroes then. Her boyfriend was a Negro, even taller than her, and he used to come for her sometimes in an Austin Mini. He was a jazz musician, pretty well known in Toronto: kids that were into that stuff recognized him, because he was the house pianist at one of the big clubs that used to have a Saturday matinee.

"Anyway, she was supposed to be weird because her boyfriend was black—this was around 1964, 1965—and people—Jesus, it's embarrassing to remember *other* people thinking this way—they thought that if she'd go out with a Negro, she must be some kind of a slut. Milner *really* sucked up to her, and people started saying that they were having an affair, that she was sleeping with Milner."

"Was she?" Rachel wanted to know.

"No, I don't think so, but Milner did everything he could to make everybody think that she was. Shit like, 'Oh, when I saw Nancy last night,' you know, fake casual mentions and stuff. Anyway, he did get close enough to be able to go in and out of her little office at the back of the physics lab whenever he felt like it, and one afternoon he stole the stencils for the grade eleven physics exam. He took them over to the Y on Bathurst Street, and ran off a whole bunch of copies on their Gestetner machine. You guys know what that is or are you too young?" They shrugged. Ava shrugged. "It's like an old copier that used to print stuff off stencils that you typed onto and then fed into this machine that turned out one copy of the stencil at a time. He told the people at the Y that they were merit badge exams for the Boy Scout troop that used to meet there and that he needed to do them right away—they didn't have to go to any trouble, he'd just do them himself before the weekly troop meeting at seven o'clock. He got the copies—I don't know how many he made—and put the stencil back in Miss Legge's office first thing the next morning.

"At first, he was going to go through the exam on his own and sell the answers. He was good in school, like I said; he didn't need to cheat to get in the nineties. Anyway, he realized that if he tried to sell answers, he'd sell one set and they'd just get passed from person to person; if he sold the exams, though, people would have to sit and do them themselves, probably in groups with their friends. Then they'd come to Milner, who could go from group to group the night before the exam and check their work for a slight additional fee, like he was Satan's TA or something."

"So what happened?" It was Randall who asked. "If he got expelled, he must have got caught. How?"

"It was my fault," Ava blushed a bit and smiled. "I turned him in. He must have liked me or something. He said he'd give me a copy for free if I'd make out with him. 'All I'm asking for is second base,' he said. I was so disgusted that I went straight to the principal's office and ratted him out."

"Did he know?"

"No. And he still doesn't. Don't tell Vanessa—he's the kind of jerk who'd still want vengeance after all these years and I don't think she'd be able to keep it to herself."

"Wow," said Randall. "He doesn't even suspect."

"What's worse is that I found out later, after Milner gave them a list of everybody who'd got a copy of the exam from him, that I wasn't the only one he tried to get that way. Dilys Himelfarb actually went for it."

"Dilys?" Randall was giggling.

"She'd come over from England. A slut. All a guy had to do to get to second base with her was ask."

"What is second base, anyway?" Rachel asked. "I never quite figured it out."

"Bare tit," her aunt told her.

· "Oh. And while we're on the subject, how come you won't let anybody know who you're married to?"

Ava thought it over. "If I tell you, you have to swear to keep it a secret. It's got nothing to do with me. Well, I guess it did a little at the beginning, when I was afraid to let my parents know that I'm a lesbian—but, you guys know Suzy Bertram?" The mothering guru, author of at least half a dozen now-canonical books about how to raise decent and upstanding middle-class children, from conception through to the age of twenty-one, when they're on their own.

"Yeah?"

"Well, we're married."

"No shit!" Rachel squealed. "I used those books. She's a dyke? That's fantastic."

"Hard core. Raised two kids a long time ago, they're about your age."

"How'd she get 'em?"

"Her brother and sister-in-law were killed in a traffic accident and she was the only surviving relative. She actually married a gay male friend—he pretended to be her fiancé right after the accident—so there wouldn't be any crap about it."

"Wow."

"You see why she has to be so careful, though. I think she goes a little far with it, but it's really the only major thing she's ever asked me to do for her."

"So, I've got to ask you," Rachel said. "What is it you do out there? That's always been the big question: What does she do for a living?"

Ava smiled and looked a little sheepish. "Really, I don't do anything. You know how much Suzy's made from those books? We have a house and some land on the Queen Charlottes and another house in Hawaii."

"Shit," said Randall, "it sounds great."

Ava nodded. "It *is* great. Don't tell Vanessa what happened with me and Milner, but see if you can keep him away from her. He really is the kind of sleaze who could talk a hasid into screwing him."

———

Vanessa and Milner were alone in the yard, and Milner was trying to get things back on track. "Getsl told me that you'd married into a hasidic family. I'm surprised that someone from outside was able to . . ."

Since Vanessa hadn't worked out that Milner already knew the important parts of the story, she spent the next hour or so telling him her whole history, beginning with Marshall and going all the way up to her growing doubts about life in a dying hasidic court run by an egoist who seemed bent on destroying everything that his parents had worked to build up.

Milner felt like he was going to come in his pants. "I know what it feels like to be stuck," he said, and embarked on a lengthy voyage into the history of his life on the Yiddish music scene, the ungrateful oldsters—so different from Getsl—whom he'd try to help, the numbers of people who seemed deliberately to have misunderstood so much of what Milner had said and done. The sun was starting to set by the time he finished his recitation, and there was a little tear in each of Vanessa's beautiful eyes. Milner headed inside when someone announced that the prayer service was about to begin.

He'd no sooner stepped into the living room than Chana, finally up from her nap, leapt at him like a guard dog and started clawing the back of his shirt, pulling the tails up and over the waistband of his Dockers. "Why are you still here?" Milner didn't know what to do. She was too old to push or even nudge, and the way she was pummelling his back didn't really hurt. It was an awkward situation nevertheless. "I told you to leave a long time ago, didn't I?"

"No, Chana. You just—"

"Well then, I'm telling you now." She let go of his shirt and stopped hitting. "And I don't want to see you back here. And one other thing: nobody ever called Faktor Getsl. He hated the name and wouldn't let anybody use it for him. He only put up with it from you because he thought you were too stupid to be worth correcting." She switched to Yiddish for the benefit of all the assembled Yiddishists. "This guy isn't human, he's a leech. No, he's a vampire who's trying to live off Faktor's carcass for the rest of his own miserable life. Don't talk to him, don't co-operate with him, don't share any memories with him, and above all, don't ever let him into your house."

Milner was trying to do his "What can I do? She's out of her mind" shrug for all the Yiddish big shots, but Chana wouldn't let him finish. "Get out of here now," she hissed, "before I call the police."

Milner left without saying anything more. He was on the verge of tears as he came through the front door and walked down to the sidewalk where Rachel and Randall were still standing. He walked right past them, gasping to keep from weeping, and headed over to the next block where he'd left his three-year-old Saturn. He got in and did nothing, just sat behind the wheel, crying sporadically and plotting vengeance while his blood was still up. "Wait till she sees how I treat her in the biography. If she doesn't like me, fine, she doesn't like me. But to throw me out like that, in front of all those people; telling them that I'm nothing, nothing, for God's sake, and that they shouldn't even talk to me. She must be jealous, but that's no excuse, no excuse at all. And I don't care if she's ninety-five years old, that doesn't give her the right to meddle in other people's business." He drove over a block to where Rachel and Randall were still standing outside the house. He even found a place to park and he sat there, cursing and gnawing the soft part of his hand between the thumb and forefinger while waiting for Feygl to come out. He didn't know that they were talking about him.

Feygl came out about twenty minutes later. She'd taken one of Earl's cars to the shiva, but hadn't told Earl or anybody else that she hadn't had a valid driver's licence in at least twelve years: hasidic women aren't allowed to drive. She could still do it, though; it was just like riding a bike, and she was enjoying the sense of freedom, the idea that she could go anywhere and do anything without having to ask permission or rely on anyone or worry about being seen or how it might look. She found an oldies station on the radio. She wasn't in mourning and was allowed to listen to music; no one could believe the change that seemed to have come over her since the last time they saw her. All of a sudden, she was helpful and solicitous, eager to perform any errand

on behalf of any of the mourners and frequently going out
of her way to ask if anybody needed anything from "the
store," as if there were only one and everyone knew what
it was. She always took the long way there and the long way
back; she still hadn't heard "Tainted Love" or anything by
Karla Bonoff. She sat in the car, puttering along on side
streets that she remembered well enough to cruise by
instinct, rolling her sleeves up in the heat—a pleasure like
you wouldn't believe after all those years in Israel dressed
for winter in Medicine Hat—and singing along, thinking
unashamedly in English, when she could be bothered to
think at all. The problem was what she was thinking.

"I think I've wasted my life," she said to herself out loud
one day on her way to pick up a few plugs of Red Man for
Niven, some apple juice for Chana and a bag of peanuts in
the shell for her father, who liked to snack on them during
the day. She'd gone into this thing with Yankel and Ruth
with a perfect, if somewhat superficial, faith. She'd never
really thought about religion before she met them, and for a
while it was quite easy for her to believe that it could make
her less of a mess and her life a lot less horrible. That was
certainly the way Ruth had pitched it to her. "I've lived in
both worlds, too," Ruth told her, "and I can tell you that
in *ours*"—she meant the religious Jewish one—"you never
see the kind of unhappiness that everybody, *everybody* in
the secular world feels. We've got strong families, and there's
not a lot of fooling around. You know how much trouble

that cuts down on right there? And after not being able to be with your husband or wife for half a month, every month, when you can act like man and wife again, it's not like a second honeymoon, it's like a real honeymoon, for half a month, every month. There's no materialism; we're all poor and we don't care. Our riches are here," she touched her right temple, "and here," and put her hand over her heart.

It didn't take Vanessa long to realize that she'd been had. Different mores gave rise to different ways of going about the same old vices; there was dishonesty and greed, and she still got hit on—plenty, and surprisingly often by women. She took things in stride, adjusted her expectations, did her best to suppress any lingering internal echoes of the world she used to live in. Then she started to travel. She was spending a lot of time in airports and on planes. Television sets blared out all over every airport. She had seatmates on every plane, and some of them wanted to talk. She was proselytizing to people who were just like she used to be, and she was starting to envy them their ability to do what they wanted and make their own decisions. She almost never felt this way in Israel; but now she was back in her native language, now it was natural for her to be who she really was. She was living in Hebrew and French and Yiddish; she still had to think to use either of the first two. Her Yiddish had improved in a way that would have made her grandfather proud, had it not ended at exactly the point where the authorized hasidic world ended for a woman. She could have sat down with Faktor and told him that Zionism was evil and anti-Torah, but she could never have discussed ideas of the national significance of territorial acquisition per se: she didn't have the vocabulary.

Fundraising in the USA let her know that she'd always be the person she thought she'd tossed away and left behind. As much as she acted on it was to buy a copy of *Vogue* or *People* in an airport and leave it in the seat pocket in front of her when she exited her plane. A large part of the reason behind her not going to Faktor's party was a fear that if she went, she'd never go back to Israel. She loved the children she'd had with Yankel and did her best to be a good and caring mother; she had no desire to lose them, which she most assuredly would in any religious divorce. Lately, she had been positively aching to be back in touch with Thomas, the son she had with Marshall. Abandoning him was the stupidest and probably the cruellest thing that she'd ever done in her life, and she'd been trying to find some way of reversing at least some of the damage that she'd done to both of them. She felt badly about her treatment of Marshall, too, but could write that off as having never really loved him, at least not the way a woman is supposed to love her husband. Same thing, really, with Yankel, except that she hadn't realized how much her feelings for him were really feelings for his mother. She'd loved Ruth, not in any sexual way, but—Yankel was still as good looking as he'd ever been, but her lust for him had grown less and less, petered out, slowly but steadily since Ruth had died. And there'd been real lust there, from both of them. The only cheating on authorized ultra-Orthodox practice they'd ever done was in their bedroom: they'd leave the lights on; Vanessa would go on top; he'd put his cock between her breasts for a minute or two, just to help it get super hard. Their paltry three children had nothing to do with Vanessa; she'd been to half a dozen doctors, all of whom eventually said that the problem had to lie with Yankel, who only went to the doctor if he didn't feel well or had been hurt. Probably a low sperm count, but no one really knew. All they could have told you—as distinct from the nothing they *would* have told you—is that they had sex an average of fourteen to eighteen times a month, as often as the laws concerning menstruation would allow them. All that screwing should have yielded more than three measly kids, but three seemed to be all that God had willed for them. And, to be truthful, it was a blessing; any more and Vanessa would have had too much trouble being able to get away for fundraising junkets. What concerned her now was that she didn't want three more Thomases that she'd never see and with whom she'd soon have nothing in common.

It was hard to keep her misgivings on hold, though, when Yankel was spending his time trying to turn Jews into goyim and letting all the work she'd done to turn semi-goyim into full-fledged Jews go straight to hell. There hadn't been enough time for her to set up any pep rallies this time around; she missed the kids like crazy, but was otherwise happy to stay over here for as long as she could manage.

She was fumbling in her bag for the car keys when Milner jumped out of his car and called her name. He was too far away to see the tears running down her cheeks. "Feygl! Rebbetsin Frankel!" She looked up, slid the Kleenex out from under her watch strap—a trick she'd learned from Chana— and wiped her nose. "It's me, Allan Milner." He was almost close enough to start speaking at a normal volume. She still hadn't spoken. "I was wondering—my God, you're crying."

She looked up at him and tried to force a smile. "I just got off the phone with Thomas." She spoke English rather than Yiddish now.

"Uh."

"My son from my first marriage."

"Oh, *Thomas*. You called him?"

After Chana had thrown Milner out, Feygl, stirred on by everything that she'd been telling Milner immediately before, found Earl and asked him if he had Thomas's phone number at home.

"I can do better than that," Earl beamed. He stuck a hand into the inside pocket of his jacket and pulled out a small leather book of phone numbers and addresses. "I've got it right here. You gonna call him?"

"I'm his mother, aren't I?"

She went into the master bedroom and sat down on the bed that Chana used to share with Faktor. She was trembling so badly that she had trouble hitting the right buttons on the phone. What if he wasn't home? Should she leave a message? What number would she leave if he did? She was in and out of the shiva, hardly ever at Earl's, where she was staying, and her Israeli cell phone wouldn't work over here.

And if he answered, what then? Would he talk to her? How would she deal with it if he hung up or started to yell? Or didn't yell, but told her exactly what he thought of her? Would she be able to take it? And what if he was happy and started to cry and say, 'Mommy, mommy, *lama sabachthani*? Why did you abandon me?' Would she be able to take that? She almost hung up while his phone was still ringing. Earl knew that Thomas was working; he'd given Vanessa his cell number.

"Hello."

"Uh, Thomas?"

"Yes."

"Thomas Nurgitz?"

"Yes, this is Thomas Nurgitz. What can I do for you?"

"Thomas, Tommy, this is, this is—it's your mother calling, Thomas." She lost it right there and burst into tears.

Nobody said anything for nearly a minute, but nobody hung up.

"Thomas?"

"My mother? I'm in a lab here. Let me go outside where I can talk."

Another long silence, then. "Why are you calling me?"

He could hear Vanessa sniffling. "Because I wanted to talk to you. I miss you. I'm at your great-grandfather's shiva. He died, you know."

"Yes, Zeyde called me."

"He did?" She had no idea that they'd been in regular touch all these years, or that Marshall and Thomas used to come to visit.

"Why are you calling me now, after all this time? I was so young when you kidnapped me, I don't even remember you."

"Not even a little? The way we used to play."

"Nothing. As if I'd never laid eyes on you." Thomas had been waiting all his life to say this. All that bothered him was that it was true; if his grandfather and great-grandparents hadn't shown him the family albums, he'd have had no idea what his mother even looked like.

"I don't know what to say, then." Vanessa was sure that she was about to have a heart attack.

"I don't think there's anything *to* say. I don't understand why you're calling me."

"I just thought, I thought that—" She was crying too hard to be able to go on now, her shoulders heaving up and down with every desolate hiccup.

"I just think," Thomas's voice was quivering, "you should go back to your life and I'll go back to mine. I appreciate your calling, but it's way too late. You should have come looking when I missed you. "

"But—"

"You don't have to worry that I think badly of you. I don't think about you at all. Sandra," Marshall's second wife, "is the only mother I have." Vanessa snorted like someone had stuck a rod up her torso to pull out a tooth. "I'd say 'Don't be a stranger,' but it's not up to me to tell you not to be what you are." Thomas hung up.

Vanessa kicked off her shoes, sat down on the floor and wept until she had to run to the toilet to be sick. She felt like she ought to be sitting shiva now, too. Not counting the silences, the whole conversation didn't last for more than three or four minutes. It was no news to Vanessa that she hadn't been any kind of a mother to Thomas, but she'd still expected *something*, some tiny spark of filial regard that could be fanned, slowly but with careful certainty, into a suitably ardent relationship. Instead, he treated her—his mother—the same way as she'd treated so many of her former suitors and lovers. She got exactly what she deserved, but nobody deserved what she got.

She'd headed straight for the car once she'd been able to collect herself enough to get through the house without attracting too much attention. Anybody who saw her weeping right after her uncle had finished saying Kaddish would assume that she was grieving for her grandfather. Even Milner thought that was what she was doing at first. He could see that part of her—the Vanessa part—wanted him to hold her, just to keep her from being so alone in her grief, but the Feygl in her wouldn't let her succumb. "It sounds to me like you could use a drink. I'd offer you one, but," and he shrugged to show how well he understood the religious strictures that made such an outing impossible.

Feygl suddenly didn't give a shit. As far as she was concerned, she'd just lost a child. Nothing else really mattered. "Do you know a place with an outdoor patio? One that's right on the sidewalk. Something totally public? Where anybody walking by could see us?" Milner knew more than one. "Then tell me where it is and I'll meet you there. We can't go in the same car." She was a stupid woman, she knew that now for sure. She might as well start to act like one.

Milner gave her an address on Bayview Avenue, just south of Eglinton, about ten minutes by car from where they were. "I'll meet you there."

Vanessa pulled her car out of the driveway and away from Faktor's house. She opened the windows as soon as she turned the corner, rolled up her sleeves, turned the radio way up and actually felt herself starting to smile through the tears. They couldn't have picked a better time to play "Born to Be Wild." She took it as a sign and stopped at a convenience store, where she bought a package of cigarettes and a disposable lighter. Most hasidic men still smoke, but for women, it's strictly forbidden. She'd just decided to see about that. She knew that smoking in the car would upset her father, and was also a little worried in case the cigarette should make her dizzy or even sick and leave her unable to drive, so she stood beside the garbage can outside the store and lit up. Let Milner wait; it'd do him good.

After the second drag, she started feeling dizzy and weak in the knees. She grabbed hold of the top of the garbage can to steady herself while she coughed. "Why am I doing this?" she wondered, but she was still Vanessa. Once she started, she was going to go through with it. And she did, then went back into the store and bought a bottle of water that she drank right down. She waited until she was feeling better, then took another cigarette out of the pack and stuck it into her mouth. This was the one she'd enjoy.

She smoked another one after that and kept Milner waiting for a good twenty minutes. He sniffed when she sat down. "You smell like cigarettes."

"Must be the cigarettes I was smoking."

"You smoke? I thought it was *osur*, forbidden."

"It is. These were the first ones in about fifteen years. When your son tells you that he doesn't want anything more to do with you, it's a special occasion. I think you're allowed. This is also the first time in fifteen years that I've been in a restaurant or bar, not counting coffee places in airports."

"This *is* a special occasion, then," Milner said. "What would you like?"

"How does beer sound?"

"Sounds good to me. Make it two," he told the waitress. "Pints."

Milner's eyes were following her as she walked away. When Vanessa turned around to see what was so interesting, she noticed that the waitress's skirt probably had less fabric to it than the kerchief on Vanessa's head. Halfway through her second beer, while stumbling to the washroom, Vanessa went up to the waitress and suggested that they swap.

Over the three pints that followed her first one, Vanessa as much as told Milner what she had only dared admit to herself in the last few days, while driving around on her errands. She wanted to be normal again, and it was only the fear of having four Thomases instead of one that was driving her back to Israel.

It was late, past eleven o'clock, when she realized that she was in no shape to drive home, especially without a licence. "I'd drive you," said Milner, "but I know you can't be alone in a car with me."

Vanessa thought for a second. "Give me your cell." Milner reached his phone across the table to her. She punched in Earl's number. "Hello, Daddy. It's me, Vanessa. I've had a little too much to drink, ha ha. Could you come get me, please?"

There were four more days of the shiva left—three, really, since Saturdays don't count—and Vanessa either saw or spoke to Milner on every one of them, except for Saturday, when it's forbidden to use the phone. She was racked with guilt because they were falling in love; they hadn't actually done anything that contravened Jewish law—as distinct from hasidic custom—or would have outraged non-Jewish morality—never been alone together in a car or a room; never touched at all, not even to shake hands or kiss good-bye; never talked dirty or even sexy; never said "I love you" or "Leave your husband" or "Help me leave my husband"—but they were both thinking about it all the time, about being alone in a room, touching, talking sexy dirt before they declared their love for each other and threw their clothes off, right there in whatever room she was imagining, and did it hard and fast and on the floor because they couldn't wait to get to a bed. With a shiver and a wet spot, Vanessa imagined what might have been with him if she wasn't already married; she saw herself putting her hand on his pants and feeling his cock get hard through the cloth.

She tried praying and saying Psalms. She took cold showers. While she'd fantasized plenty about leaving Yankel, if she only could, she had never once dreamed of doing so for somebody else. She reached a point where she stopped wanting Yankel, but she'd never wanted anybody else before. Now, though, when she was supposed to be mourning her grandfather, she couldn't help touching herself at night in ways that she knew she wasn't supposed to, while thinking about a man who most definitely was not her husband. It didn't matter, though; she knew herself and it was only a matter of time now. Not that she was going to leave Yankel. The phone call to Thomas put that out of her mind for good; there was no way in heaven or on earth that she was going to make that mistake again, so she was stuck with Yankel. But her general behaviour was already growing so iffy—flirting, driving, smoking, drinking, listening to the radio—that she could see that soon she'd be watching television again, looking at porn on the internet, violating the Sabbath and eating non-kosher food. Her attention span might have increased and grown stronger, but she'd just about come to its end. Even if she were to go on doing everything the wife of a man like Yankel was supposed to do, in her head she knew she was already gone.

Milner, for his part, didn't know what to do with himself any more. He'd had obsessions before, but this was it, the real thing, love finds Andy Hardy and about time, too: there were seventeen years between him and his pre-destined one, and he was already fifty-nine. He needed to be with her and needed to be there now, inside her arms, gazing into that incredible face and knowing that it was his. For all the glibness and superficiality of his original approach, his talks with Vanessa, which never touched on anything that wasn't themselves, had taken him so deeply inside her that a sudden loss of looks on her part would scarcely have diminished his feelings for her at all. The biggest boners he got were when he thought about her without a kerchief on her head. She was so beautiful, so modest, he was afraid to imagine her naked; or maybe, he thought, he didn't have enough imagination to envision the perfection he was sure to find under all those layers of wrapping.

"What are we gonna do?" she asked him over the phone on the day that the shiva was over. They were now speaking nothing but English with each other. "I'm going back to Israel on Wednesday and then what? I can't leave Yankel; it doesn't make sense for you to come to Jerusalem. For what? What would you do there? Wander around in the street, hoping to get a look at me as I passed? We wouldn't be able to speak. I'm better off at home with e-mail and Skype than I am with you in public in Israel, because I can't be with you in public in Israel."

"I don't know what we *can* do." Milner was running a hand through his hair. "Short of you becoming a widow, I can't see any way out, not as long as you want to be with your kids. But we've got to be together, for a little while, anyway, until we can do it forever. Spend some time together away from there, away from here. Somewhere where we can be ourselves and nobody knows us, where you can dress like a normal person and not have to worry about who might happen to see you."

"*Sure.* Why don't we pick up and go to Las Vegas? And do what? I told you already, I'm not going to commit adultery. Yankel hasn't done anything bad to me, and he did me a lot of good when I first met him. I might not feel the way a wife's supposed to feel about him, but I have no reason to hurt him and I'm not going to do it, even if it's going to keep you and me apart. We can stay in touch—we have to stay in touch, Allan; I can't imagine life without you any more—but what we both need to do is figure a way out of this marriage that doesn't involve screwing around or killing someone and that'll let me keep my kids."

"That's all?" Milner was using the same frown that he usually reserved for people who could see him. "And what are we supposed to do in the meantime? When will I ever see you again? When will you be back in Toronto?"

"I'm gonna come more now, no matter what happens. Maybe even bring the kids, show them a bit of their real heritage. It's like my zeyde gave me one last present by dying: he reminded me of who I really am and where I really come from. Now that my Yiddish is so much better than it used to be, I'd like to read some of his stuff. I never have, you know. Not a word."

"Really?" Milner was incredulous. "Wait till you see what you've been missing."

PART TWO:

The Legacy

9

CHANA AND MILNER, I

CHANA DIED AT THE BEGINNING OF NOVEMBER. No one expected her to last too long after Faktor's death. She was relatively healthy, but at ninety-five she had plenty of reasons to give up the ghost besides the loss of her life companion.

Earl had made a point of dropping by every day for those last few months, generally after the morning synagogue service where he said Kaddish for Faktor. He could see that Chana was depressed, especially by the fact that Niven and Ava both left town as quickly after the shiva as they could manage. "I don't want to be here when it starts to smell like moth balls," Ava said. Niven was worried about the paper he was supposed to present on the Old English *Deor*. The Frumkisses had all forgotten how nice Chana's children really were; self-absorbed, undoubtedly, but fairly pleasant about it and always interesting to talk to. Niven, especially; they couldn't figure out how his Yiddish was still as good as it had been on the day he left home and were impressed by the fact that he had been corresponding in Yiddish with his parents for all the years that he'd been in England; no one had ever told them. He used to send Faktor articles and even photocopies of Yiddish books that he thought his father might like, especially hard-to-find things by Faktor's old friends and rivals.

Chana was missing Faktor, and without him to keep her amused or exasperated, she found herself thinking about her children more than was probably good for her. Luz, the housekeeper, told Earl that she'd come up from her suite in the basement some mornings to find Chana looking through old photo albums while watching Turner Classic Movies and sobbing.

Milner was missing Faktor almost as much as Chana was, and he might have been missing Vanessa even more. She'd gone home with a volume of Faktor's collected poetry, as well as a two-volume selection of the best of the *Mazik* columns, both of which she hid from Yankel and everyone else. She managed to e-mail Milner six days a week and he wrote back on seven, but Milner was definitely at loose ends. Faktor had left him with enough CDs to keep him busy on the biography for the foreseeable future, but he was spending most of his time trying to figure out how he could get together with Vanessa. After Chana threw him out of the shiva in front of most of the people he'd planned to go to for help in finding a publisher, Milner was no longer sure if it paid to keep working on the book. The subject matter was too arcane for a mainstream publisher, and academic publishing depends almost entirely on recommendations from experts in the field; thanks to Chana—and God only knew what she might have said about him in the meantime—there was a very good chance that nobody was going to want to know Milner.

He couldn't be sure, though, and he spent his days transcribing Faktor's reminiscences and mooning over Feygl. Nearly sixty years old, he thought, and still behaving like a teenager. He even went back to the pub where they'd had their first, their only drink together; he started to cry as soon as he got his beer. He was sick with longing for her, and now that he didn't have to kiss the old man's ass, her grandfather was starting to get on his nerves.

Faktor's memories, spoken into his iMac in the early hours of a great many mornings, tended to be a little too heavy on particulars: cast lists, verbatim quotations from reviews, every stop on every itinerary of every show. Faktor couldn't forget and he couldn't shut up. The interesting stuff—Yiddish theatre personalities, Jewish life in Poland during the twenties and thirties, the terror and confusion at the outbreak of the War—was there, all right, but covered so deeply by the dust of unnecessary detail that Milner sometimes had to listen three or four times just to figure out what was going on. Faktor would sometimes recount every particular of any given encounter or event: what people wore, what they ate or drank, the brand of cigarette that they smoked—there were complete menus for literally hundreds of meals eaten at home and on the road. Milner had no idea that Faktor was talking to Milner's successors. "All he's going to get from anything I say is that I'm Picasso's version of Tevye," he told Chana one night when she couldn't sleep, either, "shattered, fragmented. But the next guy that comes along . . ."

"What next guy, Faktor? How can you put so much faith in a next guy coming along? Have you seen any sign of a next guy? You've got the *shmendrik* and nobody else."

"Come here, Chana." She waddled over to his desk and he took both her hands. "You were a next guy, too, remember? That's why I've got faith."

Faktor preserved the minutiae of day-to-day Jewish showbiz and literary life in interwar Poland in the hope that future generations would be able to picture it so clearly that they'd be able to smell it. "You could be blindfolded any-where in Poland, in any city or town, I mean, in the middle of an empty street, and know if you were in a Jewish or Polish area. The pork smell stopped cold as soon as you got to the Jews." He talked about spats and lapels, chewing gum brands and hasidic kids sneaking into the movies; regional delicacies, kosher and non–; long-forgotten Yiddish and Polish writers, actors, personalities. Milner was interested in some of the Yiddish artists, but none of the rest concerned him at all. He listened to Faktor distract-edly, waiting for a telling incident or another outrageous and hitherto unknown prank, something a little snappier than the ten-minute epic about Faktor's failed attempt to buy a foulard in Katowice in 1932 in the company of a soprano with whom he was *not* having an affair.

Fads and foodways didn't really fit into Milner's scheme, unless they helped to explain something distinctly Faktorian—like the announcement of his all-kugel diet. The stuff that Milner had recorded himself was more to the point and easier to use. He had Faktor answer carefully thought-out questions designed to elicit information on the kinds of topics that really interested Milner—the romance of Yiddish culture, the motivations and process behind Faktor's contributions to it, collaboration with non-Jewish artists: the events and experiences that made him unique instead of typical. He was getting about a paragraph an hour from most of Faktor's CDs and he was already sick of wasting his time. "Come on, you stupid old fuck. If you can't tell me anything good, at least let me know how to get to your granddaughter."

The hint finally came, much to his own surprise, three or four days before Chana died, about eighty hours into Faktor's self-memorializing. He was at Chana's door at ten o'clock the next morning with a copy of the CD. Luz came to the door in a pair of elbow-length rubber gloves. "Please tell Mrs. Faktor that I'd like to see her."

Luz locked the door behind her. She'd seen Milner in action before and didn't want him sneaking into the house while she was off talking to Chana. She was back in ninety seconds. "She says that you should go away, Mr. Milner. She doesn't want to see you."

Milner sucked in his stomach and squared up his shoulders. "That's *Dr.* Milner. Tell her fine, then. If she doesn't want to see me, she doesn't want to see me. She's going to want to see me soon." Milner held out the CD and gestured to Luz to take it. She reached out a glove and grabbed hold of the envelope. "Please play this for her or make sure that she plays it. It's very important. Tell her that it's Mr. Faktor discussing his marriage and that I'm going to be using what he says in my book, but I wanted Mrs. Faktor to hear it first. I'd like to talk to her about what I'm going to do with it. You can also tell her that it's very, very personal and that's why we need to speak." He leaned forward confidentially and lowered his voice. "This is really very important, Luz. We both know that Mrs. Faktor doesn't like me, but I'm trying to be nice to her. She needs to hear what her husband had to say. So, please —you know what? Here, give me the envelope again for just a second," and as she gave it to him, he reached into the inside pocket of his jacket, pulled out a hundred-dollar bill that he showed to Luz and slipped it in with the CD. "Is she in the living room now?" Luz nodded.

"Why don't you just put it into the CD player and turn it on. I'll come back in about an hour, after she's had time to hear the whole thing." He pulled out another hundred and let Luz see it. "I'll have this with me when I get here. If Mrs. Faktor has heard the disc, I won't have it when I leave."

Two hours later he was admitted straightaway to Chana's presence. She might have been ninety-five, but she'd aged visibly since the funeral. She also seemed shorter than he remembered. She was sitting in a saucer-shaped chair covered in a dark chocolate chenille, her thighs at a ninety-degree angle to her hips and her feet dangling nearly half a foot off the floor. Luz must have had to grab her under the arms when it came time to get her out of it. Chana was watching television, Turner Classic Movies with the sound down low. They were showing *Cornered*, with Dick Powell and Walter Slezak.

She motioned to Milner to sit down. He chose something with arms and a back. Chana reached up as if she were doing the backstroke and lifted a glass of pop off the table next to her chair. She drank while Milner waited. She looked at him, drank some more, and motioned for him to get up and come over to where she was sitting. Once he'd taken the five or six steps, she asked him, very politely, to be so good as to put her glass back on the table, please. As Milner was setting it down, Chana pulled her right knee back and let fly with a forward-facing mule kick to Milner's knee as soon as his hands were empty. She was wearing a pair of pumps that looked like something from the 1940s and must have weighed a good five pounds each.

"Aaugh." Milner cried out more in surprise than in pain. Chana tittered. "You shouldn't have done that, Chana."

"I can think of a couple of things you shouldn't have done, either."

He limped back to his seat and put on an earnest expression after he'd sat back down. "Oy, Chana, I wish, I really wish I'd come across this while Getsl was still alive. We might have been able to do something about it."

"What do you mean, do something about it? What are you going to do?"

"Well, as Getsl's authorized biographer—"

"Will you knock it off with the Getsl already? I told you: nobody, I repeat, nobody, in all the years of his life ever called him Getsl but you. It doesn't make you sound like his friend; it just makes you sound like a jerk."

"So what was he called over there, then, eh? What was the name on his passport?"

"Eugeniusz. And the name on his tax return and Social Insurance card was Eugene. Eugene E. Faktor. The E was for Elyokim. He hated being called Getsl."

Milner sat quietly; he didn't need to argue this one.

"The people at the CBC," Chana wasn't going to let this go, "including Willan and Healey, all called him Gene."

"Have it your way, Chana." He wanted to shut her up so he could get to his point. "As Faktor's authorized biographer, I have a duty to both Faktor and the public to include this episode in anything that I might write. It's important in itself and also as an illustration of the kind of person he was."

"Mmm hmm. And you want how much?"

"Please. It's very difficult."

"For you, perhaps. But don't get your hopes up. I don't see that it has anything to do with me. Everything he talks about took place years before I met him. He didn't commit any crimes and neither did any of the people he mentions. His first wife died in 1943; Shula Kutscher was killed in the pogrom in Kielce in 1946; Tammy died eighteen years ago and Faktor's been gone since July. Why would you think that anybody gives a damn? Any sane person would have done what Faktor did."

"Can I speak candidly, Chana?"

"No, you can't."

"What do you mean?"

"You *may* speak candidly, I'd let you, but you can't do it. It just isn't in you."

"You really hate me, don't you?"

"Now that you ask, yes. More than anybody I've ever met, and between Yiddish and china, I've met some doozies."

"You don't hate your grandchildren, though, do you? And what about your own children? You think they might give a damn?"

"No, I don't. I think *you* give a damn, though. I don't know why, but I know you. You must think there's something in it. You know what? Just to satisfy my own sick curiosity, let me know what it is that you want."

Milner walked over to the table by Chana's chair again, taking good care to keep out of her range. He took a bottle of Crown Royal from the lower shelf, opened the ice bucket and put a few cubes into the glass. He poured a healthy shot of the rye and topped it off with some ginger ale from the same can that Chana's drink had come from. He went back to his chair and took a long sip. He was smiling. "You're a very wealthy woman, Chana. And Faktor was a very wealthy man. His work, his legacy, is more deserving of commemoration than that of anybody else I can think of. I'd like to suggest that you establish an organization, an institute to promote knowledge of Faktor's work and help sponsor and guide further research into it. Call it the Elyokim Faktor Trust. And who better to preside over such an institution than the world's foremost Faktor scholar, his authorized biographer and close personal friend in the final years of his strangely eventful life? I'll settle for $120,000 a year, that's only ten thousand a month. I think you'll agree that that's more than reasonable for a post of such prominence and responsibility."

Chana was trying to push herself forward in her chair. "And if I don't?"

"This little saga, the one you finished listening to a few minutes ago, is going to be all over the newspapers. I've got an article all ready to go, if you don't want to play ball, and I've got many other copies of that CD to send out."

Chana was still trying to propel herself forward with her elbows. "Help me out of the chair, please. I can't get up." Milner looked at her but didn't move. "No tricks, I promise.

I just want to stand up. My legs are starting to cramp." He came over. She gave him her hand, and he pulled her gently up and out of the chair. "Thank you. Sit back down, please." Chana was pacing back and forth, very slowly. "What I'm going to say is hard for me, I trust that you appreciate that. I *never* thought that things might come to this, especially so close to the end of my life. I can barely believe that I'm going to do this, but I believe I really am." The expression on his face reminded her of the pictures she'd seen of Hermann Goering in the prisoners' dock at Nuremberg. "Allan—it's okay for me to call you that, isn't it? Would you prefer Dr. Milner?" Milner smirked some more and shook his head. "Well, at least you're not treating me like a servant." She walked over to where Milner was sitting. With Chana standing beside him in the chair, their faces were exactly the same height from the ground. "Allan," she shrugged, "I think you should fuck right off."

Chana, Mrs. Aubrey, grew up in very different times. "And just in case you think I'm joking, I think you should know this is the first time in my life that I've ever used that horrible word."

Expert as he was in wheedling, Milner knew when he'd reached the end of the line. A "fuck" from a woman like Chana was a sign of uncompromising finality. He stood up, not too quickly, and started to walk out of the room. "You'll regret this, you miserable bitch."

"I don't think so, Allan. We both know that you're trying to fuck"—there it was again—"my granddaughter, but I don't know what ever made you think that I was going to subsidize your diddling."

If Milner's teeth had been false, he'd have swallowed them. The old bat had figured out exactly what he was up to. He had to take his hat off to her; he finally understood how she'd managed to make so much money. "Well then . . . well," *oy vey gevalt*, a *royaume*, a whole *royaume* he would have given for a riposte, "well then, you can fuck off, too."

Well, it was a worth a try, he mused, once he was back in his car. He hadn't really expected it to work, and he hadn't really lost anything but a $120,000-a-year job that didn't really exist. At least he'd got out of the house with Luz's second hundred dollars in his pocket. He would have published what he'd found out anyway; but if she'd played ball, he would have waited for the old cow to die. It would only have been fair. Whatever happened now was her own goddamned fault; she hadn't left him any choice. The only question was timing. He ran his fingers through the front-most island in the archipelago of his hair, turned the key in the ignition, put the car into gear and backed out of the driveway. He had to go home and write an article.

10

FAKTOR'S CD

I ALWAYS KNEW THAT MY FIRST MARRIAGE was a little different from the second—I imagine anybody who's been married more than once could say exactly the same thing—but not even I knew how different it really was until after it was already over. I never told Chana what happened; I never told Tammy, my daughter from that marriage, what I'm going to talk about now, either. They would have been plenty upset—or maybe not; either way, they'd probably have been madder than hell that I didn't tell them.

I met Tamara Szulc—her name was Temme in Yiddish, Temke to people who knew her—right after Madame Kutscher let her into the troupe in 1938. For the next five years, until she died in Kazakhstan, I didn't think of any other female as a woman. The first time I saw her—it was in the Nowosci Theatre—I turned around, walked out of the room, and went straight outside. Tears were already running down my cheeks; I had to bite my lip to keep from sobbing, but I also felt like throwing up right there in the alley: that woman's face was like a kick in the balls. There was no

Cupid here, no little Nimrod with his arrows; this was like turning a corner in the desert and being talked to by a burning bush, or waking up in the year of King Uzziah's death and seeing God on His throne in front of you, surrounded by crooning seraphim—you learn what "awestruck" really means: like being smashed south of the navel when nothing has actually touched you. Temke Szulc frightened me more than anything I'd ever laid eyes on, and I still didn't know who she was. I can't say if she was the best-looking woman I'd ever seen. All I can tell you is that looking at her for the first time was like bumping into a vital organ that you hadn't known you were missing; once you're aware of it, you can't live without it.

Our daughter, may she rest in peace, looked just like her, but without the enormous bust; you could say almost the same for my granddaughter, Vanessa: she has the chest, but her parents had an orthodontist get rid of the overbite— much against my will. Temke was dark and could have passed for a gypsy, but had the manners of a girl who had been raised by hasidim: she never looked a man in the eye, never spoke to a man who hadn't spoken to her first. If her eyes weren't on her work, they were usually on the floor, though Shula—Madame Kutscher, that is—said that she was much more outgoing in a roomful of women. She was about nineteen when I met her, I was thirty-three. She never mentioned her family or background, never talked about anything that had happened to her—she wouldn't admit to having a past at all, yet the minute she opened her mouth, you knew everything about her. Her Yiddish told her story; it was more than just hasidic, it was the language of a rebbe's court: stately, a little pretentious, with just a touch more Hebrew and Aramaic than was strictly necessary, and highly euphemistic with respect to any physical activity. And she had the knowledge to back it all up. Temke's fluency in day-to-day Judaism—kosher and non-kosher; what was and wasn't allowed on the Sabbath and holidays; what prayers to omit on which special days; how to measure graves with a thread and which supplications to say when you use that thread to make wicks for candles—her expertise left none of us in any doubt that she was the daughter of one of those domestically liberal rebbeyim who insisted on educations for their daughters.

Temke knew more than the rules; she could tell you all the reasons behind them. That's why she was known as "the shiksa"—it was one of Madame Kutscher's nicknames for her—and sometimes even "the rabbi." Not the rebbetzin—the rabbi's wife—but the rabbi, as if she were also a man. "Go ask the shiksa," was all you would hear when a question came up about the minutiae of Jewish ritual or practice; when they found her, they'd say, "Rabbi, I've got a question for you." The fact that she could also speak Polish perfectly, with no trace of a Jewish accent or intonation, suggested the kind of high-level, expensive tutoring that I had also had and that was not at all uncommon among wealthier people and quite a few of the rebbeyim in Poland.

Temke never talked about her parents; never mentioned any brothers or sisters. She wouldn't even say where she was from. Her reticence fed all kinds of rumours as to which well-known rebbe had been her father and what had made her run away. All anybody knew for sure was that she buttonholed Madame Kutscher at the stage door after one of our performances in Warsaw and begged to be taken on in any capacity. Shula would normally have kept going— she wasn't a particularly charitable person—but Temke's face was so arresting, with that look of forlorn but unshakeable innocence that she kept to her dying day, that Madame Kutscher wasn't able to resist her: she'd come from a hasidic family herself and recognized the signs of a girl in trouble. "Are you pregnant, girl?"

"God forbid."

"Can you sew, then?" she asked

"Until this morning, I didn't do much else," Temke told her. "I can sew, clean, cook a little, and make a bed. I can kosher a kitchen that was just vacated by a priest and answer any questions you have about legal issues concerning your menses, if such things still matter to you."

"Do they matter to *you*?"

"They don't have to."

"Never been married?"

"Not so far."

"But you know all about it, anyway." Madame Kutscher started to laugh. "You're a regular little rebbetzin, aren't you? Or maybe you're really a rabbi, a child prodigy, a pretty little boy who likes to put on ladies' clothing. Are you sure you're a girl?"

Temke opened her coat, grabbed both of Madame Kutscher's hands and pressed them over her milkmaid's breasts. "Gevalt!" Shula yelled, running her eyes over Temke's otherwise slender figure, "Like coconuts hanging from a fishing rod. What's your name?"

"Temme, miss."

"Temme, eh? We'll call you Temme Ventke, Temme the Fishing Rod." Shula loved to hand out nicknames; it was a sign that she liked you. "All right, Temme Ventke, I'll give you a try. I need someone to look after my costumes and help me dress. Come back in with me for five minutes and I'll show you what you need to do tonight. You're not running away from the police, are you?"

"No, miss."

"Call me Madame Kutscher."

"Yes, Madame Kutscher."

"Yes, what?"

"Yes, that's what I'll call you. No, I'm not running away from the police."

"Come inside then. I want to find out why you're running away from somebody else." Madame Kutscher turned to her manager. "Zaynvl, go on ahead to Goldreich's and order for me. Tell them I'll be having the duck. I'll just show Madame—what's your last name, girl?"

"Szulc."

"Of course. A common hasidic name, Szulc. Hundreds of rebbeyim have called themselves Szulc. It's like *shul* with a *tz* at the end. And the *tz* must stand for *tzaddik*. I'll show Madame Szulc her duties." They were together in there for about half an hour, which is when the real interview must have taken place. Nobody knew what happened in there and nobody really gave it any thought. Temke came out of nowhere and was never far from Madame Kutscher again. She was a bright girl, a quick study. She seemed to have a phonographic memory: by the end of the first read-through of a script, she knew the play by heart. She was soon prompting and doing small parts on stage, and Shula was grooming her to play soubrettes: she had the perfect figure for a French maid's outfit.

It was months before I could really speak to her. I could get through things like, "Temke, could you ask Madame Kutscher to come in here, please," but the thought of a real conversation made my throat tighten up and my hands start to sweat. By this time in my life, I'd been around plenty. I was a bit of a late starter because of my weight, but once I became famous and got my weight down to sixty or sixty-one kilos—I think that's about 135 pounds—well, I'd become what you might call a real bohemian. I lived with other bohemians from the theatre or Yiddish literary circles—anarchists, socialists, bigamists—and I never lacked for female company. Some of those women were very fond of me, and I liked nearly all of them, but my inability to stop evaluating every member of every chorus line that ever danced past me was enough to let me know that I still hadn't fallen in love. Looking at Temke, though, being in a room with Temke, I felt like a boy of fifteen—except that I was never near any girls as a boy of fifteen. I caught her looking at me sometimes, too, and finally—terrified that she thought of me as a professional smart-ass who didn't do anything but make fun of people who tried to do something—I finally got up the courage to ask her if she'd like to come for a stroll and maybe a cup of coffee. I could feel blotches spreading across my face and over my arms and legs when I asked her; I remember feeling the same way when I'd get into trouble as a little boy. Usually, I'd just ask a woman if she'd like a drink and then invite her to inspect my apartment or hotel room.

We went for our walk; as soon as we'd turned the corner from the theatre, Temke said, "I was wondering when you were finally going to ask me. I already asked Madame Kutscher to tell you to get a move on."

"So she knows?"

"Everybody knows. Except you, until now."

And that's the story of our courtship. For all intents and purposes, we were engaged by the time we got back to the theatre. We slept together that night—this was the theatre, remember, but Temke was a virgin, still the only one I've been with.

The next morning I made it official: "*Khevre*, guys, wish us mazl tov and put up a *chuppah* for the shiksa and me." That's how we usually did it. We were all artists and almost all of us came from deeply religious backgrounds; we had nothing but contempt for bourgeois marriage, and most of us didn't believe in much besides. We were thoroughly Jewish and completely irreligious, except on Passover and Yom Kippur, and at the circumcision parties for our new baby boys.

The Jewish theatres were dark on all the major holidays, but you'd never find any of us in shul. And Temke, with her background, was as extreme as I ever saw; she said that there could be a rabbi at the wedding or there could be a bride—she'd leave the choice to me. I wrote up a marriage contract, dragged a couple of shnorrers out of the cemetery to serve as witnesses, and slid a ring onto Temke's finger. Madame Kutscher's tenor recited the seven blessings, we broke a glass and that's it—we were married. I went to the Tachkemoni school, remember; you can say what you want, but after that ceremony, there wasn't a rabbi on earth who would have let either of us marry someone else unless one of us was dead or we had proof of a Jewish divorce. But—and this was the important part—they would still have looked askance at our nuptials: we were married without being *married*.

For the next five years, we never spent a night apart. We were in Lvov—it's Lviv now—when the War broke out. We were booked for two weeks, and the Russians occupied it right after Rosh Hashana. All of us—Shula, Temke, the rest of the troupe and me—eventually ended up in Tashkent, then Tajikistan, and finally in Kazakhstan. We continued to do theatre—thank God I'd had tutors in Russian—and did all kinds of other things, too. They tried to get me into the army, but I was in the middle of a bout of scurvy. I dug plenty of ditches, though, stuffed sandbags, sold just about everything we had. The money I'd had in Poland was left behind with the Nazis, everything else was in Switzerland—hardly the sort of thing that I thought the Soviet authorities should know.

Temke realized that she was pregnant just before we got to Alma Ata, where we'd been sent to work in the film studios. She gave birth to a baby girl on the twelfth of September and was dead of puerperal sepsis thirty-six hours later. I decided to name the child after her; in cases like this, it's allowed by Jewish law. The Lord gives and the Lord takes away; the greatest joy of my life was the cause of my greatest strictly personal sorrow.

Shula, who was like Temke's surrogate mother, was in the hospital with me, waiting for the end. She stopped me from tearing the lapel of my jacket when the doctor pronounced Temke dead. "Stop it, Shula." I thought she was worried that I might not have anything to trade for a replacement. "It's only a jacket."

"Faktor, I need to talk to you."

"This is hardly the time." I was crying and so was she.

"This is the only time." Shula had put on her Madame-Kutscher-Star-of-the-International-Stage face and voice, so I knew that she meant it.

"What is it, Shula? You're standing right beside me. Can't you see that my wife just died?"

She asked the nurse in Russian if she'd mind leaving the room for just a minute or two, she had something very personal to tell me, "and we all know that you're able to speak Yiddish." The nurse looked angry, but stepped outside, saying "*Ikh bet iber ayer koved*, I beg your pardon," in a sarcastic tone as she did so.

"Faktor, sit." She motioned to the only chair. I sat down on the floor as a sign of mourning. "Before you *rays kriye*, before you tear your clothes, I want you to listen to what I have to tell you." What was to listen to? It doesn't matter what anybody *says*, you tear your clothes when a family member dies. What could she tell me that was more important than my grief? Temke did something? So what? She was dead now. The only way she could have hurt me was to be unfaithful, and I can tell you that if there was ever a person on this earth incapable of infidelity, it was Temke. She·still blushed if anyone saw us going into our room together at night.

"You know how we used to joke around and call Temke "the shiksa?" Yeah, so? "Well," Shula paused and thought for a second, "it wasn't really a joke. That night when she turned up in Warsaw a few years ago, when I took her inside the theatre to talk to her, she told me who she was and where she came from, and begged me to keep it a secret. She was a bastard, the illegitimate child of a Polish servant girl who'd been seduced—that's what she called it, so there were probably no knives involved—by her master's son."

Already I felt like I'd been kicked in the stomach by an elephant, a big bull elephant that didn't like Jews.

"The master was a fairly decent sort, a wealthy Dlugaszower hasid. Lucky for him and everybody else, the Torah portion that week was about Abraham throwing Hagar and Ishmael out of his house. The hasid knew that he couldn't keep the servant and her baby, and, being a hasid, was afraid that he could be responsible for the birth of a new race of Arabs right there in Poland if he threw them out. So he went to the rebbe—"

"The Dlugaszower?" I'd gone to school with one of his nephews.

"Yeah, the Dlugaszower."

"He was supposed to be very nice. Everybody seemed to like him." I didn't want to hear what was coming.

"Yes. He was so nice that he told the hasid that there was no reason for the poor shiksa to suffer for something that was hardly her fault. And he made a speech about Judah and Tamar. She couldn't stay with the hasid—the shame would be too great, all his money wouldn't be able to buy any of his children a decent husband or wife after a scandal like this—but she shouldn't be driven onto the street, either. The rebbe wanted to know what kind of a shiksa she was. 'Very nice,' said the hasid. 'Very unassuming. Behaves very modestly. You could almost take her, God should pardon my saying so, for one of us.' Whatever happened with his son, he didn't put any blame on her at all. Aside from being very pretty, she was a good worker, spoke perfect Yiddish and—embarrassed as he was to have to admit it—had a better knowledge of kitchen-based kosher regulations than the hasid's own daughters. 'A *voyle*,' he said, 'A really top-class shiksa in every way.' Smart. If she'd had any education, she could have been something more than a maid.

"'And how old is she?' asked the rebbe.

"'I don't know. Nineteen, twenty. Her mother started out working for my father, her father worked for him, too. He was our stable master.' The hasid was a horse dealer and the son of a horse dealer. 'She's been with me all her life, and, uh, and—'

"'You can say it,' said the rebbe. 'Remember why you're here. The fruit doesn't fall too far from the tree.'

"'She's looked like a woman for a very long time.'

"The rebbe stroked his beard and pondered in silence. He had three daughters; his only son was twenty-four and had just had his second child. He lived in the court and apparently had no eyes for anything but his books. His wife told the mikve lady and the mikve lady told the rebbe's wife that he rarely approached her more than once a month, right after she came home from the mikve. If his wife, for whose appearance the rebbe had the greatest respect, couldn't tempt him, he didn't think an attractive shiksa was going to be much of a problem. 'Nu, she can come to me. If the child survives, you—I'd say your son, but I already know who's going to be paying—you will pay me a monthly stipend towards its upbringing.'

"'For a goy, rebbe? I'll be paying for a goy?'

"'A father is obliged to pay for his children. Not only his Jewish children, all his children. You don't have to support all the goyim, just the ones that you've made.'

"Basia the pregnant servant girl went off to the rebbe's a few days later. She was everything the hasid had said and more. A gem. A golden find. Even in her condition, she worked hard and did everything well. She was cheerful and funny, and had spent more time with hasidim than she had with anyone else: not only did life in the rebbe's court hold few mysteries for her, she felt privileged to have been promoted to so exalted a position.

"Four months after Basia came to the rebbe, Tamara was born. She had her mother's figure, her father's colouring, and features that combined both the Jew and the goy. She also turned out to be unusually smart. She had that phonographic memory that we used to see in rehearsals. She'd stand in the room where the rebbe's grandchildren were being tutored, dusting or swabbing the floor, walk out, and repeat the entire lesson. She picked up a fair bit of Hebrew that way, just listening to teachers or the children translating biblical verses into Yiddish.

"The rebbe took a shine to her. The old Dlugaszower, you probably remember, was probably the smartest rebbe around, and he realized that, shiksa or no shiksa, this girl was something special, and that if the Master of the Universe had arranged for her to be born in his court with that kind of brain, He must have wanted the rebbe to do something about it. He started talking to her, teaching her things—stuff from the Bible, moral teachings from the Mishna and Midrash, useful halachic principles for her work in the kitchen and with the women of the court. The Dlugaszower had a head for numbers, and he also taught her some math and geometry—in Polish, yet, so she'd be able to go on with it easily if she had the chance: she didn't have enough Hebrew for the Vilna Gaon's books on the subject.

"She could have learned it without any trouble, though. The little girl was like a sponge that could soak up anything. The rebbe was practically treating her as a daughter, except that he would never have troubled to teach any of his daughters the things that he was showing to Temme. They didn't have her brains, and neither did the son who was sup-posed to succeed him. 'Temke,' he said to her one day, 'if you were Jewish and a boy, you could lead a generation. As it is, I can't figure out what the Lord wants you to do.'

"He'd have her 'cleaning' his room when litigants came for his decision. 'Don't worry,' he'd say, 'She understands nothing but Polish.' He'd examine her afterwards on the proceedings; she learned the language and logic of rabbinic arbitration very quickly.

"The rebbe died when she was twelve. His son and successor could have been the inspiration for the saying, 'vinegar, son of wine.' Not overly bright, not overly nice, not overly concerned with anybody but himself. He'd known Temke all her life and was as fond of her as everybody else in the court, but he never had the kind of relationship with her that his father had had. Where before she was almost a youthful disciple, she was now just a well-loved young domestic and was looked on as such—a servant who was a virtual chattel—by the new rebbe's son, who was a couple of years older than Temke and not half as good at Talmud.

"As long as Basia, Temke's mother, was still alive, no one dared try to mess with Temke. Basia ran the household gently but very firmly; because she never lost her temper, everyone was afraid to imagine what would happen if she did. She was like a teacher who doesn't have to threaten or raise his voice; if she was so self-assured in her calm, it must have meant that her anger was fearsome.

"She died, though, when Temke was eighteen. Yossel, the old rebbe's grandson, started to bother her almost immediately. She turned him down, put him off, pushed him away, but he wouldn't give up. I don't have to tell you how good she looked. He barged into her room one day while she was darning and caught her in a chokehold. She struggled; he wouldn't give up; she couldn't squirm out. So she lifted up one of the needles and plunged it straight into one of his eyes. She heard him scream and saw blood gushing out of the socket. No one came running, though; no one seemed to hear him in the servants' quarters. Temke grabbed a shawl and pulled the money she'd saved out of her mattress. She had her shoes on already and she ran through the compound and into the town.

"Dlugaszow is a small place and she'd lived there all her life. She found a Jew with a car to take her the twenty kilometres to Warsaw. She would just as easily have gone with a gentile. It was the car that mattered; she'd already missed the only train.

"She'd never been to Warsaw, didn't really know where to go or what to do. She was sure that she'd blinded Yossel, maybe even killed him. She needed to go somewhere, anywhere where the whole world couldn't see her and find her. She had the driver drop her near the main synagogue and she simply started walking. It was an accident that she got to me. She was walking by the theatre and saw my name on a poster. My father was a Dlugaszower hasid, you know, and she'd heard all kinds of stories about poor Pesach Kutscher, whose daughter had fallen so far off the path of righteousness that she hadn't only become an actress, she hadn't even had the decency to change her name.

"And that, my dear Faktor, is where you and I both come in."

You might as well have told me that my wife, who'd just died in childbirth, was a man. Shula pulled a flask of vodka from her bag and handed it to me. I drained it in two gulps and was unconscious ten minutes later: I hadn't had a meal or left the hospital since Temke had gone into labour.

I felt that I'd earned the headache I woke up with. I'd spent the past five years living on Mars while thinking I was still on earth. I'd always known that there was no one like Temke, but I hadn't had the vaguest suspicion that she was as unusual as she turned out to be. She was a gentile who looked Jewish, acted Jewish, spoke Jewish. She lived almost exclusively among Jews. She did business with Poles; she spoke Polish—had spoken almost nothing else with Basia and some of the other servants—but she'd never really lived with Poles. I don't think she'd ever been inside a church, and she ran to Jews for help the way that I would have run to Jews for help—who else was there for her to go to? She was one of us and one of them, a spiritual hermaphrodite. So why did she have to hook up with me?

I don't know how long I slept on the floor of that filthy, decaying hospital in Alma Ata, so I can't say if Shula was still there when I woke up or if she'd gone home, slept, eaten and come back. I looked up at her, though, as if no time had passed at all. "Was she ever planning to tell me?"

"She wanted to. I told her not to."

I was fervently hoping not. I hadn't been in touch with my bank since 1939. "She wasn't supposed to let anybody know."

"You know how frightened she was when you finally told her?"

"Frightened? Why should she be frightened?"

"A runaway servant girl pretending to be something she isn't discovers, all unknown to her, that the man she's just married is a multi-millionaire who lives just like her and the rest of the bohemians with whom he associates?"

"What are you talking about? I had a gorgeous apartment, expensive clothes."

"Which everybody thought you paid for with the money you made from writing. Faktor, you sound like a character from a play that you would have refused to write. What scared Temke was that one day you'd wake up tired of slumming and leave, and leave her behind when you did. That's why she talked to me. She was so frightened when you told her about your money that she was thinking of leaving; she wanted to know what to do."

"And you told her, did you?"

Shula leaned over and slapped me. "Shmuck! Didn't she just die giving birth to your baby?"

I was ready to give up, until I remembered the kid a couple of rooms over and how sadly I'd neglected her already. "Screw it," I said. "Shula, I'm sitting shiva." I pulled a penknife out of my pocket, cut a huge tear in my right lapel—the

"You picked a fine time to change your min

"If she'd lived, you'd never have known and
never have told you. She felt terrible keeping yc
dark, but was afraid you'd reject her if you ever fc
When you met her, you also thought *you* were a Pc
now you've got a kid who can be one, if that's ·
really want. You can have her converted easily e
just go on as if her mother had really been Jew
weren't so worried about halacha when you got n
when you used to eat ham in the middle of W
what's the big deal now?"

I didn't have an answer; I had a headach
baby to look after. I stood up and poured som
water from the pitcher warming on the window
glass was dirty, so I guess the cloud didn't matt
should I believe you?" I asked. "Where's the pro
of this? How come nobody else seems to have h
thing about it? What kind of trick are you tryir
on me, Shula?"

"The same one you tried to play on me, on
by neglecting to tell us how rich you are and tha
have bank accounts in Switzerland? Could that b

"Temke talked?"

"To me? Always. Don't worry; I haven't to
else." I was starting to feel doubly betrayed. "Doe
it a secret mean that you're not the heir to one of t
textile fortunes in Poland?"

proper side for anyone not your parent—and went out to look at my child. Even then, she was the image of her mother, inside and out. The wet nurse provided by the hospital told me that she was fine and healthy and could be taken home at any time. There was no irony in her use of "home."

I told Shula to arrange for a wet nurse who could come and live with us. "How are you going to pay her, Faktor? Nobody's going to come for free." We found a dentist. In return for a hand-job from Shula, he pulled three of my back teeth. The gold from the fillings was more than enough to pay for a nurse, at least for a while. We found a woman in the hospital, an unwed mother who had just lost her baby. She stayed until Shula started to lactate; there were no pumps around—I don't know if those kinds of pumps even existed then—so Shula got her boyfriend to suckle her three or four times a day. It took her about six weeks to start producing milk, "And," she said, "I have to thank you, Faktor. I've never been laid so much in my life."

I spent the shiva-time trying to decide what to do, trying to decide what everything I remembered from the last five years might really mean. It wasn't as difficult as it sounds. Converting the child was out of the question; there weren't enough rabbis in Alma Ata to make up the three-man rabbinical court that you need. Plus, there was no guarantee that the conversion would be granted. I had quite a reputation for making fun of the religious establishment, and they might decide to take vengeance on me: all they had to do was ask me to swear that I'd bring the kid up in strict accord with Orthodox law. If I said yes, they'd want proof: X number of years of keeping shabbes and eating only kosher food and praying three times a day with a minyan— all in front of witnesses. In the middle of Kazakhstan, yet. And with the option of telling me that I hadn't done it right and had to start all over again. If I said no, the deal would be off right away.

And even if I could somehow manage to work it out, according to Jewish law, a child who's been converted is free to reject Judaism once it hits the age of Jewish majority. I could end up doing a lot of work for nothing and losing my daughter to some callow desire for authenticity.

And let's not forget the simple Kierkegaardian absurdity of seeking to convert someone else to Judaism in the midst of the worst mass murder in the history of the world. You'd have to be nuts to demand a conversion for yourself; I don't know what you'd be if you did it on behalf of someone with no say in the matter.

My other choice was to acknowledge my daughter as a shiksa and forget about it. After all, if Temke hadn't died, I would never have known and we'd all have gone on, little Tammy and I none the wiser in our ignorance, laying the groundwork for generations of people—grandchildren, great-grandchildren and on and on—who wouldn't really have been Jewish, despite their own deep-seated belief that they were. Who knows? Temke and I might have had a few more children who wouldn't have been any more Jewish than Tammy, and neither they nor I would ever have known.

So what difference would it have made? I could accept my wife's death and cut my losses or else let one disaster turn into two. True, nobody knew but Shula and me, but that didn't affect the child's status. Would it be right to bring her up without letting her know? Would anybody believe the story that I'd have to tell her, a story that I sometimes wondered whether I should believe myself?

One night I had a dream. The Dlugaszower Rebbe's father was there. He was a famous *tzaddik*, a holy man, the founder of the dynasty, and was best known for having appeared just outside Warsaw some years after his death in the form of a talking potato kugel. Anyway, he was there— as a kugel—talking to his son, Temke Senior's mentor and former employer. "You realize that this is all our fault," the kugel said.

"Us?" His son took a snuff box out of his pocket. "Where do I come into it?"

"You treated that girl as if she was one of us, and a boy."

The rebbe tapped some snuff onto his hand and inhaled. "She had unusual talents," he croaked.

"And then your grandson tried to have his way with her."

"After I was dead. Might as well blame yourself, father; the chain of descent doesn't stop with me."

"Exactly. And it's exactly what you told the hasid who brought her mother to you in the first place."

"So?"

"The question is: so what do we do? We made her Jewish without making her a Jew, so now what happens?"

"We do like the Talmud does when it talks about bastards—some of whom probably had the wrong mothers, too. 'Rabbi Joshua ben Levi said that money makes bastards kosher.' Wealthy bastards ended up marrying into regular families despite the prohibition against marrying bastards: people were more interested in the money than the law." The rebbe sighed. "If they'd been stopped before it could happen, fine. That's probably what should have happened. Since it didn't happen, though, they decided to leave things as they were, lest the strife and accusations and retroactive disqualification of entire families from the Community of Israel tear the whole society to shreds. And these days, we need all the *yidn* we can get."

"Come over here and kiss me," said the kugel. "I'm proud of you, son. It's a case of *eyn le-dovar sof*; once you set it underway, there'll be no end to the matter. Just leave things as they are and pretend that everything is the way it looks. Only God knows what was in her heart; she chose the fate of the Jews at our time of greatest peril, maybe He's already immersed her in His own mikve, the mikve of the waters of life. So put down that snuff box and give me a kiss."

I woke up then, with the decision made for me. After the War, I found out the date of the anniversary of the first Dlugaszower's death and vowed to eat a potato kugel on that day every year for the rest of my life. The gratitude that I still felt when I was getting ready to turn a hundred moved me to expand the observance: my all-kugel diet was a subtle way of letting the world know that the Dlugaszower Rebbe and his son had kept me alive all these years. The rest of the world might not have understood what I was doing, but the rebbe and his son up there in heaven, they knew what I was trying to say. And so, I think, did Temke Number One and her daughter Tammy.

11

CHANA AND MILNER, II

CHANA WAS VERY UPSET. She hadn't been pretending when she said that contents of the tape didn't
bother her. She would have preferred to have
heard the story privately, from a Faktor who was still alive,
but Faktor had always been touchy about anything to do
with Temke. No touchier than Chana was about Milton,
her first husband, though; they had a tacit agreement to try
to avoid mentioning either of them in each other's presence.
Chana was no more jealous of Temke than Faktor was of
Milton; it wasn't so much the fact of a previous marriage
that made either of them uncomfortable, as the knowledge
that, if not for the War, each of them would probably have
stayed in those marriages. Much as Chana and Faktor loved
each other, both of them were still in love with their original spouses, even after sixty years. This had no real effect
on their marriage, but had no little influence on their manners. It was a little harder for Chana because of Tammy,
who was always asking questions about her real mother, but
it was nothing worth complaining about.

Faktor had never lied about the marriage, except to omit that one salient detail that he himself didn't know until he'd already been widowed. He simply stuck to the story that he believed for the whole of the relationship. Chana had never been religious and couldn't understand why anybody would deny Temke the "right"—she saw the word in front of her in quotation marks—the "right" to be Jewish. The rebbeyim in Faktor's dream were right, even if all they really were was Faktor talking to himself: she lived as a Jew and died as a Jew. If she wasn't a Jew, God would be sure to let her know; if God had nothing to do with it, then what should it matter to anyone on earth?

Chana was upset, all right, but only with Milner. As someone who spent so much of her life in disguise, she understood Temke perfectly and had no quarrel with Faktor's decision to keep the matter to himself: people who had known Mrs. Aubrey for over half a century had no idea that she was no more real than Aunt Jemima or Ronald McDonald, and would have been shocked to learn of the existence of Chana or even Anna Manischewitz. Not one of her employees knew who she really was.

Chana always found it strange that people characterized her as distant and unemotional, but she had to admit that she'd always done her best to contain any displays of unpleasant emotion. Her laugh, especially when she was younger and used to laugh a lot more, could be heard halfway down the block; as a single girl, as a widow, she was often told that it was one of the sexiest and most attractive things about her. She was loath, though, to show anger, to lose control in a way that could lead to unexpected consequences. Sure, there was the feigned fury of the dissatisfied boss, of the parent and step-parent charged with discipline, but she'd rarely given way to real anger in front of anybody else, not even Faktor. When she got mad, she talked to herself and paced; as she got older, she talked more and paced less. Telling Milner to fuck off, though, had pretty much exhausted her. She collapsed onto the Danish modern sofa, upholstered to match the chair where she'd been sitting before, that had always reminded her of the back of a Lincoln Continental.

"What the hell could he really want?" she asked herself, and worked it out fairly quickly. The first thing she realized, even before she threw him out—how many times had she thrown him out of different places since Faktor died in July?—was that he was going to publish the contents of the CD whether she paid him or not. "How can he not if he's writing a biography? I told Faktor to keep away from the whole thing. But that's not the main point. Whatever else Faktor was, he was famous, if that's what you want to call it, as a Yiddish writer and a Canadian children's TV personality; how many people really cared about anything that he had done, let alone whether or not his first wife was Jewish? How many people are going to pay any attention to a book or article that reveals her as a shiksa?

Faktor's Yiddish fans are mostly in the graveyard; the ones who think of him as Yankee Gallstone aren't going to care one way or the other. They might even like it."

Nobody was really affected by any of this, except for her grandchildren. Chana had never been religious, but she knew as well as anybody else that the child of a Jewish mother is considered Jewish, while the child of a non-Jewish woman can only become Jewish by converting. Earl was about to find himself in the same position as Faktor had been, only Earl's wife had been dead for eighteen years, not fifteen minutes. What could that miserable little fucker—it got easier every time—want that he . . . Fucker? That's it. Chana had it figured all along, she just hadn't known it. Not "fucker," but "fuck her." Everybody had seen Milner go gaga over Vanessa, but most men did. The fact that he chose to do so in a shiva house, and not even disguise it, only showed just how big an asshole he really was. But if she liked him back—or even if she didn't, though going out and getting drunk with him during the shiva suggested that she probably did—if the only thing standing between Milner and Vanessa was her marriage, this would put an end to it, no questions asked.

Chana was shaking her head. "Ninety-five years old, I thought I'd seen it all. I could understand a lowlife like Milner doing something like this as blackmail, but the money wasn't the main thing. It was worth a shot, sure, but he's really after the girl."

She didn't want to wait until Earl came by the next morning to let him know what was going on; he had to find out about this today. Chana was getting sleepy, though. She looked at her watch. It was early yet, not even one o'clock. She could call him after she took a nap and had some lunch.

She never woke up. When Luz came to check on her after she finished polishing the silverware, she could see at once that the ambulance was only a formality. She dialed 911, then called Earl. He did almost exactly what he'd done a few months before, except this time he didn't have to leave any messages.

12

BREAKING NEWS

SUICIDE BY KUGEL?

By Arye Tochen

W HEN THE YIDDISH POET ELYOKIM FAKTOR,
better known, perhaps, under his pseudonym
Der Mazik, passed away last July at the age of
103, Yiddish-speakers and lovers of Yiddish literature took
it as the inevitable, if unfortunate, consequence of time's
winged chariot stopping briefly to pick up yet another pas-
senger bound for eternal rest. Faktor lived a long and full
life. His literary career began in the 1920s and continued
until his death. It was supplemented, but never replaced, by
a parallel career in children's television in Canada, where
he sought refuge after the Holocaust. Starting out as a per-
former, Faktor became a successful producer of children's
television shows that were broadcast the world over. During
this time, he continued to write his weekly *Mazik* column
for a variety of Yiddish newspapers, and published a number
of volumes of new and collected verse.

Elyokim Faktor was as well known for his lively and occasionally outrageous sense of humour as for his writing. An indefatigable prankster, he was responsible for a number of notorious literary hoaxes in pre-War Europe and was alleged to have based the character he played on Canadian TV on the eminent Yiddish poet, Yankef Glatshteyn. At a party in 2005 to celebrate his one-hundredth birthday, he announced that he would eat nothing but kugel six days a week for the rest of his life.

Information recently unearthed by the present writer may well shed new light on this apparently senseless caprice. In a recording made by Faktor himself but not discovered until after his death, the poet reveals that his first wife, a minor actress in the Yiddish theatre who died in Kazakhstan while giving birth to Faktor's eldest child in 1943, was a Polish gentile who had been a servant in the court of the rebbe of Dlugaszow. Faktor himself claimed to have been unaware of her non-Jewish origins until after her death, at which time, however, he decided to go on as if nothing had happened and pass the child off as Jewish, without bothering to convert her.

Faktor's daughter, Tamara Frumkiss of Toronto, Canada, lived in ignorance of her true identity until her death in 1990. She had three children, all of whom think that they are Jewish; two of them now have children of their own, who likewise consider themselves full-fledged members of the community of Israel. Feygl, née Vanessa,

THE FR

expressed so c

supported it. M

realized that *7*

weight in the ci

York Times. The

lead time; his pi

shiva was almost

While Miln

Ava, Niven and tl

money, he thoug]

to miss any funer

selves on the next

Rachel was

shower. A local be

in the little bastar

electron microscop

decided to test H

she'd shaved off her

tattoo that she got o

where the leg shade

shape of a loonie, ar

upraised middle fing

You Suck. Her favou

like hell—was when t

of her hand on Rache

"Jesus, Rach," H

not touching. "What

Mrs. Frumkiss's eldest child, is married to the adopted son of the founder of the extremist Moginey Erets hasidic sect, the late Rabbi Shraga-Feivel Frankel, Rabbi Yaakov Frankel of Jerusalem, who is the group's current leader. She was well known a few years ago in the USA for popular lecture programs aimed at attracting unobservant younger Jews to Orthodoxy. The couple has three children, all enrolled in ultra-Orthodox schools in the Mea Shearim quarter of Jerusalem, none of whom is Jewish.

Faktor justified his behaviour on the basis of a dream he claims to have had, in which the father of his wife's employer, the first rebbe of Dlugaszow, known in hasidic circles as *Ha-Kugel Ha-Kadosh*, the Holy Kugel, decreed that the woman's choice to share the lot of the Jews during the Holocaust overrode any need for conversion according to universally accepted Jewish law.

In the recently discovered confessional recording, Faktor claims to have adopted his highly unhealthy diet as a tribute to the rebbe. The general tenor of the rest of the CD, however, makes it clear to the discerning listener that Faktor's guilt over having perpetrated so vile a crime against the integrity of *klal yisroel*, the Community of Israel, finally got the better of him, and that he chose to end his own life by means as unconventional and essentially cowardly as those by which he misled his own family and introduced an impurity into the body of the Jewish people that has migrated from half-believing Yiddishists like Faktor

to the very

hope that t

of Sabbath

stained by

None of th

interest in e

York Times,

Canadian Jeu

Family Foot

scription. Th

was *Torah Tir*

primarily by

keep them an

the week, it

demanded th

paper's editori

by signing the

Hebrew for mi

Although

a million and w

all over North

paying attentior

after I gave a d

Jewish charities

editorial positior

black hat good

She looked down as if she hadn't noticed they were gone. "Oh, that. Bedbugs, Howie. It was the bedbugs."

Howie said nothing, which upset her more than anything except for the fact that two months later, he still hadn't found the tattoo.

"Rachel?" Earl got her out of the shower. "It's your grandmother." Rachel was supposed to call Randall; Earl offered to call Vanessa. They'd been in somewhat closer touch since she came over for Faktor's funeral, although her husband didn't know about it. Just seeing each other again wasn't enough to get Vanessa and Earl talking; it was on the ride home after Earl picked her up from the bar where she'd been with Milner that Vanessa turned to her father after five minutes of "How could you?" and "A woman your age, a mother," and "Is this what they teach you in Mea Shearim? I don't think too many other married hasidic women have assignations with men who aren't their husbands in places where alcohol is served and then proceed to get so drunk that they have to find a relative to drive them home." She burst into tears. "Daddy, I'm so unhappy and I don't see any way out." She told him how dissatisfied she was; how her religious urge seemed to have passed and how meaningless most of what she did seemed to be. Earl had no answers beyond the obvious one of "leave" and wondered to himself why on earth anyone would want to maintain contact with a bunch of kids who'd look down on them, maybe even disown them, for doing the rather innocuous and hardly immoral things that she wanted to do. "If you leave, you'll lose all touch with them, right? But if you stay and go on pretending to believe things that you don't and go on doing things that you think are stupid while calling them holy or important or, worst of all, true—what kind of contact is that?" He'd been in the same situation with his own father and he knew what he was talking about.

"But if I pick up and leave, even if they understand why—which they won't—but even if they *could* understand it, don't you think they'd wonder why I'd lied to them about everything? Why I told them that things were true when I knew they weren't? *Vey iz mir*, I'm going to lose either way. I'll have nothing but Thomases—kids I let down so badly that I can't even blame them for hating me."

If Earl had been pressed hard enough, he would have had to admit that he'd never really liked Vanessa; he still wasn't able to forgive her for what she did to Rachel, and even if he set that aside, he still didn't find her personality at all to his taste. She'd always been one of those people that it was hard for him to like. It wasn't a matter of paternal feeling—he had plenty of that; it was more a question of wanting to be around someone. And he was pretty sure that she'd understand exactly what he meant; she'd certainly gone far enough out of her way to alienate him and everybody else who tried to care for her. He didn't need Vanessa's tearful explanation of how she was more interested in being adopted by Ruth, her dead mother-in-law, than in marrying her husband to understand why she'd fallen into such a crazy way of life: these people were willing to accept her completely, as long as she remade herself according to their wishes. And at the time, her wishes happened to correspond with their instruction.

But Vanessa was Vanessa. She was young enough to have two or maybe even three major phases still ahead of her. Earl could tell her to grow up, but he knew that she never would. It took him years, decades, to figure her out, but now that he had, all he could see was his daughter, his fantastically, freakishly beautiful forty-two-year-old daughter beside him in the car, crying her eyes out because she wasn't happy. And all he wanted to do was be a father and fix it.

Earl was seventy-one; he knew it couldn't be fixed, or at least not by him, but her wanting him to fix it gave him a rush of joy that he hadn't felt for a very long time: she needed him.

Phoning Vanessa didn't scare him any more. Fond as he had been of Chana, he was glad that no one could look into his head and see how happy he was to have a chance to see Vanessa again, to see all his kids together again so soon after the last time. It didn't mean that he wasn't sad about Chana, it just meant—he didn't know what. Maybe that he was feeling respected again.

Vanessa—Feygl, really—was a little uncomfortable about telling Yankel that she had to go to Canada again.

When she got home after Faktor's shiva, she found out
that the kids hadn't had a meal at home since she left.
Yankel just kind of forgot about cooking, and the kids
eventually got hungry enough that they started going to
the neighbours—all of whom were Yankel's acolytes—and
asking to stay for meals. He'd been reared to be a rebbe,
and had no idea how to do anything so mundane as cook
or wash clothes. Ruth had looked after such things when
Vanessa went off on her tours of America, and her death
was one of the practical considerations that led Vanessa to
stop travelling. If Yankel wasn't studying or praying, he
was out demonstrating on behalf of Jewish purity. He only
seemed to have one other thing on his mind; the night she
came home from the funeral, they had sex three times.

Much to her amazement, he wasn't upset at all. In fact,
he wanted her to stick around in Toronto until she could get
hold of some money. The real windfall was going to come
through Chana's estate, which had most of Faktor's money
as well as all of hers. Faktor had left a lump sum to each of
his children and grandchildren; the rest went to Chana. On
her demise, everything was to be split three ways: a third to
Ava, a third to Niven, and a third to Tammy's three children
(Earl had declined a share), to be split equally between them.
This would amount to several million dollars each. In the
meantime, though, each of the grandchildren would receive
$250,000. The will had still not been probated and Yankel
wanted Feygl to hang around and try to speed things up or

else arrange a loan from Earl against her share of the estate. He had big plans for the League, and big debts that Moginey Erets had to start paying off before they lost all their buildings. He saw Chana's death as a sign of divine favour: Feygl would get a free plane ticket to go to Canada and get things moving financially.

While Earl was on the phone with Vanessa, Rachel got hold of Randall, who was visiting his girlfriend Alexa in Syracuse. He had been spending as much time there as possible since Faktor's shiva ended and they were talking about getting married. Like Yankel, Randall was waiting for Faktor's will to be probated; he was reworking his Toyless Boy material into a one-man show and was hoping to be able to book it into real theatres. Faktor's death had hit him quite hard; he was feeling guilty about having neglected Yiddish for everything but stag parties and had been spending a lot of time reading Yiddish literature and delving into the history of the language. He was thinking very seriously of using some of the money that was coming to him to produce sumptuous new editions of Faktor's Yiddish books, along with proper English translations that might attract people who didn't know or care about Yiddish to his work. He was no more surprised by Chana's death than anybody else; he'd been a lot closer to her, though, because of the years that he lived with her and Faktor, and Earl decided that it was only right that Randall deliver the eulogy at the funeral.

After finishing up on the phone and at the funeral home, Earl decided to go to Chana's house. He himself didn't really know why—he was the executor of the estate, but it seemed a bit premature to start clearing the place out—going there somehow seemed like the right thing to do. Luz was there, looking distraught; she'd been with them since 1985, when she'd come to Canada as a girl of twenty-two. She and Earl embraced and both of them cried a little. "They were always so nice to me," she said. "I don't know where I'm going to go now." Earl knew that Luz would be receiving a considerable sum from the estate, enough to allow her to get a place of her own and hire her own domestics, but didn't think that this was quite the time to tell her.

"How did you find her, Luz?" he asked instead.

She explained that she'd gone into the living room to call her for lunch maybe twenty minutes or half an hour after Dr. Milner left and found her slumped on the sofa.

"Milner was here? Why? Chana, Mrs. Faktor, threw him out of the shiva and told him never to come back."

"I don't really know what he wanted, but he came by twice today. The first time he had a CD with him and gave me a hundred dollars to put it into the machine so that Mrs. Faktor would be sure to hear it. He wanted to talk to her after she'd listened and even promised me another hundred if she'd already heard it when he came back. He came back around noon."

"Did she listen?"

"Yes, but Dr. Milner never gave me the rest of the money. She told him to get out—in English—and I heard him tell her to f-off before he left."

"Milner told her to f-off? Did you hear what was on the CD?"

"Only the first few seconds. I was downstairs polishing the silver. It was something about Mr. Faktor's first marriage." Yiddish came so naturally to Luz after twenty-two years with the Faktors that she and Earl were speaking it now.

"His first marriage? Is it still here?"

"I think so. I don't know for sure, lemme look." They went into the living room and found it.

"Play it, please."

Luz was in tears by the end of the CD. Earl's mouth was hanging open. He wiped the drool from his chin. "My kids are all goyim. My kids are all goyim. I married a shiksa and my kids are goyim. Wait till I tell Vanessa."

Vanessa called Milner from a pay-phone in Ben Gurion Airport in Tel Aviv. "Darling," she said, "my grandmother died."

"Blessed be the righteous judge." The usual formula on hearing of a death, but Milner was genuinely taken aback. "When?"

"Yesterday." After Milner had been at her house. He felt a little sick, as if he'd just realized that that big bump he drove over a minute ago was really a child.

"That's terrible. I'm so sorry for you."

"She *was* very old."

"Still . . ."

"You know what this means, though? I'm coming to Toronto!" She squealed like a teenager. "I'm in the airport right now, I'll be there before you know it."

"Should I come to the airport?"

"My father's going to pick me up."

"I don't think it'd look very good for me to turn up at the funeral or shiva after your grandmother threw me out of the house. I got the impression that your aunt and uncle didn't like me any more than she did."

"Hmm . . . don't worry, though. This should be a lot less hectic than my grandfather's. And, oh I almost forgot to tell you the best part, Yankel *wants* me to stay in Toronto for a while and do some business for him. I'll tell you when I see you, but we'll finally be able to spend some time together."

Milner knew what he had to do before Vanessa arrived. He took a copy of his article to a court-approved translator and had it translated into French, along with a letter explaining that the article, the original of which was enclosed along with the French translation, might be of some interest to the rabbi, as both he and his wife were mentioned in it. The English version would be appearing in the forthcoming number of the esteemed English-language Orthodox journal, *Torah Times*, and the sender, who signed himself A. Fraynd—Yiddish for "friend"— thought that the rebbe had best be forewarned. He added that he thought a French translation preferable to one in Yiddish or Hebrew for reasons of confidentiality, and closed by telling the rebbe how much he admired his work on behalf of the Jewish people.

Milner had to pay extra to have the job done right away, but it was worth it. He had the package with all three documents and a copy of the CD couriered to Israel—it was a drag that he couldn't wait long enough to enclose a clipping of the published article, but he was pretty sure that the texts would get Yankel to listen to the CD. The important thing was to catch him completely by surprise. Once the article was out, rumours of it would get to him before the proof. This way, the blow—and the anger—would be all the deadlier for being so utterly unexpected.

Earl was doing a Faktor, circa 1943. Circa 1943 times nine: Faktor's delusion lasted for five years, Earl met Tammy in 1963 and had considered her Jewish for forty-five years, eighteen of them after she was already dead. If it was all a dream, he wished he'd died in his sleep.

He had no reason to stay at Chana's; he didn't want to go home. He took the CD, got into his car and drove straight up Bathurst Street to Moe Pancer's Delicatessen, so *tsemisht* that he forgot that the place had moved south from the corner of York Downs a few years ago and drove right past it and had to double back. He ordered a three-meat platter—corned beef, pastrami, and chopped liver—cancelled the fries and cole slaw that came with it and asked for kishka instead, along with a Vernor's to wash it all down.

Earl was torn. He couldn't decide if his whole life was a lie or if nothing had ever mattered. It had to be one or the other, but he didn't know which. He smeared chopped liver over a slice of rye bread, topped it with a couple of forkfuls of both the other meats and closed things up with a slab of bread covered in hot mustard. He looked at the sandwich, took a slug of Vernors straight from the can and sneezed. He wiped his nose and started in on the kishka. He knew where he was; the question was, where had he been? Unlike Faktor and Temke, he and Tammy had a real wedding under a real canopy with a real rabbi officiating. They held it in his father's synagogue, to be sure that his father turned up. Faktor, the old bastard, knew all along; he stood there and watched, kissed the bride and shook hands with his parents. Earl was pretty sure that he must have been laughing when no one was looking. Tammy taught in Jewish schools; most of her singing was in Hebrew or Yiddish; their kids had bar and bat mitzvahs, and Tammy was president of the synagogue sisterhood—twice. When she and Earl first met, she told him that she'd never felt so at home as she did in Israel. She was buried in a Jewish cemetery.

"Oh, shit." The words actually came out of Earl's mouth.

"Something wrong with the food, Earl?" He'd been a regular at Pancer's for more than forty years.

"No, no. Just remembered what I forgot to do."

"You're a member of CRAFT, eh?"

"Huh?" He was wishing that Cindy, the waitress, would fuck off and go away.

"Can't Remember A Friggin' Thing."

"Oh, right. Heh, heh." He thanked God when another customer came in.

"Oh, shit." This time he was careful to think it. "Cemetery bastards will probably make us dig her up." He took a bite of his sandwich, number one of three, and stared blankly out the window at the cars on Bathurst Street and the bearded men and kerchiefed women walking by among the blacks and Filipinos. "*I'm* Jewish, I know that. But I don't know about that guy with the beard and the big hat over there, not for sure. Or his fat little wife. And *they* know that *they're* Jewish, but they're not so sure about me. And so on and so on. Nobody really knows for sure. My kids sure think they're Jewish, especially the one that went and married a rabbi. Tell them they aren't, they'll probably spit in your face.

"I think I've just discovered Frumkiss's First Law: everybody's Jewish until they find out that they aren't. It works perfectly. There are billions of people out there who aren't Jewish and have always known that they aren't. Some of them have never heard of Jews or Judaism, but that doesn't make them any the less goyish. With people who know what a Jew is, not being one is usually something they're pretty proud of. As far as they're concerned, it's an accomplishment. The rest of us accept it on faith; our parents tell us we're Jewish, other supposed Jews consider us Jewish, people who aren't Jewish agree with them. The rabbis all say that a Jew is the child of a Jewish mother—but they never bother to tell us how we know if the mother is Jewish. Look at Tammy. And look at our kids. Tammy's mother never said she was Jewish, but she never said she wasn't. Everybody assumed that an actress in the Yiddish theatre who knows all about keeping kosher and runs away from the Nazis with a lot of other Jews is Jewish; but she knew she wasn't Jewish. Tammy didn't know that she wasn't Jewish, and she died before she could find out the truth. Therefore, she's still Jewish, according to Frumkiss's Second Law: Anybody with a sincere belief that they were born Jewish *is* Jewish. Should it emerge—" Earl was getting a kick out of his fancy syntax; it reminded him of when he'd been on the committee that drew up the charter and by-laws for the Podiatric Association of Canada—"should it emerge that they were misinformed, it doesn't make any difference. They made their commitment in good faith and cannot in good faith be made to suffer for the oversights or misdeeds of others. By that standard, Tammy was Jewish; Vanessa, Rachel and Randall are Jewish; and for all I know the guy in the turban waiting for the bus outside is just as Jewish as the guy in the yarmulke beside him. If I'm wrong, I spent thirty-five years screwing a shiksa and didn't even know it."

He was well into his third sandwich by now and held up his empty can for another Vernors.

"You feeling okay, Earl?" Cindy asked when she came by with the pop. "You're sitting here talking to yourself."

"Yeah, yeah, no worries, Cind. I'm just trying to figure something out. I'm not disturbing anybody, am I?"

"Nah. It just isn't like you, is all." Really, she figured he must have been drinking.

"I'll try to keep it down." Stupid bitch, interrupting him again. "Where was I? Oh, right. So if Frumkiss's Second Law is really a law, I don't need to say anything to the kids. They're just as Jewish as they think they are, and nothing that Faktor said or did can change that.

"And who am I fucking kidding? Even if I'm right, I still have to tell them. But none of us has to tell anybody else. And as long as it stays with us, we're Jewish even to people who refuse to accept my laws as binding." He left five dollars on the table, paid the check at the cash, and walked back out to his car. "I wonder if this is how Darwin felt."

Earl had never read Darwin, so he would never know, and he wasn't planning to explain his theory to the kids, either. Vanessa was coming in the next morning and the funeral was the day after. The funeral had had to be pushed off an extra day; it was American Thanksgiving and Niven had had to wait an extra day to get a flight. Earl called Rachel and told her that he needed to see her and Randall at his place tomorrow evening; Vanessa would be there, too. "It's important, that's all I can tell you over the phone. You might want to have Howie come along, too." Earl didn't think that his recently discovered laws called for any dishonesty. "What I need to talk about is going to affect him, too."

"Has this got anything to do with the estate, Dad? Because if it does, I think it's really in poor taste to be talking about it before Bubbie's even been buried."

"It's got nothing to do with the estate, I can promise you that."

"Then what is it that's so important?"

"I'm sorry, Rach, but you'll just have to wait and see."

They were all at Earl's the next evening. He had called his favourite glatt kosher Israeli takeout after leaving Pancer's and arranged for them to deliver dinner for nine— it never hurt to err on the side of caution. The way things had been going, the damned Messiah might decide to drop by for a nosh. And maybe even bring a friend.

They ate first. Niven took care of the Messiah's portion, Randall and Earl split the friend's between them. Earl got things started over coffee. "We're going to be burying Chana tomorrow morning, but this doesn't have any direct relationship to her, except that it might have contributed to her death. Ava and Niven, it's only about your mom insofar as she was married to your dad. Allan Milner," he was looking straight at Vanessa now, "whom some of you might remember as the *shmendrik* who made that ridiculous speech at Faktor's funeral and who Chana threw out of the shiva—"Ava groaned—"the Getsl guy"—Niven said "Oh"— "was working with Faktor on some sort of biography. To help Milner with his research, Faktor recorded a bunch of reminiscences on his computer and copied them onto CDs for Milner. This seems to be one of them. It was in the CD player at Chana's house and Chana had been listening to it only a few minutes or maybe an hour or so before she died." He gave them all the details that he had got from Luz. "Luz and I listened to it together. Milner had obviously heard it before he came to see Chana, and Luz told me that Chana had definitely played it; she—Luz, I mean—turned on the CD player herself, and she could hear Chana and Milner fighting when he came over after Chana had heard it."

The only sound in the room when the CD finished was Howie asking impatiently, "What the hell was that all about? How come I had to get a babysitter and miss a game to come here and listen to a bunch of stuff in a language I can't understand?"

"Because," Rachel started, but Niven, of all people, cut her off.

"Because you're a shmuck and we wanted to make you suffer. Actually, my mother's alive and well, we just wanted to keep you from your hockey game. The guys on your team paid us to do it; they thought that if you were here, they might win for once." Niven spat a stream of tobacco juice into a Peter Rabbit cup.

He'd been in England for so long that they sometimes forgot that he still spoke real Canadian. Earl found himself wondering again why he hadn't spent more time with Niven when he lived in Toronto, then remembered that the main reason was that Niven was still a kid then.

Howie looked so hurt that they were all afraid that he believed what Niven said. Ava got up and took him by the arm. "C'mon into the kitchen with me and I'll tell you what was on the CD."

Once they'd left, the rest of them could return to their shock. Rachel took a flask from her purse as soon as Howie was out of the room and emptied it into her Coke. Vanessa was the first to speak, and she spoke in Yiddish, in deference to the CD. "My children are goyim."

"So are mine," said Rachel.

"So are mine," said Earl.

Vanessa was the only one laughing, though. "My children are goyim." She said it again. "And so am I. And so are you," she pointed at Randall, then at Rachel, "and you."

"That's pretty plain." Randall was using his saucer as an ashtray and Earl, a vehement anti-smoker, wasn't offering any objection. "The question is, what do we do about it?"

Rachel was shaking her head. "Not quite. Remember, this isn't some goddamned artifact that was dug up by chance. Milner," she turned to Vanessa, "brought this to Bubbie for a reason."

"What reason?" Vanessa asked.

"I wasn't there," Rachel said, "I can't say for sure. He must have wanted something. What does a guy like Milner want? Fame, renown? Chana can't help him with his shitty folksinging—what, he's gonna blackmail her if she doesn't give him three Yiddish variants of 'Barbara Allan'?—and he's already sucked everything out of his connection with Zeyde that he's ever going to get. So what else does he want?"

"Pussy." It was Randall's turn to look at Vanessa. "But he's working on that somewhere else."

"So that leaves," Rachel wanted to start talking before Vanessa went after Randall, "money. My guess is that he wanted hush money from the bubbe to keep this quiet. If I'm right, if he was trying to blackmail her, then we're not the only people who have heard this CD, or at least not the only people who know what's on it. If we were, I'd say screw it, ignore it."

"How can you say that?" asked Randall. "Your whole life has just been turned upside down or inside out and you say we should ignore it?"

"I say we should have ignored it. We can't any more, because there's," she switched to English for a few seconds, "there's still another shoe that has to drop. We're getting screwed—this won't stay private—so that someone else, if you're still listening, Vanessele, can get fucked."

Vanessa slammed her coffee cup onto her saucer so hard that they both broke. "What are you trying to say,

Rach?" She was speaking English, too. "You implying that this has something to do with me?"

"I'm not implying anything, bitch." Rachel was out of her chair and fuming before anybody could do anything about the broken china—all of which had come from Chana's store. "I'm saying it. It's pretty clear that Zeyde made that tape,"

"It's a CD," muttered Randall, "not a tape."

"Shut up, Randall. This isn't a class in media studies. That's Zeyde on the CD," she shot a withering look at Randall, "and we've got no reason to doubt anything that he says on it. Your boyfriend—"

"I'm a married woman. I don't have any boyfriend."

"Your *admirer*—Look, I understand. He's supposed to be writing a biography, and I'm sure he'll finish it once he finally learns the alphabet all the way through. If he's writing any kind of decent book, he can't very well skip over something as important as this. It would have to have come out anyway. He can't have been expecting this any more than we did. If he was honest, he would have come to us and said either, 'I made this shocking discovery and I have no choice but to use it. It's nothing personal,' and so on and so forth; or else he would have said, 'Listen to this.' And when we were finished, he'd have asked us what we think he should do. And I'm pretty sure we would have said, 'Forget it. It had no effect on Zeyde's marriage, no effect on his work. The only people it's going to affect is us.

Us and our kids. So forget about it.' But he didn't. He went to Bubbie, which means he went for money. And boys and girls, *katchkes un genz*, ducks and geese, that means that we're screwed. You sure know how to pick 'em, sis."

Vanessa had gone white as a Yom Kippur yarmulke. "Allan, Milner I mean, is a decent, sensitive person. If he took it to Bubbie first, it was probably just to let her know, to make her aware of what he'd found out and was duty bound not to hush up. And he did *that* after she'd been so mean to him—I think it shows the kind of person he is. What else could he do? Go to you or Randall? You guys were horribly rude to him. Daddy? 'Hello, sir. Did you know your wife was a shiksa and so are your daughters?' And I'll have you know, Rachnik, that I've never touched him, never done anything that could even arouse suspicion. I've seen him only in public places, and all we did was talk. If I had a sister or brother I could talk to like a human being, I probably wouldn't be talking to him at all."

Randall made a lip fart.

Niven got out of his chair, spat, and told everybody to shut up. "Look, Earl was right." He was speaking English, too. "This doesn't really affect me, though I'm just as shaken up as anyone else here. I think you're talking too much about Milner. I think Rachel's right about us not being the only people who know about this and that forgetting about it is no longer an option. Blaming Milner or trying to guess his motivation isn't going to help. It's like wondering why all that rain is making the river overflow. You need to figure out how to deal with the flood. The question is: What?"

Ava and Howie came back just as Niven was finishing. Howie did not look happy. He walked over to Rachel's place at the table and would have spun her around had she not turned in her chair as he came near her. "Is this true? Ava says that you're all a bunch of goyim. I wanna hear it from you, Rach. You know I don't speak Yiddish, so I need to have this shit confirmed. Are you or are you not a shiksa?"

Rachel looked at him like he was a fatal car crash that she happened to be driving past. "According to what my grandfather says, I am. Halachically."

"Halachically." As if Howie used the word every day. "And what does that mean for Kyle and Jason?"

"It means that they're goyim, too, Howie, just like their mother. Of the four people in our house, you're the only real Jew. You happy now?"

"Goyim? I'm living with goyim? Shit. If you're such a shiksa, why don't you suck my dick?"

"I'd suck it if I could find it, He-Man. Maybe you could try getting it up, just for a change."

Earl ran to get between them. "Easy there, junior," he said. "Remember me? I'm Dr. Earl Frumkiss, and if you lay so much as the tip of a finger on my daughter, rest assured that I'll kill you, you dickless wonder." Something else Earl felt bad about was having pushed Rachel to marry this *yutz*.

Howie, who was almost crying by now, turned around to make his way out. "I'm going home and taking our babies. Don't come looking for me."

Earl intervened before Rachel could make a fool of herself. "Kidnapping's a minimum sentence of seventeen years here and no judge is going to say that being a Jew is licence to kidnap your own children or anybody else's. Why don't you just sit down and shut up while the people who can tie their own shoelaces figure out what to do."

Yankel had never heard of The Who and thus couldn't derive even a few seconds' comfort or consolation from a quick hum-through of "The Kids Are Alright." Because his kids were most definitely not all right, not any more. Feygl hadn't been gone long enough for lice to appear or vitamin deficiencies to set in; she'd left Israel only about two and a half days ago, but things were already falling apart, and she was the only one to blame.

A couple of hours before Milner's package arrived, all three of his children, two boys and a girl, had come home from school, frightened and in tears. The principal of the boys' school had been waiting for them in front of the building when they arrived. "*Avek fin danen*, get out of here. This is a school for Jews, not goyim. Go home and tell your parents that their masquerade is over. We won't get fooled again." The boys, aged thirteen and fourteen, were completely bewildered. It was the Hebrew month of Kislev, so they knew it couldn't be Purim, but they couldn't understand what else might be going on. Still, they'd been trained to obey adult Jews—or bearded adult Jews in the proper clothing—unquestioningly, so they did as they'd been told. The little girl, only eight, had been pelted with garbage and called a shiksa.

Their father was in his synagogue when they got home. He liked to say two or three hours of penitential prayers every morning—well into his forties, he still had wet dreams when he couldn't have sex with his wife, a secret that his followers, who thought of him as holy, would never have believed—and was in his little private room reciting psalms and sundry incantations when the kids arrived. Yankel's *shammes*, his executive assistant, told them to go away and then remembered to ask them why they weren't at school. "They said we're goyim and can never go back," they wailed.

B.Z. Shmulowitz, editor of *Torah Times*, was a Litvak, a deeply religious man with a wide-brimmed Panizzi hat and a Smith Brothers beard, but not a hasid. He didn't really like hasidim—their rebbe-worship struck him as idolatry— and he especially had no use for this convert who seemed to want to tell real Jews how to live. Shmulowitz had always known that there was something not entirely kosher about his pin-up girl wife who couldn't have been religious for more than fifteen minutes before she hit the lecture circuit in the States with her come-ogle-me outreach for coed audiences. Shmulowitz hadn't thought much of Yankel's stepfather, either, but he had a certain grudging respect for the old man's rigour and consistency; the Litvaks were also anti-Zionist, but they didn't see any need to make a fetish of it or advertise the fact in front of goyim. He figured that the old rebbe must have had a secret stroke and been led by the brain damage to marry a convert and disinherit the children he already had. This Yankel needed to be taught a lesson, and the lesson was that he was finished.

Shmulowitz had e-mailed a copy of Milner's article to a couple of friends in Israel the day before, telling them that he thought they'd appreciate some advance knowledge of what was about to hit the fan over at Moginey Erets. Shmulowitz knew that the article would be all over Israel, either in the original or the unauthorized translation that was bound to be made, within hours, if not minutes, of his friends' receiving it.

Milner had no understanding of the ultra-Orthodox world, which functions almost entirely on rumour; he'd hoped to have a couple of days to get himself and Vanessa ready for what was about to happen. He assumed that Yankel would read the article, freak out, divorce Vanessa and tell her to take the goyishe children and go. He'd give her a few weeks to calm the kids down and then they could be together, either here or in Israel: the children had dual Israeli and Canadian citizenship.

Things played out somewhat differently. After Yankel's shammes told the kids to wait, he gingerly opened

the door to rebbe's sanctum and walked in. Yankel held up
a hand like a traffic cop as soon as he heard the door open.
He finished with whatever he was reciting, then turned
around to see who had disturbed him. The shammes told
him that all three children were outside, upset, and none
was at school. Yankel closed his book, kissed it, removed
the tallis and tefillin, the prayer shawl and phylacteries that
he didn't take off after the morning service but kept on
until he'd finished all of the extra prayers that he said, and
went into the synagogue's main hall. The kids threw themselves on top of him as soon as they caught sight of him.
"What's going on?" he asked. "Why are you here?" The
answers made no sense to him.

"Goyim?" He scratched his head, pulled at his beard.
He had plenty of enemies—what stepson who became a
rebbe wouldn't? He'd been educated in the same schools
and could understand calling another kid *goy* as a schoolyard taunt, but what reason would the school administrators, supposedly rational grown-ups, have to call his children
goyim? He thought for a minute, then addressed the boys.
He could think of only one thing they might have done.
"Shraga-Feivel, Moyshe-Arye, have you been speaking *ivrit*,
Hebrew, again?"

"No, father. We've been very careful since the last
time you caught us. Really."

He turned to the girl. "Ris?" Which is how Ruth is
pronounced in that particular dialect of Yiddish. Ris looked

at her father and started howling. "I'm not a shiksa," she screamed. "Not a shiksa. I'm a kosher daughter of Israel."

Yankel turned to his shammes, perplexed. The shammes shrugged his shoulders. "Yossel, go outside and see what you can find out. This doesn't make any sense at all."

"Yes, rebbe." Yossel left.

"Children, come over here." Yankel folded his arms around the kids and all four of them rocked back and forth, each comforting the others. "Oy, I wish your mother was here."

Yossel came back twenty minutes later, flushed and dripping with sweat. His left stocking had slid down from under his knee-breeches and was sagging around his ankle. He was carrying a broadsheet-sized piece of paper rolled-up in his hand.

Yankel looked up. "Nu?" he asked.

"*S'i' shver, rebbe, shver in bitter*, things are seriously bad. Look at this. I had a heck of a time getting one that wasn't on a wall." Yankel gently sloughed the children off himself and reached for the rolled-up paper. It was a *pashkvil,* one of the wall posters that are ubiquitous in ultra-Orthodox neighbourhoods. They're used to announce funerals and demonstrations, get news out quickly, tell people what they should be doing and how they should be thinking. The League for the Purity of the Jewish People made frequent use of them, and as soon as Yankel saw the paper in Yossel's hand, he knew that things were serious.

He read through the poster, which contained a con-
densed Hebrew version of Milner's article for *Torah Times*.
He turned grey, then white, then grey again. He sat down
heavily. "Yossel, go into my room and bring me my cigarettes." He broke three matches trying to light one. He took
a long drag from the cigarette, sent the terrified children
into the courtyard of the synagogue to play, and read it again.
He must have misunderstood. He read it again. There was
no doubt, nothing ambiguous about it: according to this, his
wife, the woman whom his sainted mother had chosen for
him, trained into Orthodoxy, and groomed personally in the
ways of Moginey Erets, was a shiksa. She hadn't misled them
deliberately, God forbid, but that didn't change anything.

A crowd was gathering outside the synagogue. Yossel
could hear voices coming out of megaphones. Groups of his
own followers were starting to filter into the shul. Yankel
told Yossel to shoo them outside and lock all the doors.
"Yossel, can you get your wife to take the children home?"
Yossel took out his cell phone. "Don't let anyone in to see
me. Tell them I'm not in. Look outside. Is that my stepbrother's voice I can hear over the megaphone?"

Indeed, it was. Once the doors were all locked and
bolted, Yankel went out into the courtyard so he could hear
better. His stepbrother and all his step-brothers-in-law
were out there with megaphones. All the people who had
been left behind when his stepfather appointed Yankel were
coming to begin their vengeance. He could hear sirens

heading in the direction of the shul. His relatives were yelling and screaming and weeping. They claimed that his mother, the grey eminence and inspirational role model for the current shiksa, had made use of forces, sinister forces from the evil "other side," to hypnotize and beguile the old rebbe into disinheriting his legitimate heirs so that everything could be turned over to yet another shiksa who needed no instruction in the ways of unleashing impurity in Israel. The first shiksa, the old rebbe's wife, at least had a kosher conversion, and no one questioned the current usurper's Judaism. Brazenness had increased, though, and the satanic couple had injected their bastards into the very bloodstream of the community, its school system, where . . .

Yankel vomited and went back inside. He called one of his allies who worked for the Conversion Authority and who didn't wait for Yankel to say why he was calling. "The woman, never. You've made too many enemies. They'll block any attempt she makes to convert. Since she'd be converting only to marry you and be with her children, her motivation is suspect, as you know. It's one of those ulterior motives that you've been fighting so hard against, and they'll be damned if they're going to give in to you on it. The kids are a little different. They're planning to jerk you around for a year or two, send you away, make you come back, you know what I mean, then put them through a trial period for a year or two to make sure that they're really observant and not just pretending, just to cut you down to size. I don't know where they'll go to school, though—you're going to have to take them out of yeshiva, and you realize that none of them will ever be able to marry *any* member of any of the communities, not here and not abroad."

"I've committed no sin, though. We don't even know if these rumours are true."

"Have you asked at home?" This was code for "asked your wife."

"The person in question is in Canada for a funeral."

"Is it possible that one of your relatives could be behind this?"

"God forbid. They don't like me, but I can't imagine any of them committing a sin of this magnitude. They can be spiteful, but they're only human; not one of them is capable of this kind of evil, of attacking innocent children."

He could hear the Conversion Authority guy shrug his shoulders. "I don't know what to tell you that I haven't already said, except that everybody's heard. Everybody knows about it."

He looked in his desk for the piece of paper with Earl's phone number that Feygl had left with him and dialled. It hadn't dawned on him that it was 2:30 in the morning in Canada, and he wouldn't have cared if it had. This was more important than sleeping.

Earl answered the phone. "Father-in-law," Yankel spoke almost no English at all, "It's Yankel speaking from Israel."

Neither Earl nor anybody had considered the possibility that Yankel might hear about any of this. "Yankel, it's the middle of the night. Did something happen to one of the children? Is everything all right?"

"Something happened, all right. But everybody's safe so far, thank God." Earl was wondering if a war had broken out while they were trying to figure out what to do about Faktor's CD. "Could you call Feygl for me, please? I need to speak to her right away."

Earl knocked on Vanessa's door. When she didn't respond, he knocked harder and called her name. He turned the handle. "Vanessa, are you in there? Yankel's on the phone. Vanessa?" He opened the door; her bags were there, but the bed hadn't been slept in. "Oh, shit." He looked downstairs, outside, in the basement. She was gone. "Shit, she's probably out with that asshole Milner again. Just when I think we might get closer, she goes and does something like this. And with Chana's funeral first thing in the morning."

He picked up the phone in the kitchen. "Yankel? Sorry to keep you waiting. She's just stepped out for a minute"—Yankel knew this meant "gone to the toilet"— but I'll tell her to call you"—it's forbidden to talk in the bathroom—"as soon as she gets out. Is there anything I can do?"

"No, father-in-law. I don't know if there's anything anybody can do."

Soon as he was off the phone, Earl called the cell phone that he'd loaned Vanessa. It rang ten times but she didn't pick up. He called back right away. She answered on the fourth ring. She and Milner were in a Tim Horton's at Bathurst and Finch. She'd taken the car and met him there. "Yes, Daddy?"

"Where the hell are you in the middle of the night? I know you're unhappy, but even miserable people need to sleep. Anyway, your husband called from Israel. He's upset about something. I don't mean mad, I mean distraught. I thought it might be one of the kids. Anyway, when I realized that you'd snuck out of the house like a naughty teenager, I told him you were in the can and would call him right back. I think you'd better do it."

Vanessa swallowed hard. She was drinking a can of Coke through a straw. Earl was giving her instructions. "You got a long distance card with you? Use it—this account won't let you call overseas. And call him now."

Vanessa looked at Milner. "He must have found out already. Nice work."

Milner shook his head. "The article won't be out until next Tuesday. There's no way he can know."

"We'll see about that. I'm going to phone him from the car. I don't want him to know that I'm not home." She left Milner in the doughnut shop and went out to the parking lot. Suddenly, she felt very guilty.

She'd called Milner as soon as she could after the family had heard the CD and demanded an explanation of what he'd intended to do with it, why he'd taken it to Chana, why he'd had a fight with her and what did he think he was doing, messing with other people's lives like this? He'd been expecting something of this nature and told her that he could explain everything, but that he wanted to do it in person. They agreed on 1 a.m. at the doughnut shop; Vanessa thought it unlikely that she'd be able to sneak away any earlier.

She found Milner in an expansive mood when she got there, preening himself on his brilliance and getting ready for Vanessa's compliments. After the preliminaries about how he'd never in a million years have expected to run across anything like what was on that CD, he told her about the article that was going to be coming out, about the package that he'd sent to Yankel, and about how this was the best thing that could ever have happened to them. "It solves all your problems, don't you see. You said that you didn't want to leave your kids behind. This way you don't have to. Yankel isn't going to want a brood of little goyim living in his house, and no one over there would stand for it if he did. Knowingly, I mean. He'll have to give you a divorce; you'll get the kids and we'll be able to be together, you and me. With the kids." He reached his hand across to try to take hers; Vanessa pulled her hand back like he was trying to chop it off.

"You shmuck," she said. "You stupid, fucking shmuck." Milner had never heard her use this kind of language before. "You're so dumb you probably think you're smart. You destroy a whole family—not one, but three, or is it four? Mine, Rachel's, my father's, Randall's, if he ever has one; you get up to something with my grandmother—don't worry, we're coming to that, too—and all so you can put your poky little wiener inside me? Well, fuck you, asshole."

"*Sha*, keep it down. People are looking."

"Only because language like that doesn't usually get this loud here until after two. "Did you ever stop to think that there was somebody involved in this besides yourself? People like my jerk-off brother-in-law and Rachel's kids; and more importantly, *my* kids. What do you think is going to happen? I'm over here. Yankel is going to find out that the kids aren't Jewish, and then what? You think he's going to want anything to do with them? He'll give them to me, sure. But they're going to hate me. These kids have been hasidim since the day they were born. The boys have got *payes*; the language they're most comfortable in is Yiddish. They've never spoken to anyone who eats food that isn't kosher or doesn't keep shabbes. And now they're going to find out that thanks to me they aren't really Jewish? That they've been doing everything for nothing? What's going to happen to them? Where they going to go? I can't raise them as goyim; they'll lose their minds. And I can't raise them as Jews, because they know they aren't Jewish. They don't belong anywhere now."

This was so much worse than stepping in shit. Milner could see that. He hadn't just stepped in it. He'd sat down, taken a huge, stinking crap, reached into the toilet bowl, picked it up, thrown it on the floor, and then taken care to step on every part of it twice—barefoot. "If it means that much, couldn't they convert? Or be converted?"

"Not by me. Remember, I'm not Jewish. Not by Yankel, even if he should want to. He's spent the last few years railing against the Conversion Authority in Israel. Lots of people there hate him, and they'll make any conversion impossible. And what about the kids? The boys probably know more than the average Conservative rabbi— they're going to have to convert? And you think any of them will ever be able to get married if they do? What were you thinking?"

Milner tried out his sheepish, I'm-such-a-sorry-excuse- for-a-man look, the one that said, "And because I'm such a sorry excuse, I need you all the more. I'm so smart, so talented, but without you I can't do anything with my intelligence or abilities. I need you to help me be me." This was the first time in years that it didn't seem to be working.

"And my father? What about him? And what about all the shit Rachel's going to have to go through? I've caused her enough trouble; if I got anything out of all these years of trying to be religious, it's a sense of just what a horrible, evil bitch I was and how much I damaged her. She's a genius, you know, a real one, and I fixed it so she'd be so, um, negative about herself that she'd marry a shmuck like Howie. Get me another Coke."

While Milner was on his way to the counter, Vanessa pulled the kerchief off her head. "You're beautiful," he whispered when he came back, "absolutely beautiful." Minx, he thought ironically, you've been toying with me all along. Once the kerchief comes off, the rest won't be too far behind.

"Uh huh. I am. And I forgot to mention something else that makes me really want to snuggle up to you: Yankel doesn't have to give me a divorce. Since I'm not Jewish and the only ceremony we ever had was a religious one 'according to the laws of Moses and Israel,' we're not married and we never were."

Milner smiled again and lowered his eyes. "I had no idea."

"You had no clue. No fucking clue. No wonder my grandmother hated you."

This was the first thing she'd said that Milner really heard. He'd figured that the rest of it was exactly the sort of thing he would have done in similar circumstances: blow a fairly mundane problem out of all proportion in order to buy yourself a certain emotional advantage.

"I'm not going to ask what went on there," she continued, "why you turned up in a place where you knew you weren't welcome with something like that CD. Remember, asshole, no matter what I am, I'll always be Faktor's granddaughter, and that blood isn't going anywhere except to my brain. What did you ask her for? How much did you want to destroy that CD? And how many extra copies were you going to keep? After all, you *were* going to put it into the biography, weren't you? Figuring that since my bubbie was ninety-five, you wouldn't have to wait too long before you could go back on your agreement. I just wanna know how much."

"I'm offended."

"And I'm undone. You ruin my life and the lives of everybody I never cared enough about but who cared about me, and you have the chutzpah to be offended? I wish I had a dick, just so I could tell you to suck it."

It was about then that she heard her cell phone ring and went out to the car.

"Yankel, you know where I was. What's the matter?"

She pretended not to know anything about it, for *his* sake and not her own. It was the only lie she told. "What?! Come on, Yankel, Purim's not for three more months. I swear to you, this is the first I've heard of it and I don't believe it. You know what kind of family I come from—Americans, as you'd say. But actual goyim? No, never. Remember, I also spoke Yiddish when we met. And if I recall, it's you who's the *ger*, the convert, not me." And the CD? "My zeyde was always playing tricks on people. I met that biographer. He's a *shmendrik*. The zeyde must have been putting him on." Then Yankel told her about the kids and she started to cry. "I don't know what we're going to do. First, I want to find out if there's anything to it. If, God forbid, there is, we'll figure out something."

Yankel told her what she'd already told Milner about the Conversion Authority. "They aren't God, as if such a thing were possible. There's a way around them. There has to be. We can fix it, get married all over again and then take care of the kids." She might have been dissatisfied before, but at least she was herself. Now, all of a sudden, she was nobody. She'd rather be unhappy with Yankel and have her kids safe and with her than any of the other crap that she'd thought she wanted. "Your brother and your stepsisters' husbands? We'll bury them. Just hold tight. Get the kids, go to Yossel's and stay there until I can get back . . . . The children? Tell them that their mother is coming home to fix everything."

She put the key into the ignition and drove back to Earl's without saying goodbye to Milner. She wasn't finished with him yet. If she'd thought she was back on home turf the last time she was here, she'd completely forgotten what she was really good at. If it was fucking Milner wanted, it's a fucking he was going to get.

13

IT HITS THE FAN, I

THINGS WEREN'T LOOKING GOOD FOR YANKEL. AS more and more people saw the wall posters and rumours began to circulate within the religious community, Torah zealots from every part of Jerusalem—whether spontaneously or by text-messaged order, no outsider ever knew—converged outside the tiny, rather tumbledown courtyard that was Moginey Erets Central under banners prepared years in advance and kept in easy-to-reach storage against the times when they were needed: "And you shall burn out the evil from your midst."

Moishe-Shulem Frankel, Yankel's stepbrother, had withdrawn from Moginey Erets in a snit after his father willed its leadership to Yankel, the underage, adopted son of a second wife who was Jewish only by compact, not by birth: Moishe-Shulem felt like a professional boxer who'd just lost the heavyweight championship to Tiny Tim from *A Christmas Carol,* in a split decision judged by Ray Charles, Helen Keller and Stevie Wonder. He was standing on the hood of a car parked directly across the street from the gate to Moginey Erets, shouting into a microphone attached to a portable sound system that he'd borrowed from the one-man band who was doing all that season's less important Moginey Erets secessionist weddings. Moishe-Shulem was crying—screaming and weeping and coughing into a handkerchief that he pulled out of his pocket and replaced after every hawk of phlegm. "Zimri ben Salu," he was crying and gagging at the same time, going over the story in the Book of Numbers where Zimri takes a Moabite woman, Kozbi, the daughter of Tzur, and brings her near to his brethren in the sight of Moses and the whole community of Israel. "Brought her near, it says. He didn't marry her or beget children upon her or send his bastards out as if they were kosher Jews to mingle with the holy and pure, stir up the sacred sheep, and enter, God forbid, into marriages, God forbid, with holy, kosher Jewish daughters and lie with them, God forbid, in a mockery of all the laws of Moses and Israel! Zimri did not send the daughters of idolators to scatter secret bastards through the very fabric of the Children of Israel. Zimri ben Salu only brought his whore near; but for him who lives *here*, nearness was only the precondition for deeds that have appalled heaven and struck the universe dumb."

His words were met with affirming shouts of *oy*, with weeping and wringing of hands and shaking of fists. He was now shouting the slogan from the banners every few sentences as a kind of exhortative punctuation. The crowd was getting larger, growing more and more unruly. The handful of police who had been dispatched to try to maintain some kind of order was too scared and too lightly armed to venture into a crowd that was growing like a thermonuclear tumour. Their call for reinforcements had been acknowledged and ignored.

Moishe-Shulem was no idiot. He had instructed his seven brothers-in-law, each of them married to another of his seven sisters, to mobilize themselves, their families and followers, and anybody else they could find to begin spontaneous demonstrations in the middle of every road leading to any street that could get a motorized vehicle anywhere near the Moginey Erets courtyard. "Demonstrations against what?" he asked mockingly, when they pressed him for instructions. "Against anything. Who cares? Desecration of the Sabbath, immodesty in billboards—just make a lot of noise. And be sure to haul garbage cans into the street and set them on fire. This is worth a night in prison, because we're going to get rid of the *shaygets* once and for all."

The roads leading to the Moginey Erets compound were impassable. Rumours had already started to circulate that Yankel, as president of the League for the Purity of the Jewish Family, had contrived to admit thousands of out-and-out goyim into the heart of the Jewish people. It didn't matter that the rumours didn't make sense; no one seemed to recall that Yankel and the rest of the League members wanted to make conversion more, not less difficult. Once they discovered the undeniable fact that his wife, Feygl, was a dyed-in-the-wool shiksa, even if she herself didn't know it, rage took over and consistency no longer applied.

Moishe-Shulem didn't want to press his luck, though. The police were eventually going to get through, and he wanted to be finished before they had a chance to stop him. "What does the Torah tell us?" he asked, as if every one of his listeners didn't already know the answer. "'And you shall burn out the evil from your midst.' What does the Holy Torah say? 'And Pinchas the son of Elozar, son of Aaron the priest, arose from the midst of the congregation and took a spear in his hand,' and he smote them both, the man and the woman. And what happened after he ran them through?" It was like a catechism for violent Jewish rage. "What did God say to Moses? 'Pinchas, the son of Elozar, the son of Aaron the priest, has turned my wrath away from the children of Israel.' Jews! Brothers! Let us rise up and turn away the wrath of the Lord from us and from our houses!"

They all understood his call. Garbage cans were set ablaze and rolled up to the gate of the courtyard. There was no need to break in; Moishe-Shulem still had his keys, and they all streamed in behind the blazing trash cans like vengeful peasants in a hasidic Frankenstein movie. Once inside, they smashed windows, overturned furniture. The smoke from the garbage cans was burning their eyes and covering everything within in a foul-smelling mist. The cans weren't terribly dangerous, but the smoke and the stench kept everyone mindful of why they were there: Sodom was being destroyed again. The few older members of the crowd, men from Europe long accustomed to demonstrations, were as uncomfortable with the violence as they were with its cause. They'd fight to the death for God and His commandments, throw rocks at cars that dared enter their precincts on the Sabbath, but they didn't know what kind of violation could justify staging a pogrom in a synagogue.

Moishe-Shulem was strolling through the smoke and wreckage like Moses on a walking tour of hell. Groups of rioters were picking up benches in the synagogue and banging them against the walls until the benches broke and the walls were nothing but holes. They smashed every window and threw the broken benches through the ones that could fit them. The sink at the synagogue entrance had been ripped out of the wall; water was pouring from the broken pipes and forming pools, not puddles, on the uneven floor. Members of the crowd were shoving books onto shelves to prevent their desecration, and no one even thought of approaching the ark where the Torah scrolls were kept. Yossel, Yankel's shammes, was curled up on the ground, covered in dust and blood. Someone or other was kicking him in the head. Yankel had run out of his private chamber and into the middle of the fray, fists clenched and screaming. He was a big man, well over six feet, with a physique that he must have inherited from his French gentile father. He was past forty already, but fit and muscular, even though he'd never exercised in his life. It was his nature: muscles came more naturally to him than learning. When someone in white stockings and a fur hat ran up to attack, Yankel decked him with a single punch. He clocked a couple of others before fate intervened. A group of hasidim holding a bench high in the air inadvertently caught Yankel in the side of the head while they were turning around to attack an unscathed stretch of wall. Yankel went down. The part of the mob that had been heading in his direction started to kick him in the head, too.

Moishe-Shulem touched nothing and nobody. Once Yankel was down and unconscious, he mounted the dais in front of the ark, clapped his hands together and screamed as loudly as he could, "*Aroys, yidn, aroys!* Out, Jews, out!" They couldn't burn a building with Torahs and holy books inside.

The police arrived ten minutes after the crowd disappeared. Yossel and Yankel were taken to the hospital; Yossel was treated for a concussion, a broken jaw and broken nose. The lost teeth and bruised ribs hardly counted at all. Yankel was in a coma. His wife was listed as next of kin, but they couldn't get her to answer the phone.

Yossel's jaw was wired shut, but his wife let the hospital people know that Feygl was in Canada. Her children were across the courtyard at Yossel's, where they had been taken before the protest got out of hand. They hid on the floor in a back room, but could still hear and smell what was happening. They were terrified. Yossel's wife went home and asked the kids if they knew their mother's maiden name and the city in Canada where her family lived. The boys told her, she told the hospital: it was a matter of calling every Frumkiss in the Toronto phone book until they got lucky and landed Earl.

Rachel should probably have kept her mouth shut. After everything that had happened to upset Howie at her father's, her half-joking offer of a blow job before Howie started to back the car out of the driveway was probably not the smartest thing to say. He was the only man she'd ever heard of who didn't like oral sex, and Howie himself didn't know anyone else who disliked it; he'd heard lots of guys bitch about having to give it, which he couldn't even think about without feeling sick, but he was the only guy he'd ever run into who didn't like getting it, either. "Go ahead and sue me," he told the guys on the crescent. "I just don't like blow jobs. If you ask me, they're kind of gay."

"How is it gay if a guy gets head?" None of them could understand him.

"Well, isn't that mostly what they do, the gays, I mean?"

"Maybe it is," said Lorne Adelstein, " but it isn't what they do, it's who they do it with. If you fuck a guy in the ass, you're queer—"

"Or in jail," added Jerry Hoffmitz.

"But if you do it to a woman, it's just something you like to do."

"Bullshit," Howie insisted, and held fast for fifteen

minutes of argument. Blow jobs were gay even if you were getting them from a super-model, and that's all there was to it, so when Rachel leaned over and put her head in his lap and asked if he'd like to be sucked off by a genuine shiksa, he didn't see the humour, either in the blow job or the idea that his wife was a shiksa.

"Stop it."

"Hey, you asked for it inside. And I said I'd do it once I found your dick."

He grabbed the crown of her head and gave a decisive tug upwards. "This is serious and you won't stop acting like an idiot."

He didn't say anything else and neither did she. A mile or so later, once they'd got back out to Bathurst Street, Howie said abruptly, "I guess you should sleep downstairs or something until I can talk to the rabbi and see what to do about this."

Rachel turned to her left again. Her voice was an octave higher than usual. "'What to do about this?' What do you mean, what to do? Nothing's changed, Howie. Don't you get it? I was just as not Jewish when we got married, when you met me even, as I am now. Sleeping by yourself isn't going to prevent disease or keep you from getting the cooties. Whatever it is, our kids have got it just as much as I have, maybe even more."

"So what do you want me to do? Thank you for turning my kids into goyim?"

"Howie," Rachel was trying to sound patient, "they're my kids, too, and I didn't make them into anything. They were born that way."

"Thanks to you . . . That's why I've gotta talk to the rabbi. Kyle's bar mitzvah's only four months off and there's no way I'm gonna throw away all the money we've spent already for Hebrew school and the hall and the caterers if he isn't even gonna have one. We've gotta take care of the kids and then figure out what to do about you."

"What to do about me? You're gonna figure it out?"

"I said *we*, didn't I?"

"Why do we have to do anything? I'm the same person I was when we left the house tonight, or as I was last week or last year or when we first met. I keep telling you, nothing's changed."

"No, everything's changed."

"You heard my grandfather's CD and decided I'm somebody else?"

"Jesus, Rach, *I* didn't decide it, he did. Or your real grandmother, your biological one, I mean, decided it. It's like if you were having an affair—and I don't think you are, I'm not accusing you, I'm just using an example. The whole time you're having the affair, you're the same person as you always were. I come home, you say hello, we talk, we eat, maybe we even have a fight, but you're Rachel and our marriage is what it looks like. A basically happy family. And then I find out that you're sleeping with another guy, and none of that is there any more. I realize it was all bullshit, an illusion, that nothing was really the way it looked and that I've been played for a sucker. It's the same thing."

Rachel was starting to get angry. "Howie." She managed not to say, "How could you be so dumb?" and instead skipped right to, "It isn't the same. Having an affair would be a conscious choice, it's something I'd do deliberately and know that I'm doing. Committing adultery is an act, Jewishness is a state of being. Four hours ago I was Jewish enough for you. What's really changed?"

"You have." Rachel realized that they'd never get past this. "You aren't the person I thought you were. We were married under false pretenses."

"But *I'm* not the person I thought I was, either. Except that I'm still the same."

"If you were the same, we wouldn't be having this conversation. And I can't be married to a shiksa. It's that simple."

"So we're not married any more?" Rachel felt guilty for not finding the prospect half as horrifying as she wanted to make it sound.

"I don't know." Howie was quite serious. "That's what we have to ask the rabbi. I don't know if he'll give you a conversion if it's only so that you can get married."

"And what if he says he won't? Then what?"

"I don't know. But I can't be married to a shiksa. I don't know. Maybe we keep going until we find a rabbi who'll do it."

"But if we can do that, that means that there's no real standard. And if there's no standard, then the one *we* come up with is as good as anybody else's and we might just as well just go on the way we have been."

"But we can't do that."

"Why not? 'Because I'm a shiksa.' I already know. So what happens in the meantime?" Rachel was almost enjoying herself; Howie hadn't gone so long without mentioning hockey in years now. "Do we sleep in the same bed? In the same room? In the same house?"

They were parked in the driveway of their house, screaming so loudly that the babysitter could hear them inside. "I don't know. I don't think it's right. But I can't figure out what to do with you."

"We're back to that? I'm those kids' mother, Howie. Did you forget that? What if the rabbi won't convert them just to keep you from losing your deposit with the caterer? If you had any balls, if you had any brains . . . shit, forget it, if you had either of them you'd be someone else. So forget it, Howie. Forget the whole thing and go fuck yourself. 'Don't know what to do. Aren't really married.' Go inside and make a pass at the kid who's babysitting. Maybe she's Jewish enough for you, but she's still gonna laugh when you come before two minutes pass."

Rachel fished the keys to her SUV out of her purse. It was parked beside them in the driveway. She got out of the car and jumped into it, slammed it into reverse and peeled out of the driveway and back over to Bathurst Street. She was going to stop at the first bar she found. Five miles further north in Richmond Hill she came to one, a bar with a large parking lot and a huge neon sign that said Hudson House.

It was a large beer hall with green Formica-topped tables and a shaker of salt in the centre of each. There weren't many women inside apart from the waitresses, most of whom were wandering from table to table with large round trays full of six-ounce glasses of draft. The guys at the tables would hold up a certain number of fingers, and that's how many glasses the waitresses would leave them. The waitresses were wearing short skirts with little aprons over the front to hold their money, and all of them could make change with only one hand.

Rachel sat down and asked, somewhat shyly, if they had any vodka. She ordered two shots, neat, and took two glasses of well-watered beer. She sipped at the beer until her liquor came, then downed the first in one gulp, chased it with the beer, then did it once more and ordered the same all over again. Some guy sat down at her table while she was waiting for her next round. She'd planned to try to do some thinking, but noticed, over the Lynyrd Skynyrd CD that was playing, that he was talking to her. "What was that?" She leaned forward to catch what he was saying. "No, not often. I've never been here before." Her drinks came and before she could say anything, he ordered her another round and took four beers for himself. By the time Rachel realized what was happening, it was too late to try to stop him.

"Are you here for the contest?" he asked.

"What contest?" The drinks were really going to Rachel's head. Between the noise and the booze, she was having trouble focusing.

Bob, her tablemate, looked her up and down. "The wet T-shirt contest. Every Wednesday night for the last eighteen years. Biggest in the whole GTA," the Greater Toronto Area.

Rachel smiled and said she didn't think so. "No, really," said Bob. "It's the biggest."

"I meant that I wasn't here for it. I just stopped in for a couple of drinks." She looked at her watch, disappointed that she'd been disturbed. "I really ought to get going soon."

Bob gripped her forearm and shook his head. He let her go. "But your drinks haven't even got here yet. You've got to stay and have your drinks."

Rachel, who had already finished four shots and three beers, nodded and said, "My grandmother just died and I have to be awake to go to her funeral in the morning."

Bob looked sad. "My grandmother's dead, too." The drinks came. Bob paid. "Let's drink to our grandmothers." He raised a glass of beer. Rachel did the same. "Our grannies," he said, and leaned over to clink her glass.

They drank. "You're very beautiful," Bob told her. Rachel smiled, said nothing, and drank a shot of vodka.

Bob leaned a little farther over the table. "A woman like you, you could win that contest easy." Rachel giggled. She had to squint to keep Bob's head from bouncing around. "I'd give just about anything right now to see you competing."

Rachel giggled some more. She looked down and saw that she was wearing a T-shirt, quite a thick one, though. She knew that she had a bra on underneath. She'd never been to a wet T-shirt contest and all she could imagine was someone dressed up like a clown spraying her chest with a seltzer bottle. Thinking about it made her nipples feel like she'd walked into an unpleasantly cold shower. "Yeah," she said and stood up. "I'll be back in a minute." She walked towards the toilet, feeling Bob's eyes on her back the whole time, went inside and counted to thirty. She opened the door a crack, peeked outside and saw that Bob was distracted, looking towards the stage at the other end of the bar where the contestants were being herded into line. She opened the door all the way, but gently, then moved to the main entrance as quickly as she could and slid outside. She ran to her SUV, jumped in and raced out of the parking lot. She was lucky that there was no one parked too close to her. Her head was spinning and she was seeing double; she had to get out and into a cab before she had an accident or got arrested. No cabs cruised up here, though, and Rachel had no idea where she could leave the car overnight without having it towed away. Pretty soon, she knew, she was going to start being sick.

She was heading south on Bathurst, back towards Thornhill. After about a mile or so, she saw a fair-sized plaza looming up ahead; she pulled into the parking lot, hoping that the car would still be there tomorrow. She pulled her cell phone out of her purse, found the taxi number that she kept in its memory and ordered a car to the plaza. When the cab turned up, she gave the driver Randall's address.

Randall was alone in his apartment when the buzzer rang. "Ran?" Rachel's voice was tear-stained and slurred. "Ran? It's me, Rach. I'm downstairs. I'm kinda drunk, I think. Lemme in, okay?"

Randall had gone straight from his father's house to a convenience store where he bought two packages of pork rinds. He picked up six tallboys of Canadian at the Brewers Retail, drove home, opened a beer and the rinds, and sat down on his couch without even turning on the television. "Jesus fucking Christ," he wasn't sure if he was talking to himself or working on new material, "I'm living in one of my own routines. I really am the Oyless Goy, I don't have a care on earth. The world's my oyster and now I can eat it; I'm not Jewish and I'm still not dead. I just hope that oyster tastes better than these pork rinds." He grimaced, took a long chug of beer, crumpled the pork rind bags, got back up and tossed them into the garbage.

The utter weirdness of discovering that he had never been Jewish hadn't quite sunk in for him. Everything was exactly the same and so was nothing. It was as if one of those old-fashioned Protestants he remembered reading about in university, the ones who believed in absolute pre-destination, found out whether he was destined to be saved or damned: all he could do was look. Everything was the same, but knowing *what* was the same changed everything without *his* being able to do anything about it. Even, say, if he were to convert to Judaism, it wouldn't be the same as if he'd converted from being an actual goy. As it was, all he'd be doing is getting back to what he had been. It reminded Randall of suddenly getting a job after months or years of being in debt; you spent the first few months struggling to get the debts paid off, fighting to get to zero. But since nobody outside the family knew anything about it, he wondered if there was any point to fighting at all. Why couldn't he go on just the way he had been? No one who mattered to him was ever going to see Milner's article; no one but him and his father and sisters would ever know the difference. And who was Milner, anyway? Some other sap who was making a fool of himself over Vanessa? He didn't matter at all. The big thing was that Alexa wasn't Jewish, so why should he care about any of this? If it really meant that much to him, he wouldn't have got so involved with a shiksa. And the fact that he was a *shaygets*, a male shiksa—well, that just made everything that much easier.

But none of it was really that easy. Randall would have thought of himself as a Jew even if he hadn't graduated from a Hebrew day school. Really, he didn't have a clue about who he was supposed to be or what he was supposed to do about it. He walked over to the garbage can and fished out the pork rinds. The taste was starting to grow on him.

Would anything be different if he wasn't Jewish?

He wouldn't go to *shul* a couple of times a year. That was the extent of his Jewish activity. He could still read books in Hebrew or Yiddish, do stags in Yiddish, hang around with Jews and fit in perfectly. His grandmother, the biological one, didn't seem to have any trouble doing it, so why should he? By now it was a family tradition. If he didn't marry Alexa and found himself a nice Jewish girl instead, his kids would be just as Jewish as if he were the chief rabbi of Jerusalem. Who the hell was his grandfather to tell him that he wasn't really Jewish, anyway? Much as he'd loved the old man, he didn't like the idea that his whole life was really some kind of joke that Faktor had decided to play, and that the punch line was that he, Randall, got to have his identity destroyed.

He'd just finished his second beer and was feeling a little queasy from the pork rinds when Rachel rang his buzzer. Soon as he opened the door and let her into the apartment, they looked at each other and started to laugh. They didn't speak, they didn't point, they just laughed. Doubled over, falling onto the couch or into a chair, gasping and choking, pounding pillows, trying to stand up and falling back down again. It lasted for five full minutes. By the time they finished, they were both feeling slightly sick, so

Randall went to the fridge and popped open a tallboy for each of them. They drank and burped and dribbled beer down their chins and laughed some more.

"The old son of a bitch," Randall said. "We were his biggest joke of all."

"Except for Mom," Rachel said, taking one of Randall's cigarettes. "She went through the whole thing and never found out who her own mother really was."

"What a fucking prick. What are we going to do?"

Rachel lit the cigarette. She hadn't had a smoke since she was fourteen and started to cough so hard that Randall went over and started to clap her on the back. "You okay, Rach?"

She coughed a bit more, then took a hesitant sip of beer. Randall stepped away from her and went back to where he'd been sitting. "I just had a huge fight with Howie." Rachel coughed again. "He can't bear the thought of being married to a shiksa."

"Well, you've gotta admit that it's a little hard to get your head around the idea that you *are* a shiksa. I was just sitting here trying to figure out what I'm supposed to be like now."

"I'm so fucking drunk, Ran, that I don't know what I'm supposed to be." She giggled. "Except fucking drunk." She giggled some more and told him about the bar.

"As long as you didn't show them your boobs," Randall said. "But what are you gonna do about Howie? You think he'll let you have the kids?"

"I don't know if I really want the kids." She thought for a second. "God, that sounds terrible. It makes me sound like I don't love them. But they're so much Howie's that I don't think they'd even want to be with me. Sports is all they care about, just like him, and there isn't much I can do for them about that. Drive them to games, I guess, but he can always hire someone to do that or get them an account with a cab company. But I don't know what he's gonna do about them not being Jewish. He's already all upset about Kyle's bar mitzvah—what happens if he just dumps them?"

"You've been wanting out of there for a long time now, this is your chance. It would have been the same problem with the kids whether this crap had happened or not."

"I'm not feeling very good, Ran." Rachel jumped up from the couch, her hand over her mouth, and ran for the bathroom. She threw up seven times.

Howie paid the babysitter and got the kids out of bed. It wasn't ten o'clock yet and they still hadn't fallen asleep. He told them what had happened and that their mother wasn't Jewish.

"Does this mean we can stop going to Hebrew school?" they asked.

Earl didn't go to Chana's funeral in the limo. He drove himself to the funeral home extra early so that he could buttonhole Rabbi Zuckerman just as soon as he walked through the door. "Rabbi."

The rabbi nodded gravely. "Dr. Frumkiss. I'm sorry that we see each other only in such circumstances."

"Yes. Rabbi, we've got a problem here, a big problem." Earl described the nature of the problem.

The rabbi had turned white by the time Earl reached the end of the story. "I've never heard of anything like this." He was shaking his head. "It's almost impossible to believe that a man could keep a secret like that for over sixty years without confiding in a living soul. Your father-in-law must have been a very unusual person." Earl nodded. "I don't know what to tell you. I'm a Conservative rabbi, and nothing I do will be recognized by the people you're going to need. The best I can do is set up an appointment for you to talk to Rabbi Waldstein. He's the head, the chief judge of the *bezdin*, the rabbinical court. He's a world-class expert on Jewish law; people send him questions from all over the world and his decisions are considered authoritative. He's quite moderate in his rulings, though, and is a nice man, to boot. Very mild-mannered and friendly; there's no one who doesn't respect him. If all Orthodox rabbis were like him, most of the problems we now have would go away over night." The rabbi excused himself, went into another office, and called Rabbi Waldstein on his cell. He stuck his head back in a couple of minutes later. "Would this afternoon be too soon for you, Dr. Frumkiss?"

"Not at all, Rabbi."

Rabbi Waldstein shook his head and clucked his tongue. He was a child refugee himself, born in Shanghai in the same year as Tammy, and he was also familiar with Faktor's work, especially the newspaper columns. "A terrible, terrible thing, Dr. Frumkiss. It was so wrong of your father-in-law that it's easy to forget how understandable it is. It was the one way of being sure that his daughter would be safe from the next Hitler." He shook his head again. "A terrible world, doctor, when we have to run our lives around a maniac like that, or even the possibility of a maniac like that."

Earl grunted.

"In light of the circumstances, I can tell you that my colleagues on the *bezdin* will be as lenient as they can be. Conversion will be a formality. Your one daughter, the rebbetzin from Moginey Erets," he was starting to smile ironically, "can be converted immediately. I don't know if that will satisfy her husband, but my name is usually good enough to satisfy any rabbi who's sane. The same thing can be done for her children, but they'd have to be here in person and we'd have to draw blood from her sons in a symbolic—and I do mean strictly symbolic—circumcision. There shouldn't be any problems with the Conversion Authority in Israel.

"Your other daughter is a little more problematic, but it's nothing that can't be got around. She and her sons will have to undertake an Orthodox lifestyle for a year. As long as she doesn't get married in that time, she can do anything that she's doing right now."

"Except drive on shabbes and eat treyf, right?"

The rabbi smiled and nodded. "Right."

"Like that'll ever happen." Earl looked despondent. "What about their marriages, Rabbi?"

Rabbi Waldstein waved his hand in the air. "The Israeli one is null and void. The Canadian civil marriage has nothing to do with us; if she goes through with the conversion, she won't need to do anything about it. Either she or her husband will have to find somewhere else to live until she's gone through the conversion and they've had a valid Jewish marriage, because the one they have now is also null and void—it never happened and it doesn't exist, even if it was done by an Orthodox rabbi."

Earl nodded and hummed. "And now for the big question: what about my wife? Will they let her stay in a Jewish cemetery?"

The rabbi put his hands over his ears and looked Earl directly in the eye. "Don't ask," was all he said. "Whatever happens, it'll take quite a while."

14

IT HITS THE FAN, II

THAT SATURDAY AFTERNOON, Gedaliah Feinsilber, known to his parents as George, the managing director of Rock of Israel Memorial Park, felt a sweet, familiar thunder in his stomach some time around 2 p.m., not long after he finished lunching on the *cholent* prepared by his wife. Cholent, the traditional Saturday lunch in Orthodox homes, consists of beans and bits of chicken and meat that have been left to simmer for between eighteen and twenty-four hours. It is forbidden to turn a stove on on the Sabbath or to put anything onto one that's already been heated or lit. The cholent has to be prepared and brought to a heat source before Sabbath begins; by lunchtime the next day, it has attained a greasy thickness that often spurs the digestive system to quick and decisive action.

Feinsilber took considerable pleasure in what he liked to think of as his weekly pleasure dump. He rather enjoyed his own aromas, and would sit on the toilet for as long as half an hour, idly perusing that week's issue of *Torah Times*. The shlepped-out evacuation, the pomp and ritual that

went only with the Saturday crap, were among the pleas-
antest parts of Feinsilber's attempt to live up to his station.
He was young for a man in his position, forty-five or so,
portly and quite serious about himself, the kind of a fellow
who wears his paunch with pride. He'd got religion about
ten years ago, after his first marriage fell apart, and his zeal
increased from day to day. From a little knitted yarmulke
or even a plain old baseball cap, he'd progressed to a wide-
brimmed black hat and a tight-lipped intransigence in
making sure that the cemetery ran according to his understanding of Jewish law. He knew the law only at second
hand, generally from pamphlets and recorded lectures; he
didn't have the Hebrew to go to the books, but was happy
to rely on the kind of English-language distillations that
often had words like "scandal" and "shame" in their titles.
He'd got the job at the cemetery because he had some
administrative experience and a father who had been an
official in one of the larger burial societies. His second
wife, whom he'd met at an Orthodox singles' excursion to
the Carlsbad Caverns, was the renegade daughter of two
Reform rabbis. The proudest moments of her marriage
were those in which Gedaliah disallowed some previously
permitted bit of frivolous behaviour at the cemetery.

Feinsilber had just got down to business with the
newspaper when he turned a page and came across Milner's
article about Faktor and Temke. Feinsilber recognized the
name immediately—the scene at Faktor's funeral had

become something of a scandal in the local cemetery community—and the news that a shiksa had been lying in the middle of his cemetery for close to two decades without anybody knowing or doing anything about it put a sudden end to his usual pleasure. He groaned and got out of there as fast as he could; when his wife saw the article she pursed her lips and shook her head. The wig she wore on shabbes, a strawberry blonde model known as the Mindy Sue, waved back and forth attractively. "This can't be allowed," she told her husband. "It can't be allowed to stand." It's a shame that she was in her post-period state of defilement; she suddenly felt incredibly horny.

Once shabbes was over, Feinsilber called the rest of the cemetery board members to an emergency meeting and demanded, in a voice cracked by the dust of a lifetime's worth of *rugelakh*, that the gentile be disinterred as quickly as possible. "But don't we need to go through the shul? It's their section of the park and they're responsible for what happens in it," one of them objected. "Even if you're right, Gedaliah, we need to talk to them to make sure that they're the ones who pay for it."

Feinsilber stood up and bellowed in what he hoped was a leonine roar. "Money isn't the issue here! We're talking about the transgression of one of the holiest commandments: honouring the dead. We're talking about letting one of the uncircumcised rest in the same shade as the children of Abraham Our Father. It cannot be allowed. It cannot be allowed to stand! Look at the by-laws of every synagogue and burial society with space by us. The first rule is always that the deceased must be Jewish. If not, out they've got to go. We have to deal with reality, I know, so we allow Conservative and Reform converts to lie with real Jews, the way they did while they were still alive—but this? A shiksa? This is an embarrassment and an emergency. To wait for the shul is like seeing a stolen car run somebody over; first you call the ambulance. Nu, gentlemen, we're the ambulance."

The earthmover came in the next morning, and Feinsilber himself called Earl a few hours later to tell him that he'd need to have the remains taken elsewhere. "And where might you suggest?" Earl asked.

"I've already spoken to Mount of Olives," Feinsilber told him. Mount of Olives, the high-end non-denominational cemetery in mid-town Toronto, was the eternal home of thousands of prominent and well-off gentiles, including a great many political figures and Canadian celebrities. "They're willing to accept the remains and re-bury them immediately. I've had them sent already at our expense. They've got a plot all ready and are probably putting your wife into it right now. You'll have to make your own arrangements for a headstone, if you want one. We have no liability."

Earl had been half-expecting something like this and had already worked out a plan of action in his head. Even though he was still running back and forth from Chana's shiva, he had a pretty clear idea of what he was going to do. "Shmuck," he said to Feinsilber, "you better measure the hole you just dug and make sure it's big enough. I'm gonna have you in there by the end of the week."

Earl and his lawyer had become multi-millionaires together, so Earl didn't feel too guilty about calling him at home on Sunday. "Sorry to bug you at home, Kenny." Kenny told Earl not to worry. He and Mount of Olives' attorney played in the same lawyers' racquetball league; Kenny would call him right away and get back to Earl right after he talked to the guy. "Don't worry, though. They're not going to break any ground until they find out how they're going to get paid. If they've got a plot ready, it's waiting for someone with a cheque."

Earl called Rabbi Waldstein while he was waiting to hear back from Kenny. "*Oy vey iz mir.* I have no control over these people, Dr. Frumkiss, I hope you understand. I have no affiliation with the cemetery or the people who run it, but they should have spoken to a competent rabbi before they did anything. Even if there are grounds, you'll pardon the pun, to remove your wife's remains, any rabbi will tell you that there is no justification for disturbing them before those grounds for removal are established beyond any shadow of a doubt. I don't know the people at the cemetery and I can't imagine that they consulted a rabbi. They've gone ahead and taken matters into their own hands; if your wife has really been exhumed, God forbid, and moved to a gentile cemetery, you have adequate cause to summon them to a rabbinical court, not to mention a civil one; you're the owner of the plot and they aren't supposed to do anything without your permission or rabbinic authorization. I've got something to say about this, too, but as I said, I can't guarantee that they'll listen to me. Now, refresh my memory about the details of your late wife's history."

There was a message from Kenny waiting for Earl after he'd finished running through the contents of Faktor's CD for the rabbi. In order to ensure absolute accuracy, the rabbi had him quote the recording in Yiddish and even asked that he deliver a copy as quickly as possible to his home: he needed to hear Faktor himself say what Earl claimed that he'd said. Earl called Kenny while driving down Bathurst Street to get to Rabbi Waldstein's.

"I got lucky, Earl. Gavin, the lawyer for Mount of Olives, was at home, and boy, was he pissed off. One thing I can tell you right away, isn't shit going to happen over there and he's already making calls to have your wife's coffin sent right back to Rock of Israel. The shmuck over there told them some kind of BS about a deathbed conversion or something and whoever was answering the phone said to just bring the body over. There's no plot been assigned or anything like that. Gavin said that you sometimes get rogue administrators at the religious places who get more Catholic than the Pope and try to make trouble.

He's drafting a letter to Rock of Israel and *their* lawyer, making it clear that Mount of Olives had nothing to do with this and accepted delivery of the body only for long enough to confirm the shmuck's story. As such was not forthcoming, et cetera, they're sending it back."

Earl wasn't sure whether to be happy or not. Whether Tammy's bones were still in the coffin or whether they'd already turned into dust, he didn't like the idea of his wife being in some kind of goddamned warehouse like defective merchandise that had been sent back by the store that bought it. Kenny had gone on to tell him that the cemetery had breached its contract, which could hardly be voided on the basis of a newspaper story—and in an out-of-town paper, yet—written by an interested party, and was liable for a whopping lawsuit, should Earl choose to proceed in that direction. Earl couldn't see any point to doing so, except as a last resort. All he wanted was for it all to be over. As far as he was concerned, everybody involved, Tammy, his children and the grandchildren, were Jewish because they'd all spent their entire lives as Jews. This was like somebody telling him that all of a sudden he wasn't Canadian any more. What the hell was that supposed to mean? Earl never had much patience with philosophy or even with abstract ideas, but he was pretty sure that you can't turn the past into something else. If Tammy could stop being Jewish, he was thinking, then those asshole Holocaust deniers also had to be given a hearing.

Earl felt like he was going to burst. After his brother-
and sister-in-law started to sit shiva for their mother earlier
in the week, he discovered that the dead woman's step-
daughter, his late wife, wasn't Jewish, a revelation that had
already caused one of his sons-in-law to be pummelled into
a coma and the other to have such a serious fight with his
wife, Earl's younger daughter, that she hadn't been home
since the night when they discovered that she, her sister and
all their children were goyim. His only son, just as newly
minted a goy, seemed not to notice that there was anything
unusual going on—or perhaps, being childless, he had less
to be upset about—and a moronic cemetery official had
exhumed his wife. Two cemeteries were now playing ping-
pong with her remains, thanks to the intervention of at
least two lawyers, both of whom were on Earl's side. His
kids didn't yet know that what was left of their mother was
sitting somewhere—not even he knew where—waiting for
its dignity to be restored.

Earl decided to tell Randall and Rachel about it later
that evening, when they'd all be seeing each other at Chana's
shiva. Vanessa had gone back to Israel on the first flight
out of Toronto after the hospital called. She had enough on
her mind right now, what with Yankel's coma and whatever
was happening with her kids; Earl didn't need to bother
her with something else. After sliding the CD through the
rabbi's mail slot, as per the rabbi's instructions, Earl headed
back north on Bathurst Street. The cemetery didn't close

until 4:30, which gave him plenty of time to have a look at the scene of the crime.

The three-grave Faktor/Frumkiss section looked more like an excavation than an eternal resting place. Tammy's grave had just been tossed; the headstone at one end of the pile of dirt had been carefully wrapped in burlap and was lying on its back, as if it had been knocked over by drunken kids who couldn't quite get rid of a sense of responsibility. Faktor hadn't been dead long enough to have a headstone set up yet; the vaguely human-shaped pile of dirt on top of his coffin had a little sign sticking out of the middle, about where the belly-button would be, identifying the occupant of the hole beneath. There'd be no grass until the stone went up. Chana, meanwhile, had been lowered into hers only a few days earlier; the freshly tamped earth looked almost shiny next to the drier stuff that covered Faktor. Earl bent down and took a handful of dirt from Tammy's grave; it was still damp. He couldn't keep from crying. He pressed the dirt into a ball and tried to throw it. It fell apart in mid-air and came down over a couple of headstones in the next row.

He decided to take Randall and Rachel for dinner after their shiva visit, rather than upset Ava and Niven with problems that weren't really theirs. "Pancer's?" he asked. "Again?" they said. "Why don't we go south for a change?"

"I don't feel like going all the way downtown to Caplansky's, and Centre Street"—back up north in

Thornhill—"is already closed." Earl had got out of the habit of eating out anywhere but in delicatessens. They finally settled on the Steeles Deli, a block away from the funeral home that had handled the services for Tammy, Faktor and Chana. The corned beef was good, the kishka better. They didn't have a liquor licence, but Rachel had a flask of vodka in her purse for just such emergencies.

The paternal delicacy that kept Earl from mentioning Tammy's bones until they'd all finished eating was anything but unjustified. Randall's face turned as red as his hair; Rachel slammed her fist into the table, rattling the coffee cups and sloshing water from one of the glasses onto the tabletop. She grabbed her purse and stomped into the bathroom, where she drained her flask in a couple of gulps.

"Who is this asshole?" Randall wanted to know. "And where can I get my hands on him?" Rachel came back from the bathroom and sat silent and flushed.

Earl filled them in on what Kenny had told him and then told them not to worry. He also let them know about Rabbi Waldstein and promised to get hold of them as soon as he heard anything from him. Earl was also going to give Vanessa a call to find out what was going on with Yankel and the kids; he'd let them know if he reached her. He had never been a drinker, but when he got home he had two shots of Irish whisky, which gave him milder heartburn than Scotch, and went straight to sleep.

———

Randall was glad that he was doing the driving. Rachel was at least half-drunk and wasn't speaking at all. She was wearing one of Randall's T-shirts, which fit her like a tent, and a pair of his socks. She'd been rinsing her underwear out every night in his bathroom and leaving it to dry on the shower-curtain rod. Randall had gone to a drugstore to get her a toothbrush.

As close as she had been to home in the past couple of days was to have Randall drive her up to the plaza where she'd left her SUV, then follow her back to her house after the kids had gone to school. She parked it in the driveway. Howie must have taken the day off work; as soon as she saw his car, she got straight into Randall's without going inside to pick up any of her stuff. "I don't want to see him," she said.

"That's fine with me," Randall nodded. "What about Kyle and Jason, though? If you never see them again, who's going to make sure their names get changed? You don't want them going through life with jerk names like that, do you?"

"I don't know, *Randall*. When it comes to jerk-off names, I think Randy must be the prize-winner."

"I'm glad you're so concerned about your kids. Even if Howie can get them re-Jewed, you're still kind of stuck with being their mother."

Rachel opened her purse and took out four aspirins. "You think I don't know that?" She swallowed the aspirins with a swig from the open Coke can in Randall's cup holder.

"That's been there for a week, you know.

Rachel shrugged. "What bothers me is that I don't really think they want me to be. I'm just there to help out between games and practices and the rest of the Howie stuff that they do."

"Poor underappreciated baby. Force them to have better marks if they want to play. Make them do chores and crap so that they'll play less. They're kids, the only way they'll ever notice that everything's being done for them is if you stop doing it. Say you really leave Howie—"

"I'll say it once and I'll say it again—"

"And they end up living half the time with each of you." Randall lit a cigarette with the car's lighter. "You're probably going to have to get a job, but he's sure as hell not going to stop working, especially if he's got to make support payments." He liked the toast smell that came off the lighter once it touched a cigarette. "That means there's nobody to take them anywhere when they're with him. The worst that can happen to you is that you won't be able to take them, either. If you're lucky, you can get something with flexible hours and work stuff around their schedule. Any chance of teaching?"

"Not right away. I'd have to get some lab work in, publish something. I can talk to the people at York and the U of T. It's almost all people I knew in grad school. Maybe somebody needs a research assistant."

"So either you get something flexible and become the parent who actually gets them to their games, or you end up no worse off than Howie—and the kids either figure out how to take the bus three blocks or else give up playing completely."

Rachel thought about what Randall said and called the house that evening. She told the boys that she'd had a bit of an argument with their dad, who was going slightly crazy and thought that none of them was Jewish any more except himself. They told her that they knew, and that Howie also told them that finding it out had made *her* go slightly crazy and that that was why she'd taken off. She told them that they were all just as Jewish as they'd ever been and she didn't know why Dad was making up these stories. She was at Uncle Ran's right now, they could call her any time; she'd be home in a couple of days and everything would be okay. They'd see. "But how are we supposed to get to the rink with all our gear?"

"It's three blocks from school. Try walking." She felt so proud of herself. "Now let me talk to your father."

Before Howie could say anything more than "Hello," Rachel told him that she wanted a divorce.

Howie was shocked. He knew that this shiksa thing was a big problem, but not really that big. If worst came to worst, he'd been thinking, they'd just go on as they'd been before. It'd be a little weird at first, but they'd get used to it. He really couldn't believe that she wanted to leave him.

"It's going back to the way we've been all these years that scares me, Howie. If you can't see for yourself why I've been so unhappy, there's no use my trying to explain it to you. We just don't go together, you and I. It isn't personal, just a bad fit. We can do it without too much rancour, you know. It'd be better for the boys. I'll be back in a couple of days; we can take turns sleeping in the spare bedroom. Soon as I find a place, I'll be moving out." She hung up and turned off her phone before he had a chance to call back.

Whatever ambivalence she'd been feeling about how to deal with the boys and the whole religion problem vanished as soon as she heard that they'd dug up her mother. People like this weren't going to run her life for one second longer. She was only forty, still young enough to be able to do the things she liked and was good at. She was going back to her insects in a great big way and if anybody asked if she was Jewish, she wouldn't only tell them yes, she'd tell them in Yiddish. And she was never fasting on Yom Kippur again. She'd spent a lot of her life thinking about evolution and species; she knew exactly what she was.

Worried sick lest this Frumkiss business spark a purge of cemeteries and Hebrew schools all over the Jewish world, Rabbi Waldstein stayed up all night consulting his books and worked well into the next day, after a three or four hour nap, framing a response that he sent to every Jewish cemetery in Canada, as well as his professional peers, the most prominent and influential rabbis in Israel and the USA. Widely regarded as the foremost authority on Jewish law in all North America, he was the rabbi that rabbis went to for help. He'd reconsidered what he said when Earl came to his office; Feinsilber's behaviour had forced him to take a harder line on the evidence.

He decided on a strictly legalistic approach, completely ignoring the question of Tammy's parentage and focusing instead on Faktor. "We have nothing," he wrote in the English summary that he sent to Earl and a number of English-language Jewish newspapers, including *Torah Times*,

> but the word of Elyokim Faktor, a renowned scoffer who prided himself on his ability to cause trouble for himself and others alike, and who even published his writings under the pseudonym of *Der Mazik*, "The Troublemaker." Faktor had no direct evidence for this calumny and neither heard nor knew anything of it while his wife was alive. She herself left no will or confession. Faktor claims that a notorious actress and public adulteress, who was ineligible, by virtue of being a woman, to offer testimony, informed him that his first wife was not Jewish only after the woman had already succumbed to the fever that killed her. Jewish law excludes all hearsay evidence.
>
> We *could* say that such evidence as we have points to Tamara Szulc's being a true daughter of Israel, but to do so would sully the memory of a woman who fled the Nazis and shared the fate of so many of our

brothers and sisters who died as refugees. The Szulc woman is said to have been thoroughly conversant with matters of day-to-day Jewish law; to have worked and performed in the Yiddish theatre; to have fled the Nazis together with thousands of other Jews; to have stood under a wedding canopy with Faktor. We need not stress this positive evidence, because there is no negative evidence. There are no reliable witnesses to the accusation, which could be made against any Jew wherever there are no proper records: the Dlugaszow registry books were destroyed during World War II. Jewish law excludes all hearsay evidence, how much the more so then the recollection of an unsubstantiated statement utterly at odds with any known facts sixty-five years after said statement is supposed to have been made.

I thereby pronounce Tamara Szulc and all of her offspring and progeny to be full-fledged members of the Jewish people according to the laws handed down to us by Moses our teacher. It is forbidden to refer to her or any of her progeny as goyim. I order her to be re-interred in her former resting place and order further that no such desecration ever be allowed to happen again.

The humble word of me,
Shmuel-Yankef ben Ho-Rov Nachman Waldstein

Rabbi Waldstein was no fool; he knew that Faktor was telling the truth, but he also knew why the ancient sages had framed the laws the way they did; the witness requirements were meant to help prevent the guilt-stricken from balming their consciences at the cost of others' lives. The quaver in Faktor's voice, the utterly bizarre nature of the circumstances, and the fact that a guy who would normally have milked such a situation for hours' worth of shtik waited until the very end of his life to mention it, made the rabbi certain that it was true. It was nothing like the other track on the CD, where Faktor claimed to have sold Josephine Baker her first bunch of bananas and to have had a brief affair with Greta Garbo in Paris in 1924. When Rabbi Waldstein googled Garbo, he discovered that she was still in Stockholm in 1924.

Faktor's confession grew out of guilt, not the desire for a cheap laugh. But Rabbi Waldstein also knew that justice untempered by mercy can easily turn into carnage. Neither the first Mrs. Faktor nor Faktor himself stood to lose anything by having the truth come out; they had got away with their deception and Rabbi Waldstein didn't have the heart to transfer their punishment to the innocents still living and to those yet unborn. Since Faktor and anybody else involved in the deception was dead—let it stay with them. "The dead do not praise God"; we need to incline to the side of the living. To ruin all those lives—lives that would almost certainly have been forfeit under

Hitler's authority—would only hurt the Jewish people as a whole.

Rabbi Waldstein considered Moginey Erets and its leaders savages, living proof that fools can turn the noblest thoughts in the world into images of their folly. He realized, though, that Vanessa had more to lose than any of them; the Hebrew original of his declaration had a lengthy preamble about unwarranted attacks on Yankel Frankel by various enemies who were using a known adulterer and violator of the Sabbath—he meant Milner—as a front man to spread the vilest slander and calumny against the scion of a distinguished rabbinic family. The rabbi's fingers shook from laughter while he typed that last sentence. He went on to what he regarded as his *coup de grâce*: lending credence to such baseless accusations was the same as accepting the Zionists' claims that the existence of the State of Israel is the first stage of our messianic redemption. Neither had any support in Jewish law.

Every Frumkiss understood what the rabbi had done, Vanessa most of all. Yankel had suffered an epidural hematoma and was still in a coma three weeks after Vanessa arrived in Israel. The doctors told her that if he ever woke up, he would probably spend the rest of his life in a chronic vegetative state, so far as they could determine.

The only downside that Vanessa could see was that she would never be able to get divorced. Jewish law makes no provision for women whose husbands are unable to grant them a divorce by reason of incapacity, and Jewish law won't let a woman divorce a man at all: if the man doesn't do it, it doesn't happen. Otherwise, though, she wasn't terribly worried. Rabbi Waldstein's connections were so good that copies of his judgment, along with a statement of approbation signed by virtually every senior ultra-Orthodox rabbi in Jerusalem and Bnei Brak, went up onto the walls of Jerusalem as quickly as the earlier denunciation had appeared. Mobs of hasidim attacked the Flatbush offices of *Torah Times*, breaking furniture, smashing computers, and giving Shmulowitz, the editor and publisher, a well-earned concussion.

Yankel's stepbrother and stepbrothers-in-law could not very well apologize to a woman, so they went to Yossel, Yankel's shammes, hats in hand and yarmulkes still on head, expressing their regret—"We were misled. We acted only for the honour of the Torah"—and offering to pay for Yankel's medical treatment and hospitalization, as well as Yossel's. It was the price of victory; even if Yankel were to recover, by the time he was ready to do anything major he would have been so thoroughly sidelined that neither he nor his sons would ever stand a chance of recovering their earlier positions. His stepbrother would take over leadership until such time as Yankel was better, and by then it would be too late for Yankel to do anything but what he was told.

Vanessa had got rid of her husband and was keeping her kids—kind of. She explained why they'd be better off in Canada until their father woke up, and made arrangements to take them with her. She used the money she'd inherited from Faktor to make a down payment on a house in the hasidic enclave around Lawrence Avenue and Bathurst Street. Vanessa knew better than to shock the kids too much at first; she enrolled the boys in a yeshiva on Lawrence and sent Ris, her daughter, to a hasidic girls' school about a hundred yards from the corner of Lawrence and Bathurst.

She had no intention of continuing to live as a hasid, or even an Orthodox Jew, but couldn't stop immediately because of the kids. She was hoping to use the riot and Yankel's coma to wean the kids away from a hasidic way of life, but knew that she'd need plenty of time, especially as they didn't speak a word of English. She was undertaking to do the opposite of what Ruth, her mother-in-law, had done with Yankel, and, assuming that Yankel never woke up, figured she'd need between three and four years to do it. If he came out of the coma with his faculties miraculously intact—Vanessa wasn't interested in getting involved with any men at the moment, but she was planning to find somebody to have sex with just once, so she could record the encounter on a camcorder. The documentary evidence of her adultery would leave Yankel no choice but to divorce her.

In either case, Earl had volunteered to serve as chief babysitter and kid driver. Rachel said that she'd help out, too, and her kids were anxious to meet their freakozoid cousins and try to help them adapt to life in the twenty-first century.

It wasn't going to be easy for Vanessa's kids; even the most extreme hasidic yeshivas in North America—and not just in Toronto—were hotbeds of modernist debauchery and accommodation with the outside world compared to the places where her kids had been studying in Israel. The boys' fondness for speaking Hebrew when they thought no one was listening boded well for their future. With any luck, they could at least enter the mainstream Orthodox world with a minimum of pain once they'd picked up a decent English.

Rachel really did move out. One of her graduate school friends was in charge of the entomology section at the Royal Ontario Museum and managed to get her a position as an assistant curator. She and Howie were trying to work out a divorce settlement. Stupid Howie had told the kids too much about what was going on, and actually showed them a copy of Rabbi Waldstein's letter to Earl. Kyle turned out to be slightly smarter than either of them had realized. After reading it, he announced that the rabbi never really addressed the question of his late grandmother's origins. "He's just looking for excuses for us to be Jewish, but he never really says if she was Jewish or not. If it's only fifty-fifty, I'm not going to my bar mitzvah."

"Oh yes you are, sonny boy," Howie told him. "This isn't a matter of choice."

"It might be if I'm at Mom's," Kyle said. "And besides, it doesn't make any difference." Becoming bar mitzvah, attaining the age of Jewish majority, had nothing to do with ceremonies; they told him so at school. So if he was Jewish, it didn't matter. If he wasn't, there was no reason for him to waste his time learning to intone a Torah portion that had nothing to do with him.

"Yeah," added Jason, "I'm gonna do the same."

Kyle leaned over and whispered in his ear. "And once we're in public school, we can take all the Jewish holidays off."

Randall didn't mention anything about the CD or exhumation to Alexa, and asked his father and sisters not to say anything, either. He spent a few months exercising furiously and eating next to nothing, until he was down to something under two hundred pounds. Then he proposed for real. They got married in a civil ceremony at Earl's house, then had dinner at the steakhouse where they'd had Vanessa's sixteenth birthday party. Alexa's parents and four sisters came up from Arizona and were disappointed not to see one of those *chuppahs* that they always had at Jewish weddings in the movies.

That night, as he and Alexa cuddled together in bed and Alexa walked her fingers along the bald patch in the centre of Randall's head, she nuzzled him and whispered in his ear. "Ran?"

"Mmmm?"

"What would you say if I told you I wanted to convert?"

EPILOGUE

VANESSA AND RACHEL MADE AN APPOINTMENT to see the leader of the local divorce-enforcement goon squad, a strictly informal group of men who, for cash up front, would beat the shit out of Jewish men who refused to give their wives a Jewish divorce. Feygl was able to trade on her position as rebbetzin emerita of Moginey Erets: six months had passed and Yankel was still in a coma. His stepbrother had taken the group back and was sending Vanessa a monthly stipend. Whatever she wanted, she could get it for free; her boys were at the same school as the leader's kids and most of the squad members'.

Feygl almost told the truth. She explained that Rachel was her sister, but told them that Milner was the recalcitrant husband. He was such a jerk, Feygl told them while Rachel wept into a handkerchief, that he had even tried to deny that they were ever married. It was also he who had written that horrible article that provoked the attack on the rebbetzin's husband. They wanted him hospitalized. No coma, please. He needed to feel his pain.

Milner's nose was split down the middle with a

circumcision knife and both his legs were broken. As soon as he was in the hospital, Rachel turned up at his super's door and introduced herself as Milner's younger sister, come to get some of the things that he'd be needing there. She and Vanessa went into his apartment. The walls were so completely covered with pictures of Vanessa that the whole place felt like a teenager's bedroom. Rachel and Vanessa took the Faktor notes, the Faktor files, and all the Faktor CDs. It took the two girls three trips to get it all downstairs, where Randall loaded it into his van and drove it to a self-storage facility. They didn't want to throw it out, but they had no desire to see any of Faktor's stuff for a good long time. The girls went back up and took down the laminated photo of Vanessa that Milner had stuck to the centre of his bathroom mirror. In its place, they left a copy of Rabbi Waldstein's statement.

As they were leaving, Vanessa noticed a bottle of White-Out on Milner's desk. She took it into the bathroom, along with a pen that she also took from the desk. She got rid of the rabbi's signature, and when Milner came home six weeks later, he found that his favourite picture of Vanessa had been replaced by a rabbinic declaration stuck to his mirror and signed "Sorry I missed you—Getsl."

Dem Pogromtshiks Viglid
The Pogromist's Lullaby

By Elyokim Faktor
Translated by Allan Milner

Farvigt ver, shaygets oon a hit,	Get rock-a-byed, bareheaded goy,
Es nemt bald a sof tsi dayn noyt;	You'll soon have all that you need;
A tsigl brengt der tateh mit,	Daddy's bringing a baby goat,
Es esn vest az es iz toyt.	Soon as he's killed it, you'll feed.
Gekoylet s'tsigeleh, es shoyn	You'll eat the flesh and bones and blood,
Zayn hoyt mit di bayner in blit.	Once Daddy slaughters the kid.
Posmakeveh zakh, farges shoyn	Just smack your lips and then forget
Az s'tsigeleh's nebakh a yid.	That that poor little kid is a yid.
Oy, driml-zhe ooreleh mayner,	Doze off, my dear forskinned baby,
Zay shtil vi an eyfeleh past;	Be quiet, like babies should be;
Der raykher tatesheh dayner	Your wealthy father's on his way
Fin shteytl kimt inter a last.	From Jewtown—he's been on a spree.
Es zugt di mameh dir lign?	You don't believe what Mommy says?
A kik ti dortn baym ployt.	Just look at that fence over there.
Es kroket a shparber zayn nign:	A vulture's croaking out its song:
Haynt esti gur yidishes hroyt.	"There's Jew on today's bill of fare."

Fin khale'est neymen a bisn,	You'll take a bite of their challah,
Fin ling, kigl, leyber in khreyn:	Their horseradish, liver and lung.
Rosh-khoydesh iz zey haynt Nisn,	Two weeks today's their holiday,
Kayn yid vet kayn paysakh nish' zeyn.	No Jew will see Passover come.
Oy, driml-zhe yoyreshl mayner,	Doze off, little heir to my fortune,
Zay shtil vi an eyfeleh past;	Be quiet, like babies should be;
Der kliger tatesheh dayner	Your clever father's on his way
Fin shteytl kimt inter a last.	From Jewtown—he's been on a spree.
Dem tatn tsit zakh in mark tsi,	Your daddy's in the marketplace
Mekayem zayn shlulem lu-voz;	—The Bible says, "Plunder and loot."
Deym shparber tsitert der kark tsi,	The vulture's throat starts to quiver,
Im kitslt biz iber der noz.	His nostrils will soon follow suit.
Kayn elt'ren hot der shparber, oy,	The vulture's a poor orphan, oy,
Iz taylt der tateh im kitsveh;	Your dad gets him onto the dole
Nedooves shenkt er, maase goy,	And gives him alms just like a goy:
Nemt maysern di meysey-mitsve.	A tenth of the total death toll.
Oy, driml-zhe galekhl mayner,	Doze off, my dear little churchman,
Zay shtil vi an eyfeleh past;	Be quiet, like babies should be;
Der frimer tatesheh dayner	Your pious father's on his way
Fin shteytl kimt inter a last.	From Jewtown—he's been on a spree.

Der tateh arbet flink in shtib,   Your dad works fast inside the house,

Doos shparberl vart in deroysn;   The vulture sits waiting outside;

Az endlekh vert fin shtib a grib,   Once every room's become a tomb,

Ayn got kon deym shparber farshtoysn. The bird drools for those who have died.

Almekhtiker got hot indz kristn   Almighty God made us Christians

Bashafn tsi hershn di velt,   To rule his world, yes, indeed.

In yidn bashtimt indz far kistn   And gave us Jews as storage bins

Fin alts voos di shparberlekh felt.   For anything vultures might need.

Oy, driml-zhe agagl mayner,   Doze off, my dear little Agag,

Zay shtil vi an eyfeleh past;   Be quiet, like babies should be;

Der humen-tatesheh dayner   Your Haman-father's on his way

Fin shteytl kimt inter a last.   From Jewtown, he's been on a spree.

ACKNOWLEDGMENTS

Thanks to Diane Martin, the onlie begetter of this novel, without whom it would never have come into being. Also to Michelle MacAleese, Deirdre Molina and Doris Cowan.

MICHAEL WEX is one of the leading lights in the current revival of Yiddish, lecturing widely on Yiddish and Jewish culture. His books include the *New York Times* bestseller *Born to Kvetch* and its follow-up, *Just Say Nu,* and the more recent *How to Be a Mentsh (And Not a Shmuck).* He was born in Lethbridge, Alberta, and now lives in Toronto.